THE BOOTLEGGER'S DAUGHTER

DAUGHTER

A SAN FRANCISCO TALE

BASED ON A TRUE STORY BY

JOSEPH ANDREW CERNY

The Bootlegger's Daughter: A San Francisco Tale
Based on a True Story
Cover design by Golden Starling (goldenstarlingpublishing.com)

ISBN 979-8-9935475-1-0 (paperback)
ISBN 979-8-9935475-2-7 (hardcover)
ISBN 979-8-9935475-0-3 (ebook)

First Edition: November 2025

For information, permissions, inquiries, or
general correspondence, use the following address:
PO Box 4160
Auburn, CA 95603

TABLE OF CONTENTS

THE BOOTLEGGER'S DAUGHTER

A SAN FRANCISCO TALE

TIMELINE OF SELECT EVENTS

1895:
Andy's parents Mary Donoghue and Daniel Scannell arrive in the US 5/6 from Ireland on the Umbria

1899:
Andy's parents marry

1900:
Bubonic Plague starts in S.F. in March, ending with the last case in January 1908

1900:
Margaret "Maggie" Rudden (Ann's mom) arrives in the US from Ireland with her sister Mary Ann Rudden (later McGuire), September 1

1910:
Ann White is born on November 19

1912:
Katherine White is born on September 19

1914:
Beginning of WWI on July 28

1914:
Bette White is born on August 1

1915:
Panama-Pacific International Exhibition in S.F. runs February 20 to December 4. Andy rides in a bi-plane

1919:
Theresa White is born May 19

1920:
Prohibition Enforcement starts on January 17

1921:
"Billy" White is born on August 7

1926:
Ann's father William White dies on January 20

1929:
US stock market crashes on October 24 and the Great Depression begins. It unofficially lasts until the start of WWII

1937:
The Golden Gate Bridge opens

1939:
Ann's son "Danny" attends the Golden Gate International Fair on Treasure ISL with his aunt and uncle

1941:
Japan attacks Pearl Harbor on December 7 and US enters WWII a day later

1944:
Ann's mother-in-law, Mary Scannell (Donohue), dies on November 28

1945:
WWII unofficially ends on August 9 after Japan surrenders

1966:
The Beatles perform their last major concert in the world at Candlestick Park on August 29, not including a free impromptu 42-minute session where they played five Beatles songs on a London rooftop in 1969

1967:
San Francisco hosts the Summer of Love, June to October

1968:
Assassination of Martin Luther King, April 4

1969:
Ann marries Al Scully, March 15

1901:
Andy Scannell is born on May 20

1906:
San Francisco Earthquake, April 18. Andy's family loses their home on Harrison Street

1906:
Ann's father arrives in the US from Cork, Ireland, on May 27

1909:
Ann's parents, William White and Margaret "Maggie" Rudden, marry on January 17

1917:
Ann's sister Katherine White dies August 13

1917:
Entry of the US into WWI April 6

1917:
"Mickey" White is born on February 8

1918:
The Spanish Flu Pandemic starts in February, but doesn't hit S.F. until September 18. The pandemic unofficially ends in 1920

1918:
1918 End of WWI, November 19

1933:
1933 Coit Tower opens to the public on October 8

1933:
Prohibition officially ends on December 5

1934:
Andy establishes "The Old Keg Inn" on Church Street

1934:
Ann gives birth to her first child, "Danny" Scannell, March 13

1937:
Ann gives birth to her second child, Joanne Scannell, March 14

1953:
Ann's mother, "Maggie," dies on April 15

1962:
The "Escape from Alcatraz" occurs on either the night of June 11 or morning of June 12

1963:
Assassination of President John F Kennedy, November 22

1966:
Ann's husband, "Andy" Scannell, dies on January 6

1969:
Neil Armstrong walks on the moon, July 20

1976:
Ann's brother "Billy" White dies on September 1

1978:
Mayor Moscone and Supervisor Harvey Milk are assassinated, November 27

1985:
Ann dies on September 20

Ann White's Family Tree

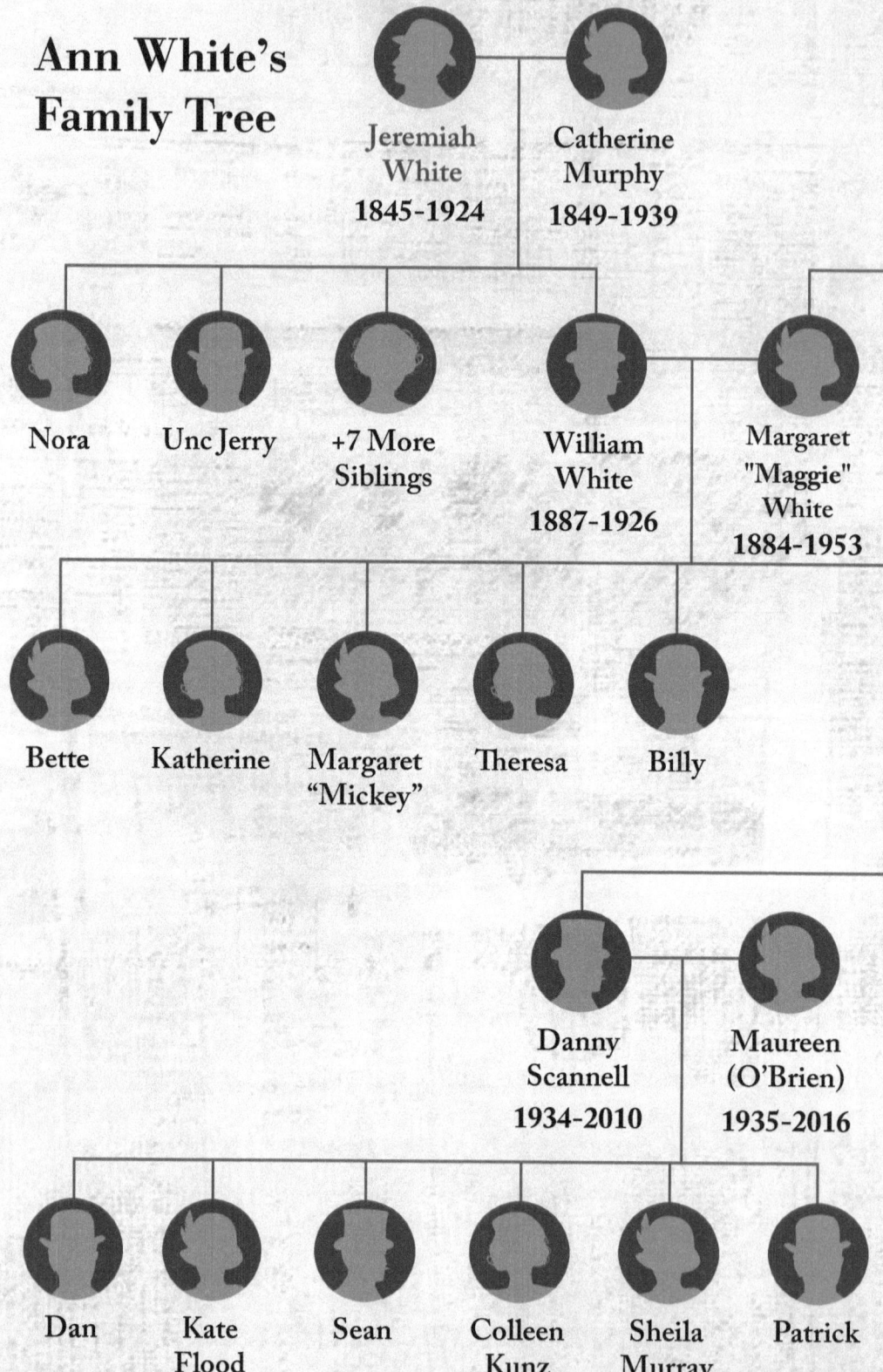

Jeremiah White 1845-1924 — Catherine Murphy 1849-1939

Nora | Unc Jerry | +7 More Siblings | William White 1887-1926 — Margaret "Maggie" White 1884-1953

Bette | Katherine | Margaret "Mickey" | Theresa | Billy

Danny Scannell 1934-2010 — Maureen (O'Brien) 1935-2016

Dan | Kate Flood | Sean | Colleen Kunz | Sheila Murray | Patrick

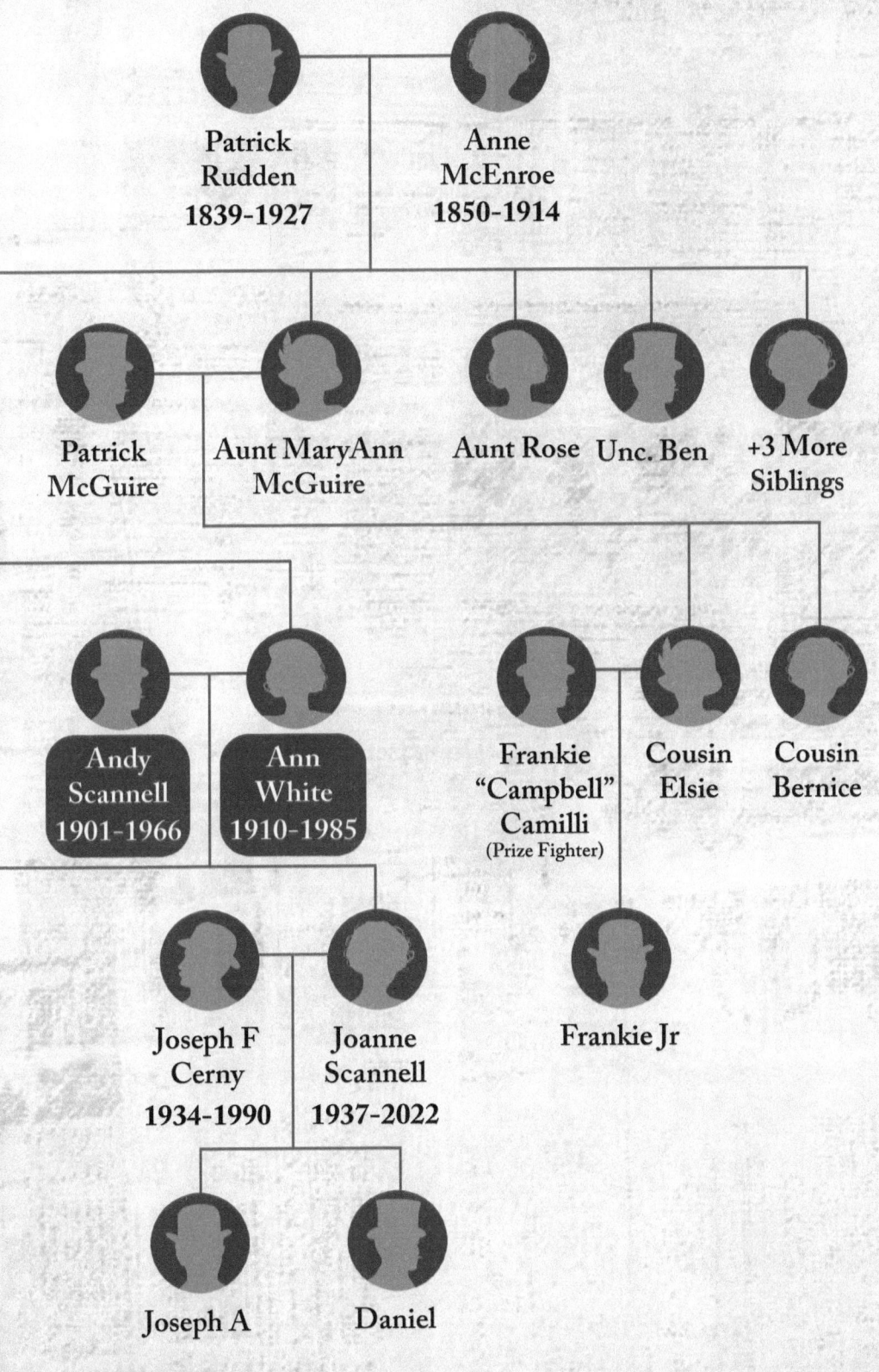

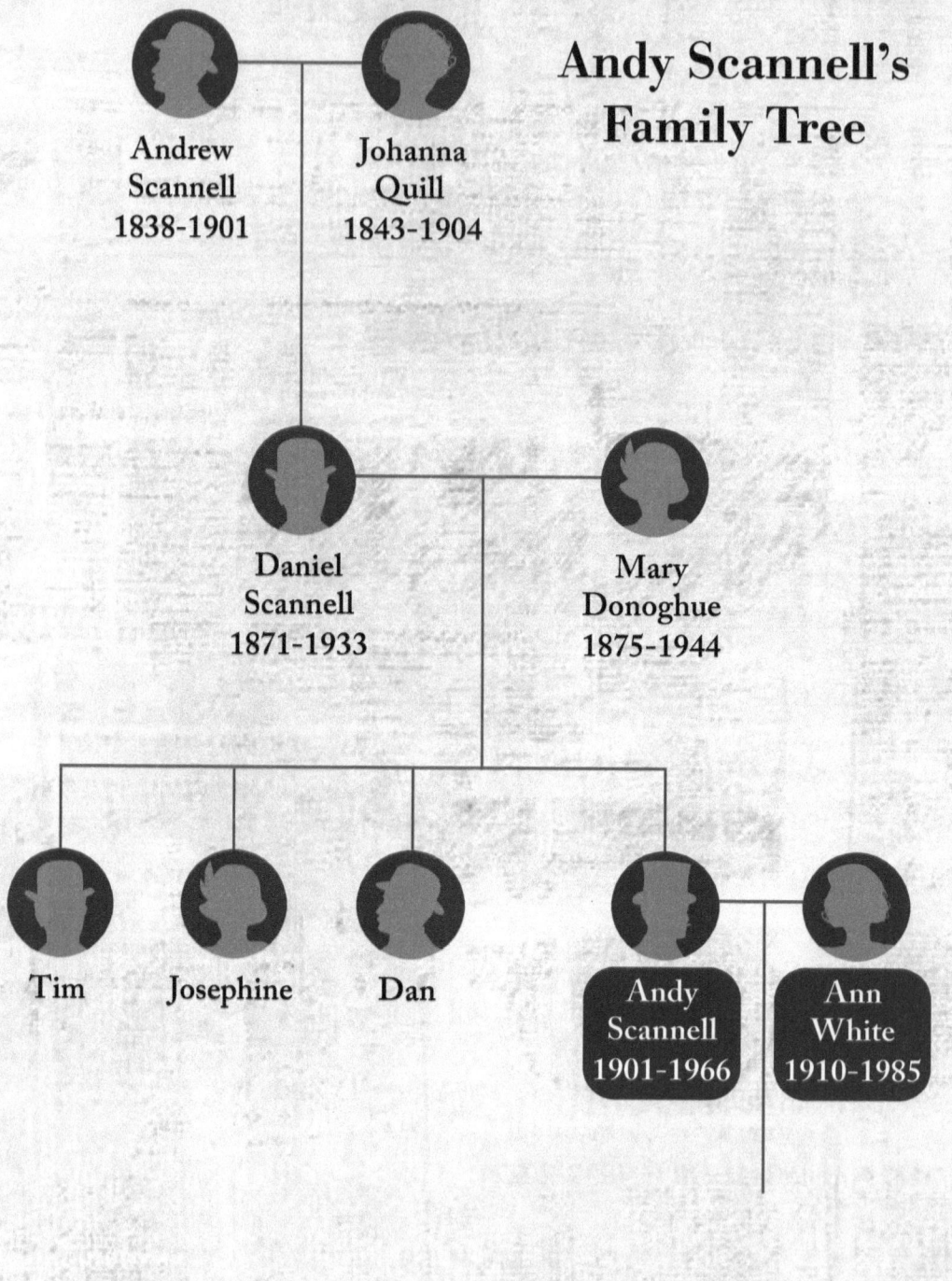

Andy Scannell's Family Tree

Andrew Scannell
1838-1901

Johanna Quill
1843-1904

Daniel Scannell
1871-1933

Mary Donoghue
1875-1944

Tim

Josephine

Dan

Andy Scannell
1901-1966

Ann White
1910-1985

PREFACE

I, Joseph Andrew Cerny, was born in San Francisco, and I am the descendant of a grandmother, great aunt, and two great-grandfathers who were all bootleggers. That grandmother was named Ann White, and she lived a remarkable life. So remarkable, in fact, that her memory inspired me to write this book.

Ann White was a child of Irish immigrants trying to survive in San Francisco in the post-1906 Great Earthquake era. Her father, William White, became a bootlegger during Prohibition, and she would play an integral role in helping him produce and transport whiskey.

Using a child's wagon stacked with dolls, Ann and her younger sister Bette moved concealed, illegal liquor through the city. This story includes a mistress, a selfish alcoholic father, occasional violence, and the unusual, unique politics of the time. Ann's family would become poor due to unforeseen circumstances, and Ann would constantly have to adapt to the ever-changing events that unfolded.

Alcohol sold or consumed by the men in Ann's life would shape her life for years to come. The bulk of this book covers her life between 1915 and 1945, with three chapters dedicated to the post-World War II period, and it is loaded with historical events that shaped the history of the United States, particularly San Francisco, during that time. The first half of the book is told through her perspective as a child, similar to the feelings and emotions expressed in books such as *A Christmas Story*, though many of her experiences were from an earlier era and involved a large family that became dysfunctional. Ann shared many sweet, humorous, and sometimes dark experiences with her high-spirited, fun-loving sister Bette, as well as a multitude of challenges they had to face together.

Life dealt Ann White a hand that most people would have balked at. Her life was full of twists and turns that involved heartache, patience, and perseverance through the Spanish Flu pandemic, Prohibition, the Great Depression, and World War II. Her life would intertwine with her cousin Elsie McGuire's and the tragic events she had to face. This story features a famous boxing match in 1930 between Max Baer and Elsie's husband, Frankie Campbell, a fight that was arguably more brutal, violent, and dramatic than the other famous Max Baer fight depicted in the story *Cinderella Man*.

The Bootlegger's Daughter is a work of historical fiction based heavily on fact. I compiled the book from my memories of the stories my Grandma Ann told me when I was an adolescent, as well as information gathered from interviews with relatives before their deaths. Most of the interviews were conducted by Ann's late son, Daniel Scannell, who appears in the story as Ann's son Danny. In addition, interviews were carried out with Jeanette Brown Ganahl, the daughter of Ann's sister Bette. The book also relies on historical research into the time periods in the book, drawing on many sourc-es, including newspaper clippings from the era. Where clear facts were not available, as all historical fiction authors do, I've filled in the details with my imagination.

CHAPTER ONE

My name is Ann. As a little girl, I went by the name Annie White. It was a crisp, beautiful autumnal day in November 1915. I was five years old at the time. My father, William White, was about to give me a ride on his horse-drawn wagon through the windy, hilly streets of San Francisco. I was tremendously excited, as it was a rare occasion that I got to ride with him. As I was the eldest child and able to hold onto the wagon, this was a privilege my two younger sisters, Katherine and Bette, had yet to experience.

Papa was a lover of horses. He had emigrated from County Cork, Ireland, in 1906 at the age of eighteen. Like most Irish immigrants at the time, he traveled by ship and was processed at Ellis Island in New York. He came from a huge family that had owned a modest farm with a few horses. Papa wanted to get a job where he could work or be around the animals. When he emigrated from Ireland, he did not have a lot of money, and at first got work as a day laborer. However, by 1909, he became a teamster, driving a horse train for an express delivery company. He transported items unloaded from steamships that had docked in the San Francisco Bay harbor to local businesses.

By 1912, Papa had eventually saved enough money to purchase his own horse-drawn cart, and he continued to work in the transportation business. He transported dry goods around San Francisco to shops and restaurants. He also worked with liquor distributors and transported kegs of beer and bottles of liquor to stores and bars.

Papa used two to four horses, depending on the load he carried. They were magnificent, smooth-bodied, clean-limbed, mixed-breed, daft horses. He always introduced me to his horses in case I had forgotten. But of course, I already knew their names. What five-year-old would forget? There were Finnegan, Aisling, Clover, and Seamus. My favorite was Finnegan. Finnegan had an exquisite brown, shiny coat with scattered white patches. Before the horses were hitched to the wagon, Finnegan would approach and greet my father at the livery where he was boarded. He would make eye contact with me and let me rub his face, something the other horses would not let me do.

Papa would pat and stroke the horses' necks and withers and talk to them gently. With his thick Irish accent, he would say things like "May God grant ya a palace full of hay," or "a shamrock full of green leafy petals." At stops, he sometimes grabbed a few carrots out from under his seat and held his hand, knuckle-side up, to let the horses have a treat.

"Tis is fur ya," he would say.

At the time, I did not know Papa's business was in jeopardy due to the gas-powered trucks that were beginning to take over the industry. Papa almost always had a cigar in his mouth, which made it look like he was smiling most of the time. His face was round with a ruddy complexion, and he had a breadbasket-shaped belly.

Papa taught me to be kind to others. He had the gift of the gab and often stopped the wagon to talk to people. He greeted people by saying, "What's doin' wit ya?" He had a good sense of humor and often said something funny about the person he was talking to, then followed by saying that he was only "coddin' ya." When people told him about something going on in the city that he was unaware of, he said "G'wan," to encourage them to tell him more.

Papa particularly liked to charm women, despite being married, especially pretty ladies. If he saw an attractive woman, he stopped and said, "Hello, how ya gettin' on? My, ya have a lovely face, and I have yet to have a pint of bee-er today." He always ended the conversation with "It was lovely talking to ya."

Like Papa, the men my father usually talked to wore suits and hats. The derby hat was popular among men at that time, with its rounded crown and broad, flat, or upturned brim. Some men wore straw hats, but they were going out of style. Others, like Papa, wore the newer style of hat, the fedora. The fedora hat was made of felt and had an indented crown. Papa wore a black suit with fine pinstripes, a long coat, and a grey fedora hat with a white band. He was clean-shaven, though nearly half of the men during that time had mustaches. Boys and day laborers tended to wear knee-high socks, knickers, plain clothes, and caps.

On that day in November 1915, I wore a white cotton dress with a sash at the waist, a pair of mittens, a white bell-shaped cloche hat, and a light green scarf that my mother had wrapped around my neck to keep the cold San Francisco air off me. Most of the women we saw wore hats with wide brims and dresses down to their ankles. The hats were often adorned with plumes of feathers, bows, or floral pieces. To keep the heavily laden, wide hat on their heads, women wore hatpins. Despite wearing these, in the strong San Francisco wind, women could often be seen clutching their hats with one hand to keep them from flying off their heads or yanking their scalps. Their dresses usually had floral patterns. Some women wore fur coats, and others wore shawls or scarves.

It was especially enjoyable to ride with Papa down some of the busiest thoroughfares in San Francisco. On that autumnal day, I rode with him down Market Street. There were no stop lights, and very few crosswalks existed at that time. I was fascinated by the people crossing the street in every direction around our wagon. In front of their businesses, some store owners quickly swept garbage or manure off the street between wagons and automobiles. I plugged my nose if the stench got too bad.

Men crossing the road dodged within the narrow spaces between cable cars. It appeared to be a major event whenever we saw women trying to cross the wide streets with their children. They always sought out the islands in the middle, where lampposts were situated, before making their way across, looking carefully all the while. My father was always polite and slowed down for such women. He would say, "Ya can go true," but others were not so gracious. We witnessed many near-misses within the span of a few blocks.

Boys roamed the street, yelling at the top of their lungs, trying to sell newspapers between the traffic. They held up the newspapers and shouted the latest headlines. "British forces successfully attack at Gallipoli, read all about it!"

Only at a few intersections did we see traffic cops. They carried billy clubs and often blew their whistles, making those junctions quite noisy.

Cars cut in front of us, and Papa's horses were so used to it that they did not blink an eye. Even at the age of five, I understood that the horse-drawn cart we were riding in seemed out of place. We saw a few other horse-drawn carts and wagons, and were outnumbered, at least in our city, by more modern means of transportation.

There were so many sounds of people, car horns, trucks, cable cars, bike bells, and street cars, but I enjoyed the clip-clopping of Papa's horses on the pavement. Following the Great San Francisco

Earthquake and fire of 1906, the 1910s were a time of major reconstruction in San Francisco. New buildings were popping up in every direction, with steam shovels and jackhammers heard echoing throughout the city. Noises of clanking steel reverberated in my eardrums.

Looking up, I saw towering buildings, some bearing flags or prominent signs. One advertised a bottle of Coca-Cola for five cents. We clip-clopped past a building that housed the world's largest millinery store, Zobel's, where you could purchase a hat of any kind. We passed ornate street clocks on posts, and elegantly designed buildings such as the Union Trust bank with its Greco-Roman columns. I also caught sight of multiple electric streetcar lines that seemed to hover above most of the city.

Papa took all this in his stride and said the day was "grand." We occasionally heard people singing and piano music emanating from bars. The air smelled like all the businesses we passed. Delicatessens and cigar shops especially smelled good, but sometimes their aroma would be ruined by the pungent stench of garbage piled up in some alleyways. We went up and down hills, and Papa often shouted in jargon I couldn't understand. Sometimes he spoke in Gaelic, a language that came from his ancestors in Ireland. Papa was fond of repeating Irish proverbs such as '*Is fearr Gaeilge briste, ná Béarla cliste,*' which meant it was better to speak in broken Irish rather than clever English. That phrase remained with me, as Papa used it frequently.

Papa's mood changed suddenly when we passed what I think was a seamstress's shop. I remember there was a man with an Irish accent arguing with a woman in front of the store. Curious as to what was taking place, Papa commanded his horses to stop with a "Whoa!" A Ford Model T nearly slammed into the back of our wagon, and the driver honked his handheld horn angrily as he pulled around us. He made what I would later learn to be an obscene gesture as he passed. Unfazed by the near accident, Papa asked the man in front of the store what all the commotion was about. The man's daughter had gone to a job interview, and as soon as the woman interviewing her found out she was Irish, she said she didn't hire Micks. My father clenched his jaw, lowered his brows, and raised his chin.

"Ya lousy feck!" Papa looked like he was going to jump off the wagon and cause a major ruckus. He told his fellow Irishman that he had every right to sue for unfair practices if he wanted to. He even offered to organize a mob to come down to the shop. The woman retreated into the store, and the irate Irishman shook his head and waved off Papa. He didn't want to create any more of a disturbance.

"What's a feck, Papa?" I asked.

"A feck is a no-good bastard." Papa looked at me and appeared a little embarrassed that he had sworn in front of me. "Don't ya repeat dat. God only knows what yur moter would do if she heard dat." He took a deep breath. "Tis is a Protestant-owned business. Ya don't ever want to do business wit dese pee-pull." He took a few puffs from his cigar, then flicked ashes which landed on the street below. "Annie … der is a lot of prejudice against da Eye-rish. Several years ago, people used to post 'Help Wanted' signs dat included da words 'Eye-rish need not apply.' But da population of da Eye-rish in San Francisco has become so huge dat people can't get away wit dat anymore. Der would be riots if dat were to occur. So, instead of advertising dat, they will instead just tell it to yur face dat dey don't want ya."

After a minute, Papa calmed down. His usual facial expression gradually returned. "Annie?"

"Yes, Papa?"

"We best get on. We don't need to waste our time here. Hold onto yur seat." Papa grabbed the reins and shouted to the horses to "Get up!" and off we went.

Papa held a hearty disdain for the British and their chiefly Protestant religion. He was very much involved in politics both in the US and in Ireland. He called the British 'Limeys'. He said he used that term when he was being kind. He called British Americans who were Protestant "W.A.S.P.S.," (White American Anglo-Saxon Protestants). At various periods in Ireland's history, there were several laws put in place by Protestants with the backing of the British that targeted Catholics. They were designed to keep Catholics poor, or at least in check. Catholics were not permitted to own land, to marry a Protestant, own horses worth more than five pounds, or to be commissioned officers in the military. Gradually, those laws were repealed, but Ireland was still occupied by the British in 1915.

Protestant British Americans had their own derogatory terms for Irish Americans, such as Paddy, Mick, bogtrotters, or bog people. I had my fair share of being called a Mick growing up. My father's hatred was so deep that I later found out he sent money to Irish militia groups in Ireland who were trying to rid themselves of British occupation.

Papa swore so often when talking about people he didn't like that I began to repeat words he would say. When I did this in front of him, he would simply holler at me with disapproval, knowing full well he was the originator of the words. However, if my mother was present and I said a swear word in front of Papa, he acted surprised, as if he didn't know where the words came from. Letting those words flow from my mouth, in front of Mama, only got me in worse trouble, and I had to suffer the punishment of having my mouth washed out with a wet, bitter-tasting, green bar of Palmolive soap.

My father's swearing only got worse after he drank too much. Often, after a busy day of transporting goods, Papa would arrange for his businessmen friends to get a ride on his cart, and he would take them to a bar such as the Old Ship's Saloon in the financial district. He would drink with them, yet still managed to steer his wagon back to the original pick-up points, then the horse stable, without getting into an accident. He would come home drunk, swearing about anything and everything. "Damn tis bugger," and "Damn dat bugger," were commonly heard in the White family household.

When Papa was not drunk, he was much more pleasant. He patiently taught me how to do math. Sitting in his brown upholstered armchair in our living room, he said, "Annie, come over here." I knelt on the floor in front of him. "If ya have four fleas jumping around a dog's fur and ya take awl of dem away, what do ya have left?"

"Zero," I replied with conviction.

"You're right … but you also have a happy dog. Dat's da important ting," Papa emphasized, with a chuckle.

Papa was always tinkering around the house, fixing radiators and other household items. However, the most useful things he fixed, in my mind at the time, were our broken toys. Papa taught me how to use a screwdriver, as well as how to properly glue things.

My little sister Katherine liked to watch us as we mended toys. She was two years younger than me. Katherine always carried a frayed pillow around the house, clenched to her chest. She would plop it down and sit on it when Papa and I got to work.

One day, Papa and I were kneeling on my bedroom floor, gluing a broken block-shaped shoe back onto our wooden Pinocchio marionette. Katherine entered the room, clutching her pillow, pausing behind me. "What are you doin'?"

"We're mending the shoe so we can play with it."

"I want to play with it!" Katherine exclaimed as she sat down on her pillow next to me.

"Not yet, Katherine."

"I want to play with it now!" She started having a conniption fit and pulled my hair from behind.

"Ouch!" Papa hadn't seen the sneak attack.

"You can't play with it until the glue dries, you cluck!" I snapped.

Papa promptly whacked me on the back of the head for my use of language. "Tell yur sister yerr sorry." He didn't hit me too hard, but I could see I wasn't getting any sympathy, so I mustered up some tears. I was trying to get Mama's attention, but she was in the back-yard folding laundry and couldn't hear me.

"She pulled my hair, Papa," I protested. He didn't listen to me and fixed me with a stern look. I glared at Katherine with disdain. "I am sorry, ... but I am really not!" I cried.

"Annie, go to yur room!" Papa barked, knitting his eyebrows. "No supper fur ya tonight."

I was mad at both my father and Katherine, but found I couldn't stay angry for too long. I couldn't say I hadn't pulled Katherine's hair a time or two. She and I got along well for the most part and played with everything together.

By February 1917, we had a new baby in the house; my sister Margaret was the fourth girl born to my parents. We referred to her as 'little Mickey'. Sitting on the living room couch, I adored holding her and smelling her baby scent. She looked just like a doll, and I loved to cradle her and kiss her forehead.

A few weeks later, in 1917, a couple of years before Papa gave up his transport business, he started giving Katherine rides on his horse-drawn wagon. By that time, Katherine was about four-and-a-half years old.

Like my father, my mother, Margaret White (née Rudden) emigrated from Ireland. She was born in Cordingin, County Cavan. Mama was about three and a half years older than Papa, and she went by the name Maggie. She was petite in stature, like me. She was pretty, with chestnut brown hair, and favored wearing very simple dresses. She possessed a soft, calming voice, but was strong-willed and could stand her ground with anyone, including Papa. Mama had traveled by ship to Philadelphia in 1900 to stay with her older sister Mary Ann Rudden, who was employed at Girard College. After a couple of years living in the US, Mama moved back to Ireland but returned Stateside for good in 1906 at the age of twenty-two. She returned by ship with her brother Bernard. Mama made her way to San Francisco to be close to her sister Mary Ann, who had married and now went by the name Mary Ann McGuire. Mama met Papa in San Francisco at a dance function sponsored by an Irish organization around 1908. He wooed her with his easy charm.

The year before I was born, my parents married in January 1909 and bought a home partly from money saved by Mama, who cleaned houses. It was a three-bedroom Victorian home on Nevada Street, in the Bernal Heights section of San Francisco. After Spanish and Mexican rule, in the mid- to late-1800s, Bernal Heights was mostly a rural cow pasture farmed by Irish, Swedish, and German farmers. There were natural springs that bubbled along some of its slopes, and the region was dotted with dairy farms mostly run by Irish immigrants. There used to be a creek that ran along its northern border, and raw sewage was dumped into it. That creek was replaced with a sewer pipe that drained to the Bay, but tidal flow sometimes carried that sewage back up marshland that bordered the southeastern portion, making that area stinky in places. Despite that, a lot of building work occurred in and around Bernal Heights in the early 1900s. It gradually transformed into a working-class neighborhood of predominantly Catholic families. Our neighborhood was mostly made up of Irish immigrants, but other pockets of Bernal Heights were populated with Italians and other ethnicities.

Mama was intelligent, creative, and incredibly well-read. She read books to us in a delightfully animated way, both visually and verbally. Mama loved reading stories written by Irish authors including Oscar Wilde and James Joyce. She usually perused the books she would read to us ahead of time, and would usually give us a fun project to do. Before reading Wilde's fairytale *The Selfish Giant*, she had us draw a picture of a giant hand on a piece of paper, which we cut out and used as a prop for storytelling time. As she read *The Selfish Giant* out loud, she adopted a deep voice and waved the hand to make the giant seem like he came alive, jumping off the pages. We particularly enjoyed listening to her read Rudyard Kipling books, such as *The Jungle Book, Rikki-Tikki-Tavi,* and *The Man Who Would Be King*.

Mama encouraged us to make up stories of our own, which I am sure were pretty bad! She utilized a black Underwood typewriter to type up our stories. Despite struggling with a key that would always stick, she was able to belt out a few pages. Those stories always had animal themes or involved our dolls coming to life, and we were pleased with the results. Mama piqued our interest in reading and taught us how to read at a very early age. However, her eyesight was deteriorating, and she wore round, nearly bottle-thick glasses. Mama had grown up in relative poverty. Her family, like my father's, was Catholic. Mama knew every Catholic saint who ever existed and had a story for each one. My favorite was Saint Michael, because he was the leader of heaven's forces in their triumph over the powers of evil.

In my early years, I had pleasant memories of our home on Nevada Street. The houses on our block were close together, and the street was steep. Our house had a pitched roof and wooden stairs leading to the front door. We had a small parlor in the front portion of the house where Mama displayed peacock feathers in a vase for good luck. We owned an RCA Victrola with a brass horn that played records, and Mama played songs like *Moonlight Baby* and *When Irish Eyes Are Smiling*. During those years, my mother spent a lot of time with us, often singing to me, Katherine, and my little sister Bette.

I had my own favorites, such as *Be My Little Baby Bumble Bee* and learned all the words to it, as well as many other songs. It became a lifelong love of enjoying music and singing songs. I especially sang when I had anxiety or felt some kind of misery or distress.

Usually, my sisters and I were not allowed to play in the parlor as that room was intended to be kept neat, to show off to guests. However, when Mama played a record on the phonograph, she made an exception.

"It's toime fur dahncen," she would call out to us. She would put the vase in a corner so we wouldn't break it. After my sisters and I gathered in the parlor, Mama played a song called *It's a Long Way to Tipperary*. I was about six-and-a-half years old, Katherine about four-and-a-half, and Bette was three. We formed a circle and sang, danced, and spun until we tumbled to the ground. I remember singing one of the verses:

"*Up to mighty London came an Irish lad one day,*
all the streets were paved with gold, so everyone was gay."

We had so much fun when listening to the Victrola.

As children, one of the things we enjoyed most was taking an insulated box containing our empty milk bottles and setting it at the base of our front porch near the sidewalk. Katherine or I would sit on the porch and act as spotter, waiting for the milk wagon to come by, which was pulled by horses at that time. Mama had given us a bell. It wasn't just any kind of bell; it was a cow bell to represent the milk that we were about to procure. Mama had acquired it at a secondhand store and was told it had come from an old dairy farm that used to exist in Bernal Heights. We were probably the only family in our neighborhood to own such a bell. Our neighbors probably thought we were country bumpkins. Once the lookout person spotted the horses from a distance making their way up our street, that person would run into the house and ring the bell. This caused great excitement, and soon my mother and sisters spilled out of the house and waited for the wagon to stop by. The milkman came wearing a vest, a tie and a hat. He let my sisters and me briefly stroke his horses while he replaced the empty bottles with new ones filled with fresh, creamy milk. Mama usually gave the milkman a new order for the next day's milk. I talked to the milkman about Papa's horses. I wasn't sure if he was impressed, but he certainly acted like he was. Papa, who trusted very few people, said the milkman's courteous behavior was all part of a ruse to keep our business.

However, it was not always fun and games growing up at our home on Nevada Street. I had chores, such as peeling potatoes, washing and drying dishes by hand, cleaning, sewing, and mending clothes. I was also responsible for pegging my washed clothes on a clothesline in our backyard and folding the dried clothes afterwards.

After I completed my tasks, I either read or played with marbles, yo-yos, or dolls. We had a wooden rocking horse that Katherine and I would take turns riding. When we weren't playing inside the house, we would often jump rope in front of our home. I even learned how to roller-skate at a fairly young age. Back in those days, you attached your own shoes to the skates. Up and down our hilly street, I went.

Within our neighborhood, occasionally on Sunday afternoons, we walked to Bernal Heights Park. It was not long before the park had a playground. At that time, it was mostly a pleasant, quiet grassy hill with a few trails. We hiked to the top and set out a blanket where we had picnics overlooking downtown San Francisco as well as the Bay. Mama would make sandwiches or red flannel hash for those special occasions.

Sometimes, as a family, we left our Bernal Heights neighborhood, crossed some railroad tracks, and walked down to the marshland to the southeast. It was referred to as the wetlands of Islais Creek. Some of that land was being reclaimed for construction projects, but there were still plenty of things to see.

One day, we walked towards San Francisco Bay and saw three boys with fishing poles pulling up smelt in one of the several foul-smelling bodies of water. I looked at the buckets of slimy fish caught by those boys and decided I no longer liked fish. The mainly stagnant ponds were made up of a mixture of fresh water, saltwater, and a little bit of sewage. The boys used some oily, drippy light brown-orange bait of some sort.

"Well, lads, what are ye us'in for da fish?" Papa inquired.

"Hello, sir," a boy, maybe eleven or twelve years old, wearing a flat cap, baggy knickers, and long socks replied. "We're using clam meat."

"Awe, dat's grand."

"Yes, we acquired the bait from the old clam shack nearby." The boy pointed in the direction of the shack. "You'll want to stay away from there if you don't want to hear foul language." The two boys he was with nodded in agreement.

"Oh my," Mama interjected.

"We went over there and asked for any unwanted broken clams. There is an irritable man who works there who runs his mouth like a sailor. At least he gave us some clams, so we can't complain too much."

The shack the boy was referring to was an old local restaurant-cum-bar on Bayview Boulevard, built when Abraham Lincoln was president.

As an adult, I realized that the establishment was the Old Clam House, and it is still in existence. It became more refined over time.

Some of my fondest memories are of playing with my cousins. When we had big gatherings at our home for dinner, I was relegated to sit at the table for kids with my cousins and younger sisters, Katherine and Bette. Mama barely ate as she spent most of the time cleaning up the messes left by my sisters. I liked to sit by my cousin Elsie, the daughter of my mother's sister, Aunt Mary Ann. Elsie was a few years older than me. We liked to make fun of the mish-mashed disarray of food, cups, utensils, and stains created by my sisters.

One evening, Elsie came over for dinner with her younger sister Bernice. Mama had made mashed potatoes with gravy and Boardinghouse vegetable soup. We had just sat down at the table, and everyone had their own napkin ring containing their own freshly laundered cloth napkin.

"I have an idea!" Elsie leaned over and whispered in my ear. "Once Aunt Maggie serves us, let's smear our napkins with mashed potatoes, then switch our napkins with your sisters."

I raised my eyebrows, dropped my jaw, and quivered with excitement. *Why hadn't I thought of that?*

We quickly pulled off the switch before Mama spied us. Before long, Katherine and Bette used the soiled napkins to wipe their faces, which became covered with mashed potato mush and a fine finishing touch of gelatinous brown goo. We snickered as they unknowingly kept eating with messy faces.

After dinner, Elsie, Bernice and I snuck around the house and scared relatives. We particularly liked to scare Mama as she would pretend that she had seen a ghost and fall to the ground shivering. This made us laugh and made me squeal. We didn't scare Papa because he would not flinch, and that was no fun. He was too much of a wet blanket when it came to those matters. He was only funny when he wanted to be.

Outside of the home, our life revolved around the church. Our family attended Mass on Sundays as well as some Catholic and Christian holidays. I attended a Catholic school where nuns taught us. They wore flowing black habits with black veils over their heads that covered a white headband-bandeau, and the lower parts of their faces were outlined with white coifs. They wore crucifixes around their necks. We were required to wear grayish-black uniforms at school with white collared blouses or shirts, with girls wearing skirts, and boys wearing trousers.

We had to recite Bible verses and learn all the standard prayers that one would recite in church. Most of the nuns lacked formal education and training in childhood behavior. They were too often quick to punish us for disobedience.

One year, I had one of the meanest nuns as my teacher, Sister Pauline. She was a bit older than the other Sisters and the lead disciplinarian at my school. Her coif was too tight for her face and grasped her loose jowl in a vicelike hold. If the sun streaming through the classroom window hit just right, you could see some rogue wiry whiskers on her chin. Brandishing a long wooden ruler, Sister Pauline ran her classroom like a medieval fortress and smacked us for the most minor infractions, such as not paying attention to a boring lesson.

I liked to make up silly, nonsense words and pass secret notes between my friends. Sometimes I said or did things without thinking too much, so that I would be as surprised as anyone else by my actions. One day, one of the boys in our class had an errant strand of hair. I felt compelled to draw a cartoonish sketch of the back of his head. It included a strand of hair sticking straight up. I labeled the drawing 'the blubstub' which I thought was hilarious, but I was caught passing the drawing to Eileen, one of my friends. Sister Pauline grabbed the note and read it. She did not find it amusing and viciously whacked me between the shoulder blades with her ruler.

Although I had a reputation at school of being funny and sometimes mischievous, my friends also thought I was sassy. In truth, most of the time I would just say things as they were. I never said anything in a mean-spirited way. If someone's hair was out of place, I had no trouble pointing it out. If someone said something pointless or stupid, I would call them out on it, which ultimately got me in trouble with the nuns. One day, I corrected Sister Pauline for using the word 'whom' in a sentence incorrectly. She had no control over the English language. She never read anything except for the Bible and a brief lesson plan. I knew this might get me into trouble, but I had to correct her at least once. I didn't correct her so that she would learn how to use the word correctly. I really couldn't have cared less. But rather, I corrected her so that she wouldn't think she had complete control over us.

"Miss Ann White, get over here at once!" Sister Pauline exclaimed with a scowl on her face. "You had better pray for guidance. Do not speak unless called upon!"

"Yes, Sister Pauline, I do apologize." I got up from my seat and walked up to the front of the class.

"I do apologize," Sister Pauline parroted in a whiny voice that did not sound like me at all. "You want to be a smart alec, do you?"

"No ma'am."

To the right of the chalkboard, in front of the class, she had me kneel before a painting of Mother Superior, who ran our local convent. The painting was a miniature version of one we already had in the school administration office. Mother Superior was an ugly woman with the face of a bulldog, I might add.

"Bow your head and hold out your arms. Turn your hands up like you're holding bowls of soup … sacred soup," the nun grinned.

"Yes, Sister Pauline." My hands began to tremble.

Sister Pauline had me count down slowly from twenty. She proceeded to swat me across the palms with her ruler until she was finished with me. I didn't shed a tear, which only made her whack me harder as I approached zero.

She was notorious for hitting classmates for the slightest transgressions. She tried to put the fear of God into us. If you used God's name in vain, such as "For God's sake, what are you doing?" she would dole out corporal punishment like Genghis Khan.

Sister Pauline also liked to grab the ears of her victims. One student named Bertie Fink would often get into trouble. He was afflicted with some sort of condition that he couldn't control. He could not sit still in class nor repeat what he had just been taught. Sister Pauline said that he had a "defect of moral character." It seemed like every class had at least two kids, usually boys, with similar behavior.

Bertie's actions would invariably annoy Sister Pauline. If his actions could not be corrected by whacking his hand with her ruler, it led to him being hauled off with her grasping his ear. She would take Bertie, or any other "misbehaving" student, to the school office first and get someone to fill in for her. While we waited for the substitute teacher to arrive, we gazed out the window to see her then march that student across the school courtyard towards our local church, which was a mile away. From what we gleaned, she made them walk on their knees the full length up and down the aisles at least ten times while they repented for their sins. Bertie had this happen to him so many times that one of his ears began to resemble a cauliflower, and his knees grew calloused.

There was a rumor going around my school that Sister Pauline had murdered children before and used their bones to decorate her room at her local parish residence. My parents would not verify this. If they knew, they wouldn't tell us.

1915. William White driving his wagon in a San Francisco parade

CHAPTER TWO

During World War I, in April 1917, the United States declared war on Germany after the sinking of some US ships by German U-boats. My father, William White, narrowly escaped being drafted into the US military during that timeframe by being a mere few months older than the age required to register. Nonetheless, we showed our patriotism by hanging flags from our house, and Papa purchased a war bond.

I didn't follow the war too closely at that age. My two-month-old sister Mickey was just starting to smile, and I enjoyed coaxing her into happy little grins.

At that time, Americans were encouraged to plant Victory Gardens to grow our own food so that more food could be used by the US military or exported to our allies. In the spring and early summer, in our tiny backyard, Katherine and I helped Mama plant and cultivate a garden that contained basil, tomatoes, carrots, potatoes, peppers, and peas. I recall how wonderful the aroma of the basil was. The fresh scent would permeate our outfits. After gardening, Katherine and I would play clapping games like pat-a-cake or Miss Mary Mack in our backyard, and we would retreat to the house with the scent of summer on our clothes.

On a Friday in August 1917, after a few days of being quieter than usual, Katherine, just shy of her fifth birthday, felt warm and lost her appetite. Mama made chicken soup, but she wouldn't take it.

By the following day, she had developed stomach pain and diarrhea, and her temperature was measured to be at 102. Mama went to the phone to contact Katherine's doctor. She fumbled through the telephone directory and found the doctor's number, then lifted the receiver from its hook and got a response from the telephone operator. She gave the number and ended up connecting with Dr. Johnson. She asked him to make a house call. However, after reviewing Katherine's symptoms, he decided it wasn't necessary. He advised plenty of fluids, rest, and a bland diet. He also recommended that Mama obtain a bottle of something called laudanum to give to Kathrine in small doses. I later learned it was a mixture of opium and high-proof alcohol.

On Sunday, Katherine appeared to be worsening, and her temperature soared to 103. She started vomiting. Mama stayed home with Katherine and six-month-old Mickey while I went with Papa and Bette to church. When we returned, Katherine was lying on the living room couch, clutching her pillow to her abdomen.

"Mama, I feel so sick; my tummy and even my hair hurts." She looked pale and her lips were cracked and dry.

"Let's get ya to bed." Mama first put Mickey to bed for a nap, then helped Katherine off the couch. She could barely stand. Papa assisted by lifting her into his arms, and he carried her upstairs to the bedroom she and I shared, while Mama followed. Papa left the room.

"Mama, am I going to die?" I overheard Katherine saying.

"Yer not going to die, sweetie." Mama reassured her, with a worried expression. She pursed her lips and her jaw seemed tense with her facial muscles flickering. I could see the deep crevices of worry lines on her forehead.

She spoke to Katherine with a strained voice. "I am goin' to da bathroom to get ya a cold moist washcloth." She quickly moistened the cloth and hurried back to the bedroom to lay it on Katherine's forehead. About half an hour later, Mama retreated from our bedroom and told Papa she was going to call Dr. Johnson again. Dr. Johnson's wife answered and said he was at the hospital delivering a baby, but would send him over when he was done.

A few hours later, Dr. Johnson arrived at our home. He came into the house carrying his brown leather doctor's bag, and Mama seemed relieved. He climbed up the stairs into our bedroom to see Katherine, and I followed. Observing from the doorway, I saw Dr. Johnson take her temperature with his own mercury thermometer and confirmed it was the same as the last one Mama had obtained, 103°F. He pulled his stethoscope out of his bag and auscultated her abdomen. He pushed on her abdomen, then raised her to a seated position where he percussed her back by thudding two fingers at different locations, while listening to her breath sounds.

"She doesn't appear to have appendicitis, and I do not hear sounds of pneumonia. I see this kind of temperature all the time. If her temperature goes up another couple of degrees, take her to the hospital. If she starts developing bloody diarrhea, then contact me. This should pass. Watch her tonight." Dr. Johnson made no new treatment recommendations.

Mama stayed up with Katherine, watching her through most of the night while I lay in my bed next to them. However, Mama, who tended to get precious little rest as it was, briefly fell asleep. When she woke up on Monday morning, August 13, Katherine had died. Mama made a heart-wrenching, blood-curdling, guttural howl like I had never heard before. She clutched Katherine's limp, lifeless body,

rocking back and forth as I heard baby Mickey begin crying downstairs. An endless river of tears streamed from Mama's eyes. I never
heard my mother scream and sob like she did on that awful day.

While grieving, later that very day, Mama gathered her strength
and got to work arranging a funeral for Katherine. She contacted
our parish and then called *The San Francisco Examiner* to place a funeral announcement which went in the newspaper the following day.
Mama refused to give up Katherine's body. I was forced to spend
the next two nights downstairs in a smaller bedroom with Bette and
six-month-old Mickey, but I couldn't get any sleep.

Shocked, distressed, and upset, I was kept home from school
for a few days. Three-year-old Bette had not grasped the fact that
Katherine would no longer be around. The day after Katherine's
death, Bette wanted to play with me, but I was in no mood. Mama
spent most of the day upstairs grieving beside Katherine's body.

Just two days after she passed away, Katherine was buried at a
Catholic cemetery. Attending the funeral was emotionally painful
for me. The whole morbid affair occurred at breakneck speed. The
memorial service was held at our house, and my sister's body lay in
a casket in our parlor, toward the front of our home. It was a practice left over from Victorian times, an era that had ended in 1914.
Given that death was much more common among children during
that timeframe, a home's parlor was often turned into a makeshift
mortuary. The term 'funeral parlor' originated from that practice.
Though not customary for most funerals by 1917, it was not entirely
uncommon. Mama had moved all the furniture, including our phonograph, out of that room. There would be no more joyful dancing.
Katherine lay in an open casket, resting on a raised platform covered
with a white cloth. A Bible sat on the lower, closed portion of the
casket. Our home was crowded with friends and relatives wearing
dark clothes. The men wore suits, and the women wore dresses and

coats. Mama wore a black veil that concealed her bloodshot eyes. We had a few chairs for guests, but most people who attended had to stand. Our family sat in chairs towards the front of our living room while our priest, standing beside the casket in our parlor, read scripture. Mama held six-month-old Mickey, who fussed and chewed her fists. As the eulogies were given, I sat next to my sister Bette with tears dripping off my chin.

After the memorial service was over, our priest led a procession of mostly Ford Model Ts, heading south from our neighborhood to Katherine's resting ground at the Holy Cross Catholic cemetery in the town of Colma. We followed a horse-drawn hearse carrying Katherine's body. Colma was and still is known as the City of Souls as it has several cemeteries, and many of San Francisco's former residents are buried there. Later it would be known as a necropolis. The cemetery and surrounding area sit on a plateau at the base of the San Bruno Mountains and are surrounded by soft green hills.

At the cemetery, I remember watching the grass surrounding the gravesites gently sway in the breeze. I came to the realization that my sister would never see grass again. A brief burst of wind ripped through the tops of the scattered trees. A solitary seagull flew overhead, possibly lost and blown off course from the Bay. I read the inscriptions on gravestones of buried individuals along with their listed dates of birth and death. There were plenty of children buried. Childhood mortality was high in those days. About every other family I knew had lost a child.

Still, most of the graves were of adults, mostly elderly. Why did Katherine have to die so young? Was it part of God's plan, and for what reason? Everything had happened so fast. The week before her death, we had played together with our dolls, and she seemed normal. Then she was gone, just like that.

At the cemetery, our priest sprinkled holy water over the gravesite, which had already been dug. He then asked for a moment of silence. I looked around and saw others crying, and I began crying again. So many tears of anguished family members and relatives dropped into the pit that it would have turned into a pond had we been there much longer. The priest said a few prayers, and after his final benediction, my father, a couple of his brothers, and an uncle, removed their coats, exposing black armbands they wore over their sleeves. They were worn back then as a sign of mourning and respect. They lowered my sister's casket into the ground, which was followed by relatives taking turns with a shovel, ceremoniously heaving dirt over little Katherine's tomb. I asked to participate and sprinkled some of the blessed earth upon her coffin, and Mama clutched my dirty hand after I was finished. I had never cried so much in my life. Family members including my Aunt Mary Ann and her daughter, my cousin Elsie, attended the funeral and gave me comforting pats and hugs.

I was sent back to school on the Friday of that week, and I remember not wanting to be there. I couldn't concentrate on anything. How could the lives of my friends and classmates go on as if nothing had happened?

For weeks and months to come, a somber mood enveloped our family. Mama developed her first severe bout of melancholy. In addition to episodes of crying, she became very distant and stopped playing with us. She ceased listening to music. Her appetite lagged, and she lost weight; her face looked thin, with her sharp cheekbones. She spent hours sitting on a chair in our living room, staring at the mantle over our fireplace. At first, Papa was understanding, but when cooking and cleaning started to diminish, he would yell at her and grab her by her upper arm, forcibly yanking her out of her chair. She did eventually snap out of her woeful, near-paralysis, but I never forgot how uncaring Papa seemed with her then.

I dealt with Katherine's passing differently. After the first couple of weeks, I tried to keep myself occupied so that I wouldn't experience too many more torrents of tears bursting from my eyes. I sang songs to lift my spirits. It did not always work, and often I could not make the words come out. However, I kept trying, and eventually it helped. Life would go on.

At the beginning of 1918, Mama learned she was pregnant again, and a renewed sense of optimism blossomed in our home. My father became excited that he might finally have a boy. Heavens to Betsy, he only came up with baby names like Jeremiah, after his father, or Thomas, Timothy, John, or Daniel after some of his brothers.

Unlike her previous pregnancies, Mama was ill quite a bit. I'm unsure if the passing of Katherine had anything to do with it, but there were entire weeks when she barely left her room due to an illness of some sort. I recall she had one episode where she developed severe body aches for several days. By late April, she went into pre-term labor. She was admitted to St. Luke's Hospital and had a still-birth on April 30. Her doctor was unable to identify the sex of the baby. Following this, Mama had another episode of melancholy, and from what I could tell, Papa may have had a bit as well. As the year progressed, Mama did recover, and my parents eventually returned to their old selves.

A worldwide flu pandemic hit that year. It would affect the US, especially as troops returned home from World War I in 1918. It was called the Spanish Flu, as the newspapers initially reported an outbreak in Spain, although it may have started at a military base in Kansas.

The Spanish Flu pandemic hit San Francisco hard in October 1918.

I recall my father reading the newspaper at the breakfast table.

"Maggie, it looks like businesses and even schools might close."

"Schools might close?" I raised my eyebrows and chimed in with enthusiasm and a sense of hope. Papa didn't turn his head towards me, or reply; it was as though I were invisible.

"People are duyin' from tis across da country in droves," he said as he raised his head above the newspaper to look up at my mother. "Tis disease is cutting true our city like a hot knife true butter. Teir even talking about a mask-wearing mandate. I don't know how tis will affect my business, but it can't be good."

"Will, we just need to follow any recommendation we're given. Ya know what a germ can do to a family," Mama warned.

"Of course I do. I don't trust doze doctors, doe."

"William … don't lettit linger."

"Well, I shan't completely neglect what da healt autorities have to say."

It just so happened, later that day my mother received a hand-delivered, typed memo from our school administration highly advising, but not requiring, that we wear masks to school. My mother, as well as most other families, complied.

At first, we hated wearing them as they made us feel itchy and uncomfortable. But soon we put the masks to beneficial use. At my school playground, which wasn't much more than dirt and concrete, I concocted a plan.

"Wouldn't it be funny if we were able to stick our tongue out at our teacher?" I said to my best friend Eileen. Sister Magdalen was our classroom teacher at the time.

"How are we going to pull that off without getting whacked with a ruler or a swat from a paddle?" Eileen replied.

"We're wearing masks, aren't we?" My spirited but mischievous mind went to work. "She isn't going to be able to see us," I assured her.

We gathered other students at the play yard who wore masks and let them know of my plan. Out of eight of us, I was the shortest. I felt like an undersized quarterback in a huddle, directing an important play that was about to unfold. Shortly after we were seated back in the classroom, Sister Magdalen gave a quick prayer and then asked us to open our lesson book. I glanced around the room to make sure everyone in our clan was paying attention to me. I gave the all-important signal by nodding my head. My friends and I looked at each other, and we started to stick out our tongues behind our masks. We could see our masks jutting forward hilariously, at various angles and distances, indicating we had just pulled off the insult. This created a brief burst of laughter from one of my classmates, but Sister Magdalen couldn't figure out who the one laughing was, nor why.

"Did I say something funny?"

We did not make another peep, and Sister Magdalen carried out the lesson. I didn't want to bother her more than we already did, as she was a lot more tolerable than Sister Pauline had been. Our mission had been accomplished. I thought to myself that a mask mandate would not be so bad after all.

As flu cases in the city mounted, superstitious methods of flu prevention started to circulate. Some children were sent to school with bags of camphor, a component of turpentine, around their necks. Others chewed on garlic or gargled seawater as a form of prevention.

Before school one morning, while sitting in the kitchen reading *The San Francisco Chronicle*, Mama adjusted her glasses and read an

advertisement. It was from the Owl Drug Company about medi-
cines offered at the Owl Drug stores.

"William, do ya tink we ought to get some medicine to prevent
tis flu?"

"What are dey offering?"

"Well, fur ten cents you can get Owl Peroxide, fur twenty-five
cents Owl Troat Gar-gal, fur forty cents ya can get Owl antiseptic
solution."

"What's da difference?"

"I really don't know. I need to speak wit da druggist."

"I wouldn't do anyting until we get more information from da
autorities," Papa replied.

By mid-October, over two thousand cases of the Spanish Flu
were reported in San Francisco. As I later learned, on October 17,
1918, the city's health officer Dr. William Hassler conducted a meeting with other members of the Board of Health. They met with
Mayor James Rolph Jr., along with members of the Red Cross, the
US Navy, and Army, as well as other community leaders. After some
discussion, the Board of Health voted to close several businesses
and banned most public gatherings such as lodge meetings, social
gatherings, and dances. Church attendance was made an exception,
as this was considered morally the right thing to do. They also decided to close all public and private schools. To ensure compliance
with the order, city police were given an extensive list of restrictions.

The school closure went into effect on Friday, October 18. I
thought that was as good as duck soup. I would not have to attend
school! Yes, I would have homework, but I would not have to con-
tend with the pious Sisters at my Catholic elementary school. On
that same day, the Owl Drug Company ran another ad in *The San
Francisco Chronicle* titled "Spanish Influenza and Some Precautions
Which Should Be Taken To Prevent Its Spread." It advised readers

to "Keep your bowels open. Intestinal Congestion invites disease."
They also gave tips such as "Make full use of all available sunshine,"
and "Fumigators should be used in the house, particularly during
and after any questionable sickness." Furthermore, they provided a
list of recommended disinfectants, including formaldehyde, an em-
balming fluid.

Hospitals began to fill up, and about four thousand were re-
corded in the first three weeks, and over fifty thousand cases were
reported in California. If one were to succumb to the flu, taking
aspirin and resting were common remedies prescribed by doctors.
It would not be known until decades later that giving aspirin to individuals under the age of sixteen could cause Reyes Syndrome, a
condition that often led to brain damage and death. Some doctors
also prescribed laxatives, believing this would purge the body of
harmful germs. One treatment during that era was to drink whiskey.
I'm sure if Papa had been afflicted with the flu, he would have opted
for that treatment.

The Board of Health reiterated that people avoid large crowds
and gatherings. Businesses, including sports venues, restaurants, and
theaters closed.

A mask-wearing ordinance was passed on October 24, 1918,
and was reported in *The San Francisco Chronicle*. Penalties for violation
were fines ranging from $5 to $100, and/or ten days' imprisonment.
The ordinance went into effect immediately. Mayor James Rolph Jr.
said: "conscience, patriotism and self-protection demand immediate
and rigid compliance" with mask wearing.

The mask mandate initially became a symbol of wartime patriotism. A Red Cross public service announcement at the time proclaimed, "The man or woman or child who will not wear a mask
now is a dangerous slacker," calling into question the patriotism of
mask refusers.

Before the end of the month, 110 people were arrested in one day in San Francisco for not complying with the new mask mandates.

Shortly after, World War I would come to an end with the US and its allies victorious. An armistice was signed with the Germans on the morning of November 11, 1918, in France. Word reached the West Coast of the US the evening before, when it was still November 10 in San Francisco, and shortly after midnight, celebrations began. Papa was so excited. He had narrowly missed being drafted. He would eventually have to register with the US military, but the war was now over. Papa could not have been more elated and animated. He woke me and my sisters.

"We have someting important ta do," he exclaimed with a feverish enthusiasm.

"What, Papa?" I asked.

"Get yur coats on and I'll show ya." His eyes flashed with excitement. He rummaged around the kitchen, on his knees, and pulled out pots and pans while Mama grabbed some spoons, barely keeping up with his hurried pace. Before I knew it, he left the kitchen floor cluttered with items he didn't need, like a cheese grater, butter dish, tin cans, and some old food pushers. He sprang to his feet and flung open the front door. Outside, we heard the echoing of car horns blaring, bells ringing, and the deep, low-pitched baritone blasts of fog horns resonating. We joined in by whacking our pots and pans as if it were the world's best New Year's celebration.

During the afternoon of November 11, crowds gathered on Market Street to celebrate. People wore masks, but the whole crowd avoidance mandate went out of the window, at least for the time being.

Just a week later, on November 16, 1918, businesses were allowed to reopen, but the mask mandate remained in place. On that very day in 1918, a boxing match was held at the San Francisco

Civic Auditorium, but most of the audience did not wear masks. Eventually, the police would crack down and enlarge photos to identify people who were not wearing masks. Mayor James Rolph Jr. and the city's public health officer Dr. William Hassler attended the match. The police identified both men as not complying with the mask mandate. Dr. Hassler said that his mask "must have slipped off" as he took a drag from his cigar. He was fined $5. A few days later, San Francisco's police chief would fine Mayor Rolph Jr $50.

When Papa found out, he said, "Mayor Rolph is a hypocrite. How can he expect all of us to wear masks if he won't comply? He is as dim-witted as a clam and as useful as a broken toilet."

Papa, like many other people during the time, poked a hole in his mask so he could smoke. He felt he was being dutiful.

The rhyme of that era was "Obey the laws and wear the gauze. Protect your jaws from septic paws."

The mask restriction was briefly lifted in San Francisco on November 21, 1918, and thousands of San Francisco residents once again gathered in the streets to celebrate. Sirens blared throughout the city. I, for one, was certainly happy. However, my glee would be short-lived. I would have to return to school on Monday, November 25. Our school day was extended by twenty minutes, and our winter holiday would be shortened, something I had not counted on.

Shortly after the New Year in 1919, the city was hit with six hundred new cases of the Spanish Flu, and a new mask mandate went into effect.

Many people felt that the government was overstepping its boundaries. An Anti-Mask League was formed in San Francisco, which would include several doctors and a member of the City's Board of Supervisors. On January 25, 1919, over 4,500 people attended their meeting. Many called for the resignation of Mayor James Rolph Jr.

On January 27, the league presented a petition to the city's Board
of Supervisors, demanding that the mask ordinance be repealed.
San Francisco lifted the mask requirement a few days later, effective
February 1, 1919, and, to my recollection, that was the end of the
mask requirement. Whether or not the pressure on Mayor Rolph Jr.
had something to do with it, I will never know. Though Papa did
not have a strong sentiment either way on the mask mandate, he
said Mayor Rolph Jr. flip-flopped his political positions "faster dan
a cockroach could scurry across a kitchen floor, in da middle of da
night, when da light bulb is turned on."

There were a few more cases of the flu that year in San
Francisco, but I was concentrating on what I felt were more important things at the time. Monday, March 17, 1919, would be an incredibly special day at our school. It was St. Patrick's Day. St. Patty's
Day, as we liked to call it, had originated in Ireland and included a
celebration of one of Ireland's patron saints, Saint Patrick. Children
of Irish immigrants made up the bulk of the student body at our
school, and our ancestors had brought the traditional celebration to
the United States. This included special church services, feasts with
corned beef and cabbage, and wearing or affixing something green
to our clothes. Green, we were told, would make us invisible to de-
vious, deceitful, nasty little leprechauns. If you did not wear green,
you gave fellow students the permission to pinch you, and this could
be quite painful. Our school, in keeping with tradition, allowed us
to wear or attach something green to our uniforms. I didn't want to
risk getting pinched, so I made sure to wear a green tie and affixed
a felt shamrock to my uniform. My friends and I enjoyed secretly
removing green items from boys' clothes, especially from the boys
who we liked. As soon as we removed the items, we pinched the boy,
often on the rear. However, this would frequently backfire, and we

would get chased around the playground screaming. This was fun until we would receive the often more forceful, reciprocated pinch.

A couple of months after that, in May 1919, my mother gave birth to another baby. My sister Theresa, nine years younger than me, was the fifth girl born to my parents. Given that Katherine had passed away in 1917, we would never be together as a collection of five girls. Theresa was adorable, with smooth, symmetrical features and rosy cheeks. Although my father pretended to be happy, I could tell he still wanted a boy. Fortunately for him, the Catholic Church encouraged procreation, and from what I gathered, he and my mother continued to try to have a boy.

CHAPTER THREE

Papa gave up his transportation business in 1919, as trucks had essentially replaced the horse-drawn wagons in the teamster industry. He thought briefly about continuing to work as a teamster driving a truck, but instead opted for purchasing and running a modest grocery store in San Francisco.

A couple of years before that, in 1917, Congress had passed the Eighteenth Amendment outlawing the production, sale, and transportation of liquor.

The amendment clashed with the drinking culture of the Irish Catholic immigrants. I had witnessed about every aunt and uncle of mine imbibe spirits of some sort, at one time or another. Even the term whiskey is thought to have originated from the Gaelic language which once dominated Ireland before the sixteenth century. Ireland, a historically impoverished country, saw a steep rise in alcohol consumption in the eighteenth and nineteenth centuries among the working class, who often lived as tenants in crowded urban areas of squalor, and used it to bring some pleasure amidst many burdens.

As a child at the time, I did not understand the roots of the Temperance Movement that led to the amendment. I would only gain that knowledge long after our family had been dragged into bootlegging in the years to come. Papa blamed the passage of the amendment on Protestants who made up a significant portion of the Temperance Movement.

When the United States was formed in 1776, consumption of alcohol was already part of our social fabric. Celebrations, communal activities, and social events all typically involved some intoxication, even if it was mild. Priests, ministers, clergymen, and politicians were just a few of the groups that regularly included alcohol in their rituals.

Many of the beverages were originally weak in alcohol content, and people drank them throughout the day and at meals. In New England towns, "grog time" became an important ritual. A bell would ring twice a day, usually at 11 a.m. and 4 p.m., to signal men to stop working in farm fields, mills, and factories, to take a break where they would drink cider.

The alcohol content of distilled beverages gradually increased over time. Hard liquor became more readily available. It became increasingly apparent that this was a problem. People were becoming drunk more often, and many became dependent on alcohol. By 1830 the average American, aged sixteen and up, consumed the equivalent of eighty-eight bottles of whisky a year. Per capita, the nineteenth century became the century with the highest alcohol consumption in the United States, as well as in many other countries. Disruptions in social life occurred. As many men became increasingly drunk, wages dwindled from missing work and spending extra cash on alcoholic beverages. Many women and children became poor. Some were victims of domestic violence or sexual abuse, often spurred on by heavy drinking.

This fueled the formation of many Temperance movements. Though Protestant groups made up the majority, unbeknownst to Papa, there were a few movements started by Catholics. One

Catholic Temperance movement was started by an Irish priest who established the Teetotal Abstinence Society.

One of the principal abstinence groups was the Woman's Christian Temperance Union. They wore white ribbons on their dresses to symbolize purity, abstinence, and membership in the organization. One of their goals was to protect the home and children from the effects of alcohol. Their slogan was "Agitate, Educate, Legislate. "

The most successful Temperance organization in the United States was the Anti-Saloon League, established in 1893. It became a major political force and used lobbying and literature to promote the Eighteenth Amendment to the Constitution.

After the passage of the Eighteenth Amendment, no one took the law seriously at first, including Papa. After he purchased the grocery store on Moultrie Street, he sold liquor there, which was technically illegal at the time. The Eighteenth Amendment had not been enforced up to that time. However, as 1919 went on, the writing on the wall began to appear. Newspaper articles printed stories regarding a strict enforcement that would go into effect on January 17, 1920.

Papa and Mama had many conversations regarding the upcoming ban. My father was concerned about losing a sizable portion of his business. While we were all in the living room, I remember Papa sipping an Old Fashioned while sitting in his favorite upholstered chair. He was irate over the mostly Protestant-led legislation. He wore an animated expression.

"Tis is so unfair. It'll ruin our business. Maggie, dey are screwing over da Eye-rish."

My mother was reading *The Dubliners* by James Joyce while sitting on the couch. She abruptly snapped the book shut. "Ya should've seen dat comin," Mama replied, with a look of disdain.

"I'll sell what I can until dat time, but I am gunna stash some liquor in our basement."

"Fur what puhrpus?"

"I'll wait until da laws get repealed, den sell it."

"Will … what if dat doesn't happen?" Mama frowned.

Papa stuck his chest out to look more assertive, but my mother did not appear to be having any of it. Papa then took a different approach. He clasped his hands together, then turned his palms up and shrugged his shoulders. "I'll figure out a way to sell anyhow, den."

"Seriously, William," Mama rolled her eyes, "ya have a screw loose." She promptly got up from the chair she was sitting in and walked away.

With conviction, Papa went straight to work. We could hear clinking and clanking sounds as he cleared out our basement. Gradually, he organized and stashed away over half of the liquor that remained at his store. He labeled every box, case or crate he brought with him. Mostly, he saved vast quantities of his favorite alcoholic beverage: whiskey.

As Prohibition was about to take place, people were allowed to keep and consume any liquor they had stored in their homes, if they didn't sell the products. This caused an absolute frenzy shortly before enforcement was about to take effect. On Friday, January 16, 1920, the last day before Prohibition, there was a frenetic rush to sell and acquire booze. Like a beehive, there was a buzz of activity that filled the streets of San Francisco. People scurried around the city with crates and boxes containing alcoholic beverages, trying to distribute the product before midnight. The remaining liquor at Papa's grocery store sold out before noon. Had he not stored some at home, he might have been able to sell it all. After work, Papa joined in the hysteria and sold a few crates from our basement. He kept a massive portion of the liquor, however, believing the value of his remaining liquor would rise.

A newspaper article in *The San Francisco Chronicle* had indicated that some people who did not get their liquor by midnight were left to stand in their doorways "with haggard faces and glittering eyes."

On the opposite side of the spectrum, the San Francisco County Woman's Christian Temperance Union, along with members of the Church Federation, the Anti-Saloon League, the Epworth League Alliance, and other organizations gathered at the First Congressional Church on Mason Street to celebrate the beginning of Prohibition. One of the speakers, a WCTU member by the name of Miss Christine Tinling, described Prohibition as "God's present to the nation." She also said that women of the "white ribbon," as the members of their union were called, had finally reached their goal of the "Never, never country," the promised land of Prohibition, despite jeers and humiliations from the liquor interests.

CHAPTER FOUR

After the enforcement of Prohibition on 17 January, 1920, Papa began to drink his stockpile of liquor. He drank it with fervor, often consuming up to a bottle a day. As shrewd as I had thought he had been, Papa's stash would gradually and carelessly dwindle.

Mama said Papa was well on his way to getting the "Celtic Curse." I asked her what she meant, and she said he was going to get liver disease and acquire a liver belly if he continued the path he was on. I wasn't sure what that meant, but it didn't sound promising.

I had associated the word Celtic with positive things up until then. Through my school, I had joined an Irish dance group. I learned a little about Celtic history on orientation day. Although the Celtic tribes originated in Central Europe, some tribes immigrated to the Isles, which would later be known as Britain and Ireland. They arrived in Ireland in 500 BC. They brought the Gaelic language with them and were known for their colorful wool clothing, including tunics, cloaks, and belts. They imported a form of dance that was associated with ancient Celtic rituals and celebrations. The dances evolved over the centuries. The Irish Celts primarily became Catholic, whereas many Scottish Celtic groups did not. Their dances were similar until the Irish Catholic dancers began to restrict their hand and arm movements. No one knew for sure why the Irish did this, and there were several theories behind it. One was that Queen Elizabeth I of England, who was responsible for taking over Irish land to start plantations and Protestant settlements, summoned a group of Irish dancers to dance for her. In protest, they kept their arms straight and rigid and refused to lift them in an act of defiance to the Queen. I knew enough stubborn Irish relatives in my extended family so I could see that as a valid postulation.

Another theory was that the clergy and nuns in the Catholic Church felt the arm movements were too sexual and provocative, and this could lead to uncontrolled smooching. Knowing who ran our local church and convent, that theory seemed very plausible to me. God forbid unbridled smooching!

The third leading theory was to simply show off intricate footwork. I could vouch for that one. To perform Irish dancing, you needed to have good balance, flexibility, and the ability to dance on your toes. It was not easy to learn, but once I mastered it, it was enormous fun.

My group performed at our school on St. Patrick's Day on Wednesday, March 17, 1920. We wore our school uniforms, but our dance group was given handmade Irish patch caps made of wool or tweed. Shamrocks were embroidered on the front of our caps, which made us look authentic, I suppose. We were accompanied by a group of four volunteer local musicians who played Irish music. One woman played an Irish tin whistle, a man beat a bodhran, which was a drum made from goatskin, another woman played the Uilleann pipes, squeezing the bellows of the instrument under her right arm, forcing air through a tube leading to a leather bag in her left arm, and another man played the fiddle. My family came out to watch the performance. First, I had the collywobbles, but my stomach settled once the show started. Fortunately, that day I didn't have two left feet and managed to perform the dances gracefully. Afterwards, while my cheeks were still red, my father said my performance was "grand" and I felt overwhelmingly happy.

The joyful mood of those days changed when Papa lost a significant part of his business. Money became tight, and circumstances abruptly changed in the White family household. By the second half of that year, Papa decided we no longer needed to get our haircuts at a barbershop. He lined us up one by one, and at the end of the line was a chair with newspaper spread underneath. Papa cut our hair using a bowl over our heads as a guide. To save more money, he didn't allow us to use much electricity. We were also not permitted to turn on the lights to read. I had to do all my reading and homework before dark or use candlelight. He often turned off the boiler to save on gas, and the radiators stopped distributing heat. Aside from the occasions when Papa started a fire in our fireplace, the house became cold. The exception would be when we had an important guest.

We did have such a guest later that year. We invited our local priest, Father O'Leary, over for Thanksgiving. It was considered an honor to host your priest for a holiday. We hadn't been able to invite our priest over for the better portion of two years due to the Spanish Flu pandemic, so, this was a momentous occasion. I was ten years old at the time, and Bette was closest in age, a little over three years younger than me, followed by Mickey, then Theresa.

Father O'Leary was a kind man with greying hair, possibly in his late fifties. He had emigrated from 'the old country' nearly twenty years earlier than my parents, but managed to hold onto his thick Irish brogue. He was of short stature but immense importance. He came to the house wearing a neatly pressed, shiny black, long-sleeved hoodless cassock with a white collar. He had the appearance of a saintly celebrity. Oblivious of how the hierarchy of the Catholic

Church worked, I imagined Father O'Leary could be in line for Pope Benedict's job at the Vatican!

At the time we hosted the dinner, Papa had already gone through his entire stash of whiskey except for a couple of remaining bottles, which he would share with our honored guest. The dinner table was laid out with our finest dishes as well as Fall decorations of acorns and colorful leaves, some of which we made in school. Father O'Leary was to be seated at the head of the table. As the eldest child, Papa said it was my duty to make our priest comfortable. I pulled his chair out so he could get into place, then pushed it back in for him to be seated. Then I unfolded his cloth napkin and put it in his lap.

"Ah, tis is lovely. Fair play to ya," he nodded his head. "Tanks to all of ya fur having me 'ere. And tanks to da Lord fur making it possible."

"Amen," we collectively responded.

On the table were cranberries and mashed potatoes with gravy. Mama brought out a staple of hers, ambrosia. It was a jiggly mess of slices of canned pineapple and oranges mixed in a mushy, almost gelatinous goo of marshmallows, cream, and coconut. Eyeing the glutinous mountain of ooze, my sisters' mouths watered, but not mine. I was more interested in the turkey and the homemade apple pie Mama had baked for dessert. After Papa carved the turkey in the kitchen Mama brought it out to the table.

As the wonderful aroma of a juicy turkey filled the air, Papa quickly lit his cigar. He liked to smoke Chinese cigars made locally in San Francisco, which he sold at his store. They were cheaper than the ones a businessman could acquire from Florida or elsewhere. Due to anti-Chinese sentiment at the time, Chinese manufacturers often disguised their businesses with Spanish names. So, Papa purchased those Chinese cigars from Chinese producers like Columbo & Co.

Sometimes Papa made special trips to Chinatown to purchase his cigars. He often described fascinating and unusual things that piqued Mama's interest. So, our family made a special trip down to Clay Street and Grant Avenue, to see it for ourselves, a couple of weeks before the Thanksgiving dinner feast. The area was experiencing a revival of sorts. There was a crime element that was dwindling. Prior to that, the overwhelmingly non-Asian population within San Francisco considered it a dangerous area, and most families did not venture there.

Papa said many Chinese began coming during the Gold Rush in the mid-1800s to escape poverty and wars in China.

"At first, dese pee-pull were welcomed. In 1850, da Mayor of San Francisco, Mayor Geary, held a ceremony for tree hundred men in Portsmouth Square. Can you believe dat?"

In those first few years, over 99 percent of the Chinese immigrants were men. Some were single; others were married and left their families in China in the hope of bringing wealth back. Some stayed in San Francisco to work in industries such as fishing, textiles, tobacco, and laundry services. Some went to the gold fields in the late 1840s and 1850s in search of a quick fortune, and others stayed in the 1860s to work on the transcontinental railroad. A number of those returned to San Francisco to live in Chinatown. Gradually, an anti-Chinese sentiment developed among European immigrants seeking employment as the Chinese took lower-paying jobs. A series of anti-Chinese laws were put into place beginning in the 1850s and continuing throughout the 1800s. In 1870, San Francisco even passed an ordinance prohibiting anyone from using poles to carry merchandise on sidewalks, which was prevalent among Chinese merchants at the time. Tongs, organizations within San Francisco's Chinatown, and Chinatowns across the US, were formed to help protect Chinese Americans, and many offered monetary assistance. However, as time went on, some of the Tongs became involved in criminal activity.

In San Francisco's Chinatown, the imbalance of sexes contributed to the development of houses of prostitution, and opium and gambling dens. This fueled already existing anti-Chinese sentiment. During that period, most Chinese Americans did not allow girls to attend Chinese schools in Chinatown. Many women entered the sex industry, and some became slaves who were sex trafficked. By the late 1800s, 90 percent of its population was still male, and feuds began between Tong groups. Different factions targeted the illegal markets and forced Chinese merchants to pay protection fees. Tong wars broke out in San Francisco's Chinatown. In one instance in 1879, fifty men from two Tong gangs fought in an alley over the ownership rights to a Chinese slave girl, and four gang members were killed.

"From my understandin', i'twas bad." Papa flicked ashes from his cigar onto the ashtray on the table. "It just takes one bad Chinaman to ruin Chinatown. Not awl Chinamen are bad." Papa had a look of concern. I'm not sure if Papa realized that the term Chinaman was offensive. It was ingrained in his vocabulary.

To quell the criminal activity, the San Francisco Police Department formed a special police unit known as the Chinatown Squad, and some inroads were made, some officers took bribes from the Tong gangs, so it was generally ineffective.

Unfortunately, while attempts were made to root out criminal activity from Chinatown, the sprawling neighborhood would experience a bubonic plague epidemic beginning in 1900. Its first casualty was a resident named Wong Chut King, who died on March 6,

1900. Bubonic plague was thought to have originated from infected rats, transported by ships, containing a specific disease-causing bacterium. In 1898, a researcher discovered that fleas feeding on infected rats could pass the bacteria to humans through their bites, but this theory was far from widely accepted at the time. Instead, many people thought that the germ infected humans through open wounds or ingestion of contaminated food. City officials quarantined Chinatown the day after Wong Chut King died, but it would only last three days after an outcry from those living in Chinatown, as well as business leaders in San Francisco, and protests from local newspapers. Views were expressed in one prominent newspaper that the quarantine was a way for the board of health officials to increase their budget appropriation.

"'Twas all about money!" Papa became animated. "Da business leaders inside and outside of da Chinese community knew how important Chinatown was economically fur da area. Der was no way dey would let dat quarantine last."

Many people did not trust Dr. Joseph Kinyoun, who was the physician responsible for investigating tissue samples from corpses in San Francisco. Local and state officials downplayed the threat to protect interstate trade and travel. Newspaper reporters mocked him in print and with a cartoonish illustration indicating the plague was "bogus." California Governor Henry Gage claimed that Dr. Kinyoun and other federal employees had falsified evidence for the plague by injecting cadavers with bacteria. Dr. Kinyoun resigned from his position in 1901 after intense scrutiny. However, deaths mounted, and in 1903 the new physician in charge managed a city-wide clean up that included trapping rats, tearing down shacks, replacing sidewalks with asphalt, and spraying carbolic acid into Chinatown's cellars. Other city-wide efforts included trash clean-up, fumigations in the sewer system with sulfur dioxide, and a bounty for citizens to turn in rat tails. Ships arriving from ports known to have plague were quarantined. Eventually, through a combination of those efforts it was eliminated. By 1904 there had been 121 cases resulting in 119 deaths, and more in the greater Bay Area.

More tragedy struck in 1906 when the Great San Francisco Earthquake destroyed much of the city, including Chinatown. Along with its destruction went Chinatown's gambling halls, ghettos, and houses of prostitution. The power of the criminal Tongs was drastically reduced. When Chinatown was rebuilt, it became a less arduous task to regulate. The bubonic plague did return to San Francisco in 1907, but it would not be centered in Chinatown, and would be eradicated by November 1908.

One of the topics of conversation at the Thanksgiving meal with Father O'Leary was our family trip to Chinatown.

Papa removed his cigar from his mouth briefly. "Fader O'Leary, i'twas absolutely fascinating." Papa, like my other relatives from County Cork, liked to exaggerate. He could not say something was simply good or bad. It either had to be the best or the worst thing he had ever seen. He held his arms out and shook them. "It was brilliant. It's a triving neighborhood. No one gave us a hard time. Not-tat awl. 'Twas lovely."

"Aw, what did ya see?" Father O'Leary was curious. San Francisco's oldest Catholic Cathedral, St. Mary's, was and still is in Chinatown, and he knew a lot of the history. Though he was not a member of the church's clergy, he worked with the church and had made numerous trips into Chinatown. Originally established by Father Henry Ignatius Stark, St. Mary's Cathedral was built in 1854 by Chinese laborers. Its mission was to teach the Catholic faith to the Chinese community. When it was completed, it was the tallest building in all of California. Though essentially destroyed by the

1906 earthquake, its brick and bell towers remained, and it was rebuilt in 1909.

"Well, Fader, we did go to Saint Mary's and saw awl da stained-glass windows, beautiful woodwork, and grand murals."

"Of course ya did, good man. Dat's lovely. Ya know da Catolics have been doin' good tings der for years. In times of need, we have provided food and medical supplies. We've also been teachin' da word of God and have provided teaching in da English language. 'Twas almost fur notin', however."

"How so?" Mama chimed in.

"Well, in da 1870s der was an economic depression in da United States and unemployment rose. Chinese immigrants began taking lower pay, undercutting da wages of da Eye-rish who already were paid poorly. Do ya understand dat?" Mama nodded her head. "Dis led to resentment, and in 1877 a riot broke out in Chinatown between da Chinese immigrants and da mostly Eye-rish Catolic immigrants in da nearby and surrounding neighborhoods. It lasted ah-boat two or tree days. Many businesses in Chinatown were set ablaze, and windows were smashed. Eventually da police squelched da riot, but some people died in da disturbance."

"Oh, my." Mama was not aware of that part of San Francisco's history.

Father O'Leary continued. "From my understandin' it took quite a bit of time for da Catolic church to regain da trust of da Chinese people, even dough da church had notin' to do wit da matter. Do ya understand?" We all shook our heads in agreement. We did not dare disagree with anything that our priest had to say. "I hate to say it, but some Protestants have done a lot of good work in Chinatown." It was rare for an Irish Catholic priest to say anything positive about Protestants, given the oppression in Ireland. "In da 1870s dey started a Presbyterian Mission House called da Cameron

House on the edge of Chinatown. A woman of Scottish descent, along wit a former Chinese slave, rescued Chinese girls and young women who had been sold or kidnapped into slavery. I tink over da decades, dey rescued over eight hundred pee-pull. Anyhow, what else did ye do when you were der?"

With excitement, I knelt on my chair to make myself more visible, and raised my hand. I desperately wanted to tell Father O'Leary what we saw. In those days, as a child, you could not just speak your mind in front of a guest, especially a priest. You had to wait to get permission. Papa controlled the actions of the White family. He was like a gatekeeper at Buckingham Palace.

Mama looked at Papa. "Should we let Ann tell Fader O'Leary ah-boatit?"

As I awaited approval from the grandmaster, Papa, shrugged his shoulders and turned his palms slightly upwards. "Why not?"

"Thank you, Papa. Well, Father O'Leary, it was a lot of fun. It was like digging a hole in your backyard and ending up in China; like entering a different world! There were a lot of people, and they were packed into small areas … packed like sardines, I would say. And about half the men were smoking."

"Is dat so?" Father O'Leary perked up, paying attention to every important detail I had to say.

"We saw a lot of buildings with Oriental architecture. Some of the lampposts looked like giant balls and others looked like paper lanterns. There is a building called Sing Chong that has a three-tiered pagoda at the top. And some of the structures have balconies that look like Chinese boats!"

My little sister Mickey, being three-and-a-half and not knowing the protocol as to when to speak, piped in. "Big boats!" She held her hands wide.

"Ya don't say!" Father O'Leary smiled and became wide-eyed, pretending to be exceedingly interested.

Mickey happily nodded her head in affirmation before I went on speaking. In the meantime, my one-and-a-half-year-old sister Theresa was in her highchair mashing a corn muffin she had been given.

"We saw some buildings that were painted in wonderful colors of red, green, yellow, and blue. Some had detailed Chinese lettering. On some streets, there are wires strung between the buildings holding dangling Chinese lanterns. Real ones, not like the fake ones on the lampposts."

"Oh, dat is lovely!" Father O'Leary smiled. "When Chinatown was rebuilt after da 1906 earthquake, buildings were reconstructed mostly in da Edwardian style, but many were built to include Chinese-style architecture."

Papa looked at me and interjected. "Ya know why dey did dat, don't ya?" I shook my head. "Dey did it to attract tourists. Tis all about money!"

Father O'Leary went on. "Well, it's a lot more dan dat. Some of it was done because dey are proud of der Chinese heritage. A lot of changes occurred after dat earthquake. God works in mysterious ways. In 1911, China issued orders dat da Chinese should adopt customs in da country in which dey were living. Pretty soon, men in San Francisco's Chinatown started cutting off braids on da back of der heads; they called them ques or bings. Children began attending schools in greater numbers and learning English. Anyhow, dey are starting to assimilate better but at da same time have preserved some Chinese culture.

"Despite da good tings dat are happening, some say dat der is discrimination against da Chinese goin' on right-tas we speak. Over on Angel Island, in da San Francisco Bay, an immigration processing center opened ah-boat ten years ago, in 1910, to process immigrants coming in from nations like China across da Pacific. It is supposed to be like da Ellis Island of da West, but it hasn't worked out dat way. Over on Ellis Island, immigrants are usually processed wit-in hours or a few days, but over here, fur da Chinese it's apparently an average of two weeks to several months. To be fair ah-boat it, da immigrants coming true over here face many more helt problems requiring quarantine but der are many being held wit no medical problems for lengty periods."

Papa took a puff of his cigar and then temporarily pushed it to the side of his mouth. "Why is dat, Fader O'Leary?"

"It has to do wit da Chinese Exclusion Act passed in 1882. It halted awl immigration of da Chinese to America except fur students, teachers, merchants, returning laborers, diplomats, and temporary autorized travelers. And doze pee-pull dat are currently allowed in have to show extensive documentation, have enough money to get to der destination, and I tink dey have to have a sponsor. A lot of dem must go true extensive medical exams, including laboratory testing. Awl of dem have to fill out long questionnaires and go true lengty interrogations. If just one piece of information is incorrect, den dey can be held for prolonged periods while dey make an appeal. To be fair to da government, a lot of phony documents have been given to da immigration center. But dey have no means of handling da situation. Doze pee-pull are understaffed. Der are backlogs occurring. From what I hear from da clergy at Saint Mary's, der congregation is telling dem about a lot of bad tings goin' on at Angel Island. Da Chinese are being segregated and kept in locked, cramped quarters. Dey are saying dat da living conditions are inhumane. Da reports I am getting are dat der is poor sanitation."

"Father O'Leary?"

"Yes, Ann?"

"If what the Chinese are saying at Saint Mary's is true, that is absolutely terrible what is going on there."

"Dat-tit is indeed."

Mama interjected, "Dey-ur God's children an'awl."

I pondered for a few seconds. "When I grow up, I would like to work with the department responsible for immigration. I would be fair and treat people humanely. I would treat them with dignity."

"Dignity is awl ya can ask fur. Dat's what da Eye-rish have been asking fur, fur several years … Well, den, from here on out, when-ever ya go outside, may raindrops fall lightly on your brow. Dat's a blessing."

"Thank you, Father O'Leary. You are so knowledgeable and wise." I smiled up at him.

"Well, you know what dey say, don't ya? An old broom, like me, knows da dirty corners best. Anyhow … what else did ya partake in?"

I sat up. "In Chinatown, we saw the Chinese Telephone Exchange. It's a tall, red and gold building with a curly roof. The telephone ladies wore headphones and their arms were always moving, pulling and pushing plugs and cords. We even learned that those ladies had to memorize thousands of telephone numbers by heart!"

"Aw, dat's interesting; it sounds like ye had great craic … did ya visit any of da markets or eat in Chinatown?"

My six-and-a-half-year-old sister Bette started to raise her hand, bouncing up and down in her chair, eager to get a word in. Papa looked at her and nodded at her to speak.

"We saw chickens in cages. We even went to a fish market, and they had eels in glass tanks. There was a fish on ice with lots of sharp teeth. Papa, what is that called?"

"Monkfish."

"Oh, ya, that's what it's called. Also, we saw lots of dried fish in boxes, and some still had their eyeballs." Bette made her own eyes look wide by pulling her eyelids apart with her thumbs and forefingers to drive home the image. She shuddered, remembering it. "There were dried squid also, and they looked like parachutes." She made a sour face.

"Yeah, it's pretty exotic," I interjected. "After we visited the fish market, we went into some stores, and there were a lot of beads hanging down. They use them for partitions. Mama and Papa bought us a couple of paper fans to share. We're going to use them next summer to cool off our dolls when they get hot … after that, we looked for a place to eat. They have lots of noodle and chop-suey cafes and restaurants, and we ate chop suey!"

"Did ya like it?"

"Yeah, it was my first time eating chop-suey, and it was pretty good, but my sisters didn't like the ginger in it. Mine had pork, bean sprouts, celery, onions, umm … mushrooms, and water chestnuts. Oh, and I almost forgot, just like a lot of Irish dishes, they use a lot of cabbage!"

Father O'Leary looked me directly in the eye. "Cabbage is not da only ting dat da Eye-rish and Chinese have in common. Do ya know dat da Eye-rish and da Chinese were da ones dat were responsible for most of da construction of da transcontinental railroad?"

"Yes, we learned about it in school."

"Do ya know why da railroad companies liked to hire da Eye-rish and the Chinese to work on da railroad?"

"Cheap labor?"

"Ya are correct wit dat statement, but dat is not what I was fishin' fur. Well, let me tell ya. Boat cultures liked to drink tea."

"Father O'Leary, why would that make railroad companies like to hire them?"

"To drink tea, ya must boil water. If ya boil water, den you are less likely to get da diarrheal condition called dysentery. If you didn't get dysentery den you didn't get sick. So, da railroad companies had less people dat were sick… At least, I tink so."

"But we drink coffee!"

"I know, times are changin' but dat was someting da Chinese and da Eye-rish also had in common besides eatin' a lot of cabbage."

Bette raised her hand. "Father, Ann forgot to tell you something."

"What is that, my little angel? G'wan."

"After we left Chinatown, we took a streetcar to one of the Japantowns in San Francisco and went to a bakery. Or was it a candy factory? Mama, what was it called?

"Benkyodo," Mama replied. "It's boat a candy factory and bakery. I heard dat dey were making treats called fortune cookies, wit special messages inside, so we decided to go der before we ended our day. One of my friends said dat dis establishment is making cookies for da Tea Garden at Golden Gate Park."

"What are dey like?" Father O'Leary was captivated.

Bette took over. "They are like sweet, folded, thin cookies that contain important messages." She gestured with her hands to demonstrate the shape. I couldn't tell for sure, but it looked like Father O'Leary's mouth began to water.

Fortune cookies were invented in Japan in the 1800s and were more like crackers than cookies. Originally, messages were not in the center of the treat but rather in the crevices. They were made from rice or miso paste (fermented soybeans) or sesame, and tended to be darker and larger than cookies, and were not sweet. In the early 1900s, at the Japanese Tea Garden in San Francisco's Golden Gate Park, the caretaker made them sweeter and began serving them with tea. He then hired Benkyodo's candy factory in Japantown to mass-produce them. It was Benkyodo that added butter and vanilla and transformed them into cookies. Chinese immigrants in Los Angeles and San Francisco produced something similar following this, but Chinese restaurants would not routinely adopt the practice of handing out fortune cookies on a wider scale until World War II when Japanese Americans were interned, leaving a void in the industry.

"Oh, what kind of fortunes did ya get?" Father O'Leary asked Bette.

"Mine said 'a stranger will be your friend,'" she replied.

Mama interjected. "Hers said, 'A stranger will cross yer path who later becomes yer friend.'"

"Dat's nice. We can't be mean to strangers. Annie, what did yur fortune cookie message say?"

"Mine said, 'Fall down seven times, get up eight.' Papa's said, 'The child of a frog is a frog,' and Mama's just said, 'Thank you for your business.' Mickey got an odd fortune cookie message. Hers said, 'I am a slave in a fortune cookie factory, please save me!'"

"Oh, my!" Father O'Leary covered his mouth in disbelief.

"Yes, we were concerned and took it up to the counter. We were pretty steamed up about the whole thing. Bette started to tell Mickey that there could be a slave making the cookies in the back room."

Mickey piped up. "We were going to take the poor little girl," she paused for a moment and shook both her hands, "or boy, home with us, and let them stay in our room and play with our toys."

"Is dat so?" Father O'Leary appeared concerned and put his hand under his chin.

I resumed our story. "At the counter, we showed the message to a woman who, in broken English, said it was a joke and gave us another fortune cookie."

"Well, den, it sounds like yur trip turned out quite lovely."

"It sure did, Father O'Leary."

Mama soon lit up a cigarette. She did not smoke except for special occasions. Before long, the room became smoke-filled, dampening the delicious turkey aroma. Father O'Leary congratulated my mother for finally gaining the right to vote. The Nineteenth Amendment had been ratified in August of that year, allowing women to vote in the United States. Then he spoke about what was going on at the church, including upcoming Christmas events and church services that our parish had planned. He also talked about all the charitable deeds that the nuns had been doing for our community. I didn't want to be reminded of the nuns. I supposed many were doing right by God, but there certainly was a vile lot of them that were not.

After about an hour, it became apparent Father O'Leary had drunk more whiskey than Mama and Papa combined. As the night wore on, laughter began filling the air. To my delight, after becoming inebriated, Father O'Leary started making fun of the nuns. Perhaps he saw what I had seen, or the whiskey made him speak more honestly. He must have known the truth. How could anyone not know the heavy-handed ways of the Sisters?

Father O'Leary began telling jokes. He even began telling ones about the drinking culture of the Irish. "Tree men walk into a bar: an Englishman, an Eye-rishman, and a Scotsman. Dey each ordered a bee-er. And da fly lands in each of der mugs. Da Englishman pushes aside his mug and asks fur a new bee-er. Da Scotsman pulls da fly out of his mug and continues to drink. Da Eye-rishman pulls da fly out of his bee-err. He lifts da fly to eye level and turns da fly around so dat dey are face-to-face. Den he says, 'spit it out ya little bugger!'"

I remember laughing so hard I almost peed right there. I fell to the ground laughing. Even my youngest siblings Theresa and

Mickey, who did not understand the joke, giggled as the laughter in the room became contagious.

Between Father O'Leary's drinking that night and the jokes he told, I would never see him in the same light again. Though I still admired him, he would no longer be the godly figure that I had once made him out to be. The uncomfortable reality was that I had an upcoming confession scheduled with Father O'Leary.

Being Catholic, we were expected to go to confession to confess our sins. Given I had plenty of sins, I was no stranger to confession. There was a dark cubicle where I kneeled by myself on a hard wooden bench, and the priest was sitting in another, as I imagined, more comfortable cubicle adjacent to mine. There were drapes between us. The purpose, I was told, was to confess the dreadful things I had done to absolve myself of all my sins, so I could make amends with God, and live a dutiful, holy, faithful life within the Catholic Church.

At school, we knew all too well it was better not to divulge too much at confession, especially something committed against a teacher, or else you faced a lot of trouble, or at the least, had to perform community service. So, I would say just enough to get some consternation and a tongue-lashing, and yet feel like I was doing right by God.

Before Christmas that year, I gave my confession to Father O'Leary.

Father O'Leary partially pulled back the drapes, but I was unable to see him. "Aw, Miss Ann, welcome to confession. It's good to know yur 'ere. How is yur family doin'?"

"They are doing well, thank you."

"As ya know, 'tis is an important encounter wit Jesus da Good Shepherd. Da priest is da messenger to convey furgiveness of yur sins to Jesus. Let's begin ... " I knew the basic format, as I had done this a few times. Together we said: "In the name of the Father," and we raised our hands to our forehead, saying "and of the Son," then we touched our chests, saying "and of the Holy Spirit," and then we touched our left shoulder, then the right. We both finished with an "Amen."

"What sins are keeping ya from loving God, Miss Ann? What do ya ask da Lord fur furgiveness?"

"Bless me for I have sinned. I have disrespected my parents on a few occasions."

"How so?"

"I didn't pick up my dolls and put them away after my mother asked me to."

"G'wan."

"I slapped my sister Bette's hand after she tried to grab food off my plate at dinner time."

"And?"

"My father asked me to apologize to Bette, but I didn't. I already got punished for that one, Father O'Leary."

"Anyting else?"

For a few seconds, my heart raced, and my palms began to sweat. I tried hard to suppress my thoughts about my other sins. I did not dare tell him I had disrespected a nun. I think God forgave me for that without having had to confess. "I can't think of anything else at the moment, Father."

"OK, den. Tis is what I want ya to do. Be grateful to God for da family dat has been given to ya. I want ya to say da Hail Mary and the Our Fader prayer at home. Dat would be the right ting to do, wouldn't it Miss Ann?"

"Yes, Father."

He said a prayer and absolved me of my sins ... at least the sins I spoke of. My sin bank was half empty at that point. I was glad to get that out of the way. I knew I could then enjoy Christmas.

CHAPTER FIVE

Despite 1920 being a year of relative frugality in the White family household, my sisters and I had a happy Christmas season. Mama had cut down some evergreen branches of trees at a local park. The house smelled like the holidays. My sisters and I helped Mama decorate our Christmas tree a few days before Christmas. Papa adorned the tree with strings of Mazda lamps, clear glass electric bulbs that gave off an invitingly warm, yellowish-white glow. For previous Christmases, we used real candles clipped to branches.

In keeping with tradition at the time, we fastened upside-down paper cones to the tree branches. Santa Claus would later fill the cones with candy and hide small gifts worth a few pennies inside the tree, such as a bag of jacks with a red ball. We would typically receive one major gift from our parents, such as a doll, and sometimes some knitted items from a relative. Christmas carolers often came to the front door to sing songs.

The one thing my sisters and I did not enjoy around Christmas was hearing what would happen to us if we didn't behave. It was difficult to discern at our ages what stories Papa told were true and which were fictitious. Papa repeatedly told us that when he grew up in Ireland, his father Jeremiah banished one of Papa's sisters, Norah, to a convent for misbehaving. He never saw her again. I later found out that the frightening story was true. However, he told us fictional stories too. Most families would tell their children they would get a lump of coal if they fell out of line. That would have been simple and a fate I could have lived with if I had truly been disobedient. However, Papa took it a step further, for some inexplicable reason. He pulled out sets of old Christmas cards showing us hideous drawings of a creature that you did not want to come across.

"Dis is Krampus," Papa smirked. He pulled out a colorful card depicting a half-human, half-goat character with gnarled horns, a long tail, and a slithering tongue. In the illustration, Krampus was stuffing a misbehaving boy in a sack while his sister sat forlornly on the floor, near a coil of chains. Krampus seemed ready to lock her up if she made a misstep. "Krampus is evil. He likes to carry a bundle of birch switches to whip and punish naughty children." He made a whipping motion with his hand. He pulled out another card showing Krampus snaring a child with his tongue. "If yur extra careless and ya have egregious, rotten behavior, den he'll snatch ya up in no time … " Papa slowed the ending of his sentence, "and steal ya from yur home." Bette burst out in tears upon hearing this. Papa put his arm around her. "Now, now don't ya worry. Dis only happens to bad children. If yur good, den Krampus won't visit yur home. Instead, Saint Nicholas will bring ya someting nice." Somehow, Papa felt he was being comforting!

We behaved better than any other family I knew around Christmas after hearing all the tales, real or fabricated. The one involving Krampus deeply bothered us. Despite knowing this character was a fabricated, mythical, horrid beast, I had plenty of nightmares following the creepy tales. I believed at the time that the fables about the creature came from Ireland, where there were a lot of goats and sheep, but I later learned that the tales originated from the Austrian Alps several centuries earlier.

Although Krampus had not come from the old country, there was an unusual oddity that did come from Ireland near Christmas time.

In Ireland, Saint Stephen's Day, also known as Wren Day, was celebrated with a traditional bird hunt. Some Irish people, like my mother, would send Christmas cards depicting a deceased bird. This was meant to give a family good luck and holiday cheer. Mama had left a stack of cards she had yet to complete on the kitchen table, next to a plate with remains of some scrambled eggs. I peered at the illustration and saw a dead bird lying on its back in full rigor mortis. It had an orange, bloated belly, and its feet were curled. "My word," I said out loud as I wrinkled my nose and raised my upper lip in utter disgust. I thought to myself that this tradition must come to an end.

On Friday, Christmas Eve 1920, I helped Mama in the kitchen as she prepared some Irish soda bread pudding. It was a Christmas tradition my mother had grown up with in Ireland. It was a variation of bread pudding that people in the US and England often had at their dinner tables. The Irish began making soda bread as a cheap way to make bread during challenging times in Ireland in the 1800s. The bread was made from baking soda rather than yeast, which tended to be more expensive. The pudding was a concoction of brown sugar, Irish soda bread, vanilla, eggs, butter, and whipping cream. Sometimes whiskey was added. It certainly did not suit my palate, but it was a tradition that made the creation somehow appealing.

Mama hid objects in the pudding that would predict how your life would go for the next year. If you pulled out a penny, it meant you would make money; if you pulled a ring, you would get married; a wishbone brought luck; an anchor charm brought safety; and a thimble meant you were destined for hard labor and had to remain frugal.

While we were busy making the pudding in the kitchen, Papa was standing in the living room talking to his older brother Jeremiah White, whom we liked to call Uncle Jerry. He was a respected fireman in the community. They were blabbering animatedly about something. I could hear the excited inflections of their tone of voice and inched closer to the entryway between the two rooms to hear what they were saying.

Uncle Jerry had put in an illegal still in his home in Noe Valley, a few blocks away from us, northwest of Bernal Heights. He was making several barrels of whiskey a month.

"Will, you ought to get into da business," Uncle Jerry urged. "I am making money hand over fist, and I only started a few months ago."

"Aren't ya a bit nervous about da cops?" I strained hard to listen to the conversation. Little did I know at the time how much it would alter the course of my life.

"No, ya just give dem a few bucks and dey will look da utter way."

"Jerry, I wouldn't even know how to get started!"

"Listen to me, lad. I will give ya a few pointers and some contacts. Besides dat, half da businessmen ya used to give rides to are in da business."

Papa was intrigued by the money his brother was bringing in. Aside from that, the idea of generating an unlimited amount of whiskey for personal use seemed to be of interest to my father.

Papa and Uncle Jerry somehow became aware that I was eavesdropping. I thought I was out of eyeshot of their conversation, but they likely saw movement as I went back and forth between helping Mama and listening in.

"Annie, what are you doin', snoopin' around like dat?" Papa snapped. I walked out to the living room to face the inquisition. "Ya can't be pokin' around in utter pee-pull's business!" Papa licked his lips then pressed them tightly together staring at me. He gave me a piercing glare. "You shan't let anyone know about tis." His eyebrows furrowed and his jaw tensed. "It could lead to us being carted off wit nippers on our wrists and sent to da slammer. Do ya understand me? It could mean hard jail time. You don't want dat fur da White family, do ya?"

"Papa, I'm not going to be a stooge." *Some extra money would be useful, as we could sure use some heat and lighting in our house,* I thought to myself.

Papa let the conversation go. Soon we would eat our Irish soda Bread pudding. Bette pulled out a wishbone, Mickey acquired the anchor charm, and my parents hauled in coins. I fished out the thimble. It was all baloney! Perhaps Mama put it in my serving when I walked out to the living room. There was no wedding ring. Mama made sure not to include an item like that.

Within a couple of weeks, Papa began bringing other men to our house, men whom he had associated with when he had been a teamster in his transportation business. Some of these men had entered different facets of the illegal trade of alcohol, from the distilling process, delivery, and sale of liquor.

After gaining the requisite knowledge, Papa plunged headlong into the business in early 1921. He built a still out of copper he had purchased, and from leftover pipes he had in our garage. At first, he thought about constructing the still out of radiator piping, but learned that some people were getting lead poisoning from the toxic metal being leached from radiators. According to newspapers, one could get brain damage or even die from lead poisoning. He was also careful not to use wood in the distillation process, as methanol, a byproduct, was causing cases of blindness. Due to these potential hazards, bootlegged liquor back then was often referred to as "coffin varnish."

Papa placed the still in our basement. His still had a chamber where he used a combination of cornmeal, potato peel, water, malt, and yeast to ferment the product into a hot mash solution. He poured in a touch of juniper oil for flavoring and added glycerin. The mash was heated using a furnace, and some of the solution turned into a vapor and went through tubing that led to a worm box, which consisted of a series of coiled tubes inside a vat of freezing water, to condense the product back to liquid. From fermentation to the final product, the process took about two weeks. Some bootleggers were producing their product sooner than that, but Papa was meticulous and wanted a high-quality product. This required significant monitoring of the boiler. At first, when he went to work at his legal business, Papa employed Mama to do the monitoring. But she had too much to do, and soon she employed me at the age of ten. I didn't mind as it was the warmest place in the house.

Papa produced booze he branded as 'White's Whiskey.' Before a batch was ready for bottling, he tested it for lead contamination. Though the still was mostly made of copper, he was not sure about some of the piping he had used to build it. He taught me how to check for lead using flame testing.

"Come 'ere, Ann," Papa called from the basement. I walked down the stairs to where he was. The basement smelled like nail polish. "Scoop some of da whiskey up wit tis spoon." He handed me a spoon with burn marks on it. Then he lit a match and flipped off the light. I observed the whiskey evaporate. "Listen to me, Ann. Tis is very important. Der is a saying ya got ta remember." My ears perked up. "Lead burns red and makes ya dead. Remember dat."

The vapor that emanated did not burn red. "Papa, I only see blue and yellow."

He flipped the light switch back on and had a wide grin on his face. "Well, den dat's a mighty good batch of giggle water, I would say!"

Lead testing became one of my favorite things to do. There was a small window near the basement ceiling that provided some light during the day. When we turned the light-switch off, it was dark enough for testing. However, it was particularly fun to test the whiskey at night, when it was completely dark. We watched in awe as the flame turned countless shades of blue and yellow.

Hundreds of speakeasies began to pop up throughout San Francisco, and opportunities for Papa to sell his whiskey were plentiful. Saloons were converted to old-fashioned soda fountains with secret backrooms or basements where booze was served. Even the swankiest hotels like Sir Francis Drake and St. Francis had speakeasies underground and within secret, hidden rooms. Papa mapped out all the speakeasies, stores, and homes he would sell to. He memorized all the passwords to get through various barriers. The main risk in the whole operation was not necessarily in distilling the liquor; but in the delivery. He would initially carry out his clandestine deliveries at night by car. He drove a black 1919 Model T Ford touring car that he modified to contain a secret compartment to hide the liquor.

He began to make money, and us older girls were allowed again to go to the barber to get a haircut. Soon our radiators began emanating heat in our house again. It was a good thing, because my parents soon had another mouth to feed as my brother William, or Billy, as we liked to call him, was born in August of 1921.

Mama and Papa slept in the main bedroom on the main floor, beside the cramped, tiny room Mickey and Theresa shared, while Bette and I stayed in the medium-sized room upstairs. After baby

Billy's arrival, Mama and Papa played musical chairs with our rooms. Billy was placed in the smallest room with Theresa, who was a toddler at the time, while Mickey moved upstairs with Bette and me. That arrangement fell apart quickly because little Billy cried often, prompting Theresa to wake up and drag her blanket upstairs to be with her three sisters.

Eventually, my parents moved upstairs and took the medium-sized room, and all four of the girls took the main bedroom, leaving Billy with his own room.

Papa bought a cigar shop on Courtland Avenue because it had a backroom basement where he could sell some of his moonshine. He sold the grocery store as it was not particularly profitable, and he did not have enough time to manage two stores. It made me a little sad because Mama used to take us to his grocery store to meet him for lunch. The store had a few tables where you could sit down to eat and watch people walk by the windows. Papa moved the tables to his new cigar shop and put them in the backroom, where my siblings and I were prohibited from entering.

The whole trade was called moonshining because the bulk of the operations were carried out at night, under moonlight. Papa was competing with moonshiners who transported copious amounts of liquor by trucks from Oregon. The trucks were sophisticated, often with phony logos and special concealed compartments. To carry the extra weight of the booze, they had extra springs for shock absorption to facilitate going up and down hills and to avoid the truck appearing too low, which would have raised the suspicion of law enforcement.

When Papa delivered his product, some businesses rang bells in certain ways, indicating incoming booze. On other occasions, bells chiming at a faster pace were used as warnings of impending police raids. Enforcement of the illegal sale of liquor in San Francisco was lax, and it became known that members of the San Francisco police department were receiving kickbacks in exchange for leaving the illegal operations alone. Fortunately, the police had not found the secret room at Papa's cigar shop, so to my knowledge he was never extorted.

In 1922, the bribes were exposed in the newspapers. San Francisco's police department's Chief O'Brien and Captain Goff indicated a supreme shake-up would result. And sure enough, shortly thereafter, they began cracking down hard on operations. Papa began to comment on newspaper articles, such as one in *The San Francisco Chronicle*, detailing successful police raids in the city. He also heard about raids in nearby towns. In one town near Sacramento, a friend of Papa's told him that there was a sheriff who seized so many weapons from bootlegging operations, including shotguns and brass knuckles, that he created his own trophy case to show off his cache.

December 1921. Maggie & William White and children.
Left to right: Bette, Theresa, Mickey, Ann and Billy

CHAPTER
SIX

P apa had confidantes who had been arrested. He had friends and associates who carried firearms, ready to shoot the cops should they raid their illegal operation. He didn't want anything to do with a violent approach, as he knew it would mean more jail time should he be caught. After the police stopped receiving kickbacks to look the other way, Papa also saw a major new crime element creeping into the industry. Mobsters began extorting money from some of the establishments selling the liquor in exchange for "protection," which was just a ruse. The mobsters had not penetrated San Francisco as deeply as other major US cities, but nonetheless, Papa did not want to get extorted. He didn't want to walk into any of those establishments when mobsters were present.

Papa tried to think of ingenious new ways to conceal the whiskey. He learned of some bootleggers hiding whiskey in meat trucks, or inside pig carcasses. Others transported liquor in trucks carrying bricks that had secret compartments. He concocted a novel approach. We owned a red children's wagon. Papa had seen me pulling the cart containing my dolls down the sidewalk in front of our home. He got the idea of placing whiskey in the cart and then concealing the liquor with burlap bags and placing our dolls on top. He got me and Bette, aged twelve and eight respectively, to carry out many of the deliveries in the afternoons, after school. Bette and I were both petite and looked much younger than our ages, a fact I am sure Papa considered when he put us to work.

Our operation was unique in that we made the deliveries in broad daylight. His new daytime operation gave Papa a bit of an advantage as his booze was the first to be consumed in many of the illegal joints, some of which opened at 4 p.m., well before the after-dark delivery times of his competitors. Daytime deliveries also avoided contact or confrontation with some of the seedier elements of the night. However, this did not mean that what we were doing was not dangerous. We often went to dreadfully run-down areas of the city to make deliveries, some of which were rat-infested dives.

At first, Bette and I were accompanied by Papa, Mama, or a trusted relative, but as we grew up, we carried out many of the deliveries on our own. Looking back on it, I don't know how we were not kidnapped and sold to gypsies. Our cart only had room enough for a couple of crates, so we had to go back and forth between our house and all the businesses several times a day. Bette and I typically walked about five to six miles a day after school, and in the summer sometimes up to eight to ten miles in a day.

Papa became so busy with his businesses that he stopped attending our school functions. Earlier in the year, in the spring of 1922, he missed Bette's first Communion right around the time she turned eight years old. He also started to dote on our middle sister, Mickey. She was only five years old and highly intelligent. He called her Mickey Dooley.

A few weeks before Christmas in 1922, Bette had asked Santa Claus for an oil-paint set and let my mother know about it. I asked my mother for a new set of roller skates. I wanted a fun mode of transportation, one where I wouldn't have to walk so much. My feet were growing, and my shoes no longer fit into my old pair of skates. I hadn't skated in over a year, and hadn't yet been allowed to skate beyond our street. I tried to convince Mama to get a pair for me, and I offered to give my old set of skates to Bette.

"Dey're too expensive!" Mama balked.

"But, Mama, they are good for balance. I can practice better posture!" I wheedled. Mama shook her head in a firm no. She wasn't buying my story. I had to lay my sales technique on thicker. "We could do our deliveries faster and come home sooner ... so, I could help more with chores." I was being a bit dishonest, but the ploy got her attention.

"Da two of ya can break a leg in dis hilly city." *Applesauce*, I thought. Mama wasn't a pushover and was always concerned about our safety.

"Mama, you do realize that I already know how to skate. I'm ducky at roller-skating and not a Dumb Dora." I spread my arms, palms up, to drive home the point.

"I doan't know, Annie." *Annie, why did she call me Annie?* She hadn't called me by that name since I was six or seven years old! She was treating me like a little girl. She shook her head only slightly that time, looking off in the distance. At least I had planted the seed about the skates.

On a Saturday afternoon, about nine days before Christmas, Papa borrowed a truck from a friend so he could pick up our Christmas tree. In the past, our choice of Christmas tree had been limited due to what size tree could fit into Papa's Model T. He came home first to show us the truck, and to get some extra rope to tie the tree to the truck bed. We filed out of the house to look at it.

After getting the rope, Papa jumped back in the vehicle, which was the first gas-powered truck he had ever driven. "Look at dis magnificent piece of machinery!" he crowed, puffing on his cigar.

The truck he had borrowed was a flatbed Sandow Motor Truck. It was enormous and impressive with wide back wheels. The front seat was probably five feet off the ground. I jumped up into the vehicle using all my leg muscles. Then I barely squeezed into the seat beside him. The steering wheel was larger than a pizza pie.

"Papa, I am going with you." I had made up my mind.

"Ya are, are ya?"

"I know how to pick a good tree," I said cheerfully. "You wouldn't know a good one if you saw it."

"Is dat so?"

Mama thought I would just get in his way and asked me to stay home. Papa told her it would be fine.

He started up the engine, creating a deep, roaring noise. As he pulled away from the curb, he initially drove the truck slowly the first couple of blocks, getting used to its raw energy. I happened to see a classmate of mine walking along the sidewalk with her younger sister, coming towards us. Her name was Grace, like the quick prayer we uttered before dinner. Grace was a show-off and always had to be the center of attention at school. She was also a little Miss Know-It-All. She showed everyone at school how the English queen waved her hand and then proceeded to tell everyone there was a difference between how a queen and a princess waved their hands to common folk. She had bragged that her family was related to the Queen of England. I didn't believe any of it and found out later that my hunch was correct. In fact, her birth name wasn't even Grace! Mama discovered one of her relatives had been part of the security force that protected the Queen of Denmark, who had apparently traveled to England. Mama said that if Grace was genuinely related to the Queen of England, she wouldn't be living in our neighborhood!

As we drove closer to her, I hollered "Grace!" She turned her head towards us. I couldn't help but spring into a standing position.

Maintaining good posture, appearing prim and proper, I started waving like a queen, first putting my arm up in the air showing the back of my hand, then turning it slowly from side to side as though I were screwing in a lightbulb. Grace's jaw dropped as we drove away. Papa gave me a quick swat on my back, and I sat down. Grace's expression was priceless, and it was a moment worthy of the annals of any child's diary.

We then headed to Market Street, where Papa said there was a Christmas tree lot. I recall Papa working the clutch and shifting the gears to get the vehicle up and down the city's streets. He muttered choice words along the way as he was learning to operate the vehicle. I recall the sensation of floating as we passed over the top of a hill. It must have had good suspension. When we got to the Christmas tree lot, I think the owner, after seeing our truck, saw dollar signs. He must have thought we were going to purchase a 15-foot tree. Papa was treated like royalty.

The lot was surrounded by tall buildings with painted-on advertisements and billboards pitching every vice known to mankind. In addition to ads for tires there were advertisements for chewing gum, undergarments, pipe tobacco, and cigarettes. There was also an old advertisement for lager, then illegal at the time, the faded paint peeling off the bricks. Some of the advertisements included striking women with perfect smiles.

We looked around the lot and I spotted a majestic seven-and-a-half-foot Monterey pine. Papa thought it would fit in our home and purchased it. I'm sure it disappointed the owner of the lot, who was trying to unload the last of his taller trees, but we were happy. After Papa dropped me and the tree off at our home and returned the truck, he came home and set to work on the tree.

Mama played Christmas music on our phonograph. I remember hearing *The Twelve Days of Christmas* many times, but the song that got me in the true holiday spirit was *The Carol of Bells*. I recall humming to the lovely melody. Papa erected the Christmas tree in our parlor while the music was playing. Mama was busy in the kitchen baking bread and Christmas cookies with a friend of hers from our neighborhood. The house was filled with sumptuous scents of nutmeg, cinnamon, vanilla, and butter, mixed with the delightful aroma of fresh pine.

After Papa sawed off a few branches to allow the tree to fit into the space, he wound a new set of electric-powered red, green, and blue lights around the tree. This was our first tree with multi-colored lights. My youngest siblings were jumping up and down and twirling around in anticipation of lighting the tree. Papa plugged the light strand into the nearest socket, and it didn't work. He had almost no patience and quickly became furious.

"Da dam crooks! Dey sold me a bad batch of lights!"

Mama entered the living room from the kitchen and walked toward the parlor. "William, button your lip, we have a guest." She was embarrassed that her friend could hear his quick-tempered remarks. Sighing, Papa clenched his fists and quickly unscrewed each bulb, before screwing them in again, one at a time until, about twenty bulbs into the process, the tree lit up. We all cheered. Papa then unplugged the tree, waiting for the moment when all the decorations were complete before plugging the lights back in.

My siblings and I went to work decorating the tree. We had made a few items in anticipation of the event. We gently placed red tissue honeycomb balls and chains of popcorn and cranberries within the bows, and added precious old ornaments such as glass balls and glittered stars.

Mama had asked Papa to monitor my sixteen-month-old brother Billy while she worked in the kitchen. Putting Papa in charge of protecting Billy around a Christmas tree was like putting a blind puppy in charge of monitoring a bull in a china shop. Papa paid absolutely no attention, and within no time, Billy had grabbed tinsel and stuck it into his mouth. I quickly picked him up and pulled shredded silvery strands of material from his mouth. Billy began crying, and I took him to the kitchen to pawn him off to Mama.

Before long, we got back to the joyous task at hand. After hanging the ornaments, we began to sprinkle on the silver tinsel. It was uneven, as my younger siblings couldn't get the ornaments or tinsel up past the lower third of the tree. Bette and I were too short to get the items much above the middle part of the tree.

A few minutes later, Mama walked Billy back through the living room to the parlor, holding his hand. He had apparently stopped crying and whimpering, eager to get back to the shiny objects that lay before his eyes. Mama let him place some tinsel in one big lump on a solitary branch. Some of the tinsel stuck to his hands, which were constantly sticky from his incessant drooling. Before washing his hands Mama pulled off the decorations on the lower branches and placed them above the reach of Billy's tacky fingers. She retreated into the kitchen with my brother and washed his hands in the sink.

Papa finished the tree by grabbing a ladder and placing a few last decorations on the upper third of the tree, and topped it off by placing an angel on the top. With the drapes open, the whole neighborhood could see our tree. The angel wore a white dress and had a halo glued onto its head.

I headed to the kitchen with Mickey, both of us gleaming with joy, to tell Mama that we had finished decorating our tree and that Papa was about to light it again.

Upon reaching the kitchen doorway, I overheard Mama's friend asking what my mother had procured for our Christmas gifts. Her friend, who was seated at the kitchen table, faced us as we entered the kitchen. Mama's back was turned. Her friend looked back and forth at our eyes as well as Mama's to alert her that we were in earshot of her voice.

Mama started speaking in Pig Latin, trying to outsmart us. Pig Latin, previously known as dog Latin, has been around since Shakespearean times. You take the first consonant or consonant cluster of each word and add it to the end of the word, before adding the suffix *-ay* at the end. It had become popular again when a song came out in 1919, called *Pig Latin Love*, sung by Arthur Fields. Pig Latin was used so you could speak in code to someone without those around you knowing what you were talking about. The faster you could speak Pig Latin the harder it was to decipher. Mama had not realized just about every kid I knew had mastered the language. In fact, it was a common language on school playgrounds used when a schoolyard supervisor or teacher was nearby. Mama gave a wink to her friend, then quickly listed some items. At first, it sounded like mumbo jumbo. Then, suddenly music came to my ears, and it wasn't the music playing on the phonograph.

"Oller-ray ates-skay." There it was, I knew I would be getting roller skates! I quickly left the room and walked up a few stairs to get out of view of everyone, and I sat down on a step bursting into tears of joy. I would miss the first official lighting ceremony involving multi-colored lights at the White family home, but I didn't care. I was so happy dreaming of skating. In my mind, I performed amazing tricks and pirouettes, gracefully sweeping through the streets of San Francisco, in the wind, while wearing a flowing, shimmering dress. I even skated past my classmate Grace, waving my hand like a princess. A very similar wave to that of a queen, I might add!

That December, our church had a food drive. Despite being from a lower-middle-class family and only a footstep away from being poor, Mama said that we needed to collect some canned food so that we could give it to families that were less fortunate than ours. Bette and I went through our cabinet and rounded up all the food we didn't like. We gathered cans of wax beans, okra, sardines, prunes, white and black cherries, boiled cabbage with beans and succotash. Succotash, why would Mama have ever bought that? We stacked the kitchen counter with the cans that we would never miss.

Mama took one look at the stack and shook her head in consternation. "If we were poar, would we want to get items we didn't like?"

"No, Mama," we said in unison with subdued voices.

"OK, den. Put tree of dees cans back in da cupboard and pick tree tings dat dey might like."

Reluctantly, Bette and I put on the counter things that we did like, such as peaches, green beans, and pineapple. Back into the cupboard went the wax beans, black cherries, and sardines.

During the weeks leading up to Christmas, I volunteered to participate in a Christmas production at my church as part of our special services, and sang in a small choir that consisted of children about my age. Mama talked to the organizers, and they allowed Bette to join so we could practice together. For the production, we dressed as angels. We rehearsed songs like *Silent Night, O, Tannenbaum*, and *Joy to the World*. About four or five days before Christmas, carolers came to our door one evening. Unlike most of the groups that paid a visit to our house, that particular collection of vocalists consisted solely of men. They were World War I veterans, and some were missing limbs. One gentleman had a sleeve sewn to his shirt. Another was on crutches, and through his pant leg you could see the outline of his stiff, thin, probably wooden prosthesis. They began singing *O Come, All Ye Faithful*. It happened to be one of the songs that Bette and I had practiced. She and I started to sing along with the men, and there arose a melodious contrast of voices. We were by no means in perfect harmony; far from it. But somehow it sounded even better than when we sang in synchrony with our church choir. Looking around at all the singers, I could see many men with tears in their smiling eyes, and I will never forget that.

Mama always prepared extra cookies for Christmas carolers, but with this particular group,. she went a step further. After a few songs, she invited them in for cookies and hot chocolate. One of the men in that group even ended up attending our church production a few days later.

A couple of days before Christmas, Mama received a package. She placed it on the console table near our entryway. I didn't know it at the time, but Bette noticed that the package was addressed to Mickey and had been sent by Aunt Frances. There was no package for Bette. Mickey was already getting special treatment. When Papa ate an egg, he would slice off the top part and give it to her and not to Bette. When she saw that no-one was looking, Bette tore open the package and found a wrapped Christmas gift. She unwrapped it to find a strikingly beautiful doll of a woman wearing a frilly, ivory satin dress, with delicate lace trim and a red velvet ribbon sash tied at the waist. She had deep brown eyes made of lustrous glass. Aunt Frances must have spent a fortune on that high-end porcelain masterpiece. Bette stared at the doll for maybe half a minute with extreme jealousy, and then fetched a hammer. She placed the doll flat over a cutting board and smashed its face. Then she wrapped the doll back up in its wrapping paper and stuffed it back in the package.

Christmas Day 1922 finally arrived. After performing our songs at church, we headed home and ripped open our presents. Bette and Mickey were twirling around with excitement. Bette couldn't locate her gift from Santa Claus, but discovered one from Aunt Frances. She had not forgotten about Bette after all! Mickey opened her present and there was the exquisite doll that Aunt Frances had given her; but puzzlingly, her face was angelic, intact, and in perfect shape. Baffled, Bette opened her present, and there lay the doll with the pulverized face. Bette wept and ran to her room where she sulked. Somehow, my parents found out what had happened. In the meantime, I acted surprised at acquiring my new roller skates and gave Mama a bear hug.

About an hour after Bette's exit, Mama walked downstairs holding a wrapped-up Christmas gift. She said Santa Claus had accidentally left it in her room. She knocked on our bedroom door and entered to find Bette lying face down in bed. "Bette, Santa Claus did bring something fur ya. He must have misplaced it." Bette opened the present, and it was the oil-paint set she had asked for. She began crying again, hugged Mama and apologized. It was a lesson she would never forget.

My shoes fit perfectly into the skates. I implored Papa to allow us to use the skates to deliver whiskey, as it would cut down the time we spent roaming the city on our deliveries. Papa emphatically told us he would not allow it. He thought it might attract too much attention. And thus, with the little free time we had on weekends, Bette and I skated around the neighborhood visiting friends and neighbors. This would be perhaps our most joyous time during our childhood.

When it came to our bootlegging business, we continued walking up and down the hills of San Francisco. Bette and I developed impressively strong leg muscles. I would later use those muscles to jump high playing basketball as a freshman in high school, despite being the shortest person on my team at only five feet tall.

Papa was so inspired by driving the truck to haul that Christmas tree that he got an itch to become a teamster again. A friend of his, Jimmy Smith, got him a part-time job hauling warehouse supplies, and he did this a few hours a week in 1923, to supplement his income. He didn't want to give up his bootlegging business.

Papa was intensely meticulous about making White's whiskey. He was diligent about everything, from the temperature controls of the mash solution, the delivery of the product, and the accounting. We never had a distillery accident aside from a few overflows that stunk up our basement. Our Uncle Jerry, whose operation was nearby, was not as careful, and his distillery blew up frequently.

Papa kept a ledger documenting every penny he spent and who owed him money. He made sure that the ledger was unintelligible to anyone on the outside who might come upon it. He did this in case our house was raided. Papa disguised the names of the people, their locations and the amounts people owed. He would write things in the 'Owed' section like "Donnie: 1 sack of oranges, 72 cents ents," when he really meant two crates of whiskey sold and owed from a person named Danny for $72.

We became adept at memorizing the passwords and all the steps needed to get through venue barriers and became familiar with all the people we needed to trust. There was a sharply dressed man with dwarfism who worked for a movie theater selling tickets at the box office in the evening, and he occasionally worked the street to bring in moviegoers. During the day, he had a side job dressed in plain clothes. We would locate him in the afternoon and ask him what time it was. Whatever time he gave us, our password was to say we thought it was an hour later. This prompted him to look around in all directions, and when the coast was clear, he spun around and walked briskly around a corner. We then followed him down an alleyway, where there was a tarp hiding stairs to a basement. He pulled the doll wagon close to the stairway, quickly unloaded the hooch, and disappeared.

When Bette and I visited one grocery store that had a concealed back-room saloon, we always headed for the back right-hand corner of the store and looked for the floor sweeper, a tall thin man with greasy hair named Ed. We weren't allowed to address him by name. We would say "The floor looks extra shiny today," prompting him to guide us to a back room that had an enormous mirror on the wall. He would remove the mirror, revealing a secret door through which our cart would be permitted to pass. Once inside the room, there actually was not much to see. The bar was never open for business when we entered. There were no windows, and the lights had yet to be turned on for that evening's libations. There were usually crates and boxes of liquor stacked up, preventing us from venturing too far into the space. From what I could tell, the bar itself looked rudimentary. It most definitely was not a high-end establishment.

In March 1923, Bette and I entered the store. We headed to the right back corner with our cart loaded with dolls and whiskey. Only this time, the floor sweeper ignored us after we said the code phrase. At first, I didn't understand what was happening, but soon it became apparent what the problem was. A police officer had entered the store, apparently to buy something. He saw Bette and me with our red cart in the aisle. Pretending not to notice him, I grabbed the cart, turned left, and rounded the back corner of the store with Bette, and we came down another aisle heading toward the front of the establishment. Somehow, the officer cut us off and managed to get into that aisle. Paralyzed by fear, I froze, and we came to a standstill. My heart started to pound. As he approached, he smiled. Before I realized it, he stood towering above us. He bent over and picked up one of our dolls.

"What's her name?" the cop asked, in a friendly tone.

"You're holding Marlee," I simpered in a cutesy voice as I swung my body back and forth as I smiled, pretending to be an eight-year-old child. Why, I even managed to throw in a little curt-sy. Mama had dressed us to look as young as possible for situations like this. She had curled my hair, and I wore a ruffled cotton dress and a silly bonnet with stripes. "Marlee does not like to be touched," I warned, as I tried to outsmart the cop, but I soon realized my mistake. This only made the officer scan the cart more thoroughly, prompting him to pick up another doll. The one he picked up was one of my favorites, a bisque doll with a fancy pink dress and frills. I was sure we were going to get caught. My life flashed before my eyes, and I thought we would be thrown in jail. I imagined Bette and I would be attached to a chain gang and would have to do hard la-bor the rest of our lives. I'm not sure how he did not feel the hard wooden crates of whisky covered with burlap underneath the dolls. I couldn't even think of the name of the doll the officer was now holding.

In a hurried, befuddled state, I made up a name. "It's Trixie you're holding."

"It's Edwina, silly," Bette chimed in. *Did she actually say that?* I thought. *Was she really trying to get us busted?*

I was not sure if the officer could tell, but I began to perspire. A bead of sweat slowly trickled down my chest and moistened the upper mid-section of my dress. My fingers clenched as if I had no control over them.

He looked me directly in the eyes. "Is her hair real?" The officer gazed at the doll's hair and ran two fingers through it.

I tried to slow down the rate of my speech to look more as-sured. "Well, I believe so."

"Do you know what I discovered after looking closely?" The cop was looking directly at the empty space where he had picked up the doll. There, a corner of one of the underlying crates of whiskey created an indentation in the material. It was so obvious.

Scared beyond belief, I gulped and nearly passed out. "No ... what did you discover, officer?"

"There is a marking on your doll that says it's made in Germany. My daughter has a doll like this, and her doll was also made in Germany."

"Oh, I didn't know that." I sighed with relief.

"Well, you two take good care of them."

"We will, officer." And off he went. I could not believe our good luck. At first, I wasn't sure why he did not ask where our parents were, but then I realized a woman was standing close to us. He likely thought we were with her.

After the policeman made a purchase and left the store, the owner walked back to us. He was a stout, menacing man with a ruddy, hardened face, a bristling mustache, and a tiny derby hat perched atop his head, dressed in a long-sleeved shirt with a bow-tie.

"You better get the hell out of here ... and I mean now," he rasped harshly. "For Pete's sake, don't come back unless you are with one of your parents. Now scram!"

We rushed out of the store, briefly dropping and then replacing one of our dolls back on the cart in a haphazard way.

I told Papa what had transpired, and he cut that business off our route. It did not make much of a difference, as we still had plenty of businesses we delivered to.

On Saturdays, we mostly delivered to the homes of people my father trusted, including friends, relatives, and their close acquaintances. We were done with those routes before noon and had most of the afternoon to catch up on homework, read, roller-skate, play, or go to the movies.

One Saturday afternoon in May 1923, my cousin Elsie McGuire, who had recently turned sixteen, stopped by with her mother, my Aunt Mary Ann. Elsie's father, my Uncle Patrick, had died the previous year. Their family ran a grocery store just a few blocks away on Randal Street. Elsie looked much more mature than the last time I saw her, and a beaded necklace with a cross adorned her neck. She was attractive and had wavy, russet hair with the body of a full-grown woman. She wore pretty, pointed Oxford strap-shoes. She was petite like me, but taller and had good muscular tone. She was on her high school's rowing team at Mission High school, and was the team's pilot.

They came to pick up my mother, Maggie, and take her with them via streetcar downtown to see a Rudolph Valentino movie. Mama wouldn't let me go and see it with them. She felt Rudy Valentino was too steamy, and the movie they were about to see, *Blood and Sand,* had something to do with an affair. Apparently, that was a taboo topic for a twelve-year-old to learn about. Mama and Aunt Mary Ann went to the kitchen to chat for a few minutes, and my cousin and I talked outside the front of our house. I recall feeling left out and disappointed that I would miss out on all the fun. I folded my arms close to my chest and semi-jokingly bent my head forward and nudged it into Elsie's shoulder.

"There, there." Elsie, trying to be silly and calm my nerves, rubbed my back and patted my head like she was petting a cat. "I can't believe your mother won't let you see the movie." She turned her head sideways and looked at me. "I've been to three Rudy Valentino movies already and was probably your age when I saw my first one."

"It's so unfair." I disengaged from leaning on her shoulder. "Mama thinks I am eight years old still. Why, that's applesauce!" I looked up at Elsie. "I heard that some women fainted in a movie theater when they saw Valentino in *The Sheik,*" I sulked.

"I know. I almost fainted myself!" Elsie sighed and fingered a bead on her necklace. "Rudy has handsome, pomaded dark hair and such dreamy eyes. He is so dapper and wears the most elaborate, expensive wardrobes. And I hear that in real life he wears fancy fur coats. Did you know he recently divorced and is now married to Natasha Rambova, his costume designer?"

"Yeah, I read about it in a gossip magazine."

"Well, she's probably a hussy who squashed his first marriage. I'm just waiting for him to divorce her so I can marry him," Elsie grinned.

"That will happen as soon as I become president." I rolled my eyes.

"You never know, Ann. If I don't marry him, I plan to marry a dapper Italian man just like him."

"You will, will you? You are living in a fantasy world, Elsie."

"Maybe … speaking of fantasies, don't you see the glitz and glamour of speakeasies, in your world?"

"Are you kidding me? Bette and I deliver to dozens of establishments, and most of the time we never get to go inside. Usually, we only see the middlemen and there is nothing glitzy or glamorous about them. They usually wear plain clothes, baggy trousers, and ruffled sleeves. They are not usually the most clean-shaven people. You wouldn't be able to spot one from a police line-up if you tried. In fact, their names aren't even interesting. Bette and I know them by names such as the tall guy, the little guy and the guy with a pointy nose. Our contact is usually very brief, and generally they won't allow conversations."

"Oh, that's awful. So, you haven't seen anything?"

"There have been a few exceptions, however. A few of the places will allow us to pass through to unload before they open. One of those places is a dark, dingy dive with only six or seven tables and a pile of garbage in the corner. We've seen rat poop in there!"

"Oh, my!" Elsie lightly bit her lower lip.

"But we have been inside a fine establishment, and you wouldn't believe what it looks like. It has red, lovely, upholstered leather chairs, candelabras, and a long, shiny cherry wood bar with a footrest. There are bottles of booze of every type, shape, and color, and behind the bar are elegant mirrors and interesting paintings." I pulled Elsie close to me and whispered in her ear, "Don't tell Mama or Aunt Mary Ann, but in that place, there are nude paintings!" I felt like I was then starting to give Elsie a bit of an education.

"Honestly?" It piqued Elsie's curiosity.

"Before you get too excited, those paintings I am referring to are of women," I teased.

"You're right! I am not too excited!" Elsie chuckled.

"The first time we were let into that upscale bar, the owner asked us if we had the foot juice. I didn't know what he meant at first, but I put two and two together, and he was asking if we were delivering wine. I don't know how many other little girls are delivering to his joint, but I found his confusion amusing."

"I'll bet."

"There is just one bar that we do get to go in while it's operating, however." I sat down on the street curb.

"Tell me about it!" Elsie sat down on the curb next to me and leaned in to hear the important things I was about to say.

"You have to keep this confidential," I whispered with conviction. "You have to pinky-swear you won't tell a soul." I held out my pinky finger and Elsie locked it with mine. "One of the closest speakeasies we deliver to is owned by a friend of Papa's, and he's involved in local politics. I can't tell you what his name is or where it is located, but a lot of locals drink there. Why, half the people on this block have probably been to it. His place opens at four o'clock, and if we don't spend too much time there, the owner lets us hang around for a few minutes. You wouldn't believe who we saw seated there drinking some booze!"

"Who, the mayor?"

"Good guess, and I wouldn't be surprised if he did. But that's not who. There is a cop who lives down our street and who frequents the bar. Papa already knows he won't cause trouble for us. When we spotted him at the bar with a glass of whiskey in hand, he recognized us and gave us a wink. I think he's seen us jumping rope out in front of our house on the sidewalk before. He followed that up by placing his finger to his lips and gave us a shush signal."

"Wow, I can't believe it, Ann! What a crazy life you live."

"I'm picking up a lot of lingo from that bar. Two young women walked in with men the other day, holding their arms around them. They said they invited their 'jellybeans' for a drink and a snack. And some of the men call money they hand the bar tender 'lettuce.'"

"'Lettuce?'"

"I guess if a dollar bill in one's pocket gets crinkled up it can look like lettuce?"

"Ah, that makes sense."

"The latest term I have heard is to be on the lookout for a "house peeper." Elsie looked at me with a blank expression. "You know … a detective. You don't want to get busted. You could get locked up in the caboose for years, and the cops will smash all your barrels of liquor on the street, in front of news photographers, to make an example of you. I've seen it in the papers."

"Wow, Ann, you get to spend time around some interesting people."

I carried on excitedly. "Time is not what I have, Elsie. I have a schedule, and we have to be back home before dark. Bette thinks this whole thing is an adventure. She wastes so much time and is a complete gigglemug. She likes to be silly and babble. During the week, in the few places that we are allowed in, she will chat with anyone who will allow her to speak. She is a free-spirited, curly-haired moppet. A little chatterbox. She always uses the term 'grand.'"

"Doesn't your father say that a lot?"

"Oh, yes, but Bette uses it more often. How can anybody be that damned happy? For crying out loud, I'm on a schedule."

"What does she do?"

"She blinks one eye rapidly in a funny way to make her look crazy, and it makes people laugh. She also has a knack for imitating the thick Cork Irish accent of some of our relatives. She also uses a singsong rising and falling intonation when talking and moves her head up and down. The other day, she mimicked a conversation between two Irishmen in a pub, speaking from the side of her mouth."

"How so?" asked Elsie.

"How's it doin'?" I put on a high-pitched voice, imitating my sister's mimicking. I paused before adopting a lower-pitched voice for the reply. "I am duying! It's hot in here ... utter dan dat, it's grand!"

"Tanks for da pint and da biscuit."

"Tis nadaboter, boy. Would you like a wee bitabutter for da biscuit? Tis so good."

"Tanks lad. Noting better den blabberin' about slatherin' a bitabutter on a biscuit."

"That's a gas!" Elsie giggled, then gave me an affectionate hug. "I can see what you're up against."

"I try keeping her in check, but it almost never works," I grinned.

Just then, Mama walked outside with Aunt Mary Ann. "It's toime fur us to go, so it tis," Mama said abruptly.

In a blink of an eye, the three of them went off to see that scandalous movie. I wouldn't get to see the heartthrob on the silver screen the man who every woman in America was talking about. Instead, I was stuck with Papa and my siblings.

Papa noticed I was sulking that afternoon and felt bad for me. After coming into the house, I sat on our living room couch with my knees curled up to my chest and my head down. He came and sat down beside me.

"Why do ya want to see dat movie anyhow?"

"Papa, you wouldn't understand."

"It's da allure of Rudy Valentino isn't-it?"

I nodded.

"What's a twelve-year-old girl have in common wit dat man?"

I rolled my eyeballs then looked directly into my father's eyes as if he were the village idiot. "He makes women faint."

Papa reached over and put an arm around me. "Ya know dat's all phony, don't ya? Why, it's all hogwash. It's a boonch of hooey."

"What do you mean? Elsie said she almost fainted when she saw a movie he starred in!"

"Da trute is dat da big cheeses in Hollywood and utter parts of da movie industry pay women to faint fur publicity."

It couldn't be true. "Fiddlesticks!" I responded, not wanting to hear what Papa was saying. There was nobody in the entire world more handsome than Rudolph Valentino. The conversation reminded me of when he told Papa the truth about Santa Claus, and he was correct about that myth.

"If ya wanna be wit a spiffy young man, I can send ya to da house across the street to talk to da toofless boy wit pimples."

"Papa, don't make me laugh." I smiled.

"Ya know Rudy Valentino is in fact an ugly man," Papa continued. I shook my head. "Oh, yeah. He wears tons of make-up. And I mean tons of it. Rumor has it, under all dat pancake concoction he has a face like a donkey."

"No, he doesn't, Papa!" I chuckled.

"Oh, yes indeed." Papa balled his left hand into a fist and stuck his left thumb out to mimic Rudy Valentino's nose. "He probably has a skilled crackerjack plucking his nostril hairs every day." He took his right index and third finger and made a snipping sound while he grabbed his left thumb. I slipped down the couch, lying on my back, laughing harder.

"Dey probably put a pint of oil and vinegar on his hair to kill da lice." Papa grinned. "Dat's what makes his hair so shiny." I could not stop giggling.

When I did finally calm down, Papa offered to take me to the movies the following day, Sunday, after church. As a reward for participating in the bootlegging business, he gave my sister Bette and me spending money and would sometimes take us to the movies on weekends with Mama. Only Mama now had two-year-old toddler Billy, and would have to stay home to give us a turn to go to the movies. Papa offered to take us to see some Buster Keaton shorts. Sure, Buster was not Rudy Valentino. But he had a knack for escaping perilous dangers, such as collapsing houses and avoiding auto collisions. We enjoyed the live piano accompaniments, which only heightened the excitement. I promptly accepted the offer but tried to press my luck.

"Maybe we can go to a penny arcade after? There's one at Ocean Beach."

My father looked at me, unfazed. "Doze penny arcades make ya penniless. In fact, der nickle-nabbers." I couldn't argue with that logic, but gave him a sad face.

"How about we get ice cream afterwards?" I clamored with a wide-eyed expression.

Papa looked at me discouragingly as he shook his head. "Ah, Annie, I am already spoiling ya by taking ya to da movies."

The following day my sisters and I would see a medley of Buster Keaton short films including *Balloonatic,* where Buster was accidentally launched into the air riding on top of a hot air balloon. He had to rappel down the balloon in midair to get into the basket, where his feet then busted through the wicker floor, putting him in yet another dangerous situation.

We went back to reality on Monday. After school, we resumed our deliveries. White's Whiskey grew, and locals started to recognize us on the streets of San Francisco. When people saw our cart, they would say it was "The bee's knees."

As per my observation, despite his success, Papa became the number one consumer of White's Whiskey. His belly had become distended and his face ruddier. Whiskey at that time was called rot gut. Papa called it "hooch." Though my father became more successful in the production and selling of his signature booze, he also came home inebriated more often after work. Prior to that point, he held his liquor well. However, he became increasingly short-tempered and at times belligerent. This prompted Mama to come down hard on him. She incessantly nagged him and refused to do his laundry unless he ceased consuming his whiskey. He did stop a few times but would develop the shakes. He felt he was better off just trying to limit his alcohol consumption, and it seemed to work for a while.

Papa did so well in the business that he was able to expand his operation. Before long, he rented out the house next door and installed another distillery in that basement. He used his work truck to haul the equipment there. The new distillery was made of all copper, including the piping, which negated the need for flame testing. However, this still was much larger than the still at our house. He subleased the house next door to a young woman named Dorothy, who ran the still. When she was not expected to be home, I was given the task to monitor the still and was given an extra house key.

That house's basement was eerier than the basement in our own house, with steep steps leading down to a dark basement. There was no natural light, and the dingy room was full of bottles and crates. I had to use a stool to climb up over the gas-heated boiler to measure the temperatures and monitor for signs of overflow. In addition, that still was louder and had a stronger odor than the one at our house.

Papa spent a lot of time next door, at the new location, monitoring and tinkering with the still. At his tobacco shop, he became increasingly busy selling merchandise and operating the back room. Mama used to meet him at his tobacco shop with my youngest siblings, Billy and Theresa. They would go out to a nearby park to eat lunch while Bette, Mickey and I attended school. However, Papa became so busy that he said he couldn't do that anymore, and he stopped giving my mother his schedule. She tried to surprise him a few times, hoping to catch him on a break, but had trouble tracking him down. His employees never seemed to know where he was.

Papa also became so preoccupied with work, the two stills, and his part-time business that he had less time for Bette and me. He stopped taking us to the movies and no longer attended school functions. He even missed a school play that Bette participated in. He also became a lot less patient and would lose his temper easily, especially when drunk.

One evening, we were all seated for dinner, and Papa, who was inebriated at the time, sat at the head of the table. Mama was next to him on one side, and I on the other. The rest of my siblings occupied the other seats, including Bette, who was seated to my left. Mama had baked a large chicken pot pie. Before dividing the pie, Mama served us artichoke halves with a dollop of mayonnaise. We had eaten artichokes once before, and I liked how they tasted, but some of my siblings did not care for them. Bette and Mickey had sour faces and were picking at their food.

"Fur Christ's sake, der are pee-pull in China starvin'," Papa snapped. "Dey'd be gra-effel fer fude like dis. Ye all need ...," he hiccupped, "... to get some scran inta ya, yeh eejits!"

"William, simm-ar yer temp-ar! Mama barked.

Mickey promptly obliged and ate her artichoke.

Bette speared her artichoke half with her fork. "I'm not going to eat mine. Ann likes them." She plopped her artichoke half on my plate.

Papa's face turned beet red. His eyebrows furrowed, causing a crease to form between them. His nostrils flared. Before I could even take a bite, Papa sprang to his feet and knocked over his chair. He grabbed the artichoke off my plate with one of his bare hands and proceeded to shove the artichoke down Bette's throat.

"William, stop it!" Mama screamed.

Bette gagged, retched, and eventually threw up. This was followed by a long episode of crying and panting. My father's behavior shocked and sickened me.

Even when Papa was sober, more appalling behavior began to appear.

He started to give my younger siblings menial tasks. A cop who had emigrated from Ireland helped Papa protect his business from getting raided by the police. To show his gratitude, he had Bette or Mickey wash the officer's feet and trim his nails. Mickey said the officer's feet had a foul odor. She desperately wanted to plug her nose but knew she would get a scolding, at minimum, if she tried.

During that period, Papa gave us less spending money, often forgetting about us altogether. We felt like we had entered a state of involuntary servitude to keep his business afloat. He told us it was our duty to help our family and that we should be grateful we had a roof over our heads and food on our table. Although we did not mind making sacrifices, Bette and I did not see many kids our age having to do what we did. After learning in school about how Irish women in some of the colonies in the seventeenth century became indentured servants, we could not help but make the comparison. We protested to Mama, hoping Papa would give us a steady allowance or at least throw us a bone more often, but it fell on deaf ears. It did not make one iota of difference.

During the summer of 1923, we saw a noticeable change in our surroundings. The spot where we used to picnic on top of Bernal Hill suddenly became a huge advertising platform. An automobile firm, the Maxwell Motor Company, paid for the placement a gargantuan sign of whitewashed letters on the hill reading *MAXWELL*. It was 24 feet high and 120 feet long! Two of Maxwell's cars were parked at the summit. They were driven to the top of the hill to demonstrate their climbing abilities. An airplane flew over to take aerial views for an advertisement that was posted in some of the local newspapers. Most people in our Bernal Heights neighborhood thought it was tacky, but Papa didn't see it that way; he admired the gall of the automotive company, seeing it as an effective business strategy. Had he not been running an illegal business, he said he would have done the same and put a giant logo on the hill advertising *WHITE'S WHISKEY*.

Without a choice in the matter, Bette and I continued to support Papa's illegitimate business. We were directed to go to the new location next door to pick up batches of the newly minted whiskey. Dorothy would let us in whenever Papa wasn't around. She opened a narrow side-yard gate for us, and we pulled our cart around to the back of the house and loaded the whiskey. She would sometimes offer us lemonade or juice. Dorothy was kind and considerate, and always smiled at us. She was about ten years younger than my mother, and I thought she was lovely-looking. She had dark brown hair like Mama's and a similar petite figure, only Dorothy didn't wear glasses. Also, unlike Mama, she didn't constantly have a child in one arm and dish rags in the other after a hard day's work. Mama always seemed to have a loose wisp of hair dangling from her head, whereas Dorothy, who had no children, always appeared to be immaculately put together. She had better posture, and her make-up was skillful, applied in all the right places. She wore a variety of fine-looking dresses and pieces of jewelry. She often wore a pearl necklace paired with a powder blue dress, as well as elegant white gloves and a white hat with a blue band that matched her dress. She looked like a younger version of my mother.

Shortly after we met, Dorothy answered the door one afternoon. "Hello, darlings. Why, you two girls look so pretty!" she beamed.

"Hi, Dorothy, we're here to pick up some firewater," I chirped.

"OK, I'll let you through the gate, but then come right in. I'll leave the back door open. Don't be running off so quickly. That wouldn't be ladylike."

After positioning the cart behind the house, where Dorothy had a couple of crates of liquor stacked and ready to go, we let ourselves in. She was standing in the living room. Her home was tidy, not cluttered and disorganized like ours. That said, there was very little furniture in her home.

"Have you played the Game of Graces before?" Dorothy asked us.

"No, ma'am," Bette and I chorused.

"You don't have to call me ma'am. I'm not a ma'am yet. Just call me Dorothy."

"OK, Dorothy," I replied.

"This was a game I used to play when I was little. My grandmother, who grew up in France, used to play it when she was a child.

She taught me how to play it, and now I'll teach you. Hold on a minute." Dorothy walked over to a closet with her elegant posture and reached into a box to retrieve some sticks and a leather hoop decorated with dangling ribbons. She pulled out six sticks and gave Bette and I two sticks each. She proceeded to move her phonograph out of the room so we wouldn't run into it. "OK, now, let's get into a circle, or perhaps we will call it a triangle." She put the leather hoop around her two sticks. "Now, if you're the one to toss the hoop, you need to cross your sticks and then rapidly pull them apart." Dorothy did it, and the hoop flung and whacked me on the chest. Bette laughed. "All right, you just need to use your sticks to spear the hoop." Dorothy did it again, and I was able to catch the ring on the second try.

Eventually, Bette and I learned how to play, and we became adept at tossing the ring around as fast as we could without it falling to the ground.

Dorothy would sometimes play a board game with us, or a card game like the Ace of Spades. Occasionally, she would even tell us a quick story. We gradually became fond of her. Mama used to play games with us, but with five children, domestic chores, and part of the bootlegging business to look after, that be-came increasingly rare.

One day, when I was nearly thirteen years old, and about to head out next door to pick up crates of whiskey, I noticed blood trickling down my leg. I started to cry softly; I had no idea what was happening to me. My mother rushed over and found me standing over drops of blood on the floor.

"Ya 'ave da curse," Mama announced. This frightened me even more. What was the curse? Was I possessed? "No need to worry, it's a sign you're becoaming a woman," Mama continued. Other than that, she really gave me no explanation. She was not a cold woman, but she clearly didn't want to talk about it. It was a taboo subject. A subject that a proper woman would not say too much about. Mama drew a bath for me. I recall crying while I sat in the tub, bewildered and terrified. After I cleaned up and changed my clothes, Mama attached a rag to my underwear using some safety pins. *How horrible*, I thought, *to have to live with rags pinned to my underwear,* and then I realized why some people, especially men, would sometimes say things like, 'That woman is on the rag.'

Later, I went next door with Bette to pick up some whiskey and whispered in Dorothy's ear. "Can I tell you something in secret?"

"Sure, sweetheart," Dorothy replied. She told Bette to go to the basement to check the temperature of the mash solution. She then took me into a bathroom away from the earshot and the prying eyes of my sister and closed the door.

I told Dorothy what had happened. She explained to me what it meant and that all women had to go through this, and usually on a regular basis, for a few days each month. I was relieved to know that this was normal, and that took the sting out of finding out I would be dealing with this for years to come. I was also happy I could confide in her, as she had become a vitally important person in my life, a person I could sincerely trust.

During the fall of 1923, for my thirteenth birthday, my mother gave me a set of delicate white gloves. This was a gift I had asked for. Of course, I wanted to emulate Dorothy.

Maxwell Sign on Bernal Hill, 1923. Courtesy Greg Gaar and the Bernal History Project

CHAPTER SEVEN

By 1924, Papa became so busy with work that he had to give up his part-time job.

That September, I had just started a new school year. Papa had had an accident the week before. Late on a Wednesday afternoon, after Bette and I had completed one of our last summer bootlegging routes, Papa had shown up unexpectedly at the house when he was supposed to be at work. He came into the house swearing. He was sweaty and shaking and appeared to be drunk. Only later, I realized he may not have been drunk, but instead was going through alcohol withdrawal. He wielded a hatchet in his right hand and was wobbling as he entered the living room.

"Will, what are ya doin?" Mama spoke with apprehension.

"Where are ya?" Papa stared right through her.

"I'm right here. In front of ya … Will, can ya please put dat hatchet down?"

"Where are ya?" Papa turned his head to the side as if she were invisible.

"I implore ya to put dat hatchet down!" Mama slowly shook her hands with her palms facing down "Yerr scaring da children."

Through our parlor window a beam of light shone into the living room. It struck half of Papa's almost expressionless, drenched face, and the other half appeared to be in the shade, which gave him the appearance of a madman. He swung the hatchet through the stale air in our living room with such force that it disrupted dust particles in all directions.

Mama shrieked. "Kids, lock yerselves in da bathroom!" All five of us darted into the bathroom, but I didn't lock the door. I peered out to make sure that Mama was OK. Three-year-old Billy was petrified, and tugged on my arm to shut the door while my sisters yelled at me to do the same. Mama was trying to reassure Papa that everything was OK.

Papa swung the hatchet again as if he were attacking an imaginary foe. "Get off me!" His speech was not slurred, but he seemed confused.

"It's OK, Will," Mama choked, her voice trembling. "Everting will be OK. Now, listen to me … ya have to listen to me, Will. I need ya to go to da backyarrd and pick some green beans fur me. Can you do dat?"

Papa followed Mama through the kitchen, and she opened the back door. Like a puppy he went out the door and Mama locked it behind him.

"Ann!" Mama yelled.

"Yes, Mama?"

"Lock da front door! Now!"

I bolted out of the bathroom to do as she asked, with my siblings following me. After the house was secured all of us ran to the back of the house. We peered through the windows into the backyard to observe Papa's unusual behavior. Billy pulled up a chair to stand on and pressed his face against the windowpane so he could watch the chaos.

Papa grasped for green beans but also managed to pull up some weeds. He fell on his side on a dirt patch while holding the weeds in one outstretched hand, as if holding a bouquet of wilted flowers, while he wielded the hatchet in his opposite hand. His face became dirty and bruised. It was so degrading to witness. As he clumsily started to try to right himself, he fell again, and we couldn't help but laugh. Fear had turned into comedy; the whole scene was so surreal. Papa grasped the cinder blocks outlining our vegetable garden, trying to steady himself. He took a few more swings with his hatchet, which caused another burst of laughter amongst my siblings.

Mama was still frightened and was unsure what to do. She headed for the telephone. I'm not sure if she went to call the doctor, the hospital or one of her siblings, but as she lifted the receiver, Papa took another swing with his hatchet. We all screamed in unison, followed by a collective "Ew!"

Papa had chopped off part of his left index finger and staggered backward onto our wooden porch. Blood started to squirt from his hand in rhythmic pulses. Mama grabbed a dish towel and flung open the back door as if a grenade had exploded. She immediately applied pressure to his hand. She yelled to Bette to get Papa's belts. A trail of blood lay on the porch, with tiny globules of blood scattered on each side of the porch steps.

Fortunately, Papa then passed out and we were able to grab the hatchet and bind his arms with the belts so he could not harm himself further. While we waited for the ambulance she had called, Mama opened the front door to listen for the bells. Then she came out the back door where we were hovering over him. She chastised us for laughing at Papa.

"Ye should be ashamed of yerselves lahf-in at your fader like dat! Put a sock in-it right now!"

We deserved the tongue-lashing and felt guilty about it. This was something we later divulged to our priest during confession.

Fortunately, Papa got medical attention, and his wound was cleaned and bandaged. He looked like a prize-fighter when he returned home. His hand was covered in a bulky gauze dressing, and his face was black and blue and a little swollen. Papa apologized for putting us through that harrowing situation and said he just needed to control his drinking better.

As the school year started, Papa had left for a doctor's appointment for a one-week check-up on his wound. That afternoon, Bette and I were not asked to do our deliveries nor monitor the still next door. Nonetheless, I looked forward to spending time with Dorothy and took it upon myself to walk over to her home without my sister or a cart in tow. I remember the day being relatively warm. The front door was locked. I knocked on the door, and there was no answer. I used the spare key I had and entered the home, where I could hear the boiler running downstairs, and a record was playing on the phonograph in the living room on the main floor. It was *Sunshine of Mine* by Charles Dornberger and His Orchestra. I recognized the semi-slow but upbeat clarinet-heavy melody because I owned a copy of the record.

As I slowly approached the phonograph, I realized the record belonged to me. In the center there was a label, and within it, a logo. It was illustration of a dog, a terrier named Nipper, staring into the horn of a Victrola, a symbol of the Victor Talking Machine company that produced phonographs and records. I had accidentally scratched the area where the dog's left ear was located, and I recognized the abrasion. Perplexed, I stood over the spinning record, double-checking my discovery all while keeping my head still and moving my eyes around in synchrony to view the label more clearly. I knew without a doubt that it was mine and paused while I brought together my eyebrows in a state of confusion. I pondered for a moment. How on earth had Dorothy got hold of my record?

"Dorothy?" I called out once but got no response. She was nowhere to be seen. I thought I briefly heard some noise, but I wasn't sure where it was coming from. Into the kitchen I peered and noticed an open container of whisky on the kitchen table, and two plates. Both plates had crumbs, and a half-eaten sandwich lay on one of them. An uncomfortable, eerie feeling crept over me. Everything seemed out of place. I then heard some female laughter tinkling down from upstairs. It sounded like Dorothy. I slowly and gingerly walked up the stairs and started to hyperventilate a little as I was afraid of what I might encounter. Her bedroom door was ajar. I slowly opened the door and saw my father and Dorothy naked in bed. I screamed.

I scurried downstairs and Papa chased after me. I fell awkwardly on the stairwell, landing hard on my right elbow. Papa caught up to me. In his left hand, bandaged with some dried blood showing, he held his pair of trousers. He stood looking down upon me, wearing nothing but underwear.

"You dirty bastard!" I cried. "I am going to tell mother what's going on here!"

He then abruptly yanked me up by the arm and slapped me on my face with vigorous force. The slap knocked me back to the ground, causing a cruel scrape to one of my knees. He had never been violent to me in the past aside from a few spankings and well-deserved swats to the back of my head. This level of violence was something I hadn't seen before. Papa had metamorphosed into a savage beast.

Papa hovered over me, breathing rapidly. Scowling, his face appeared redder and more florid than usual. I soon found myself on the receiving end of a livid, glaring stare. "If ya say anyting to her, dat will ruin her life. Do ya understand me?"

I began weeping.

Papa's facial expression softened. His eyebrows straightened and his eyes widened, looking more concerned. He dropped his head "Annie, I had a moment of weakness. Can ya please furgive me?" I did not respond with voice but looked straight at him disapprovingly. "I'm gunna go to confession. Will ya please pray for me?" I stopped crying and averted my gaze. "Look at me, Ann." Out of the pair of trousers he was holding, he pulled out some money and grasped my hand. "Here, take tis." He proceeded to give me an outlandish amount of pocket money. About $10 in total. I was traumatized and felt like I had received blood money.

At dinner that evening, at home, all seven of us sat at the dinner table. I recall the meal included Italian meatballs, noodles, and green beans. I was in a sour mood and remained mostly silent while I picked at my food. Mama noticed my seemingly odd behavior and asked if I had trouble at school that day with one of my classmates or the new teacher. I frowned but said no, and didn't say much. All the time, my father was staring straight at me with piercing eyes, in a threatening way, hoping I would not crack. Seething, I reciprocated by looking steadily and angrily into his cruel steel blue eyes. I utterly hated him in that moment. I wanted to spill the beans but held my tongue.

Mama hadn't even noticed the physical wounds I had suffered. She appeared to be completely oblivious, focusing on her domestic duties and doting on Billy and his seemingly incessant whining.

Following that encounter, I had many sleepless nights. The bruise on my elbow and scrape on my knee were just reminders of that awful day. I did sing to myself to ease the pain. I felt like I had lost my father. I sang the song called *After You Have Gone*, by Turner Layton. One of the verses resonated with me.

"After you've gone, you left me crying,
after you've gone, there is no denying.
You will feel blue, you will feel sad,
you'll miss the dearest pal you've ever had."

I remember weeping and singing myself to sleep.

I never saw Dorothy in the same light again, and all the smiles I had received from her now felt fake. I began to think that the fancy jewelry she wore may have been gifts from my father. At that point, I suspected he wasn't even charging her rent. Maybe he wasn't subleasing to her after all? Maybe she was married to another man and was only living there for some of the time? I would never find out.

After the incident, I barely talked to Dorothy when Bette and I went to the house for a liquor pick-up. I simply could not trust her.

"Au revoir, you trollop," I muttered under my breath as I left her house one afternoon.

"Darling, what did you say?" Dorothy asked, pleasantly.

"Ma'am, please don't call me darling," I chirped, without looking at her, and off we went.

At least not talking to Dorothy saved us time. We got onto our routes a little earlier. When carrying out deliveries some neighborhood kids told us that they admired my father. William White was a hero in their eyes. They told us he would sometimes toss coins to them. Little did they know what he was truly capable of. He certainly was no hero of mine.

Mama started to suspect my father was having an affair. She increasingly questioned him about his whereabouts. Mama demanded his schedule down to the hour, stating she required it in case of an emergency or if she needed his help. She also told him she wanted to resume meeting him for lunch, but I didn't buy it. I knew the real reason she wanted his daily agenda. My father procrastinated, telling her he would get it to her, but didn't. After she persisted, he finally gave her a schedule but only wrote in general times and remained as evasive as he could.

At times, Mama became short-tempered and snapped at him. She began talking about handsome, dashing silent movie stars like Douglas Fairbanks and John Barrymore as if to make him jealous that he did not possess their looks. At other times, I could tell, she was trying to look more attractive. She spent more time brushing her hair. She started putting on make-up during the week, which she had not typically done except for special occasions. When I would occasionally go upstairs to talk to her, I noticed in the upstairs bathroom plenty of lipstick, eyeliners, powders, and liquids lying on the counter. I could tell Mama spent time plucking her eyebrows as they became thinner. Her cheeks were covered with plenty of rouge. Her eyelids took on a smoky blue look. Her lips were drawn with the pattern of a Cupid's bow, which was popular at the time. She lathered mascara on her eyelashes.

Mama even stopped wearing glasses for a while but that meant she bumped into the walls. In the kitchen she knocked over pots, pans, bowls, and glasses. She once even misjudged how close she was to a boiling pot and burned her forearm, resulting in blisters. She reluctantly resumed wearing her spectacles.

As time went on, I gradually forgave my father and naively thought that was the end of all of that.

However, Papa became increasingly short-tempered and was unpleasant to be around. One day, Mickey invited a few friends over to play. They were playing hopscotch on the sidewalk out front. Bette and I were busy monitoring the still downstairs in our home's basement. We could hear sounds of Mickey and her friends playing above us through the vent I was perched on a ladder monitoring the temperature, and Bette was on the lookout. The mash solution overflowed, hitting the basement floor, and the stench wafted up through the vent in the upper part of the wall that was just above the ground level. Just as the still accident unfolded, Papa walked into the room down the stairs with a cigar in his mouth. I had a pit in my stomach as I was unsure how the event would unfold.

"What's doin wit ya?"

"Smell is doing." Bette tilted her head up to the vent to warn my father that other kids were near. She was trying to be funny at the same time. He cracked her to the back of her head, so hard that it knocked her over. She sat on the cold basement floor, rubbing the back of her head while tears were streaming from her face. She didn't say anything. His behavior was frightening. It was ruthless and appalling, and I felt infuriated and powerless. He was not the man I once knew.

We implored Mama to do something about his behavior, but she did nothing other than to minimize it. "Yer Papa loves ya. He works long hours and just wants to make sure everyting is operatin' smootly."

Mama tried to take our minds off the situation by inviting us to go swimming at an enormous outdoor public swimming pool that had just opened in San Francisco, in April 1925. The Fleishhacker Pool was one of the largest swimming pools in the world, located in the southwest portion of the city off the Great Highway on the opposite side of the highway to the Pacific Ocean. Water was pumped from the ocean, then filtered and heated, although the temperature rarely got much above the high 60s. The pool contained 6.5 million gallons of seawater. The saltwater pool was so huge that some of the lifeguards used wooden row boats to patrol the waters. There was a rumor going around at the pool that there was a shark on the loose. Though I knew it wasn't true, I couldn't help but scan the water from time to time.

Girls at that time were expected to wear bathing caps for fear that our hair would clog swimming pool drains. We only owned two, so we initially took turns sharing. However, with thousands of swimmers to patrol it, it was not strictly enforced, and within no time all of us swam at the same time.

The Red Cross sponsored swimming lessons, and we all took them except for our parents. My father did not attend, and Mama preferred to sit on the steps, wearing a black dress, watching us from afar. Papa was too cheap to purchase bathing-suits for all of us. We had to wear undergarments covered by long undershirts, which, in addition to being embarrassing, would get waterlogged and affect our buoyancy. I was on my way to becoming a woman, and Mama had sewn a piece of cloth in the bust area so my nipples would not show. She also pinned cloth to the private areas over all our undergarments. I thought we were going to get busted by the lifeguards or the moral police, but instead we were just gawked at. I had been to nearby Ocean Beach in San Francisco in the past with a friend and her family. My friend lent me a bathing suit, and I recall a bathing beach cop going around to women and measuring the distance from their knees to the bottom of their bathing-suits to make sure the exposed area of skin was not too long. I remember being mortified at first, but then I realized that, with my short frame, it wouldn't be a problem. My calculation was correct, and they didn't bother me.

In the late summer of 1925, when I was almost fifteen, I saw Bette pass a note to my father while he was sitting in the living room, and Mama was in the kitchen out of view. When I got the chance, I pulled Bette aside and asked her what that was all about. She said that Dorothy had been handing her notes to give to our father and that she was sworn to secrecy not to let Mama know about them. I resented my father and was gathering the courage to tell Mama, but soon found out that that she already knew about the relationship by then. I overheard my parents arguing about it. Mama started to experience deep melancholy and became distraught.

Papa came home drunk more often. His face grew puffy, his eyes bloodshot, and he developed webs of little red spidery blotches on his cheeks.

One evening, Mama tried to confront him when he came home late after drinking. He ignored her, walked straight past her, and proceeded upstairs. She yelled at him and followed him up the steps as I trailed behind. Her voice did not carry like my father's, and it appeared to have no impact on him. After they reached the room, Papa had his back turned and was putting away his coat in the closet. I stood in the doorway witnessing the argument.

"Will, you've been fooling around wit dat hussy, haven't ya?"

Papa turned around, lowering his eyelids and scowling at her. "Button yur trap, ya shrew!"

For once in my life, I fervently wished that Mama would sock him. She didn't go that far, but she grabbed his face with her right thumb and index finger and forcefully pinched his cheek. Papa shoved her away from him and flared his nostrils, balled his fists, and his face became beet red. I could see Mama shaking with fear.

"Stop it!" I screamed.

Ignoring me, Papa grabbed Mama by the collar, turning her sideways and slammed her head into the wall. It caused the plaster to shatter, and an indentation in the wall appeared from her crown. Fortunately, Mama did not break her skull. My mother wept, and I spoke through choked tears while I said a few choice words to my father. He left the house again but came back home later that evening.

CHAPTER EIGHT

The next morning, Papa apologized and promised to stop seeing Dorothy. He said he would make it up to Mama. He started
by buying her a necklace and told her it was made of real gold. We
found out later that it was imitation jewelry.

Papa proceeded by trying to butter Mama up with his charm.
"Yer a right dote, Maggie. A daycent woman. Ya shift my gears, and
ya are as beautiful as da day we met." I knew he felt guilty because
he then went into overdrive and in a soft-toned voice said a Gaelic
phrase that I had heard him use in the past: '*Is tu mo storin,*' meaning
'*You are my little sweetheart.*'

He then promised to take the whole family on a vacation. It
would be our first and only White family vacation. He rented a cabin
in Sonoma County along the Russian River, and reserved it for several days just before the school year began.

Although recent events were quite unsettling, we were all incredibly excited to go on vacation for the first time. Mama tried to
look past everything my father had done. He finally gave Mama an
allowance for us to buy bathing suits. We all got tank suits, one-piece
suits with mostly solid colors made of a springy, ribbed jersey material. My sisters got red, blue, and grey suits, my father and Billy got

black ones, Mama bought a white one, and I found a Kelly green suit with contrasting stripes. The bathing-suit shapes did not differ a whole lot between men's and women's, except that girls' and women's suits flared at the bottom like a skirt.

While at home, in preparation for lounging at the beach, Mama pulled out all the hats she owned, including a smaller hat she would stick on four-year-old Billy's head, making him look like another sister. Mama, who liked to feed stray cats in our backyard, hired a boy to come over and feed the cats daily while we were on vacation. She called the male cats Tom and the female cats Minnie.

We woke up early preparing for the lengthy trip that lay ahead. We had fun making sandwiches, potato salad, and fruit salad. Mama also prepared fried chicken for that evening's dinner. We helped load Papa's Model T with all our supplies. Papa used his hidden compartment to stash his whiskey. "'Tis is goin' to be fun," he grinned with excitement.

My three sisters and I crammed into the back seat. The Model Ts did not have dedicated trunk spaces back then. Papa removed the back seat cushions to allow more room. He rammed in a couple of heavy, hard suitcases. My younger sisters had to sit on top of one of them and one partially sat on top of Bette and me, making it an exceptionally uncomfortable ride. We didn't pack a lot of clothes and were prepared to do laundry in the Russian River. In the front passenger seat, Mama balanced both Billy and a picnic basket on her lap on her lap. Papa coughed intermittently throughout the trip. He drove down to Hyde Street Pier in San Francisco. There was a hubbub of activity there with a long line of autos on the dock waiting to board diesel-fueled ferries with long smokestacks spewing dark noxious vapors into the atmosphere. All of us except Papa got out of the car. He then drove his Model T onto the auto-ferry where we boarded.

During the journey across the Bay, I turned around to look at the skyline of the city. Though scenic San Francisco gave the impression of being smaller when viewing from afar. It was a perspective I had never seen before. Papa lit his cigar and walked around the ferry chatting with people and charmed women while Mama sat on a bench with my younger siblings. Seagulls followed us on our journey across the Bay, gliding and occasionally flapping their wings, some of them squawking. I reasoned their bird brains figured we were a fishing boat of some sort about to bring up the catch of the day in pots or traps, and they were hoping for scraps.

As the wind picked up in the middle of the Bay I went to the bow of the boat with, Bette and Mickey. We crouched down, jutting our heads forward to look at the churning water below. We watched waves as they curled under our ferry. We went over a few whitecaps, and when the seawater from the Bay lightly splashed on our faces we could taste the ice-cold saltwater on our lips.

After reaching the Sausalito Ferry Terminal, we squeezed back in the car to resume our journey. I had never been out of San Francisco in my life aside from going to a funeral in Colma. It was like going to a new world. Where were all the people?

I was so excited to see the countryside. It was not covered in concrete, and there were so many verdant trees and picturesque farms. We drove past old wineries, surrounded by withering grapevines, that had closed due to Prohibition. The weather was much warmer than San Francisco. Fruit stands dotted the route. We stuck our heads out of the car to let the wind blow on our faces, where we breathed in the surrounding air and smelled the familiar and sometimes unfamiliar scents. The sweet new smells sometimes mingled with the aroma of slightly rotted fruit. Papa, at times, drove faster than the twenty-five-mile an hour speed limit posted on the state highway. It may have been the first time he was able to see what his

Model T roadster could really do. He drove as fast as forty miles per hour causing Mama to almost lose her wide-brimmed hat with its flowery bow-tie. We breathed in the breezes and experienced the exhilarating sensation of warm air blasting on our faces, with the heightened sense of the surrounding environment, until Mama spoiled our fun.

"Slow down, Will! Tis isn't a race. Yur gunna get a speeding ticket!" Papa begrudgingly obliged after she repeated her demand a few times. He shifted the gears and gradually slowed to the pace of other drivers. He became annoyed when a well-dressed couple, driving in a sleek, shiny red Lincoln Beetle-back roadster, zoomed past us.

"Look what ya made me do." He lifted his hands in the air with his palms up briefly disengaging from the steering wheel. Perhaps he was summoning the racing gods to help propel the car faster? Papa must have thought he had entered the Indianapolis 500 where the average speed had finally topped 100 mph three months earlier. Much of the ride to our destination was uneventful except when a rude driver abruptly cut in front of us. This prompted Papa to yell "Ya blockhead!" This was followed by an Irish curse. He skipped the Gaelic version and went straight to English. At least his version of English with an Irish accent. "Da devil may prepare a fire for ya!" This caused a burst of laughter among us. His coming undone was entertaining to watch.

As our journey continued, we passed by a number of charming towns, scattered across the countryside. Mama observed that some of the green hilly countryside resembled places in Ireland. Being out of San Francisco, to her, everything must have felt like her home-land. When we had to drive through the center of a town, Papa slowed down and he was as courteous and polite as ever, letting cars merge in front of him. It was as if Dr. Jekyll had turned back into Mr. Hyde.

Before settling into our cabin, near the town of Rio Nido, we passed by a candy store, soda shop, bowling alley, grocery store, and an outdoor theater. We saw families holding hands together and children playing. Bette and I looked at each other with wide-eyed expressions. Had we just entered heaven?

After the long journey, we arrived in the early afternoon.

"Mama, are we close to Ireland?" Billy piped up. "No, my love, dat's a place far, far away. An enchanted land I will probably never get back to." I could tell Mama was yearning at the thought.

The area was surrounded by a mixture of oak, tanoak, Douglas fir and redwood trees. We had a few hours of daylight left before nightfall. The first thing we spotted near our cabin was a woven hammock tied to two oak trees. As soon as we got out of the car, Bette, who was eleven at the time, ran and jumped onto the hammock and fell back to the ground laughing. She managed to climb back on, face down and my younger siblings started to pile on top of her. I wanted a turn but had to let the clown show unfold first. Bette's face was smooshed into the mesh, and she started blowing raspberries through the open spaces between the woven material. My other siblings followed. Eight-year-old Mickey jumped off and began swinging the hammock trying to dislodge the rest of the rambunctious bunch. Sure enough, my calculations were correct, and their attention got diverted elsewhere in no time. My youngest sister, six-year-old Theresa, spotted a black-tailed jackrabbit in the grass near the cabin, and the whole gang proceeded to chase the startled creature, who easily out- maneuvered them, zig-zagging and leaping, before disappearing from sight.

After helping unpack, I got to relax and read in the hammock for a little while. Bette pulled out her paint set and began painting the jackrabbit she had seen. My other siblings spotted some cute ground squirrels and were busy collecting some acorns and stacking them in a pile on top of a tree stump in hopes the furry creatures would approach. I was reading a book that I had started at home, *The Man in the Brown Suit* by Agatha Christie. My peace wouldn't last long as my siblings were clamoring to go down to the river and play. They were jumping like pogo sticks, raring to head out.

Most people back then did not use sun protection other than to carry umbrellas or wear hats and long sleeves if they felt it necessary. We didn't know about sun damage but did know we did not want to get an unpleasant sunburn. With our pale Irish skin Mama insisted on some defense against the sun rays. I suppose she was right. When 'flesh-colored' Band-Aids came out in the early 1920s they were too dark for our skin. The only people who were offended were black people and us! Mama slathered olive oil on the exposed areas of our bodies and zinc oxide on our faces. By the time she was finished with us we looked like the byproducts of Grecian wrestlers who had mated with Geisha girls. It didn't matter; our friends were not present to make fun of us. I just didn't want to come across a good-looking boy. God forbid I scared off a potential boyfriend and gave him a case of the screaming meemies!

Our cabin was fairly isolated and away from the main town. As Mama applied the oil and zinc oxide, I scanned the interior. The cabin was old and rudimentary. There was a small kitchenette with an iron, wood-burning stove and an old ice-box. The kitchenette was loaded with gadgets from the era that my mother had grown up in. There was a waffle iron, a Bissell floor sweeper and a hand-cranked chopper. There were bins for flour and sugar. Also, there was a pyramid toaster where you could put up to four slices of bread around the rim at one time, but you had to remember to flip the bread to toast the other side.

Aside from the kitchenette, the cabin was simply one big room with several springy cots with overlying mattresses. The exception was one bed that was attached to the wall that folded out. They were called Murphy beds, but sometimes the bed was referred to as 'The Disappearing Bed' or the 'In-A-Door Bed.' William Lawrence Murphy, the son of two Irish immigrants, invented that type of bed in San Francisco around the turn of the century. The story I had heard about Murphy's invention was that he had an opera singer girlfriend who he wanted to invite to his studio-type, one-bedroom apartment, but it was considered improper for a woman to enter a man's bedroom in those days. So, he designed the foldable bed to hide it in his closet and turn the room into a respectable parlor. He ended up marrying the opera singer the following year. Though the reasons for the foldable bed could certainly have been true, I believed the account was hogwash. I had read enough steamy novels by then to know that he could've done that so any heavy petting or other pre-marital improprieties could be swept under the rug, or into the closet, so to speak, should their families come to visit.

Up to that point, most of my education on sex came from gossip, or novels shared among friends that we hid from our folks. Parents back then, or at least mine, would not broach the subject with us. The book *Ulysses* by James Joyce had been passed around my neighborhood so many times among the girls I knew that the binding was coming loose. The book contained sexual language and imagery. It was considered highly indecent for the time. *Ulysses* was banned in the US, but had managed to make its way to young ladies in San Francisco, coming of age.

I wasn't sure about Murphy's original intention, but despite a patent he had on that type of contraption, the bed at our cabin looked like a second-rate imitation with poorly-made hardware and shoddy craftsmanship. Certainly, it was not a true Murphy bed, but rather a cheap knock-off brand, if not homemade. It screeched when Papa pulled it out of its resting place against the wall. It would be the bed that my parents decided to sleep on.

Inside the cabin, there was a stack of blankets and pillows on a shelf. A tiny fireplace partially covered in soot was on the back wall. Next to the fireplace were some board games. One was a game, *Ring My Nose,* which featured a hideous, scary-looking clown missing a tooth. It included rings that you threw from ten feet away, trying to get them to stick on a nose peg. There was also a board game by Milton Bradley that you could play checkers on one side with, and baseball on the other. Also present was the *Gee-Wiz* horse racing gambling game. It was a tabletop game with a metal track and tin horses. There was also an old stereoscope next to sets of black and white photograph cards. It allowed you to look at a photo in three dimensions. Stereoscopes had been popular in the late 1800s. We looked at some photos for a few minutes of people, pets, landscapes, monuments, and exotic places. I couldn't believe all the fun we would be having for the next several days.

Papa picked up the metal horse racing game contraption. "I've seen tis game played at one of da back-room bars back home." It was a wind-up game, and the horses made their way to the other end of a straight track. "Pee-pull place bets on dez horses." I could tell his wheels were spinning, only his wheels were more like a slot machine being fed by a bag of nickels. In fact, Papa said having one of these racing games was as good as owning a slot machine, which happened to be another San Francisco invention from 1894.

"Maybe I'll ask da owner of tis game if he would sell it to me." He had a starry-eyed expression, as I could tell he was imagining it in his own illegal bar. Papa certainly never lacked ambition. He inspected the game closely, lifting it up and turning it on its side, searching for any sign of damage. "Dis is sound … der is money to be made here." Papa set the game down and filled his canteen with whiskey.

Once we had slipped our pasty-white coated skin into our bathing-suits, we dashed along the pebbly riverbank while my parents followed, hollering at us to slow down. We located one of the few sandy patches remaining where no one was occupying the space. My parents found a boulder to sit on adjacent to the sandy area where we put some of our belongings. Papa wrapped his arms around Mama while they sat, but she did not reciprocate, keeping her arms by her side. The tension was still palpable.

As we had fun playing in the river and chasing ducks, Papa managed to refill his canteen with whiskey several times. We saw damselflies and dragonflies hovering over the water.

By that evening, Papa was inebriated again, and his cough had worsened. He did not help Mama with a single thing. When we returned to the cabin, he lay down on a bare mattress on one of the cots with squeaky springs, forgetting that he and Mama had staked out the folding bed. He didn't even bother to make his bed. He just plopped down while still wearing his clothes and fell asleep. Mama covered him with a blanket and became quite upset.

She had to help some of us get our bathing-suits off then set up a clothesline to dry them. She used a hose to wash off all the sand stuck to our creamed bodies. Billy had a cut on his ankle he must have sustained while playing in the river. Mama got him to slow down and applied some antiseptic and bandaged him up. We changed into warmer clothes and gathered blankets from the cabin. I was directed to locate a box of matches we had packed, and Mama started to prepare for a campfire by collecting some wood.

I witnessed Mama struggling to start the fire, something Papa usually did at home. She was tired, her face sunken with droopy eyelids. At first, she seemed overwhelmed with the tasks at hand.

I noticed she briefly buried her face in her hands, and I offered to
help. With perspicacity, she sprang to life and directed me to find
some smaller pieces of tinder like twigs and dry moss. Bette and
Mickey were tasked with rounding up some chairs. Billy and Theresa
were entrusted with locating the marshmallows we had packed without eating them on the way to the campfire. Marshmallows back
then came in a can, not in a clear plastic bag like they do nowadays.
That assignment was quite difficult for them as they opened the can
and were pointing to which particular marshmallows they wanted.
They squeezed individual marshmallows to mark which ones would
be their special gooey treats.

In no time, Mama had managed to start some flamelets and was
able to coax a fire into life. As we sat around the campfire, I realized
Theresa had not seen Papa lie down when we returned from the
river.

"Mama … where did Papa go?"

"He's fully scuttered from drinkin' whiskey. He is in da cabin
passed out," Mama answered in a matter-of-fact tone. Theresa just
shrugged her shoulders as if that were normal.

Soon we became settled and devoured Mama's delicious fried
chicken. A gorgeous, warm orange glow filled the skies as the sun
set. The air was cool and crisp, but we were more than comfortable
around the warmth of the fire. After eating the chicken, we carefully
and methodically found the best sticks for roasting marshmallows.
Smoke began to cling to our clothes as we roasted the fluffy white
treats.

We enjoyed ghost stories told by Mama beside the campfire.
They were a bit tame, though, so as not to scare my youngest siblings too much. Bette did not hold back, however. She added her
own ghost story, told with haunting fervor. It included multiple
voices, accents, wolves howling and an ax man who was ready to

chop up unsuspecting innocent tourists visiting the Russian River. Theresa provided some comic relief. She told a story about a giant marshmallow man who was sad because no one liked him. He handed out marshmallows that would stick in your teeth and rot them, but then revealed that simply by brushing your teeth, you could stop the rot. So the people did, and their teeth no longer rotted, and so they became great friends with the marshmallow man.

"What-a lovely story!" Mama beamed with over-enthusiastic expression. "Y'awl have splendid imaginations. Just splendid."

As the surroundings grew darker the night sky was illuminated with brilliant stars, brighter than I had ever seen. Prior to that time, I had only seen the celestial bodies from the perspective of living in San Francisco. I did not realize that all the artificial light from the city's buildings, lampposts and automobiles' headlights interfered with viewing the magnificent astronomical displays above us. We viewed the Big and Little Dipper as well as the Milky Way like we had never seen before. Mama didn't know much about astronomy, but she pointed out a couple of things she had learned when she was a child growing up in Ireland. Growing up in farmland, in County Cavan, she had seen the night sky with all its luminous stars and planets. She knew how to identify a few objects and asked us to find something that looked orange in the night sky. We spotted it in no time.

"Dat's Maars. Ya can always locate-tit by its color. Der might be Maartians living der! We just don't know."

Then she asked us to find the brightest object in the sky besides the moon. It took us a little longer to spot but we located it in nearly the opposite direction.

"Do ya want to guess what dat is?"

After a plethora of wrong guesses like Jupiter and the North Star, Mickey, perhaps the smartest of us, shouted: "Venus!"

"Yerr correct!"

Little Billy perked up. "Mama?"

"Yes, my angel?"

"Are the stars the same in Ireland?"

"Why, yes, dey are, dear! Dat's a wonderful question. When ya look in da night sky, ya might see more clouds, but utterwise, it looks very similar." Mama gestured to Billy. "C'mere." She held her arms wide. Billy got up from his chair and embraced her. She picked him up, gave him a kiss, and put him in her lap. "Before we head back to da cabin, I would like to give ya awl a lovely Eye-rish blessing. I'm goin ta modify it-a little. Tomorrow morning, when we wake up, may da road rise to meet ya, may da wind always be at yer back, may da warm rays of sun fall upon dis cabin and may da land of a friend always be near." Mama always had a calming way of making us feel good.

Before bedtime, we stood outside the cabin brushing our teeth using Colgate's Ribbon Dental Cream. We rinsed our mouths with water from the hose. All of us then took turns using an outhouse up on top of a hill, behind our cabin. We shared a flashlight so we could make our way there without slipping. The wooden structure was old and dilapidated, and I found the surrounding area to be rather disgusting. It stood above a slope and there was a trail of dirty liquid, perhaps urine, mixed with who knows what, meandering from its base. Flies swarmed the murky stream as if they were in a feeding frenzy. One even appeared to have a peculiar oddity, as a red growth bulged out from one of its eyes. Conceivably, the noxious waterway brought life to the area. Earlier in the day, I could swear I had seen a lizard sunbathing and doing push-ups near one of its tributaries. The whole area was malodorous, but wasn't half as bad as the inside of the latrine. There was a wooden seat with a hole cut out in the center and noxious vapor emanated from its cavity. We were all forced to hold our breath and set personal speed records for using an outhouse. Mama made sure to clean Billy's hands well before settling into our cabin. This was a minor inconvenience, I felt.

Despite sleeping on a springy cot, I knew I would not have to get up early to go to school nor do a hooch delivery, so I slept, snug as a bug in a rug. I dreamt about all the other things we might do on our vacation. In addition to going to the beach, relaxing, and reading in the hammock, and playing games in the cabin, I thought perhaps we would rent a boat, go fishing, or hang out at the soda shop.

The next morning, as my eyelids were still shut, I sensed the sun had come up by the variation of light filtering through its translucent membranes. Just as I was wiping sleepy sand from my eyes, I heard an incessant wet cough. Papa had awoken with a fever, and his cough had worsened. He was hacking up yellow gunk, which he spat along the side of our cabin. He was pale and languid.

Mama, already dressed and appearing ready to go somewhere, hovered over me as I sat up. Her face wore a somewhat ominous expression. "Yer fader is ill. He is goin' to drive da Tin Lizzie to find a doctor." My mother didn't know how to drive a car. "I'm going wit him and we'll take Billy wit us. I want ya girls to stay togeter. Here is some money." Mama handed me about forty cents. Ya can go to town to dat candy shop and buy some candy. Get somting for Billy."

That sounded like fun. An adventure without adult supervision, only one in which I would not have to transport illegal, hidden liquor. At that point, I figured my father would be prescribed some medicine and we would be able to continue our vacation.

The four of us girls headed into town, which was over a mile's walk from our cabin. Theresa preferred holding my hand while we walked. Upon reaching the resort village, we walked past a penny arcade and decided to take a brief detour wandering through. We passed strength testers, including one where you could shake Uncle

Sam's hand. Then we located racing games, fortune teller booths, and hand-operated Mutoscopes where you could watch a movie created by rapidly-flickering photo cards. We didn't have enough money to both play in the penny arcade and buy candy, so I rounded up my sisters and redirected their attention to focus on the task at hand.

We located the candy shop in no time. Vibrantly colored candies of all kinds were displayed in neatly separated containers. There were bins containing mostly hard candy, and a couple of buckets full of chewy candies. There was also a small display of uniformly wrapped candy bars. The smell was absolutely delightful; a mixture of intoxicatingly sweet aromas of caramel, chocolate, vanilla, cherry, and cinnamon pervaded the air. There were too many scrumptious choices. Would I get a peppermint stick or some other hard candy, or would it be chocolate or taffy? I certainly was not going to leave with just a measly piece of hard candy. My sisters left the store with items like sherbert fountains and Charleston Chews. I ended up getting a Baby Ruth Bar, a mostly chocolate, peanut, and caramel concoction named after the former President Grover Cleveland's daughter Ruth. After we exited the store, we sat on the sidewalk and enjoyed consuming our candy. It felt like we were in heaven.

We gradually made our way back to the cabin and within two to three hours my parents and Billy returned from the doctor's visit. Our nirvana would then come crashing to an abrupt end. Mama emerged from the car, crying. "We have to leave," she sobbed. "Da doctor said yur fader has pneumonia and we need to be near a good hospital in case it worsens. He wants him to be isolated, in a different room."

"Why can't we stay in a different cabin with separate rooms?" I retorted.

"Der all filled up. Der are no vacancies. Aside from dat, da doctor didn't tink it is a good idea to be so far away from a major hospital. Der is a small hospital in Sonoma County called Burndale, but dat's about fifty miles from 'ere. We've got to go home."

All of us, excluding my father, who was too ill to express much emotion, burst into tears. It was so sad that we would have to leave paradise in less than twenty-four hours since we had arrived. The journey back was awful. I felt every bump in the road and every cough as Papa spat phlegm out of the driver's side of the car. The only joy I got was seeing the image of the black-tailed jackrabbit that Bette had painted and held in her hand for nearly the entire ride home. The jackrabbit appeared realistic and seemed to spring to life, giving me moments of joy, in between bouts of tears, every time I peered at it. We made it back to San Francisco by the early evening.

To add insult to injury, when we got home, we discovered that the boy Mama had hired to come over daily to feed the cats had just chucked dozens of fish heads all at once into the backyard, over the fence, without ever using the side gate. He had taken a shortcut by doing the work all at once. The backyard stunk up to high heaven.

CHAPTER NINE

My father recovered from that pneumonia, and my parents continued arguing with each other for months. My mother never used the word divorce in front of us or when she knew we were listening, but I overheard her use the word during an argument. Divorce was forbidden by the Catholic Church, and my mother's threats to divorce him seemed empty. She had told us in the past that good Catholics did not get divorced. An annulment was an option, but it was taboo to talk about it, and even then, it meant the marriage had never existed.

Mama was upset about Papa's drinking, but she was infuriated by the affair between my father and Dorothy. She would occasionally go outside late at night when she couldn't sleep and throw rocks at the house next door so that Dorothy wouldn't be able to sleep as well. Over time, my other siblings learned of the affair and of Mama's rock throwing. They began to toss rocks at the house as well.

My parents' bickering continued into early November 1925. Papa, at the age of thirty-eight, developed pneumonia again and was in a weakened state. His doctor put him on medication. It wasn't an antibiotic, as penicillin, the first antibiotic, would not be discovered for another three years. We tried to keep our distance from Papa as best we could. Sometimes my mother brought him food in bed, and other times he managed to get down the stairs, coughing and wheezing, and ate in the kitchen, separate from us children.

One evening, Papa made his way slowly downstairs, heading toward the kitchen. He was so sick I don't think he'd drunk an ounce of booze for nearly a day. He had a tremor and could barely hold onto the stair banister. His skin was yellow, and his face bloated. He had a moist, rattling, loose cough. Once he made his way into the kitchen, he coughed violently, and I briefly peered in to see if he was OK. He hacked up some green-brown, milky, purulent sputum and spat it in the sink. My mother rinsed the sink, and a stream of cloudy, fetid liquid made its way down the drain. I gagged and came close to throwing up.

My mother turned to Papa. "Will, perhaps it's time for ya to go to da hospital."

My father was breathing rapidly and could barely talk. He shook his head sideways. "Da quacks ... dey don't ..." He paused to catch his breath. "... know anyting." Perhaps he was still bitter about the loss of my sister Katherine back in 1917.

Mama set a bowl of her homemade vegetable soup before him, which she made with carrots, parsnips, and leeks, and gave him a, piece of Irish soda bread on the side. He was in the kitchen for nearly half an hour and barely touched any of it. He scratched his skin and was confused, asking what day it was. Then he stared at a cutting board. "Get dat cat outa here!" he exclaimed. There were no cats in the house.

"Will, yer seeing tings. Der is no cat in da house. Ya look exhausted. I'll help ya upstairs." Mama wrapped her arm around him getting him up to a standing position, and they gradually made their way upstairs. They stopped at a landing so he could rest for a minute and catch his breath.

As they got close to the bedroom, I heard Papa say, "I got it … g'wan," and Mama retreated downstairs.

We all did the dishes and cleaned up. Mama knitted while sitting on the couch. Bette and I caught up on our homework. After completing our work, we listened to the radio, the first one we owned. My father had purchased an Atwater Kent radio the year before. He frequently polished his prized possession to keep it looking just like new, as if it had just come from the factory. Made from shiny, glossy wood, it was rectangular in shape with a variety of dials on the front to help with tuning, volume, and frequency. Papa had mounted a bell-shaped metal horn speaker on its top. I was highly impressed with the technology. We tuned into one of our favorite new radio stations, KFRC, and listened to some music while I curled my feet beneath the couch sitting next to Mama.

Around 9:30 p.m., Mama prompted us to go to bed. As we were getting ready, she went to her bedroom to check on Papa. For no clear reason, he had locked the door. When Mama called out, he didn't answer.

"Why did he lock the door?" I asked.

"I really don't know. Since he has had trouble breatin' today, he has been a bit confused," Mama replied, with a look of concern.

After repeated failed attempts to get him to answer, Mama felt it was necessary for one of us to get into Papa's room through the bedroom window, which he kept partially open to let in breezes. Usually at night he closed the window, but it had been left open. The only way to get into the room would be to climb onto the roofline below the bedroom window, which was two stories up.

"Ann, climb up to da bedroom window and see if ya can get in and unlock da door," Mama ordered.

"Mama, why don't you do it?" I protested.

"Jesus, Mary, and Joseph, I have weak knees and can barely climb upstairs as it-tis!" she squawked.

"Why don't we get a friend or relative to come over?"

"It's late and I don't want to get dem sick. Yer fader could spread germs."

"Heights frighten me, Mama. Besides that, he could just be sleeping," I reasoned.

Mama faced me squarely and put her hands on my shoulders. "'Tis is important, Ann," she said, sternly. "Who else is goin' to do it? I shan't send little Billy ... why, he'll break a leg!"

"Who's to say I won't break a leg, Mama?" I tried to appeal to her, to no avail. Reasoning with her was like reasoning with a cat stuck in a tree. There was no coming down from her position.

"Listen to me!" Mama raised her voice. "I know tis is unpleasant, but I am concerned about your fader. Ya must do it."

I sighed. Being the oldest child, at fifteen, I knew it was only right that I should be the one to climb up to the bedroom. Aside from that, I may have been the most agile one, and small enough to fit through a window.

Mama turned on the porch light and grabbed a flashlight. Bette and I carried a ladder up from the basement. Standing in front of the house we could see the master bedroom window was open. It was a vertical sliding-type window. I wasn't sure that the gap was big enough for me to squeeze through. I could clearly see that I would have to gain access to the roof from the right side of the house, as the street angled upwards on that side, meaning the height between the street and the roof was shorter.

After setting the ladder in front of a tall but narrow fence between our house and the house to the right, I took a deep breath. My siblings and mother watched me climb up the steps. I grabbed onto the roof with both hands as I stepped up on top of the fence, bare-ly balancing myself. My whole body quivered. I said a quick prayer asking the Lord to strengthen me. As I hoisted myself onto the roof, my legs dangled briefly in the cold night air.

Before I knew it, I found myself lying face down in the prone position on the roofline. I knew the roof pitch was steep on top of our house, but I didn't realize that the roofline below the master bedroom was as steep as it turned out to be. The wind turned out to be stronger than when I was standing on the ground.

"Mama!" I shrieked. "I am going to roll off and die!"

"Just crawl slowly. I'll catch ya should ya fall!" Mama called. *How was she going to do that?* She probably weighed no more than 110 pounds. She didn't own a fireman's safety net. How could she guar-antee that?

I tried to look up to spot how far away the window was but the sweater I was wearing briefly snagged on a roof shingle, and tilting my head caused a slight sensation of being unbalanced. "Mama, you're just going to have to tell me how far to crawl." I unfurled my sweater.

"Yer head is only about four feet away from da window." By that time, a neighbor, an elderly man who lived down the street, had come out to see what was happening.

I kept my head down without looking up and crawled until my siblings yelled out for me to stop. I tried reaching but couldn't feel the windowsill. "Yerr going to have to crawl upwards. It's uh-boat anoter foot," Mama called.

My heart beat quickly and my body shook uncontrollably. I wasn't sure how much strength to use to prevent me from rolling off the roof, so I used nearly all of it and exhausted myself. Lactic acid built up in my arms, and my hands were turning numb. I let go of one arm at a time, trying to get the feeling back. As I tried to catch my breath, the wind kicked up and howled. The nearby window reverberated from the turbulent air. I paused for a few seconds to regain my strength, breath, and senses. With no other choice and the daunting task at hand, I lunged toward the window and managed to grab the windowsill with my right hand. In the process, I kicked off a roof shingle. Like an inchworm, I crawled toward the window and was able to get my other hand on the sill. I popped my head through the gap and was able to get my chest partway through but briefly got stuck and started to hyperventilate. I tried to lift the window up with one hand while the other clutched the wall inside the bedroom, but was unsuccessful. Gradually, I shimmied my way through the space, exhaling then pushing, resting then inhaling. I repeated this pattern until I got all the way through.

The gawking neighbor who had come out to watch started clapping. The room was nearly pitch black, and I landed upside down on my right hand and left elbow, nearly hitting my head. I felt like I had just landed a plane without any flying experience.

After I gathered myself, I called out. "Papa!" There was no response. However, I could hear rapid breathing. I wasn't sure if it was from Papa or me. Mama had apparently made her way back into the house and up the stairs. She began pounding on the door.

"Just a minute!" I felt around for the light switch and turned on the light. My father was pale and dripping in sweat. I let Mama into the room, and Papa began mumbling incoherently. Mama called for an ambulance, and he was taken to a local hospital. There he was, hydrated, injected with something, and given some paraldehyde. He recovered from the worst of the pneumonia, but his physician said he had something called delirium tremors. It was from alcohol withdrawal, and it was life life-threatening. He also said that Papa was retaining fluid and showing signs of liver failure.

After spending several days in the hospital, Papa was released. Less than a week after he was discharged, he went back to work, against the doctor's orders. He seemed to do OK at first, but this only lasted a few weeks. He resumed drinking. About three days before Christmas, he began feeling ill again and started coughing up sputum. Papa was too sick to work and stayed home. He refused to go to the doctor or have one come to our home to make a house call. Papa instead opted to take some cough elixir.

Mama kept a close eye on him and kept the doors locked. She listened out for a click or thud of the deadbolt should Papa try to leave. She even locked their bedroom door at night. On New Year's Eve she and Papa went to bed right after midnight. She woke up sometime after five in the morning, feeling a cold draft in the room. The sound of bedroom drapes could be heard fluttering. She felt around, and Papa wasn't lying next to her. Upon flipping on the light switch she discovered the bedroom window was open. Somehow, he had managed to climb out the window, probably hop down to the roofline, drop down to the front-side fence, then leap to the street level, all without killing himself or breaking his neck. There was no sign of him. Mama called the police but was told it was too early to file a missing person's report.

She woke us shortly before sunrise on the morning of January 1, 1926. Papa's car was still at home, and we weren't sure where he was. Mama grew concerned again and asked Bette and I to take turns babysitting our younger siblings while Mama and one of us went out to look for him. That winter was unusually cold for San Francisco. We could see the breath vapor emanating from our mouths. Naturally, we first stopped next door, but Dorothy was not home. Mama and I walked to Courtland Avenue. Papa's cigar shop was locked and appeared empty. We scoured the area. The streets were littered with garbage and empty bottles from the previous evening's festivities. After no luck, Mama contacted Papa's brother, my Uncle Jerry. He advised that she contact the local hospitals. Mama started to call every hospital she knew of in San Francisco. Sure enough, a man with no identification on him was picked up after being spotted in a sewage ditch and taken to Mission Hospital. I listened to Mama talking to someone from that hospital on the phone.

"My husband is missing a fing-ger. Is tis man missing a fing-ger on his left hand?" There was a long pause. I could see that my mother was exhausted both physically and emotionally. The creases in her face were exaggerated. She had bags under her eyes, and her hair was coming loose. She exhaled so forcefully that her hair briefly wafted away from her face. She rocked back and forth, holding the phone in her left hand by its candlestick part and with her right hand held the receiver to her right ear. Her lips began to quiver, and then the silence ended. "Dat's him," she said, almost expressionlessly. "William J. White."

After providing the information the hospital needed, Mama contacted Uncle Jerry again. They went down to the hospital to see him. They learned that the person who found him noted he was gurgling in the sewage ditch. He was found in an area that is now paved over. Back then, there was an exposed swampy area of Islais Creek at the foot of Crescent Avenue.

I'm not sure why Papa did not drown right then and there, but he was confused and in acutely bad shape. X-rays determined he still had a right-sided pneumonia, but he also had a fluid collection on the left side within the lung lining, called pleura.

He was transferred to San Francisco General Hospital the following day for a higher level of care. During his hospital stay, he was injected with horse serum, which was the treatment for pneumonia back then. He didn't respond, and his physician ended up removing a pint of thick, purulent fluid from the fluid-filled cavity around his left lung. This temporarily helped his breathing, but Papa remained disoriented and unable to have a meaningful conversation. His condition gradually worsened, and his physician told Mama to prepare for his death.

My siblings were not allowed to visit him due to hospital age restrictions present at that time. Due to concerns about infection control, this was a common practice in those days. I went with my mother to see him. Mama had already visited him a few times. I will never forget the pungent scent of ammonia emanating from the rooms and hallways. As we approached his cast-iron bed, the man in the bed next to him was spitting up something into a metal basin and swearing. A nurse wearing a white uniform with a long-sleeve button-down top, a belted skirt, and a crown-like white cap came running into the room and scolded the man for his foul language.

Upon reaching Papa's bed, we heard coughing and wheezing emanating from my father. His eyes were closed, and he looked deplorable. His face was puffy, and he was as white as a ghost.

"Papa, can you hear me?" There was no response other than some incoherent mumbling, and his eyes remained closed. Mama grasped his right hand on one side of the bed, and on the other side, I leaned over to touch him gently. As I lightly touched his cheek and forehead, his face was dreadfully cold. I desperately wanted to have a conversation with him. I felt awful because my relationship with my father, though rocky at times, had been relatively good until the last two or three years. I wanted to tell him I loved him despite his faults, but I also wanted to confront him about his transgressions, which were hard to forgive. Because I couldn't have a conversation with him, I decided not to say anything. I just told him that I was there and kissed his forehead. That would be the last time I ever saw him. I walked away feeling hollow.

Bette, who was not allowed to visit Papa, was indifferent about the situation. She had not seen as much of the kinder side of him and had been cracked on her head more times than anyone in the family. Aside from cheating on Mama, drinking excessively, and being sporadically physically abusive, Papa never attended any of Bette's school plays or recitals, nor did he attend any of my other siblings' school functions.

As Papa's death became imminent, Mama asked the hospital staff if she could stay with him overnight. Visiting hours were awfully strict in those days, and an overnight stay was not allowed, so she was unable to. Sometime after five in the morning on January 20, Papa passed away. Mama was called and awoken with the news. I had stirred from sleep with the sound of the phone ringing before my brother and sisters had awoken, and Mama told me the news. Uncle Jerry drove her to the hospital to say their final goodbyes. That was it; there would be no happy ending to his life.

Shortly after sunrise, before Mama had returned from the hospital, my siblings and I gathered around the breakfast table, and I gave them the news. No one shed a tear. Not even one of us. In our minds, our father had died long ago.

Though none of us saw him lying in sewage water prior to his hospital stay, that image of him struggling to breathe in the most sordid, awful, dreadful way became implanted in our brains, causing many sleepless nights and nightmares for days to come. At least he had not drowned in the swamp.

Mama became completely overwhelmed after his death. She had trouble coping with the situation, let alone with trying to organize a proper funeral for my father. Our family's income had been abruptly severed. Friends said they would help, but after a few days of cooked meals, the help dried up. There was no Social Security at the time. Little did we know how much our lives would change and how much more difficult it would get.

At first, Mama tried to continue the bootlegging operation, but she could not make heads nor tails of my father's ledger, and she certainly did not trust Dorothy. She tried to rely on me, but with two adults out of the picture and not understanding the scope of the operation, she gave up.

When one of my father's older brothers, who resided in New York, learned of Papa's demise, he came out to attend Papa's funeral and paid a visit. He agreed to help Mama settle my father's estate, which included some sort of investment property. By then, the coroner issued the official cause of Papa's demise, confirming pneumonia with the contributing factor of alcoholism that caused his death. Mama gave my uncle the death certificate and estate documents. He also said he would help my mother sell the two stills she had, and he took them apart, but he left for New York and was never seen again. He never responded to my mother's correspondence, and she was unable to track him down to get the money he had promised he'd get for her. She enlisted his brother, our Uncle Jerry, to help, but he, too, could not locate him, and she was unwilling to travel to New York to try to find him. I don't know if Mama paid for an investigator to search for him, but she would never discover his whereabouts. We were left nearly penniless, aside from a trifling amount in a joint bank account that my parents had.

The situation was awful, but in some ways, I was relieved not to be involved in the bootlegging business anymore. Perhaps breaking free from that aspect of my life was for the best. My sister and I would no longer have to sneak around the city. Aside from that, despite my slight stature and looking younger than my age of fifteen, I was starting to look too old to be transporting a cart with dolls.

That same year, in August 1926, the silent movie actor Rudy Valentino died unexpectedly after a bout with appendicitis. I didn't talk to my cousin Elsie at the time, but I'm sure she was devastated by it. An estimated 100,000 people stood out in the rain in long lines to attend his funeral in New York. At the Frank E. Campbell Funeral Home, there was a rumor that Mussolini sent four men wearing black shirts as bodyguards, but it turned out they were hired actors participating in a publicity stunt. There were women who were hired to faint, but there were also real suicides that occurred following his death. There was an element of hysteria. So, my father had been only partially correct. Some people in the crowd smashed the windows of the funeral home, attempting to enter, and a riot ensued.

Back in the sphere of the White family household, there would be no hysterical grief for Rudy Valentino. We had other things to worry about. Lack of income was the number one issue. To save money, Mama took us out of our private Catholic school and put us in public schools. It was quite an adjustment at first. We were so used to being around mostly Irish and some Italian Catholic kids. Although the student bodies at the new schools were still primarily white, we were exposed to a few Chinese, Black, Hispanic, and Protestant kids. We learned more about other cultures. I suppose this may have made us a little more well-rounded than some of our former classmates, although we felt some of the classes were not as challenging. I certainly didn't need the new stress of having to adjust to new teachers. And I had to find new friends at school to eat lunch with.

Initially, although Mama did not have a lot of money, she gave food and clothes to hobos and continued to feed stray cats in the neighborhood. However, this gradually ceased. With six hungry mouths to feed, the money dried up quickly. In the subsequent years,

Mama would become a full-fledged cheapskate. I suppose the other way of looking at it was that she was resourceful. She continued to grow vegetables in our backyard as she had since the latter half of World War I, and grew her own fruit, including citrus. It was quite a feat to grow citrus in the chilly San Francisco air, but Mama somehow managed to accomplish this. She canned or jarred everything that we would not eat right away.

Up until my father's death, we had continued to get milk deliveries except that the milk was now transported by truck instead of a horse-drawn cart, and Billy and Theresa had assumed the cow bell responsibilities. Mama cancelled those milk deliveries, and we would never hear the high-pitched resonant sound of that cow bell again. Instead, powdered milk became the norm in our household.

Mama stopped paying for the newspaper delivery service. She used to get free magazines from Papa's stores and declined to purchase any.

She refused to ask for help, except that she took us to a few free dinners, but only those hosted by our church. She would only take us to the ones that were disguised as celebrations of a holiday, though we knew they were really for poor families. We previously had volunteered at some of these events when we were more well-to-do and it suddenly became exceedingly uncomfortable for us.

My mother would buy a whole chicken and find ways to stretch meals out, so the chicken lasted for an entire week. We began to appreciate all the trimmings, as well as all the carcass of a chicken. Parts were used to make chicken broth, pâtés, soups, and casseroles. She also liked to use breadcrumbs in casseroles and meat patties to stretch the dollar out.

Despite not having smoked much, Mama gave up the trivial amount of social smoking she once did. She never again bought another pack of cigarettes.

Mama was frugal with everything. As Bette was adjusting to her new public school at Paul Revere Elementary, her class was having a celebration of some sort, and the students were required to contribute food to a feast. Mama tried to make some taffy. In order to make taffy, you had to get the perfect balance of sugar, butter, oil, corn syrup, corn starch, salt, egg whites, salt, jelling agents, and flavorings. Mama skipped the egg whites and was stingy on sugar to save money. Instead, her concoction was heavy in oil and cornstarch. She created an oily mess that looked like a big lump of grease, and she handed it to Bette in a brown paper bag to take to school. The bag leaked. Bette left the house with the goods in hand, and her fingers became greasy. As she walked to school, quite embarrassed and upset, she met up with her new friend, Gloria. Gloria brought elegant afternoon tea finger sandwiches that her mother had purchased at a local bakery. Bette said, "Who would want fancy sandwiches when they could have candy?" She convinced Gloria to trade, and they made the switch.

At school, Gloria pulled the taffy out of the bag to put it on display. It looked like the taffy had come to life, draining oil from its pores, like an adolescent's popped pimples. Most of Bette's classmates were disgusted by it. Bette tried it and said it was awful. It tasted like a mixture of clay and lard, and wasn't sweet in the slightest. The teacher didn't even bother to taste it, but instead went for an afternoon tea sandwich and raved to the class about how wonderful they were. Poor Gloria became upset that no one liked the pile of sticky goo that Mama had made. I'm not sure if she tried to tell the teacher that the afternoon tea sandwiches came from her, but somehow, Gloria was sent to the coat closet, where she remained for the rest of the party. Bette felt terrible. She thought at first that she had been cunning and skillful to hide the fact that we were poor. However, it had unintended consequences, and she spent the next several weeks repairing the damage done to her newfound friendship.

In the meantime, Mama continued to find ways to save money. Like my father had in the past, she began to cut our hair, only she did not use bowls in the process. Perhaps she should have, as there were a few disasters at first. She called us into the kitchen, where she set up a chair against the sink. She covered the basin with towels.

"Who wants to go first?" Mama looked directly at me.

"No, Mama." Did she honestly expect me to be a guinea pig? Was I wearing a dunce cap? Would I end up with peach fuzz or worse, bald?

My mother then looked at Bette. She and I, as older siblings, were too wise to offer our heads of precious hair. "No, no, nope!" Bette replied firmly, as she rocked her head from side to side, almost violently.

"Yerr awl are behavin' like a bonch of wailin' banshees! Why, tis is gunna be grand!" Mama beamed, holding up a pair of basic scissors, normally used to cut paper.

Our younger siblings didn't know any better and were jumping up and down wanting to go first. Mickey ended up with a significant chunk of hair missing on the left side of her head, which necessitated her wearing a cap for about six weeks. After receiving our hatchet jobs, Mama ran water from the sink faucet through our hair. Once the cut hair separated from the hair that was still attached to our head, did we realize what we had. Theresa's haircut looked lopsided. On everyone else, she did an adequate job, but nothing to write home about.

However, Mama did get better at it. Before long, she taught all of us, except for little Billy, how to cut each other's hair. Billy wanted to take part but was shunned from the practice when he attempted to join in. He silently took matters into his own hands. At the age of four, he retreated into his room and cut off most of the hair on the front of his head and stored it in a shoebox. Despite being reprimanded, he did it again at the age of five. On his second attempt, he managed to cut off all his hair, except for a few wispy dangling strands. He was the only boy I knew who managed to cut his hair twice.

Mama initially made all our clothes. However, she did expect that the clothes would be given to a sibling, as a hand-me-down, once we outgrew them, regardless of the condition. All my siblings aside from Billy, the only boy in the house, wore hand-me-downs. I was the shortest girl in the family, so even I had to wear hand-me-downs from my taller, younger sister, Mickey! This was incredibly embarrassing for me. I just hoped no one would notice that the clothes had once belonged to my sister.

Several years earlier, Mama had taught me the basics of mending clothes, but after that embarrassment, I implored Mama to teach me how to make my own clothes. Although I knitted only one sweater, I learned some practical skills that helped me throughout my life.

Mama didn't have enough money to buy us new shoes, and all our soles were developing holes. Sometimes an aunt or uncle would help us out with a new pair. However, there were plenty of shoes that did not get replaced. There was a city center where one could get free used clothes and shoes, but Mama refused to take us there. She felt it was a matter of pride despite the painful blisters that developed on our feet.

However, there was an incident where I believe she did accept help, but she did it in her own way. One day, she asked me to babysit my siblings. The day was not unusually cold for San Francisco, but Mama wrapped a wool scarf around her neck so high that it covered part of the lower half of her face. She also put a veil made of lighter material on her head, which was unusual for her, and a much more common practice among the elderly in our community. She donned a pair of one of her sister's sunglasses that she must have borrowed, which was extremely odd since she could not see well without her regular glasses. She left the house and told me she was going to a friend's home. She was gone for several hours. I didn't realize she had come back into the house, as she must have come through the back door. The following day I noticed towering stacks of canned foods in our kitchen cabinet; not the kind of canned food we would normally eat. Among other things, there was oxtail soup, canned peanut butter, mashed canned pumpkin, olives, sauerkraut, deviled ham, pickles, moist mincemeat, jellies, Mexican tamales, relish, and loganberries. Loganberries? What were loganberries? What was mincemeat? How disgusting! I asked Mama where she got the canned goods, and she got upset with me and told me it was none of my business. I noticed the red wagon that Bette and I had used for transporting whiskey was leaning against the kitchen wall in a vertical position. I hadn't seen that cart since Papa had passed away, as it had been in our garage collecting dust. There were no canned food distributions in our area. Mama must have walked a few miles in disguise, barely being able to see, towing the wagon to another parish or distribution center to get the cans. The next several meals were odd to say the least, but I did not dare question Mama again.

When things at our house broke, they would not get fixed. Our home gradually fell into disrepair. And this would only worsen during the Great Depression. Mama stuffed newspaper in holes that had developed in the walls as insulation and constantly talked about money.

My mother's brother Bernard Rudden, whom we called Uncle Ben, lived nearby in San Francisco on Somerset St. with my Aunt Frances. Uncle Ben was a San Francisco fireman like my Uncle Jerry. The Ruddens were better off than we were, and their children, my cousins Jimmy and Bernadette, were well-behaved and always dressed in nice clothes. Bette would say they were always 'dressed to the nines.' Their home was far nicer than ours and usually spotless. We liked to visit their family often. Mama dressed us up as best she could before we made the two-mile walk to her house. She lent Bette an old velvet cap of hers. Aunt Frances always fed us a hearty meal. Aside from having to monitor our sometimes rambunctious behavior, we added a lot of mouths to feed with every visit. We eventually wore out our welcome.

One time, Bette and Mickey headed over to Aunt Frances' house and rang the doorbell, and there was no answer. They tried to peek through the windows but saw no movement. They rang and rang the doorbell several more times. After still no answer, Bette told Mickey to wait by the front door. Bette then proceeded to walk through a vacant lot next to their home and pulled herself up to look over a backyard side fence. She spotted my cousins hiding along with Aunt Frances in the backyard, cowering underneath a tree, away from any window.

According to Bette, she called out: "Aunt Frances, you didn't answer the door!" Aunt Frances turned her head and stood up straight as if nothing had happened.

"Oh, I didn't hear you," she replied, and then welcomed them in. They ate another substantial meal and played with my cousins Jimmy and Bernadette until Uncle Ben came home. He then offered for them to stay for dinner. Bette said she had to call Mama and practically beg to let her stay. Aunt Frances pretended that it was no big deal to prepare another meal and insisted they remain.

Before dinner, Aunt Frances set up a children's table for the four kids with a white tablecloth and gold trim. Bette knew the rules of their house. There was to be no laughing at the dinner table when you were eating. Before devouring the meal, while our aunt and uncle were not looking, Bette described making a volcano out of mashed potatoes with oozing gravy. She also put peas between her teeth to make her cousins laugh. They couldn't stop laughing and snickering. Aunt Frances kept scolding her kids. Often, she yelled out, "James!" She didn't scold Bette or Mickey because they were guests.

After dinner, Aunt Frances loaded a sack for Bette and Mickey to take home, which contained extra food and magazines. Uncle Ben drove them back to our home on Nevada Street. We probably had more out-of-date magazines from Aunt Frances' house than anywhere else. In particular, we obtained many old copies of the movie magazine *Photoplay, Good Housekeeping,* and *Reader's Digest,* and we read those old magazines from cover to cover.

After hearing about how Aunt Frances tried to hide, I advised my sisters not to press their luck, and we agreed to limit our visits. Also, Mama was starting to get upset that Aunt Frances was giving us extra food and items, and she didn't want to feel like a charity case.

In late 1926, just two weeks shy of my sixteenth birthday, money became even tighter at home. Mama's bank account was dwindling, and she asked me to get a job to help with the family expenses. She also wanted us to become less reliant on our relatives. I began applying for part-time jobs and did not have much success.

At that time, I attended Commerce High School. While I was in science class, we were doing an experiment creating a battery out of a potato. *What a poor use of a perfectly good potato,* I thought. The experiment was also deeply boring. I recall asking my science teacher, a kind, meek man, for an extra potato, falsely claiming that mine was too hard and couldn't generate much energy. He let me rummage through a sack of spuds, and I picked the largest one I could find that wasn't growing roots. I quickly pocketed the extra tater to use as food for our family table. When I got home from school that day and handed the potato to Mama, she put it down on the counter without thanking me. My mother had other things on her mind.

"So, I have good news, I tink. I talked to yer Aunt Mary Ann. I was visiting her at her grocery store to see if she had any extra work fur ya at her store. It turned out she does not, but she knows a person who works at one of da best department stores in San Francisco. It's on Post Street between Grant and 3rd Street. I got ya an interview on Tuesday afternoon. Da store is called O'Connor, Moffatt & Company."

"Oh, good! Thank you, Mama."

"I'll have Bette watch yer broter and sisters and I'll go down der wit ya by streetcar." Mama rarely paid for streetcars. Obtaining the job was of utmost importance to her.

Mama contacted my high school and arranged for me to leave school at lunchtime. I'm not sure if she told them it was for a doctor's appointment, but whatever she said worked. She wanted me to leave early so that we would have enough time to reach our destination and explore the store a little before my interview. When we arrived at the department store, the building looked intimidating from the outside. It was wide, had enormous windows, and Renaissance-Baroque style ornamentation on the upper portion of the edifice.

The interior of the building was much prettier. I felt like I had walked into another country. It was spellbindingly amazing, with Roman columns, giant windows, and exquisite mahogany woodwork throughout. Huge, elaborate floral pieces were displayed on each level, and well-placed ornate mirrors abounded. This was quite a contrast to our home life at the time. The store catered to the upper middle-class, a class to which I certainly did not belong. There were imports of perfumes, fabric, and dresses from France. There were hundreds of shoppers, mostly well-dressed women. The whole store was buzzing with activity.

The first floor smelled of a delightful mixture of perfumes with notes of citrus, spices, and flowers. There were fine linens, silk, satin, laces, gloves, and hosiery. Brass light fixtures hung from the ceiling, containing globe lights. The aisles were wide, and the ceilings were tall. In the center of the store was a giant light-well that extended all the way to the ceiling, bringing in natural light from the sky above.

On the second floor, there were suits of all kinds for sale, as well as a millinery department dedicated to hats of every imaginable shape, color, and price. In another section on that floor, there were cases made of solid mahogany and plate glass that displayed imported dresses. There was a French Room with gold and white enameled walls and French evening gowns on display. There was even a miniature French Room, dedicated to infants and toddlers, where you could dress up your little one in the frilliest clothes imaginable. In the back of the store were draperies, upholstered furniture, and throws.

Exquisite French lingerie was sold on the third floor along with undergarments. There were also vases and dainty trinkets. The carpet was made of green velvet. I left Mama on that floor gawking at all the items, hoping not to be spotted by anyone I knew. She said she was only going to spend a few minutes on that floor, and after my interview she would meet me on the second floor.

I nervously made my way up the steps to the fourth floor, on my own. There was a hubbub of activity just as frantic as on the other floors. People were talking, typewriters were clacking, and I heard the pressurized sounds of a pneumatic system in operation. I walked past several secretaries, all women, in front of offices inhabited by their male bosses of various departments. I tried to look confident, holding my head up as I slowed my pace and strolled past the offices of accounting, advertising, and shipping, and made my way to the administration department, which was even fancier.

The desks were huge and gaudy, and I was rather intimidated. I found where I was supposed to be and arrived ten minutes before my scheduled meeting.

The interview was difficult, as I had no real job experience. It was conducted in an office by an executive who was in his late thirties, sitting behind a massive maple desk. To his side, sitting in a tall, upholstered chair, was a woman in her mid-to-late forties who was the lead cashier in the ladies' clothing section, whom I would be working closely with. They had me sit down in another upholstered chair; and I realized the back was taller than my head. With my diminutive stature, I am sure I looked like a child. I had to rely on talking about my organizational skills at home, and even brought up helping my father with the books when we had the bootlegging business. Although I helped very little in this regard, I was trying to see what would stick. I'm sure they were thinking *pauper* when they were looking at me. I added that I was able to mend clothes too, which seemed to get their attention.

After the interview concluded, I smiled and shook hands with them. They told me to wait in the hallway for a few minutes. I began pacing, unsure if I made a good impression. Looking down at the carpet, I could see the flooring in the area where I was standing was worn down. Perhaps it had been trodden by countless other interviewees?

Before I knew it, the executive opened his office door. "Have a seat." I nervously reached for the chair I had just sat in. It was still warm from the interview. "Well, Ms. Ann White, we think you are polite and capable of doing the tasks required for this job. So, we are going to offer you the position."

"That is music to my ears, sir. Thank you, I will not disappoint you!" I bowed my head more times in a few seconds than I had in my entire lifetime.

"Now, I am going to lock up my office and head downstairs to meet with one of the other supervisors, while Clara here is going to take you to a table in another section on this floor. She will go over the details." We got up and exited the office.

Down the hallway, I followed Clara to a communal area, where there was a large round table and a few wooden chairs, and we sat down. Clara leaned toward me. "Congratulations, Ann. I'm sure we will get along just fine. The wage is forty cents an hour to start. You will be working as a cashier with me most of the time, but we decided to also have you work with our seamstress as well, to help with alterations."

"That's grand." Why did I say grand? I sounded like Bette and Papa. Perhaps it was just my nerves, as I was not thinking clearly. Or maybe the word was ingrained in my Irish roots, and I would never be able to rid myself of it.

"The first two weeks, I will be training you." Clara pulled out a booklet, wrote down the hours I would be working, and tore out the page.

I took one glance and realized she had given me the schedule for a full-time position with hours starting in the mornings during weekdays and Saturdays. There was no room for high school. "I thought this interview was for a part-time position?" I ventured.

"Oh, did your aunt or your mother not tell you that this interview is for a full-time job?"

"My mother knew this was for a full-time position?"

"I don't see how she could not have known. I am friends with your aunt, and we talk all the time. Is there a problem?"

Dumbfounded, I just shook my head, but she could tell I had reservations.

"Let us know by tomorrow. We can't hold the position too long. We have a long list of applicants. If you decide to move forward, your start day will be on Monday."

In shock, after thanking Clara, I headed downstairs to the second floor to locate Mama. She was holding up a light peach-colored dress with an art deco design, in front of a mirror, turning her body side to side imagining what she would look like in the outfit. She was already wearing lipstick she must have sampled at the cosmetic counter. I was enraged that she had deceived me.

"How did yer interview go?"

"I don't know, Mama," I said tersely, as I frowned. "Why don't you put down that dress? For Pete's sake, you know you can't afford it. Let's just leave."

I abruptly pivoted and purposefully walked ahead of her, scurrying rapidly down the stairs, while Mama tried to catch up with me. We exited the building and no sooner than stepping two feet outside did I go into a rant. "Why didn't you tell me this was for a full-time job? Am I supposed to quit high school! Are you off your rocker?!"

"Button yer lip. Don't talk to me dat way!"

"When were you going to tell me this, Mama? When?!"

Mama grabbed my arm and tugged me down the street, out of earshot of any store employee. She didn't want anyone to see me making a scene.

"Listen, Ann, I'm running out of money. I am sorry fur not telling ya but I was afraid you wouldn't agree to do da interview. I do need yer help."

"I just wish you had been honest with me."

"Did ya get da job?"

"Yes, Mama," I snapped.

As we rode the streetcar on the way home, I pondered our predicament. It sank in that we were in dire straits. My goodness, I had even pocketed a potato from science class like a common criminal! Quitting high school would be the right thing to do. I had no choice in the matter.

"Mama, I am going to take the job." Mama leaned over and gently kissed my head, pulling me in for a hug. "I just wish I had time to say goodbye to my friends at school."

"Ya can still go to skull tomorrow, can't ya?"

"I'm not going to want to sit through classes all day just so I can say goodbye to a few people." And just like that, life as a student at Commerce High School was over.

I began working at O'Connor, Moffatt & Co and found it to be rather enjoyable. I mainly worked on the second floor. I was amazed at the pneumatic system they had in place. It was made of an extensive highway of pipes that ran through the bowels of the department store. The network ran to nearly every counter with a cash register. After a sale was made, I placed the cash in a tube along with the sales receipt and sent it to the accounting office via a vacuum-air-pressured conduit. It was a whole new world to me, and a far cry from home.

CHAPTER TEN

Most of the money I earned working at O'Connor, Moffatt & Co went to Mama to purchase things like groceries. I felt proud about it, and throughout 1927 it gave me a sense of pride that I was contributing to our family. I even had a little leftover spending money for the first time since the days of my father's elaborate bootlegging operation. With the money I was bringing in, for the first few months I worked there, I had a sense that our lives would gradually improve. I enjoyed a certain degree of freedom at work that I hadn't had before at home. I felt like I was growing into an adult. To and from work, I took the same streetcar route I had taken with Mama during my interview.

The sense of hope and optimism I had would, unfortunately, be short-lived. Mama, by then in her early forties, started acting strangely. First, she had marked mood swings. I thought she was joking when she became unusually heated over something minor, only to realize later she was being serious. Mama began to count the money I gave her incessantly, in a frantic manner.

Bette informed me that Mama was talking to herself and was possibly hearing voices in her head. I refused to believe it until one day when I was off work I witnessed some unusual behavior. Mama was standing in the kitchen and appeared to be looking in the direction of the cupboard. She looked disheveled, not having taken a bath or shower in a few days.

"Get da hell out of 'ere," she blurted. "Quit followin' me!"

"Mama, are you OK?" I ventured.

She turned to face me. "I am fine, sweetie."

"It sounded like you were talking with someone."

"Yerr mistaken."

I was dumbfounded and frightened by her behavior.

Soon, she unplugged our radio when we were not using it. She denied doing it at first, then I caught her in the act. "Mama, why did you do that?"

"Dey are sending signals. Dey are trying to control my brain."

"What signals?" I replied carefully.

"Dey know."

"Who are 'they'?" I wrung my hands in frustration.

Mama grew irritated and impatient with my line of questions and told me to leave her alone.

Before long, without telling any of us, she sold our beautiful Atwater Kent radio. Aside from reading books and playing records, listening to the radio was one of the few things I enjoyed in my little spare time. I had heard of a distant relative of ours having a nervous breakdown, but couldn't imagine that it would happen to my own mother. I had trouble processing everything that was going on. *This could not be happening*, I thought.

Mama became aloof and detached. Dirty pots and pans began to accumulate in the kitchen sink. Meals became simpler and devoid of vegetables, despite having access to them in our backyard garden. There were only so many nights we could tolerate eating boiled potatoes and bread. Gradually, cooking fell by the wayside altogether. I began to cook meals, and Bette chipped in. We perused cookbooks but we could not afford most of the ingredients. Who wouldn't want steak or Beef Wellington? If we could have, we would have. We had to be creative. We cooked a variety of pasta dishes, vegetable soup, and our own version of chop suey using what we had.

Over time, Mama stopped cleaning the house. The carpets grew dirty. Worse yet, the toilets became grimy and mucky. I began playing the role of mother to my siblings when I was home. I assigned tasks and organized the house cleaning., Bette and Mickey protested. They didn't appreciate my new role, and there was nearly a mutiny. They were not accustomed to being bossed around by their sister, but things would not have been accomplished without my efforts. Theresa and Billy, being the youngest, went along with it. We had no good cleaning agents but found vinegar to be effective.

I notified a few of my aunts, who also lived in San Francisco, and let them know how Mama was behaving, but they were unable to help much other than take her to the doctor and occasionally come over to help her when I wasn't at home. They were sweet people, but had families of their own and certainly didn't have the money to take Mama to a private, rural hospital outside the city for care. And I didn't want her committed to a state-run asylum. They were known to mix the criminally insane with the general population of mentally ill patients. Back then, such people were treated cruelly, and some illnesses were not well understood. Even people with normal mental capacities, such as those who had a tic disorder such as Tourette's Syndrome, were sometimes committed to asylums. I had no grandparents to turn to, as they all resided in Ireland. I desperately wanted out of the whole situation. I wanted to run away, or at the very least move out of home when I reached financial independence.

When Mama was at a doctor's visit with her sister Mary Ann, I decided to snoop around the house and went into her bathroom and bedroom. I suppose I was trying to find a medication that was causing all her unusual behavior. I poked around her medicine cabinet and rummaged through drawers. *Perhaps I could put a stop to all of it*, I thought.

There were no devil's pills. Instead, in the top drawer of her dresser, I found a strange letter she had typed. She used the same old black Underwood typewriter that she used to type our stories on. It was folded neatly into an envelope that had not been sealed. I gradually unfolded the letter and read it. I imagined her typing the letter with her accent, but the letter was in perfect English.

"They are using radio towers to control our minds. They want us to succumb to evil forces and scoop up the riches through our labor.

The mayor is using new technologies to stretch and alter our brains. This needs to cease immediately!"

Oh my God, I thought, *Mama has gone mad! How is this going to end? Who does she intend to give this letter to?* I burned the letter in the fireplace so it wouldn't reach the mayor's office or some other government official. Mama would have been carted away had that occurred. As the letter went up in flames, I sat on the living room couch rocking back and forth, staring at a loose thread in the area rug over our hardwood floor, feeling helpless. Where had our intelligent, warm, caring mother gone?

Mama appeared to stop hearing voices after several months, but she continued to act strangely. One evening she came into our bedroom late at night. I was asleep at the time, and Bette nudged me awake. Mama was about ten feet from our bed. There was just enough moonlight coming from our window where we could see her, but she couldn't see us. She stood holding a long, serrated kitchen knife close to her chest. Her pupils were fixed and dilated, and she had a piercing gaze. She did not raise the knife above her head but stood and stared in our direction for several minutes. Bette and

I looked at each other with extreme fear. We slowly lifted and drew down the bed covers. We bent our knees, ready to make a run for the door, and I said a silent prayer. We didn't say a word and kept our breathing shallow so as not to startle her into doing something regrettable with the knife. We briefly grasped each other with our hands squeezing tightly together. It crossed my mind to pounce on Mama should she have approached any closer. I'm not sure what I would have done, but Mama turned and left the room and that decision would not have to be made.

The next day, Bette searched the house while I scoured the neighborhood for anything we could use as a weapon. We met back in our bedroom a few hours later. Bette pulled out an object from underneath our mattress.

Bette whispered, so Mama could not hear. "Look what I found." She displayed a menacing piece of metal piping about three feet long with some sort of elbow fitting on the end.

"Where did you get that?"

"I found it in our basement, earlier today, but couldn't bring it through the house because Mama was around. I waited until she was in the backyard watering the plants."

"Wow, Bette, that's a great find."

"So did you come across anything useful?"

"Well, first I searched some alleyways and went through garbage cans, but I found nothing. Then I went to a friend's house. Her grandfather used to be a policeman."

"Yeah, so did you get a pistol of some sort?"

"No, but I got this." From underneath my coat I pulled out a billy club. We looked at each other with trepidation. Though our weapons were not necessarily lethal, we figured they might save us in case of an attack. We hid the items underneath our mattress during the day and kept them under our bed at night. We had many sleepless nights for several weeks to come as one of us stood guard. We felt like prisoners in our own bedroom. Fortunately, Mama never entered our room again in that manner.

Surprisingly, Mama's odd behavior gradually dissipated, except that she was a little more aloof and distant than she had been in the past, and so we never saw her in the same light again. Our youthful innocence had been shattered by bootlegging, primarily due to our father, and now our trust and caring attitudes toward our remaining parent had been destroyed by mental illness.

As Christmas 1927 approached, Mama realized she could not afford to buy us Christmas gifts. She told us she would knit gifts for us and asked us what we wanted. We all accepted the fact that we would not be getting anything that we really wanted. None of us would receive anything remotely like toys, a paint set, skates, or records, and my younger sisters would not get dolls like Bette and I had received in the past. Mama spent hours upon hours knitting us sweaters, hats, scarves, and gloves. She made sure to add designs we wanted. It felt as though the warmer, kind side of Mama was beginning to reappear.

Mama tried to do her best by taking us to free Christmas events like concerts in a local park or Christmas productions at our local church. When Mama found out about something free of charge she jumped on it like a frog leaping onto a log covered with flies. The exception that year was a free visit to Santa at a local department store. She knew if she were to take my younger siblings to see St. Nicholas, she wouldn't be able to fulfill Santa's promises.

A neighbor gave Mama a newspaper advertisement for free stuff for children. The neighbor realized we were not well off. It was an advertisement in *The San Francisco Chronicle* that said: "Kids! Free balloons and candy and Big Doings at Fell and Baker Street at 7 p.m. this evening. Have your Daddy drive you over!"

Big Doings!? What were they? It certainly sounded fun. Were they going to give away presents? Would we get a new house, or a new parent, perhaps? My imagination ran wild. The problem was that the advertisement came from a newspaper dated December 10, 1927, and it was already a few days old. The neighbor said that a big Christmas display was being built, and she heard they were still giving away goodies. She had planned to take her grandchildren.

I was not familiar with the corner of Fell and Baker Street. Was this the location of a new department store? The advertisement did not say. Instead, it depicted a happy camel, an inquisitive elephant, and a couple of clowns, including one clown with a stretched-out body. I checked a crinkled old road map of San Francisco that we had. It was a full four miles away. Upon learning this, Mama asked if I could pay for streetcar fare for the whole family. I was the only person with a job in our household at that time. Though I hated to give away cash for anything other than food for our dinner table, I made an exception and paid for the transportation.

We made a trip out to the location on a Saturday afternoon, when I was off work and my siblings were out of school. As we approached the intersection, there was a long line of cars waiting to turn onto that corner. A familiar smell permeated the air. It was the pungent, acrid, semi-sweet odor of benzine in gasoline. That is when I discovered that the location was a new Shell Gas station. After we got off the streetcar and walked to the site, I noticed that the gas attendants were dressed as elves pumping twenty-one cents a gallon gas. Some had bells tied to their shoes. They looked like Peter Pan, only dressed in red. Some had oil-stained dirty rags draping from their waists. I recognized one of them as a junior at the high school I had attended. He was a good-looking fella on the football team. Only he looked like a complete doofus in that setting, and I laughed heartily.

There was a canopy over the gas pumps. Behind that section, there were about two hundred people who had gathered around a massive Christmas display. Little kids were riding on the backs of their fathers to get a good view over the crowd of gawkers. The display must have been at least four stories tall. There were several cut-outs of hills and mountains that gave the scene a three-dimensional look. Meandering in front of the monstrosity was its own boardwalk. Within the boardwalk there were posts which had little houses the size of giant mailboxes with owls on top. I think it was for mailing letters to Santa, but I forgot to ask. In the center of the display, there was a twenty-five-foot Santa Claus, who appeared to be sitting on a throne, flanked by two Christmas Nutcracker-like soldiers holding rifles. Santa was directly in front of a giant shell representing Shell Gas. One of the posts on Santa's chair looked like a peculiar-looking owl-like man, with a mustache, thick eyebrows, and buck teeth. The creature was wearing goggles. The display had a hideous clown with a prominent nose and three puffs of curly hair sticking up from the top of his head in front of a cone-shaped hat. He also had a ruffled collar.

The whole display was strange and bizarre, but at the same time it was fascinating. It was designed to catch a person's eye so they could stop and pump gas at that location. Within the display, there were elves dressed in tights, standing on toy blocks, arching their backs looking up at Santa. The blocks bore letters of the alphabet as well as detailed drawings of animals such as a rooster, leopard, and a dog. On the backdrop, within the hillside, there appeared to be a mineshaft or railroad tunnel of some sort. There was a donkey climbing up the hillside approaching a windmill, and an oversized cow standing on its hind legs with its udders fully exposed.

The people within the display were odd as well. There was a Spanish conquistador talking to an odd-looking monk wearing glasses. Or perhaps it was a pilgrim talking to Mrs. Clause? I couldn't tell.

Mama made a beeline to where the servicemen were pumping gas, to see if they were still offering free popcorn and candy. There was no popcorn to be had, but she made it back with pockets full of hard candy. As we sucked on the candy, we continued to eye the display and find more strange items. Theresa pointed out a monkey-like man on the hillside wearing earrings.

As outlandish as that exhibit was, it was quite fun and amusing and gave me a lasting memory. Had Papa still been alive, he would have said that the people who owned that gas station were marketing geniuses. As cars became more prevalent in the city, gas stations were popping up everywhere. There was a lot of stiff competition among gas stations. Shell was competing against Standard Oil. In 1926, Shell had fourteen gas stations in San Francisco. By the end of 1927 they added twenty more service stations.

Back at the White family home Mama struggled to finish knitting our Christmas gifts on time. She must have spent twelve hours a day knitting toward the end.

Bette wanted to chip in to help our struggling family. She managed to get a job at an ice cream parlor. She worked in the morning, making ice cream before school, then had to run to class to make it on time. Following school, she went back to work at the parlor. Her boss Mr. Roy held illegal card games in the back of the store. When Bette told a neighbor named Hazel about it, Hazel told Mr. Roy, who then fired Bette the next time she returned to work. During Prohibition, illegal activities, even if they were not alcohol-related, were rampant, and you simply didn't mention those things to anyone. Later, Bette found out Hazel had taken her job.

After that, Bette found part-time work as an usher at an opera house on weekends. She was probably only fourteen years old at the time. One of the singers, a dapper man who seemed to be getting a lot of attention from young women, took a liking to Bette. I can't recall if he was Italian or Eastern European, but he was dark and handsome and had an accent. She said he could teach her how to play the piano in private, and she could earn a lot more money.

I had a frank conversation with Bette while sitting with her on the steps in front of our house. "Open your eyes, Bette. Don't be such a rube. Playing the piano is not what he really wants to play with."

"Oh, he wouldn't do that."

"He is a cake eater, and I am sure he fools around with a lot of girls." I looked directly into Bette's eyes. "You could end up in the back seat of a struggle buggy." That was the term we used for old cars back then. "You could end up getting the drip, or worse yet, pregnant!"

"Ann, I can fend for myself!" Bette stomped her foot. "I'm not stupid."

But I was older and wiser and felt I was giving her solid advice. Despite her initial protests, Bette took my advice and stayed away from him. It turned out the piano lessons he had offered were legitimate. He trained one of the other girls in the opera house, and Bette never let me forget about it.

Just around that time, I began to attract the attention of a local boy named Earle Swensen. He was one and a half years younger than I and two years older than Bette. He lived close to us just outside Bernal Heights. He and his friends would come over to our house, and we would roll up our carpet and dance, playing records on our phonograph. Though handsome, he was too young for me. I tried to redirect his attention to Bette, but they didn't click. However, we enjoyed dancing and singing songs like Gene Austin's *Ain't She Sweet* or swaying, gathered in a circle, to *Baby Face* performed by Jan

Garner and his orchestra. I can't say that it was the first time we flirt-
ed with boys, but it was the first time we had boys of a similar age
to us over to our home.

CHAPTER ELEVEN

At the age of seventeen, I met a young man named James who came into the department store on a regular basis doing deliveries, and I couldn't help but notice him. He often came by my cash register grasping a long-hand truck, balancing several wooden crates. His arm muscles would flex when he balanced the loads he was carrying. He was ruggedly handsome with curly blonde hair and had chiseled features. He was, as we would say back then, "the cat's meow." He was only a few years older than me but looked like a mature man, especially on his sleek red Indian G20 motorcycle that he kept well-polished. He looked like the adult version of the 'it boy,' you know, the 'it boy' at school with dreamy looks who every girl wanted to date …

I wanted to impress him, so I dug out my best, as we called them at the time, glad rags. Before I met James, I had found a buttery yellow flapper dress in a secondhand store. I began wearing that dress to work, trying to impress him. It had pretty, understated fringes. I had sported a short, bobbed hair and wore a headband, prominent earrings, and stockings. I could have borrowed a pearl necklace from a friend, but I didn't want James to think that I was trying too hard to impress him. Eventually it worked and he stopped by the counter I was working at in the women's clothes department.

"Ann, you look like peaches and cream. You're such a doll," James grinned.

"Stop it, you're making me blush." I smiled and tilted my head slightly while lightly batting my eyes.

"How did you get so smart?"

"What do you mean?"

"From my observation, you kinda look like the boss around here. It looks like you got your supervisor running around doing work you should be doin'. Everyone around here seems to respect what you say. You got everything so organized."

"Maybe," I replied.

"Would you like to go to a special talkie movie with me? You know, the one with Al Jolson?"

"*The Jazz Singer?*"

"Of course!"

"Sure, I have wanted to see that movie."

"I'll pick you up on my motorcycle. Where do you live?"

"I get off work early on Saturdays. You better pick me up from here. I don't want my mother to see me riding on a motorcycle."

"OK, then this Saturday it is! I'll take you to the new Avenue Theater in the Portola neighborhood."

In preparation for the date, I bought another dress at a second-hand store. That one was light black, and it had three-quarter sleeves with cream-colored fringe borders. The dress went down to just below the knees, and I teamed it with black stockings. When I sat down, it exposed the reinforced lacy edges of my hosiery as well as my bare knees. Perhaps James would get a glimpse, I hoped.

I had difficulty deciding whether or not to wear high heels as I would be riding on a motorcycle, but decided I wanted to look as pretty as possible. I didn't like the new style of rounded Cuban shoes with two-and-a-half-inch heels at the time. They did not match my petite frame. At a neighborhood rummage sale, I managed to find a pair of only slightly worn black Tango-style shoes with two-inch heels that tapered toward the toe box. They were narrow but not pointed. New women's shoes at the time typically ranged between $2 to $20 with a few exceptions. This particular pair of shoes was being sold for $1.25, and I managed to haggle the price down to a dollar. I negotiated the price of a few other items. With my newly acquired pocket change that I earned from working at O'Connor, Moffatt & Co, I also bought a short necklace with a heart nearly the size of the palm of my hand. I also found a long necklace that I draped around the shorter necklace.

A friend of mine, Ruth, and I took turns giving each other haircuts. She suggested a fresh new look. She parted my hair on the left, and trimmed it so that my bang on the left was shorter than that on the right. She curled my hair slightly to give me a sophisticated, elegant look.

At our department store we sold perfumes like *Guerlain Shalimar* and *Chanel No. 5*. A relatively new perfume, *Coty L'Aimant*, had just come out. Before James came to pick me up, the girl behind the perfume counter let me spray a bit of it on my neck from the sample bottle. Its fragrance was a delicate mixture of vanilla, flowers, and sandalwood.

James arrived at the store to pick me up wearing a black leather jacket. He had parked his gorgeous motorcycle out on the street. On the fuel tank was the Indian logo in perfect cursive. He had modified that cycle so that his little brother would be able to easily ride with him. He had installed a small back seat over a basket, and there were foot pegs to set your feet on. It was my first time riding on a motorcycle. James told me it was a good thing I was petite because it would make it easier for him to climb the city's hills, and there was no shortage of hills in San Francisco.

James kickstarted the motorcycle and revved up the engine. It required nearly all his weight. Then he had me get on the bike and instructed me to hold onto his waist. That was the first time I had touched him. It was a little awkward at first, as girls did not typically hold onto men on their first date.

He took a quick peek at my legs. "Nice gams." I'm sure I blushed. I rolled my eyes and smiled. In addition to the smell of leather emanating from his jacket, I detected a light scent of herb and citrus. Men did not typically wear cologne back in those days, but if they could afford it they would spray some eau de cologne on their handkerchiefs. James told me that he had gone to the perfume counter on the first floor and sweet-talked the ladies working there, who gave his hanky a quick spray.

I said a little prayer, which made him laugh. He throttled the engine, and before we knew it, we were off. With the engine humming and blistering, we rode about five miles through the city, passing the neighborhood where I lived to reach the theater.

The art deco movie pavilion had a huge, illuminated, shimmering marquee. There was a glass ticket booth below the sign near the street. James purchased our tickets, and we waited in line before the theater opened. The inside of the theater resembled a glamorous palace, with delicately-carved molding on both sides of the screen. The ceiling was colorful and ornate. It looked like a picture I had seen of the Pantheon in Rome. Only this theater was dark, without an oculus in the center. I was bubbling over with excitement.

The movie was full of music, and I managed to learn a few lines of some of the songs. *The Jazz Singer* was one of the first movies that transitioned from silent film to sound. After the movie ended, we walked down the sidewalk and I moved my knees in and out, shifting my elbows side to side while I sang a verse from a song, from that movie, *Toot, Toot, Tootsie*. I was wrapped up in the moment.

> *"Toot, toot, Tootsie, goodbye,*
> *toot, toot, Tootsie, don't cry,*
> *that little choo-choo train that takes me*
> *away from you, no words can tell me how sad it makes me,*
> *kiss me, Tootsie, and then, do it over again!"*

James abruptly grabbed my face and kissed me. This caught me off guard, but I didn't resist. I couldn't think of anything to say except repeating the word "Tootsie," and he dipped me back slightly and kissed me again. I felt his tender grasp and melted into his arms. From that day forward he became my boyfriend. Before long, we became an item at our place of work. Not an uncommon practice at the time, I planted a hickey on his neck as a sign of affection, and I thought it was funny. Other girls did it to mark their territory.

I rode on that motorcycle with him everywhere. I made my mother aware I had a boyfriend, but I conveniently left the word 'motorcycle' out of our conversations. James eventually taught me how to ride it on my own, but I preferred being the passenger, hugging onto his body, whizzing through the city with the wind in my hair.

One day, James said he was going to take me on an adventurous ride. He kept it a surprise, and my imagination ran wild as I pondered where he would take me. Would it be to Lake Tahoe or Los Angeles? Surely he couldn't afford that? Besides, Mama would not allow me to leave the area, let alone be with a young man by myself overnight. I had to tamp down my expectations.

After hopping on the bike, we rode toward the northern part of San Francisco where there was a steep winding road, Lombard

Street on Russian Hill. It used to be a relatively straight, steep cobblestoned road with a 27 percent grade that had wildflowers growing between cracks. Prior to 1922, it had been mostly used as a pedestrian pathway as most vehicles could not climb it, and those that attempted to go down it were prone to sliding. So, the city re-engineered it to include eight hairpin turns between Hyde and Jones Streets, and reduced the grade to 16 percent. The old cobblestones were removed, and the redesigned street was paved with red brick. Back then, it was a two-way street, though most tourists preferred going down its slopes. Not James, he wanted to take it both ways. We started by going up against most of the traffic as he used full throttle at times to get us up to the top. People in cars heading down the slope waved, hollered, and cheered us. We didn't wear helmets, which was not unusual at that time. I thought to myself, if only the nuns who taught me in school could have seen me, then they would have snapped their rulers and choked on their veils.

James then made a loop, and we headed down the hill as the wind whipped through our hair. We saw spectacular views of San Francisco's skyline, including a huge swathe of the Bay as well as Goat Island. In the mid-1930s that view would change to include the new structures such as Coit Tower and the Bay Bridge, and the view of the Bay water would become limited. By 1939, it became a one-lane downhill road. It was later dubbed the crookedest street in the world.

After we got to the bottom of the hill, James pulled over, beaming at me. "Ann, what did you think?"

"That was breathtaking! If that isn't the bees knees, I don't know what is! That is the windiest road in the world!" I exclaimed.

James shook his head. "No, it's not." We merged back into traffic and in less than half an hour we leisurely made our way through the Mission District and then into the Potrero Hill neighborhood.

On the western slope of Potrero Hill there was Vermont Street. We took the down slope between 20th and 22nd Streets. We wound around seven sharper turns than those on Lombard. James took the turns faster, making the descent somewhat treacherous. I got a rush of adrenaline. Though the views were more filtered it was still thrilling, and before we reached the bottom, I cried out "Uncle, uncle!" Though I had never been on a rollercoaster before, when I got home, I experienced the sensation of being on one, turning and swaying, when I lay down.

My escapades on that motorcycle would eventually come into jeopardy. After an argument with Bette, I was ratted out. She let Mama know I was riding with James through the city up and down busy, steep streets. Mama was furious and argued with me often about it. I knew she was just looking out for my best interests, but it was just so annoying.

When James would drop me off, he was careful to approach from the higher portion of our hilly street so that he could coast down eliminating or minimizing use of the throttle so that my mother would not be alerted. He usually dropped me off a couple of houses before reaching my house. Mama caught on to this. As we glided to a stop one Saturday afternoon, she came from what seemed like almost nowhere. She must have been lying in wait, sitting on a neighbor's steps, tucked behind some wooden railings and in line with a bush that concealed her as we approached. As I got off his motorcycle she was already standing on the sidewalk with her arms folded, almost in James' face.

"Oh, hello, Mrs. White. I'm James."

Mama did not introduce herself. "So, yerr da one riding tis contraption."

"Yes, ma'am."

"Yerr da nitwit dat's letting my daughter ride wit-out a helmet. I don't plan on attending anoter funeral … especially one in which my daughter is da featured guest. Do ya understand me? Do I make myself clear?"

"Yes, ma'am. I do plan to get her a helmet."

After his response, Mama suddenly gave less importance to a motorcycle helmet. "Der just ledder caps. Dey won't protect you from bustin' yer skull!"

"No, ma'am, but I don't ride fast when Ann is seated."

"Ya shan't be riding fast at-tal."

"I will be extremely careful, Mrs. White." James tried to look as polite and humble as possible, maintaining eye contact and turning up his palms up. He bowed his head in an exaggerated fashion as if he were a polite Japanese businessman listening to every word she had to say. He went into full-blown charm mode. He had some in-side knowledge about his motorcycle. Trying to appeal to our Irish heritage, he said that the Indian G20 motorcycle was designed by an Irishman, Charles Bayly Franklin.

"You don't say!" Mama exclaimed with a wide-eyed expression, as she suddenly took interest in the conversation.

"Oh, yes, he is a smart engineer who went to school in Dublin. He takes immense pride making these motorcycles safe." James knew he was lying. The Indian motorcycles were designed to go fast, and he had knowledge about Franklin's racing history. He aus-piciously left that fact out of the dialog. He got Mama to calm down and had a civil conversation with her.

Though James was not the most sociable person, he had a way of talking to people to get what he wanted, whether it be my mother or anyone else. He certainly found a way to my heart through sweet talk.

Early in 1929, a few months after I turned eighteen, James asked me to marry him, and I accepted. I had discovered that he was a bit temperamental at times and would anger easily. This concerned me a little bit going into our marriage, but despite that, I was giddy and happier than I had been in years. James was from a poor family and had no religious affiliation. His parents worked on assembly lines. I thought my life would continue as a lower-class American, but that it would be a happier one in comparison to the life I had lead in recent years. I desperately wanted to get out of the situation I was in at the time. I enjoyed planning our wedding, although it would be on a shoestring budget. Though not religious, James had agreed to become Catholic and have a Catholic wedding at our church. Mama seemed to recover a little more from her mental affliction and was happy to find out that James had purchased a leather helmet for me. She again warned him not to drive too fast when I rode with him. For the most part, James did honor that. Mama began helping me prepare for the wedding and started to become familiar with James' family. His parents invited her over to their home for dinner on a couple of occasions.

I rode the streetcar back from work one evening to find Mama waiting for me at the door, which was most unusual. She wore a pained, strained expression on her face. The unthinkable had happened. She took my hands, and gently told me the horrible news: James had been killed in a motorcycle crash. He had rounded a corner too fast and crashed into a building earlier that morning.

My life imploded. Another funeral to attend, and the tears would not stop coming. I didn't want to think about anything, as I had trouble suppressing all the bad memories in my past that came flooding back into my mind. Maybe I had been destined to live a loathsome, lonely life. I felt so hopeless. I even had fleeting thoughts of ending it all and wondered if the world would be any better without me. The Catholic Church considered suicide sinful at the time, and I knew I couldn't carry out such an act. Back then, cannon laws of the Roman Catholic Church since 1917 prohibited one from having a funeral ceremony if one committed suicide.

I refused to go out with anyone for several months and slept whenever I could. Friends came to the door, often in groups, trying to pull me into their cars. They goaded me with young men they brought with them, and finally they persuaded me to go to a picnic at a hilltop park called Buena Vista, overlooking the city. It was a mostly sunny day with a few clouds moving fast overhead, carried by strong breezes. Several children were holding kite strings as they ran laughing along grassy knolls. Their dancing kites of blue, green, and orange and even one with stars and stripes, floated over us. I was amazed to see a red kite in the shape of a long, serpentine dragon attached to a cute child with straight black hair and almond-shaped eyes. We climbed up the pathways and steps that led to the top of the park, and I felt my heart pounding and the wind blowing against my face as I peered toward the city skyline, with the distant choppy Bay glimmering like diamonds. I exhaled deeply, and at that moment felt that maybe I could go on after all.

CHAPTER TWELVE

As time went on, I wondered if I would ever find another man I could love. By that time, Bette had procured a part-time job at O'Connor, Moffatt & Co and worked alongside me on Saturdays. We were sometimes invited to social events after work. Some of my work colleagues belonged to various bridge or athletic clubs that would host get-togethers called tea dances at St. Francis Hotel, located near our work. We did not attend most of the dances, because such events required wearing formal clothes, which we couldn't afford. However, some events included jazz bands, and women were allowed to wear sleeveless dresses at those affairs. Bette and I went shopping at a secondhand store so she would have a nice dress to wear and a pair of high-heeled shoes. We and our co-workers would meet under the Great Magenta Clock, the grandfather clock in the hotel lobby which was built in Vienna in 1856. We enjoyed listening to the jazz music and dancing the foxtrot and the Charleston in the hotel's various ornate venues such as the Fable or Mural Room. The men wore suits and ties. Despite some freedoms that women gained in those days, such as being allowed to kiss in public and go on dates unchaperoned, it was still not protocol for a woman to ask a man to dance. We had to wait patiently to be asked. Attracting attention was an art that included eye contact, smiling, giggling, subtle body swaying, and graceful positioning near the dance floor. Occasionally it worked, and a dapper young man would ask one of us to dance. However, we had our fair share of unwanted suitors. It was also an art to shake them off.

A co-worker of ours named Mildred gave us advice. Mildred had grown up in New Jersey.

"Sistuhs, it's simple. If they ask ya to dance, ya just tell 'em your legs are tiyud. If they persist then ya go to step numbah two."

"What's step number two?" I replied.

"Well, then, the two of yous work in tandem. In front of the dumb palooka, one of yous just tells the otha that 'yowa boyfriend would not be happy if he soaw ya here with this fella.' Then ya just grab the otha one's arm and go to a different area of the bawlroom."

Bette and I tried it once and it worked, but we felt guilty. It seemed so cold-hearted! Instead, we decided to put up with it and oblige, which led to a lot of wasted time. We still enjoyed the dances, but it never led to finding a beau.

Sometimes when I was off work, my friends and I would drive to North Beach, an Italian American neighborhood in San Francisco's northeast side. We rode in one of my friends' parents' magnificent Franklin sedan with a prominent, shiny, impressive grille on the front end of the car. I suppose we were looking for a strong, dark, and handsome Italian man. My cousin Elsie McGuire, the cousin I played with as a child and who liked to watch Rudy Valentino movies, had found an Italian man just as she had predicted. He was right under her eyes all along. She had known him since they were children, but had not paid much attention to him when she was young. He grew into a good-looking muscular athlete. He was the Catholic Italian American prize fighter Francesco Camilli, who went by the name Frankie Campbell in the ring. Elsie had married Frankie

Camilli the previous year, in 1928. Why couldn't I find a handsome man like that? Someone who could sweep me off my feet and pay for nice things? Instead, most of the time we would end up sitting at a restaurant cafe on Columbus Street. I couldn't afford to pay for lunch most of the time, so I usually sipped a cup of cheap coffee slowly while my friends ate.

One day, while sitting at a cafe, we peered through the window from our booth and looked at happy couples walking down the street, wondering what their lives were like. After one look, we would pretend to know everything about them.

"Look, Ann." My friend Ruth turned her head toward a woman kissing her man right in front of the cafe. "There's a bear cat." I turned and saw a woman in her early twenties, wearing long white gloves, deep red lipstick, and a silver headband. She was wearing a V-neck black dress with silver beads and sequins, and multiple geometric patterns. She also wore high-heeled shoes with silver buckles. She was trying to draw attention to herself, in an aggressive way, grabbing her man and kissing him in a full display of affection, for all at the cafe to see. Then, after the kiss, she pulled out a cigarette and slotted it into a flashy silver cigarette holder. She held it out without saying anything.

"She has him wrapped around her finger," I responded. Sure enough, without missing a beat, the gentleman she was with pulled out a lighter and fumbled with it for a second before lighting her cigarette. Then she took a puff and grabbed him by his short tie and pulled him forward before they began walking down the street. "I don't think they are married, but she thinks she's hotsy-totsy."

"That's for sure." Ruth lit up a cigarette in the cafe. "He must carry a torch for her as she has him all balled up. You know, she's from old money, and I don't think it'll last. If he makes one misstep, she will replace him in a jiffy and won't have any trouble doing it."

"Ruth, since when did you start smoking?"

"I'm keeping my figure slim." Ruth was already as thin as a toothpick.

"You don't need that. Besides, where did you get the idea that smoking will keep you slim?"

"Don't be such a sap, I'm smoking a Lucky. You know their motto, don't you?"

"'Reach for a Lucky instead of a sweet?'"

"Ya, but there is a new ad with that motion picture star, Constance Talmadge."

"I must have missed that one. What does she say?"

"'Light a Lucky and you'll never miss sweets that make you fat.' Besides that, the ads say that they won't make you cough."

I grabbed Ruth's cigarette and took a puff, causing laughter among the group. My friend Helen then took a drag. She began to cough, which caused quite a guffaw among our booth. Our waitress came over and told us to keep the noise level down.

After our laughter subsided, a few minutes later, we saw a couple, in their late thirties, walking by wearing their best Sunday clothes, only it was not Sunday. The clean-shaven man wore a full suit and tie, a perfect short haircut, and sported shoes that must have been polished by a shoeshine boy earlier in the day. Without holding hands, his arms were locked at the elbows with a woman wearing a white dress and short white gloves. She held her head up-right while she wore a brimmed hat and held a dainty umbrella to keep the sun off her.

Helen and I looked at each other, and at the same time we said "blue noses," then laughed. Blue noses were the ones who typical-ly did not drink, and their life revolved around the church more so than mine. They were people whom you would never see at the lingerie counter at O'Connor, Moffatt and Co. In my eyes they were the ones responsible for Prohibition.

"I'll bet they are happy," I sighed.

The day ended without finding any good *uomini* (Italian men) to date.

I continued working for O'Connor, Moffatt & Co and they moved to a new location on O'Farrell and Stockton in the center of San Francisco's Union Square. In the summer of 1929, a recession hit the country. It worsened into what became known as the Great Depression. In October 1929, the stock market crashed, and the slide continued into 1932 when stocks, on average, lost nearly 90 percent of their value. I was lucky I was too poor to have any money in the stock market. Fortunately, I still retained my job and began to appreciate what I had. Gradually I saw more homeless people and beggars on the streets.

Though I still lived at home I had a roof over my head. The roof of our home on Nevada Street, however, would become leaky and Mama did not have enough money to fix it. The upstairs window broke, and she boarded it up. My mother's finances worsened. I gave all that I could to help her out. Billy, at the age of eight, began stealing money from Mama, but she refused to punish him. She began to hide money in various places. He also began stealing from friends to buy ice cream. He began to act out at home and Mama truly didn't know how to control him. He had no father figure, not even a drunken one, and she felt sorry for him. Being the only boy in the house, my sisters and I resented him a little for not having to wear hand-me-downs and for having his own room. We saw him getting special treatment from our mother.

During the Great Depression unemployment eventually hit 28 percent, and at one time, 20 percent of Californians were on public assistance. Inexperienced day laborers competed with seasoned longshoreman for work, unloading and loading crates from ships that would enter San Francisco Bay.

Mama sometimes went to a local park with my siblings to pick wild blackberries, a practice she had done since my father passed away in 1926. However, for the first time, she soon found competition among others affected by the Depression. When she got to the parks, the only berries left were often hidden high up in sharp, thorny brush. She continued to grow vegetables in our backyard which barely sustained us. We weren't starving, but there were days when we experienced real hunger.

Our house became cold as Mama refused to let us turn on the heat. The exception was running the fireplace. If we could find wood, we were allowed to start a fire. You couldn't just chop down a tree branch in San Francisco unless it was in your own backyard. My siblings and I would go to alleys to find crates and rummage through trash bins to find pieces of wood. There were no large metal dumpsters at the time. George Dempster's dumpster invention would not be known until the mid-1930s. There were no standard garbage cans back then and they tended to be heavy. Some were made of wood, others were derived from metals like steel and copper, and others were made from a combination of concrete and metal.

We had to time our trips before trash pick-up days. Garbage collection in San Francisco was carried out by a group of Italian immigrants known as the Scavengers. There were two companies in operation at the time. One was the Sunset Scavenger Company, and the other was the Scavengers' Protective Association. An enormous group of them resided on one section of Oakwood Street near 18th and Delores Streets in a rundown cul-de-sac. Many of them lived in boarding houses next to horse stables. That section of town was known as Dago Alley. 'Dago' was one of the many derogatory terms for Italians. Just like the multiple names given to belittle Irish immigrants, there were a plethora of disparaging names used to call Italians as well. 'Zips' and 'wops' were among the other common names. The immigrants operated one of the few remaining transport businesses in San Francisco which still relied on horses.

Most of the time we had success. However, one day we came across a hobo. He had made an encampment from crates near a collection of garbage containers, in a vacant lot, behind a restaurant. At first, we didn't see him amongst a pile of garbage that littered the ground. Smoldering embers from a previous night's fire were visible in the back of one of the garbage can lids. He stirred when we approached. Bette nearly stepped on him and gasped, "I'm sorry sir!" The hobo was in a seated position on the ground with his knees bent, leaning against a wall. His face was weathered and dirty, and his head was adorned with a brown, wool felt hat with a floppy brim. His eyes were haggard and expressionless. He wore a ratty old tweed coat and common work pants rolled up at the cuffs. His clothes were baggy, and he wore fingerless gloves exposing his grimy digits. His fingernails were discolored with a yellow tint, and some of them were broken. The hobo had a bone polisher with him; a gargantuan Pitbull, was tethered to a nearby pole by a chain. The dog darted towards us so hard that his forelegs shot up straight into the air when he reached the end of the chain. The pole that anchored the leash made a loud thundering sound as it darn near toppled over. We all screamed. The vicious mutt must have come within six inches of biting Mickey.

"Let's get out of here!" The mangy canine leapt into a frenzy, moving from side-to-side barking, snarling, drooling, and exposing its teeth. I could almost smell human flesh emanating from his breath as we bolted away, running for our lives.

Aside from that one incident, we managed to find wooden boxes, cardboard, and crates that we used as firewood. Often the boxes were painted, and when we burned the wood, it gave off a chemical smell in our home. I'm sure it wasn't good for our health, but it did keep us warm.

On the brighter side of the Depression era, one of our favorite things to do to fill up our bellies was to go out on Halloween. Halloween was another tradition brought to the United States by our Celtic ancestors. Thank goodness for that. My mother made scary black cats out of paper mâché and a scarecrow out of burlap bags and old clothes stuffed with newspaper scraps. Our church organized trick or treating nights, and Bette and I volunteered to escort kids, including our siblings, to various houses. Given she and I were petite and went as ghosts, we blended in with the kids and got treats along with everyone else. Back in those days, it was common to get cookies, fruits, nuts, and toys. Sometimes we would even get a little money. We looked forward to the Hershey's chocolate bars and candy corn that some people handed out.

I was on a quest to bring some food into the house, and Bette had her own mission. She liked to play tricks and scare people. When the time came to stop by our own house to trick or treat, Bette got an idea.

"I'm going to run ahead to our house and scare everyone," she whispered in my ear.

Off she ran. On our porch, Mama had sat her scarecrow on a bench. Bette covered herself in burlap and sat down near the scarecrow, holding still. When our group arrived at our house, she leaped out. "Boo, you little hooligans!" She scared the living bejesus out of everyone! Everyone screamed.

When we finished the night's trick or treating, we came back with a glorious haul, and hunger did not exist in the White family household in November.

Shortly after this, a mouse infestation developed in our home, likely entering from cracks in our roof. Perhaps the mice smelled our stash of candy. Instead of calling an exterminator, Mama made her own mouse traps and baited our house. We often had to throw the dead creatures away in the garbage. It was utterly disgusting, but we had no choice.

One day, Bette scraped her calf but didn't recall how it occurred. She forgot about it and was over at a friend's house helping wash their dog. Bette kneeled inside the large dog wash basin, felt a stinging sensation, and realized that her wound had opened and some dog fur had entered the wound. Her wound festered and gradually became more painful. A pus pocket had developed, and my mother squeezed it frequently to express purulent, foul-smelling gunk. Mama refused to take her to a medical professional, trying not to spend any money.

I let one of my aunts know what was going on. Aunt Rose contacted a school nurse to come to our home and help care for the wound. I'm not sure if she was hired or was going to treat her for free but Mama refused to let her in the house. My mother would rather have let Bette die than accept any kind of assistance. Fortunately, Bette did make a full recovery aside from a noticeable scar, the size of a silver dollar, which would remain with her for the rest of her life.

Mama steadfastly refused to go on public assistance. To earn a little pocket money, she babysat other kids at our house when I went to work. However, when it became apparent that she was not mentally present much of the time, families plucked their children out and took them to other sitters in the neighborhood. She then began selling items we had. To our detriment, she sold our phonograph and all the stacks of records we listened to. All the fancy dinnerware went. She sold some of our better furniture as well.

To help support our family, Bette also had to quit high school and to work full-time at O'Connor, Moffatt & Co's department store. And later, when Mickey and Theresa got to high school, they also had to give up on their education. This was particularly hard for Mickey. She was the middle child and was the most intelligent out of our lot. She would later tell Bette, "You could have talked to Mama for me. There had to be a way for me to stay in school." But at the time, Mama wouldn't hear of it. It was an issue of fairness; if one of us left school, then we all had to leave.

CHAPTER THIRTEEN

E arly in 1930, at the age of nineteen, I finally met a nice Irish-American man named Andy Scannell. He initially came in as a customer at O'Connor, Moffatt & Co and introduced himself, but later he got a job working as a cashier clerk at the department store. Andy was nine years older than I and stood a foot taller than me. He was a little quieter and gentler than my first love James, but incredibly sweet and dapper, though he had a receding hairline. He had a steady, assured, confident, measured voice. Though thinner than my ex-fiancé, his posture was upright and his chest broad. At first, I thought he was trying to look manly, but then realized it was a trait that many of the Scannell men in his family had. He had asked me out on a date, and at first, I turned him down due to our age difference. However, he persisted. One day, while I was on a break at work, unbeknownst to me, Andy spotted me reading a book I had borrowed from a friend, *A Farewell to Arms* by Ernest Hemingway. A couple of days later, he stopped by the counter I was working at to say that he had seen me reading the book and told me that he had read it too. He wanted to compare our experiences. I didn't know it at the time, but when he saw me reading it, he hadn't yet read it. He bought his own copy of the novel and read the entire book in two days, just to have a reason to strike up a conversation with me. He was highly romantic and sent me flowers and poems he had written along with clever notes. Eventually, I couldn't resist, and I agreed to go out with him.

Andy was a sports buff and had been a good athlete growing up. He used to play baseball with a child prodigy named Joe Cronin, who was a few years younger than Andy. They had grown up in the same neighborhood. Cronin would eventually become a Major League Baseball star who was later inducted into baseball's Hall of Fame.

Andy's main vice was that he had an affinity for booze, not unlike my father, and Andy tended to get, as we used to say, "swacked." At least, at that time, he was careful not to drive drunk.

On our first date, he picked me up in a handsome burgundy 1928 Ford Model A. It looked sleeker than the old Ford Model T Tin Lizzies. There was a dazzling blue logo on the grille. The car had a hood ornament with wings and looked brand new, though he had just purchased it used. Andy had previously worked as a salesman at a used car lot and got a good deal on it from a friend. He wanted to impress me with the car's performance. He had a fascination with speed. "Do you want to see how this baby performs?"

"Sure!" What did I have to fear? After all, I had ridden a motorcycle around the city on numerous occasions.

Andy drove me outside the city limits and found some open road overlooking San Francisco Bay. While the car idled at a stop sign, he began revving up the engine. Then, before I knew it, he had the car running over sixty miles per hour and we hit a downhill section. "Slow down!" I screamed and closed my eyes. I thought I was going to die at that point and hugged him tightly until he gradually slowed the car down. I had never ridden in a car traveling that fast before. It's funny to think about it now.

"The excitement has only begun," Andy smirked. He then took me to a boxing match where we met up with some of his friends to round out our date. I was only one of a handful of women to attend the male-dominated exhibition. I thought it was brutal, but at the same time thrilling.

On our second date, Andy took me to the horse races. He bet on some of the races and was pretty good at it, studying the handicaps before race time. I was attracted to his childlike, enthusiastic behavior. I began to know Andy better and started to fall in love. My friends warned me about him, given my father had a similar drinking pattern. They tried to dissuade me from continuing to date him. I chose to ignore their warnings.

Through dating him, I got to know a lot about Andy and his upbringing. He was from an Irish Catholic family like mine. Andy was proud of the fact he had an ancestor who had worked for the owners of the Blarney Castle, in Ireland, and was either granted or somehow managed to purchase some land from that family, after laws prohibiting ownership of land by Catholics were repealed.

Andy's parents had emigrated to California from Ireland. His father came from County Cork like my father, and his mother hailed from Kerry. Only they came in 1895, a few years before my parents arrived in the US. They initially settled in the town of Crockett, less than thirty miles outside of San Francisco, in the northeast Bay where there was a mini enclave of Irish settlers. His father, Daniel Scannell, worked at a nearby hotel as a clerk. Andy was his parents' first child and was born in Crockett in 1901. He moved to San Francisco around 1904, and their family would expand, adding two boys and a girl.

Andy's father Daniel was no longer working at the time I met Andy. He had recently sold a dry goods store. Like my father, Daniel had once worked in the liquor industry. He had been a bartender and later a liquor distributor. One of the things that struck me was that when Andy's father was twenty-four-years-old and still living in Ireland in 1895, he had an altercation with a local policeman over an illegal poteen (Irish moonshine) still that he owned, and he assaulted the officer. Andy was unaware of the injury his father had caused, but it was bad enough that he fled Ireland, never to return. So, both our fathers had been involved with illegal stills at different points in their lives. I should have recognized that as a red flag at the time, but simply thought that was normal in an Irish family.

Daniel Scannell also supported the rebellions against the British in Ireland, like my father had. In fact, when an Irish rebel, Major MacBride, was on a lecture circuit in the United States he hosted a reception in Crockett, CA, where he kept ties to the community.

Andy's mother Mary was strict. Their house on Sanchez Street in San Francisco was immaculate, with everything was in its place. It was almost too perfect. There were two pianos, one on each level. Couches were covered when not in use. Shelves were organized in such a way that one could see every item from various angles. There were always at least two jars of apple cider on the back porch in case guests got thirsty. Mary had a reputation for being a good cook, at least among the Scannell household. She cooked a generous pot of soup every week and had 'clam chowder Fridays' which were a favorite of Andy's.

When Andy and his parents originally moved to San Francisco in 1904 they moved to a house on Harrison Street. His father co-owned a liquor store called Scannell and Donoghue Liquors. Andy didn't remember much about it but was later told the store was on 7th Street.

On April 18, 1906, Andy was a month short of his fifth birthday. He awoke to violent shaking that occurred just before sunrise, and he recalled glass vases shattering and tin cans striking the ground. The shaking lasted a minute, and then a pipe burst in their home, flooding their kitchen. A massive earthquake had struck San Francisco. He recalled running out to the street with his parents while wearing night clothes. Throngs of people were shouting. Before long, the sun rose behind a strange-looking brown cloud. Fires had started, and he later learned that they were progressing towards his father's liquor store. Andy remembered his father leaving quickly to check on its condition.

Andy's mother Mary tried to get on the telephone to reach relatives living nearby but she had no luck. The earthquake severed parts of all the telephone lines in San Francisco. On that day, Andy walked with his mother to various relatives' and friends' homes, the majority of which had also suffered damage. Mary gathered a group of people, and along the way he saw destruction. Some streets appeared almost untouched, and others looked like a bull had gone through a china shop. Some cable car rails were ripped straight out of the street. Many houses and businesses had collapsed or were turned sideways. He saw a dead horse that had been crushed under rubble. Over thirty fires erupted from ruptured gas lines, and some buildings were on fire. The group Andy was in climbed up a steep street to get a better look at the city. He saw several other masses of people gathered at intersections with vantage points. What he described was apocalyptic. He saw fires and destruction all over the place. Sadly, his father would lose his store to one of those fires. Furthermore, the house the family lived in had major structural damage, rendering it uninhabitable. They had no insurance and lost everything. Fortunately, none of the Scannells lost their lives in the earthquake or the fires that followed, but about 3,000 people residing in the city died in the tragedy.

Despite all this, his family went on to prosper, and Andy eventually grew up living in a middle-class household.

When Andy was about eight years old, he had invited a friend over for dinner one evening, and his friend told Andy's mother, "Look, Mrs. Scannell, I've finished everything on my plate."

She snapped back sharply, raising her voice. "Is me food so bad dat ya want a compliment fur finishin' it?" Her tone terrified the little boy, and he slunk out of the house, embarrassed and scared. I found out firsthand during my marriage just how cutting and unpleasant Mary could be.

Despite some unpleasant childhood memories, Andy mostly recalled his younger years fondly. His family attended the World's Fair in 1915. This was the same year I remember having ridden with my Papa in his transportation wagon, down Market Street. Only Andy was nearly fourteen years old at the time the fair began. "Ann, the World's Fair was an amazing spectacle. You would have been astonished!"

It was called the Panama-Pacific International Exposition, held to celebrate the completion of the Panama Canal a year earlier. It was also used to showcase San Francisco's recovery after the 1906 earthquake. It was held in San Francisco's Marina District, and on its opening day, 255,000 people attended. In all, 18 million people visited the fair in 1915 over a nine-month span. Thirty-one countries were represented, and the French brought Auguste Rodin's famous bronze statue, The Thinker, and put it on display. The Liberty Bell was transported across the US at the request of 500,000 school children in California who had signed a petition. It was brought by train from Philadelphia and also put on display.

Andy remembered a Grand Prix car race taking place adjacent to the fair. "You could hear the engines roaring from any place you were standing. The smell of gasoline and cotton candy filled the air.

"I saw Charlie Chaplin walking around the fairgrounds. I suppose I should have obtained his autograph. The auto maker Henry

Ford also attended, and the Ford company even had an assembly line where I witnessed an automobile built right there at the fair!"

Andy saw the new Palace of Fine Arts. He described the well-manicured landscape surrounding the palace, which itself had intricate sculptures, Corinthian columns, and a Greco- Roman rotunda. There was also a magnificent building over 400-feet-tall called the Tour of Jewels. It had larger arches than the Arc de Triomphe's in Paris. Andy described it to me as an awe-inspiring structure that was covered with faceted jewels, each backed by a tiny mirror that scattered light in all directions and gave the appearance of precious gems. At night it was even more spectacular to see. A device called the Scintillar was used to shoot beams of glimmering light into the night sky.

Andy recalled getting excited watching biplanes fly over the Bay. His father Daniel saw how elated he was. He told Andy a barnstormer was giving airplane rides at the fair and asked him if he wanted to fly, a privilege very few Americans had had then. Andy agreed but had to experience the flight without his father as the flight cost $5, which was a lot of money in those days. He climbed into an open-air biplane with skids. There was only enough room for the pilot, himself and one other passenger. He sat in the plane wedged between the pilot and a stranger. His mother had given him a scarf to keep warm. The ten-minute flight over the San Francisco Bay was spine-chilling. The plane's motor was loud, and it vibrated violently in the Bay wind. Momentarily, his scarf blew into his face, blinding him. Andy described sucking so much air that he could barely speak. Just a few days later a famous stunt pilot Lincoln Beachey was killed flying over the Bay in full view of the fair-goers when the wings of his biplane snapped and plunged into the water right near a dock. As a result, Andy would never fly again.

By the time Andy was in his late teens his family went on regular vacations, and they gradually started to acquire vacation rentals
in Marin County, north of San Francisco. He had lovely memories
of fondly playing with his dog, an Airedale named Queenie. One
summer, some ranchers posted $5 gold coins as rewards for killing
mountain lions and bringing in their pelts. Daniel bought Andy a
30-caliber lever-action rifle and they went on hunts with his dog
Queenie through the hills near Lagunitas. Initially, Andy was unsuccessful, but the following summer he killed three mountain lions
and acquired $15 in gold coins.

CHAPTER FOURTEEN

Andy informed me about an upcoming ten-round heavyweight fight between Max Baer and the Italian American boxer Frankie "Campbell" Camilli, the same Frankie Campbell who was married to my cousin Elsie. Frankie was about three years younger than Andy, and Frankie's brother Dolph was also a sports prodigy. Dolph would later play Major League baseball as a first baseman and earn Most Valuable Player for the Brooklyn Dodgers. Though Frankie had played baseball he was more successful at boxing, with thirty-three wins, three losses, and two draws. He met Andy in the past and was excited to know that Andy was a boxing enthusiast. In August 1930, in San Francisco, Frankie was given a shot at Max Baer, one of the top prize fighters in the country. Both fighters lived in Northern California, and the fight was billed as the Pacific Coast Championship. There was so much excitement about the upcoming fight that Andy got together with a few of his friends and relatives, and they bought seats close to the ring. I was invited too. Given that the Great Depression had already started, it was rare that Andy would spend so much on one thing. But this was a special occasion.

He organized a pre-event get-together two days before the event. We went to one of the popular speakeasies in town, at a hotel in North Beach, in the center of bootleg activity. The speakeasy was in the basement, and it accommodated about eighty people or so. It was a swanky little joint with exquisite woodwork, murals on the wall, and an ornate bar.

We were accompanied by two of my friends who wanted to come but would not be attending the fight. Andy brought several of his friends. He looked so sharp in a black single-breasted suit with a wide-peaked lapel and a black bow-tie.

I wore my old buttery yellow flapper dress with fringes. I updated and accessorized it by wearing a pair of off-white silk gloves and a long strand of faux pearls that ended in dangling faux pearl tassels. I adorned a headband with a solitary short feather at one end that spread out, but was not overstated. Usually I didn't smoke much, but on that occasion I did. It gave a woman an air of sophistication, so I thought at the time.

We enjoyed the drinks that the establishment had to offer. I sat at the bar with Andy and our friends, sipping on giggle juice. I drank a Gin Rickey while Andy downed an Old-Fashioned. At the speakeasy, we listened to current popular tunes like the guitar-laden *Tiptoe Through The Tulips*, the Dixie-like sound of *Ain't Misbehavin'* and the pleasant, gentle swaying beat of Rudy Vallée's *Honey*. We were interrupted with an announcement from a gal named Marlene, a regular there, that anyone who wanted to dance the 'Black Bottom' was encouraged to start lining up. That dance had surpassed the Charleston in popularity. It was more complicated, and I had learned a few steps at home before my mother sold our phonograph. I was anxious to give it a try and grabbed Andy's hand and yanked him from his stool. He was in no mood to dance and rewarded me with a sour facial expression.

"Don't be such a wet blanket. This'll be fun!" I cajoled. Andy reluctantly followed me to a cluster of about twenty people who were assembling in a corner.

Marlene, who was organizing the dance, was dressed in a stunning art deco-style, sleeveless black flapper dress with gold trim and sequins. Her hair was in the style of the actress Clara Bow. It was short and had a cutie curl dangling over her forehead. Someone mentioned that Marlene's voice sounded a little like the new cartoon character Betty Boop, who had appeared in the animated film *Dizzy Dishes*.

Marlene broke the group into two, with the guys on one side and the gals on the other, facing each other, and asked the group to follow her moves if they didn't know the dance steps. Andy made his way toward Marlene like a puppy dog, as he was clueless as to how the dance went. Then the fast-paced song began. Pretty soon, we were swaying our hips, bending our knees, shuffling forward, and sliding back with 'mooch' and 'doodle-back' steps followed by slapping our bottoms. Most of the men, aside from maybe two, could not keep up, which made the dance hilarious and entertaining. It wasn't until one of the other men fell down that Andy laughed and loosened up. Towards the end of the dance, he was enjoying himself, making exaggerated moves. He even stuck his finger on his tongue and touched his bottom, and other men in the dance line began imitating him. We had such a wonderful time that evening.

Before long, the fight date had arrived. Early on the evening of August 25, 1930, we headed for the match at Recreation Park in San Francisco, at an outdoor open-air baseball stadium. We took a streetcar to the stadium which was in a bustling area of town with limited parking. It was located on Valencia Street, between 14th and 15th Street, and was surrounded by mostly three- and four-story buildings. As we approached the area, we saw a man had set up a shoeshine stand on the block, and there was a lengthy line of customers waiting to get their shoes shined for this special event.

After getting off the streetcar, we met up with some of Andy's friends and then hooked up with two of his relatives as well.

Recreation Park was the home to two minor league baseball teams, the San Francisco Seals and the Mission Reds. It had also hosted many boxing matches as far back as March 1915. In fact, Frankie Campbell fought a match there in 1925. Before Prohibition, the park was known for its booze cage. It was a long section along the third base-line where whiskey was served, and gambling occurred. I'm sure if my own father had been a big baseball fan, he would have been in attendance during that period.

Ticket booths dotted the main entrance, and there were several people in line both at the booths and at the gate waiting to get in. Excitement filled the air. Quite a few people were already liquored-up prior to the event.

"Andy, there must be a gin mill around here."

"Ab-so-lute-ly."

Profanities were rife. Some men acted out the match before it started, bobbing and weaving and doing wind-ups. They imitated Max Baer as he often pretended to be staggered by a punch, drawing his opponent close so he could get a good shot off. This got the crowd laughing at times.

After the gates opened, we shuffled forward, taking tiny steps at a time, along with a teeming herd of mostly men. I couldn't see anything except for the tall backs of everyone before me. I had the advantage of being able to see the ground more readily and avoided splats of tobacco and wads of chewed, discarded gum. I felt like a little child and was briefly squished and nearly crushed a couple of times as the mob surged forward. Rattling around like an ice cube in a cocktail shaker, I grabbed onto Andy's hand tightly, as I was afraid I would lose him.

We made our way into the stadium where suddenly I became free of the horde of warm bodies surrounding me and felt a blast of cold air on my face. The temperature had been in the seventies that day but had dropped into the fifties by the time we made our way to our seats. Our seats were only a few rows behind the boxing ring. The ring itself was centered over home plate.

Frankie was riding a fourteen-match win streak, according to Andy. His nickname was the Italian Dempsey, named after the legendary fighter Jack Dempsey, who had retired after a fight in 1927. Frankie's parents were Catholic immigrants from Italy, and he was raised by an abusive father after his parents had separated. He grew up poor as a child living in the Mission District, and he never finished grammar school. He dropped his family name of Camilli and went by the name Frankie Campbell in the ring because the last name Campbell was thought to be more appealing to the droves of Scottish and Irish boxing fans in the San Francisco Bay Area at the time.

His wife, my cousin Elsie Camilli née Maguire, would not be in attendance. She and Frankie had a son, Frankie Junior, who was eight months old. Elsie lived with her husband and son above the grocery store owned by my Aunt Mary Ann on Randall Street, near to where I lived. In years past, Frankie used to visit Elsie at the store where she did the books and worked as a clerk.

Frankie Campbell was pitted against Max Baer to determine who was the best fighter on the West Coast. The winner would be catapulted closer to a shot at the world heavyweight title. Frankie was a crowd favorite, as he was undersized at one hundred and seventy-nine pounds, quick, and had brought down heavier opponents in past fights. He was known for his left-hook but had developed a good one-two punch. He had a square jaw, good muscular tone, and dashing good looks.

Andy talked avidly about Frankie's opponents in the past, who had names like 'Sailor' Hughes, George 'Buster' Trenkle, 'Racehorse' Roberts and 'Bad News' Johnson.

Frankie's opponent, Max Baer, had grown up in a middle-class family that owned property. He moved around a few times before his family settled in Livermore, California, and owned a ranch with livestock. He also had a limited education. He was Catholic but had a Jewish grandfather, and his father had been initially raised Jewish. Baer had wide shoulders, a five-inch reach advantage, a stiff punch, and stood four inches taller than Frankie. His nickname was the 'Livermore Larruper.' The term 'larruper', in the boxing world, was used to describe a person who beats or flogs someone. Baer weighed in at one hundred and ninety-four pounds, a full fifteen pounds more than Frankie. Though he was the favorite to win, he was only twenty-one years old, five years younger than Frankie and considered immature. He was flashy and liked to spend money on fancy suits and nice cars, and to go out with older women. He was known for clowning around in the ring and for sometimes taunting his opponents. He was also said to have demonstrated how tough his head was by banging it against steam and radiator pipes in his dressing room before fights.

Baer had twenty-four wins, only lost one fight on points, and in just two matches, he was disqualified for fouls. In one instance, he threw a fighter to the ground, and in another, he pushed a fighter when he was being given a count. He had dispensed with a list of opponents with names like Chief Caribou, 'Tiny' Abbott and 'KO' Christner.

Upon reaching our seats I noticed there were probably thirty men in the crowd for every woman. The smell of shaving cream and aftershave floated through the air. Many in the crowd stomped their feet in anticipation of the fight, creating a deep rumbling noise that went through the wooden stadium. I could almost feel the testosterone permeating through my seat.

Gradually, the smell of tobacco and hotdogs replaced the scents of men's shaving products. Patches and rings of cigar and cigarette smoke wafted in the air and over the ring.

We were already seated when Frankie's entourage reached the stadium as it started to get dark. Frankie had led a grand procession, organized by friends from his old neighborhood. People next to us in the crowd told us Frankie's lead car was adorned with flowers.

Initially, the wind that evening was light but began to pick up. As the sky grew darker, fog started to roll in off San Francisco Bay. A cool mist moistened my face, and the lights above the arena flickered as patches of fog danced in and out. Visibility of the ring was good. The attendance was over fifteen thousand people. Numbering about ten people, our group made a small but respectable cheering section. Our seats were only a few rows back from the ring, close to the action. Seated around the ring were some professional and ex-professional boxers and sports reporters.

Before the fight began, I talked with two of Andy's close friends, Tim and Johnny. The pertinent topic of discussion amongst the crowd was that a boxer had been killed in a boxing match in San Francisco four days earlier on August 21. A teenage fighter, Johnny Anderson, lost his life against a fighter named Red Kuehl in a four-round bout. The fight had occurred just a block away from where we were seated, on the corner of 16th and Mission Street in a smaller boxing facility, National Hall. I vividly remember Andy's friend Johnny pointing out the direction of the hall.

Another fellow in the crowd overheard our conversation and said that earlier in the year another boxer, Mickey Darmon, died following a knockout in Olympia, Washington. The discussion distressed me. I had seen fights before, but I had not witnessed any tragedies like those being batted about.

Sometime after eight o'clock, a series of short preliminary bouts started while the distant sound of a foghorn could be heard.

Andy looked over to me with a wide grin. "Isn't this great?"

"Yes." I smiled. My jaw was set, and he could see I was anxious. I had butterflies in my stomach. "I'm a bit nervous."

"Frankie has nothing to lose. He's the underdog." Andy had not heard the dialog I had with his friends. He must have been engaged in another conversation at the time. He didn't seem to understand that losing was not what I was concerned about.

Before we knew it the grand finale was about to take place. It must have been sometime after ten o'clock when the boxers emerged from the centerfield clubhouse and walked towards the ring. The crowd roared along with a cacophony of sounds from various musical instruments. There were huge sections of fans in the stadium that cheered for each fighter, but it felt like there were more Frankie Campbell supporters. You could hear the Frankie chants above the chants for Max Baer.

Most people rose to their feet as the boxers entered. I tried my best to get up on my tiptoes to see around the hordes of people. Most men wore fedora or trilby hats, and a few wore the taller more formal Homburg hats. I couldn't see past any of them. I had to stand on my chair which allowed me to witness the unfolding hoopla. This was something I had to do several times during the fight, to be able to see the action.

The boxers gradually made their way to the ring wearing striped robes. The fighters were introduced in grand fashion as the ring announcer fluctuated his deep voice intonation. After Frankie was introduced, he gave a salute. After Max was announced, there were some boos, and he made a point to bow to the crowd. Max had broad shoulders, was taller and bulkier than Frankie, and looked so much more menacing.

A photographer took a pre-fight photograph. When the flash-bulb went off it caused a metallic odor which permeated the area for a minute or so. The fighters then disrobed, with Frankie wearing light trunks and Max in dark.

The bell rang, and the fighters soon went after each other. Frankie pressed first, going to work right away with one-two combinations to the body. Max followed by striking blows to Campbell's jaw. Frankie's punches were shorter and more compact. Max tended to have long, loopy punches that originated from beyond the width of his shoulders, coming in almost sideways. Baer's shots looked like they were coming in at times from both right and left field. The fighters went back and forth, and Frankie looked be getting the better of Baer. Max was pushed against the ropes a few times, and Frankie was quicker and landed more blows. However, Max connected on a left hook to the side of Frankie's head which dropped him. On one knee, Frankie took a ten count. Before reaching ten, he sprang up as if nothing had happened and went back to attacking his foe until the bell sounded.

The second round was a brawl until Frankie landed a blow to Baer's left jaw, which caused Max to slip and fall onto the canvas, on his caboose. Some people in the crowd laughed. The referee, who was a short man wearing a bow-tie, signaled to Frankie to go to a neutral corner. Campbell headed towards the corner, stepping over Baer's feet. Enraged, Max rolled over and popped up immediately. Before Frankie even made his way all the way over to the corner, Max sucker-punched Frankie as his back was turned. With vicious force, Frankie was struck in an area that included part of his neck and the back of his jaw, causing him to be catapulted into the ropes. The referee untangled one of Frankie's arms from the ropes and was turning him around to get him back on his feet when Max slugged him again. A chorus of boos and insults filled the air. "You dirty rat!" was among the crowd favorites. Someone in Frankie's corner clamored for an immediate disqualification of Max Baer for the fouls. However, nothing was done, and the bell rang, ending the round.

As Frankie sat in his corner, he said something. We couldn't make out what he uttered, and Andy started to ask people in front of him. I don't know what Frankie's exact words were, but it was relayed to us that he felt that something was broke or had broken in his head. We all became exceedingly concerned.

"That wasn't necessarily mafia, but those were cheap shots," Andy declared, scornfully.

"Oh, my God, I hope he isn't hurt badly!" With trepidation, I moved my head sideways between a gap of fight fans in front of us to get a better look. I really couldn't gauge how badly he had been hurt. He was given smelling salts, was sitting upright and looked to be alert and engaged with his cornermen.

After being briefly assessed by his corner, the bell rang, and Frankie seemed to spring up just fine to start the third round. We briefly forgot about the incident as Frankie certainly came to life in the third and fourth rounds, striking bigger blows than Max, staying in attack mode most of the time. In the fourth round, Max got a bloody nose and was pushed up against the ropes multiple times. He seemed to be running out of gas. Frankie gave the impression of stalking his prey. For a minute, we thought he would knock his opponent out, but Baer survived the onslaught until the bell rang.

In between rounds, the wind picked up and the air became dense and cold. My teeth began to chatter. "Look, Andy, I can't control myself."

"Doll, that's because you're with me."

"You're so funny, Andy," I retorted with sarcasm. "Can't you see I'm cold?"

"Of course I do." Andy wrapped his arm around me. Being a lover of poetry, he decided it was a good moment to start quoting a line from *Annabel Lee* by Edgar Allan Poe. "*In the kingdom by the sea, a wind blew out of a cloud, chilling my beautiful Ann … *"

The bell rang again, and the fifth round started. Suddenly I forgot about being cold as I once more became engrossed watching the fight. As Frankie continued to put on the pressure, Max Baer experienced a resurgence. Baer used his reach advantage, holding his left arm out against Frankie's head and body, then began to connect with some solid punches, which pushed Frankie forcefully back to a corner. I developed a terrible sinking feeling in the pit of my stomach, and this was followed by an overwhelming sense of impending doom. Baer lunged forward and eventually connected on a hard uppercut shot to Frankie's jaw followed by a right cross to the chin. There was an uproar in the crowd, and people started to leap to their feet. I jumped up onto my chair and bent my head a little so I wouldn't block the view of fight enthusiasts behind me. That's when I noticed Frankie was knocked out cold. He slumped like a rag doll, and was hung up on the ropes in an almost seated, semi-standing position. Like a possessed madman, Max pummeled him violently and relentlessly, striking multiple blows to Frankie's head. Frankie became Max Baer's punching bag, and the referee didn't step in. I raised my hands to my forehead and almost covered my eyes in horror. I couldn't believe this was occurring before my eyes. Frankie's head kept bouncing off one of the metal turn-buckles that was used to cinch one of the ring's upper ropes to a corner post. Although the barrage may have lasted less than ten seconds, it seemed like an eternity. Everything felt like it happened in slow motion before the referee finally intervened and grabbed hold of Baer.

I'm not sure how many punches Baer threw, but Andy thought it had to be at least twenty.

Unconscious and battered, Frankie "Campbell" Camilli's limp body toppled to the canvas, blood oozing from his nose and mouth.

The referee raised Max Baer's left arm above his head to signal victory. A photographer took a photo of Baer and the referee while Frankie's motionless body lay on the canvas before them. There was a deafening chorus of boos from the audience.

There was an attempt to get Frankie up onto the stool in his corner, but that was unsuccessful as his lifeless body slithered back onto the floor. Then Frankie began to convulse. After screams and shouts from the audience, some people in groups, including ours, began to pray. This is when some of those prayers that the nuns had belted into our memories came flooding out of our mouths.

"Oh, Lord," I began to pray out loud, "we come before you in the need of a healing hand. Gracious God, we ask you to guide Frankie back to health. He has suffered greatly and needs your salvation. Please lay your hands on him and grant him, as well as all those who are injured, a speedy recovery."

As Frankie's body lay on the canvas, a group of people, including some cornermen started to surround him. I was hoping they were doctors. From that point on, it was difficult to see what was going on. A rush of photographers began to make their way into the ring to try to take pictures of the critical situation. One of them managed to take a photo. Some people in the ring, as well as spectators trying to make their way in, became enraged and started to kick and punch the photographers, and chaos ensued. Police tried to break up the melee as people tried to smash the cameras. The police began grabbing hold of and escorting the photographers out of the ring, bumping into furious fight enthusiasts, including those who poured out from the bleachers, racing through the outfield, toward the ring. The wind lifted swirls of hotdog wrappers into the air. People shoved and pushed each other. I later learned that at least one of the photographers was assaulted once outside the stadium.

Shouts to get a doctor in the ring echoed through the crowd. It took several minutes before a doctor was able to make his way through the hordes of people clogging the pathways and surrounding the ring. Everyone was on their feet watching the horrific scene as it unfolded. In the meantime, Max Baer left the ring, escorted by the police and some men in plain clothes.

By that time, some people began exiting the stadium, and seagulls from San Francisco Bay circled overhead waiting to swoop on garbage from the dispersing crowd. It was another ten minutes before an ambulance arrived. The ambulance had been caught up in traffic and had to drive through the exiting crowd to the stadium. The medical personnel worked on Frankie in the open-air ring for half an hour. He was loaded onto a stretcher and lifted by some police officers who carried him to the waiting ambulance. That is when I got a good look at Frankie. The poor man's face looked like hamburger, all swollen and bloody, and he remained unconscious. He was first taken to Mission Hospital, where the doctors who examined him determined he had a broken skull, and then he was transferred to St. Joseph's Hospital for a higher level of care.

This was one of the most harrowing nights of my life. Only the deaths of my father and fiancé James superseded this.

I felt sickened for my poor cousin Elsie. The two hospitals' medical personnel, including physicians and nurses, cared for him for several hours, but he died the following day. He had suffered a cerebral hemorrhage, and his brain had been knocked loose from the connective tissue inside his head.

Max Baer met with Elsie at the hospital the following morning on August 26. Frankie died before noon. Elsie had not witnessed the fight, and publicly did not blame Baer.

Max Baer was taken into custody that afternoon by San Francisco's Police Captain Fred Lemmon and was charged with manslaughter. Bail was set at $10,000, which was a lot of money in those days. There was quite a lot of talk about it in the community. I wasn't sure whether to put all the blame on Max Baer, the referee, or the sport. Boxing was brutal and risky. I would never attend another boxing match again.

In the days that followed, my mother was in close contact with her siblings, my Aunt Rose, Uncle Ben, and my Aunt Mary Ann. Everyone was shocked and upset. I attended the church service at Frankie's funeral with my mother three days after the fight. It was held at St. Paul's church in San Francisco. Andy had been a member of that church for years, but was unable to get off work that day so was not in attendance. The church was packed beyond its 1,400-seat capacity, with hundreds of mourners standing. I only got a brief window to comfort Elsie as she had done for me when Papa and James had died. Frankie was laid to rest at the same cemetery, Holy Cross in Colma, where my sister Katherine had been interred thirteen years earlier.

I found it ironic that when the famous young Italian American actor Rudy Valentino died it would be hosted by the Frank E. Campbell funeral home in New York City, and now the young Italian American boxer with the fictional name of Frankie Campbell would have his own funeral in San Francisco.

The state boxing commission suspended Max Baer, the referee, and other people associated with the boxing match while the fight was investigated. Eventually, the charges were dropped, and Max Baer's next fight would be four months later, at Madison Square

Garden. In the newspapers, it was alleged that the referee in the Baer-Campbell fight had been involved with some gamblers. Though I don't believe anything came of it, a recommendation was made for future bouts to have three judges determine the outcome of a fight and not one. In the end, it became a boxing standard. Also, because of fights like this one, eventually it became mandatory to pad all the metal turnbuckles and posts of boxing rings.

On June 14, 1934, Max became heavyweight champion of the world by defeating a fighter by the name of Primo Carnera. After intense public pressure, on February 16, 1935, Max Baer held a benefit fight for Frankie Junior, at Dreamland Auditorium in San Francisco. Over $10,000 was raised for Elsie's son's future education.

Later that year Max Baer lost the heavy-weight title to a fellow by the name of James Braddock, an under-sized fighter who was raised by Irish immi-grants. James Braddock was called 'Cinderella Man' because of a quick second rise from obscurity to fame, and had once been on pub-lic assistance.

Pre-fight photo of fighters
Max Baer on the left and Frankie "Campbell"
Camilli on the right. Source: AP Photo

CHAPTER FIFTEEN

Life went on, and I went out with Andy on several, much more pleasant dates. He eventually asked me to marry him, and I gleefully accepted. Given his family was more well-to-do than mine I thought we would have the vast Irish Catholic wedding, one I had always dreamed of. I was giddy all over again. However, Andy's father Daniel Scannell had developed intestinal cancer and was in no shape to attend a wedding. He became weak, and following a procedure on his colon in 1931, he had a colostomy bag, which required regular maintenance. Andy quit work in 1932 for a while at the department store and got odd jobs near his home so he could be with his father and help his family, and he stopped taking me out. I was almost twenty-two at the time. The home on Sanchez Street, where the Scannell family lived, was a couple of miles away from the White household where I resided with my family on Nevada Street. I didn't have a car or a driver's license and had long hours at work. I managed to walk to his house a few times, but visits were too few and far between. Bette, who was about eighteen years old at the time, was still working alongside me at O'Connor, Moffatt & Co's department store, helping to support our mother. I stopped diverting as much money as I had been to Mama and tried to save up money before starting my marriage to Andy. Bette and I got jobs modeling for the department store to make extra cash. Bette often heard me at work complaining about the limited time I was able to spend with Andy.

As sisters we were exceptionally close, and she got sick of me complaining about the whole situation. When we were at home, she developed an insane idea. I was sitting on the couch in the living room mending a dress that had torn. I looked up and she was hovering over me holding a pair of my dusty old roller skates.

"Ann, see if you can still fit into these." They were the same skates I had acquired when I was twelve and I had not skated since I was fifteen.

I looked up at Bette. "What kind of bird-brained idea do you have in mind?"

Bette also pulled out a set of skates for herself that she had borrowed from a friend. "We, my darling, are going to skate over to the Scannell home and visit Andy."

"Oh, Lord!" I imagined myself crashing into a car. "I haven't skated in seven years. What if I forgot how to skate?"

Bette looked directly into my eyes. "Well, there is only one way to find out, isn't there?"

I called Andy to make sure that it was OK to come over to visit, as I did not want to disturb his dying father, and he said it was OK. I didn't tell him we would be arriving by roller skates.

Bette and I took our skates to the last step, below our porch, where we sat trying to get them on. The frames were forged out of metal. One's boots, or in my case, shoes, went in one at a time. To secure one's footwear, the skates had leather straps. They also came with a key which was used to tighten or loosen metal toe-grips that anchored one's shoes. Since my shoe size was larger than when I had originally acquired the skates, I had to loosen the toe grips to allow my shoes to fit. Fortunately, they still fit me. Bette had no trouble getting on the skates she had borrowed. The skates did not have toe-stoppers back then and the wheels were made of wood, and the ball bearings were crude. To turn, one had to shift one's bodyweight in the desired turning direction and push one skate slightly forward, not unlike snow skis. I apparently forgot how to start that maneuver.

The portion of Nevada Street where we lived was steep. To get to Andy's house we had to turn downhill to reach Courtland Avenue. We stood up and precariously rolled to the sidewalk, and to avoid going over the curb, I started a highly imprecise turn and cut in front of Bette. I did a half-pirouette. We almost crashed right then, and Bette grabbed onto my left hand and stopped me, facing her. She was facing downhill, and I was facing up.

"Loosen up your legs, Ann, don't be such a gobstick!"

"I won't be a gobstick if you don't behave like a little ankle-biter," I retorted.

We gradually got into a sideways stance facing the street, and I turned my head, looking downhill. I had no idea why this had suddenly become a scary venture. My heart started beating briskly. Blood coursed through my arteries as if I just had consumed a massive pot of coffee. I used to skate all the time. Why did this suddenly seem so daunting? Little by little we skated down the sidewalk, turning sideways to slow us down or stop.

We got into one stretch where we were rolling too fast. I started wobbling at first, then like greased lightning, zipped ahead of Bette and was forced to make an abrupt stop. I somehow managed to terminate my land speed record, chipping one of my wheels due to sudden friction, but Bette overcorrected and turned uphill to slow down and then started rolling backwards. I could see her coming straight at me. For a split second, I thought I would just leap out of the way and let the action unfold naturally. It might have been hilarious to watch. However, I knew if she couldn't stop, there was a slight risk she could glide all the way down to the upcoming inter-section and be smashed by an oncoming car. My protective instincts took over, and I tried to catch her. She bowled me over like a bowl-ing pin, causing me to fly into the air and land in a patch of dirt. Bette fell partly on top of me.

"Strike!" Bette could not help herself from making that remark. She scraped her left wrist a little. She would have gouged her left hand had it not been for mittens she was wearing. She ended up with dirt stains on the left sleeve of her blouse and on one of her cream-colored mittens. She also tore her blouse.

I landed on my side, tearing my turquoise sweater, which had now become dirty along with my skirt. We sat up and gradual-ly flicked off the pebbles, twigs, and leaves stuck to our clothes. We tried to brush the stains off as much as possible and decided to press on. We made our way down to a busier street, Courtland Avenue, where we had to make a left turn.

The first part of Courtland Avenue was the steepest part of our journey. We had to use all our strength to sidestep up the hill, push-ing off with one foot followed by turning the other foot sideways, zig-zagging our way up. Finally, we made it up to the peak near Gates Street. From there, it was a gradual descent. We dodged around peo-ple, pets, delivery men unloading their goods to the local shops, lampposts, and signs. Sure, we looked ragged and lost our dignity, but we quickly got the hang of roller-skating again. We passed by our father's old tobacco shop cum illegal bar, and turned left onto another busy thoroughfare, Mission Street, where we had to climb another hill. Then, after crossing the busiest intersection at San Jose Avenue, we made our way up Randall Street, where Elsie had grown up, and eventually onto Sanchez Street, where Andy spotted us roll-ing toward his house. He came out bursting with laughter and then gave both of us an exuberant hug. He kissed me on the lips and gave Bette a peck on her cheek. He helped clean Bette's wrist road rash.

From then on, we made a trip to his house on roller skates at least a couple of times a week. He always laughed when we arrived. I didn't want to be apart from Andy more than I had to. He was sweet, gentle, and funny. I wanted to get married as soon as we were able.

Weeks turned into months. Before I knew it, 1933 came, and still no marriage. In February, Congress proposed the 21st Amendment to end Prohibition, given the unintended consequences such as higher crime. To pass, thirty-six states needed to approve and ratify the amendment, a process that would take several months.

Franklin D. Roosevelt replaced Herbert Hoover as the president of the United States on March 4, 1933. He started 'The New Deal' in March 1933. It was a series of programs aimed at leading us out of the Great Depression. San Francisco was among the first cities to receive aid, and more jobs were created. It included public work projects and financial reforms. San Francisco benefited greatly. Among other things, it provided funds for improving fire stations and underground drainage systems, as well as the building of roads, libraries, and bridges.

Meanwhile, I had other things on my mind. At first, Andy and I postponed the wedding, thinking that his father would pass away and his mother Mary would eventually attend our wedding if we delayed long enough. Aside from that, Mary forbade us to get married until after the inevitable. However, Daniel Scannell's cancer lingered on for almost three years. Even then, we knew if he died then Mary wouldn't be able to attend a wedding for some time, and we were tired of waiting. I suppose we were being selfish, but we made the decision to elope. We got married in Watsonville, California, about a two-hour drive from San Francisco on April 26, 1933. I had not even bought a white wedding dress because I didn't initially know when we would have our wedding. Given the spur of the moment decision, I wore a powder blue dress and pinned flowers to my outfit. Only Bette and one of Andy's friends attended the ceremony. Almost as soon as we got back, Andy's father died, on May 4.

Given Daniel Scannell had been a devout Catholic, I felt solace from believing he was in heaven. I felt sorry for Daniel, because he was unable to attend his own mother's funeral back in Ireland, back in 1904 when she died. After he had fled Ireland over the poteen still altercation in 1895, he was never able to return to his homeland.

Once again, I stood at Holy Cross Cemetery in Colma. I remember singing the old Irish song *Danny Boy* at his funeral. Only I imagined *Danny Boy* as being Andy's father Daniel arising from his grave before us that day in San Francisco, coming back to Ireland, then running towards his mother Johanna's grave in the village of Ballyvourney while she sang to him, lying in her coffin, yearning for him to come kneel over her. The words in the latter half of that song especially resonated.

"Oh, Danny boy, oh Danny boy, I love you so!
But when ye come, and all the flowers are dying,
If I am dead, as dead I well may be,
You'll come and find the place where I am lying,
and kneel and say an Ave there for me.
And I shall hear, though soft you tread above me,
and all my grave will warmer, sweeter be,
for you will bend and tell me that you love me,
and I shall sleep in peace until you come to me!"

CHAPTER SIXTEEN

Though Andy's mother, Mary, would continue living at her home on Sanchez Street, she owned another property on 28th Street that she rented out to a family. There was a humble-sized cottage behind that property that she let us stay in rent-free. That's where we lived when we started our marriage.

By the late summer of that year, I discovered I was pregnant and was thrilled to learn I would become a mother. The only major hiccup I had was morning sickness. Andy and I took a stroll through Golden Gate Park, a park that was built over sand dunes back in 1870. On our way to visiting the 'singing falls' we passed by a couple of musicians in front of a small crowd, playing a version of Duke Ellington's new song, *Sophisticated Lady*. I suddenly developed nausea and lightheadedness. I ran on a pathway trying to find a restroom, but ended up vomiting behind an oak tree with that song playing in the background. I felt anything but sophisticated! Then came laughter from Andy. If I had been close to him, I could have bopped him on the lips right then and there. Fortunately, the morning sickness didn't last too long, and the rest of my pregnancy was uneventful.

Later that year, on December 5, 1933, Prohibition was finally repealed. The few wineries that operated during that period, selling their wine to places of worship for the sacrament, were in the best position to capitalize. One of those wineries in Sonoma, the Italian Swiss Colony, paraded fifteen decorated trucks from their warehouse on Beach Street to San Francisco's Civic Center, including City Hall. Their trucks were loaded with cases of Chianti, ready to sell to eager residents.

On December 6, at the Civic Auditorium, the California Restaurant Bureau sponsored a two-day-long Repeal Carnival. An orchestra, jazz band, and entertainers performed on stage, and dances were held both in the afternoon and evenings, lasting from noon to midnight each day. Andy had long had a dream to own a bar, and he had heard that liquor distributors would be present, so he wanted to attend. He was able to get the afternoon off on the second day and invited me to go. I was already showing and didn't feel up to drinking, so I decided not to attend. He spent a few hours there and he said there were thousands of attendees, with multiple liquor distributors displaying exhibits, as well as other retailers, including those for adding machines, music products, and even Chlorox. Chlorox? Well, why wouldn't you want bright white blouses and shirts after you had stained them with wine?

Prohibition had taken a toll on our country. It was said that there were twice as many illegal bars as there were legal ones operating before Prohibition. I later found out in a book written about Prohibition, *Ardent Spirits* by John Kobler, that between 1920 and 1930, some 577,000 suspects were taken into custody. How my father, mother, Bette and I were never discovered and arrested was a miracle. I felt like a survivor from that aspect alone.

During that period, across the country, agents seized 1.6 million stills and other liquor-making devices, 9 million gallons of hard liquor, 1 billion gallons of malt liquor, 1 billion gallons of wine, hard cider, and mash, as well as 45,000 cars and 1,300 boats. And those totals were only for what was confiscated. I could only imagine what the actual numbers were.

A columnist for *The San Francisco Examiner* said that the official estimates were that there were "five hundred to seven hundred speakeasies in San Francisco" alone. Bette and I had only serviced a fraction of those. Many people predicted the downfall of those speakeasies, if enough businesses sold liquor and the taxes were not too high. Those people were correct. Within weeks after Prohibition was repealed, the California Board of Equalization, which was responsible for issuing liquor licenses, determined that any place serving a meal could qualify for a license. Taxes were placed on the sale of alcohol, but weren't so high that the illegal businesses could undercut the legitimate establishments. In no time, businesses such as restaurants and legal bars began selling booze, and the illegal establishments dwindled.

Shortly after Prohibition ended, San Francisco, along with other cities, became littered with secret basement speakeasies, many of which became abandoned. In my eyes, Prohibition had been a disastrous experiment. If it had categorically eliminated alcohol, perhaps my father wouldn't have died so young. However, it just encouraged illegal activity and paradoxically increased alcohol consumption. Maybe he would have lived to a ripe old age if Prohibition had never taken place? I would never know.

Though I was not anxious to re-enter the spirits industry, my husband was ready to run a bar. No longer would there be the same level of threat from selling booze.

Certainly, a new opportunity arose. Using some money he had acquired from the passing of his father and with help from his mother, Andy finally opened a bar which he named the Old Keg Inn, located on Church Street, which I helped him decorate. It had a sports theme, and we displayed photos of baseball players like Babe Ruth and boxers such as Jack Dempsey and Gene Tunney.

"You forgot one," I pointed out.

"No, I haven't!" Andy pulled out a picture of the late Frankie "Campbell" Camilli and added it to a wall.

I made it my mission to include some female athletes and mounted photos of American tennis players like Helen Wills. Andy rolled his eyes, but let me post the pictures, nonetheless.

The Old Keg Inn was a cozy tavern. In addition to serving liquor, Andy cooked food for the patrons, making French bread and kettle dishes like clam chowder and pork and beans, recipes which he'd learned from his mother as he grew up.

Andy and I made special trips by car out to Fisherman's Wharf to purchase fresh clams. Back then, most of the merchants that we saw were Italian. There were stalls that consisted of wooden tables with platters and bowls of clams and oysters, and every fish you could imagine, on ice. There were tables covered with lobsters and crabs, and vendors standing near steaming pots of boiling water lining the street, ready to cook them up. Growing up, I hadn't eaten a lot of seafood as my family could not afford it, especially shellfish. I didn't particularly care for the fishy smell of the market mixed with hints of seawater and seaweed.

It made Andy happy, as he had good memories of the wharf. He made it a point not just to make a purchase and leave. After acquiring the clams and storing them on ice, he would take me to a nearby pier where we would find a bench and cuddle, watching the fishing boats and ships travel in and out of San Francisco Bay. We often sat for an hour or two, and usually wore warm coats or sweaters for the occasion. Seagulls would fly overhead, screeching out their high-pitched, excited cries. They would land on the pier's long wooden pilings sticking vertically out of the water at different heights. We also enjoyed watching sea lions sunbathing on boulders.

While sitting at the pier one day, Andy made up poems about the Bay. He sprinkled in some San Francisco history and talked about things I had not heard of. Sure, I knew a little about cable cars and the 1906 earthquake, but who was Emperor Norton? I had heard the name before, but knew nothing about him.

"Ah, Emperor Norton. Where do I begin? Where did all of this begin?" Andy had a wide-eyed expression. He was a history buff and wanted to share his knowledge of all the books he read. "Well, to understand Emperor Norton, you have to understand how San Francisco began."

"Do tell, wise man," I smirked, then rested my head on Andy's chest while he held me.

Andy went on to talk about how the Spaniards arrived in California in the 1760s and established missions and *presidios*—fortified military settlements. By 1776, in the area that would be later named San Francisco, the Spaniards built the Presidio of San Francisco and Mission San Francisco de Asís. The missions were run by priests backed by Spanish military forces. Native Americans were encapsulated and exploited in the Franciscan mission system. Around those structures, a town gradually formed and was named Yerba Buena, meaning 'good herb' in Spanish, after an aromatic, naturally growing mint vine that covered much of the area. The Mexican government eventually overthrew the Spanish government, and by 1847 the name of the town was changed to San Francisco, as settlers more often referred to the names of its mission and presidio.

Early in 1848, in the foothill town of Coloma, gold was discovered at Sutter's Mill on the American River by James Marshall. In the meantime, Mexico sold land to the US that included the territory that would become the state of California.

The town of San Francisco only had about 1,000 residents at the time. Sam Brennan, a Mormon businessman, started buying up gold mining equipment for his store near Sacramento. Then, in May 1848, he walked into San Francisco's Portsmouth Square with a vial of gold flakes, shouting: "Gold! Gold from the American River!"

So much excitement was generated that nearly three-quarters of all the men in San Francisco left for the gold fields. Some of the newly-arriving ships to the port were abandoned and left to rot. The town of San Francisco nearly collapsed. Rushing out to Brennan's store and the gold fields were shop owners, blacksmiths, masons, laborers, clergyman, merchants, sailors, and soldiers.

"When all was said and done, Brennan eventually became California's first millionaire, and he wasn't even a miner!"

"So why didn't San Francisco become a ghost town?" I sat up for a few seconds and brushed a piece of lint off Andy's sweater before I lay my head back down.

"It darn near did. Near the end of that year, President James Polk gave a State of the Union address to the nation proclaiming the gold discoveries. That's what set off the worldwide mass migration to California in 1849, hence the name '49ers.' Nearly half came by sea, and close to 100 percent of those came through San Francisco's port. Though many people headed for the gold fields, so many people came that new businesses formed, and several people stayed. The population of San Francisco swelled from nearly one thousand in 1848 to twenty-five thousand by the end of 1849!"

"That's faster than mice could multiply at my old house on Nevada Street!" I laughed.

Andy smiled. He explained that about one thousand ships were abandoned in San Francisco's harbor, and some were repurposed to become saloons, warehouses, hotels, boarding houses, and even jails.

Some were burned in fires and sunk. Others were buried along with dirt, sand, and debris to create landfill to enlarge the city.

"There are hundreds of buildings in the Embarcadero and in downtown San Francisco built on top of these old ships."

"That's amazing. Perhaps there are ghosts lurking underneath the ground!" I turned my head and looked up at Andy. "What does that have to do with Emperor Norton, though?"

"Aw, I almost forgot. So, there was this fellow by the name of Joshua Norton, originally from England, who came here during that Gold Rush. He started a real estate investment business and became exceedingly wealthy. Then he made a bad investment decision that left him bankrupt, and he became a pauper living in a boarding house."

Andy said that Norton proclaimed himself Emperor of the United States and issued his own currency. He acquired old military officers' uniforms, including a blue one with gold-plated epaulettes that draped over his shoulders. He used to walk the streets of San Francisco in uniform, wearing a tall hat with peacock feathers, carrying an umbrella. He walked into newspaper agencies, issuing proclamations and decrees which would sometimes be printed in the local papers. He didn't like citizens of San Francisco calling our city 'Frisco.' He issued a decree stating:

'Whoever after due and proper warning shall be heard to utter the abominable word "Frisco", which has no linguistic or other warrant, shall be deemed guilty of High Misdemeanor, and shall pay into the Imperial Treasury as penalty the sum of $25.'

Norton walked around town knighting people for good deeds or just for having a bad day. He was known for his support of a woman's right to vote as well as fair treatment of the Chinese.

Some businesses honored his currency, thereby giving him free lunches, train and ferry rides, and free tickets to the opera where a balcony seat was reserved for him. He rented a tiny room on Commercial Street, and many locals paid for his rent. Mark Twain worked for a popular newspaper, *The San Francisco Call*, nearby Emperor Norton's residence, from 1863 to 1864. Later, Twain based his character 'The King' in *The Adventures of Huckleberry Finn* on Norton.

Emperor Norton was eventually arrested and committed to a mental institution. This outraged many in the city who felt he was not harming anyone. Under intense pressure, Police Chief Patrick Crowley ordered that Norton be released and issued a public apology.

Norton decreed that a worldwide Bible convention be held in San Francisco. He received the unwanted attention of a celebrity preacher, Edward Hammond, known as the Children's Evangelist, who brought a traveling revival show to San Francisco. Hammond scared children into believing they were sinners and performed thousands of conversions. Some of the youngsters were frightened into hysterics with prolonged singing, quivering and spasms. Emperor Norton felt Hammond's practices were cruel and issued a proclamation, that he preach to children about 'God instead of sowing the seeds of imbecility and bigotry in their little minds.'

"Hallelujah, Emperor Norton. I think I would have liked you," I interjected.

"He became so popular that some local merchants capitalized, selling souvenirs with his image. He was San Francisco's first tourist attraction until he passed away in 1880."

"Wow! To think I have lived here my whole life and never knew anything about him apart from his name!" I gave Andy a hug and he reciprocated. "With the success you are going to have at the Old Keg Inn, you're going to be my butter and egg man, so you won't have to walk around the city a poor man making proclamations."

"Well, if I fail, what proclamations should I make?"

"You are not going to fail. You are too intelligent for that. But, if for some unseen reason that were to happen, your first proclamation will be that you will remain kind to me my whole life. The second is that you will never cheat on me like my father did to my mother. The third proclamation is that we will raise a family and take them to a magical place like the Russian River, where families stay together and are happy." I began to tear up, recalling the painful memories of my childhood. I kept wiping off the tears, hoping the steady wind would make them evaporate. I became a little embarrassed as I couldn't turn off my internal faucet, no doubt due to my pregnancy. My face just needed more time to dry. Andy grabbed his handkerchief, dabbed at my wet face, and gave me a soft kiss on the lips. I took a deep breath while I collected my thoughts. "And lastly … lastly, we'll raise a family that will be better educated than we are. If you can do that, I will promise to always be by your side." I forgot to include no heavy drinking. Quite an oversight, as I came to realize later.

"Ann, I can do that. I'm going to repeat those proclamations right now." Andy went through the whole list that I had given him, and it made me feel warm inside. We sat embracing each other for another couple of minutes. We got off the bench and made our way to the car, with the clams in hand, and went back to fixing-up the tavern.

Andy painted the interior of the Old Keg Inn to have an antique look using grey and silver. He said that he didn't want it to look "shit brindle brown," a term he used frequently when he did not like the color of something. It turned out to look pretty nifty.

The bar had comfortable, private booths for women. Local union officials found the booths convenient for conducting union business and collecting dues. One of Andy's regulars was an agent for the Laundry Drivers' union named Jack Shelly. He had been a friend of his father's and was now a friend of Andy as well. Shelly later became a Congressman and then the Mayor of San Francisco. Those booths would often get smoke-filled by the end of the union meetings. Andy did smoke cigarettes, but didn't do it too often at work. He did, however, carry a lighter in case a patron at the bar needed to light one up.

He also kept a pack of cards at the bar in case someone wanted to play a game of something like poker, pinochle, or war. Most of the time, however, it was just used by patrons to bet against Andy for a free drink. They would each draw a card and the highest number won. If the patron won, they would get a free drink. If Andy won, he made that patron pay for someone else's drink. It didn't make sense to me as the recipient of the drink from the losing patron would've had to buy their drink anyway. Half of the time it was just money down the drain and the other half of the time it was a whitewash. I tried to convince Andy to change that habit, but he wanted to keep people happy.

Andy often turned the radio up at the bar when sporting events like boxing matches or football games were broadcast. He particularly liked it when the Catholic college of Notre Dame played a football game. Andy couldn't sing well, but when I would stop by during the first few months of the tavern's operation, I would catch him singing with patrons and would join in.

Andy had two brothers, Tim and Dan, and a sister, Josephine. They came over to the bar to celebrate our opening. Instead of calling me by my first name Ann, they called me 'Anna Banana.' At first, I thought it was funny and endearing. However, after every other sentence became Anna Banana, I jokingly said they could call me Queen Ann instead. Boy, that was a mistake. From then on, any time they thought I was controlling an action of Andy's that they didn't like, they would say that the Queen or the Grand Duchess was behind it.

Perhaps they had forgotten that I hadn't grown up in a wealthy family. Far from it. I tended to wear nice clothes, but they had no idea everything would come from garage sales, flea markets, second-hand stores, and rummage sales. I carried a fine leather handbag, and when I wanted to look stylish, I wore an over-the-wrist Avenue bag. When they made a Grand Duchess comment, Andy reminded them that I was a member of the White family. He said the Whites living on Nevada Street were known for being "so poor that they don't have a pot to piss in nor a window to throw it out of."

By late January 1934, I'm sure I looked less stylish than before. My belly had expanded, and I was about seven and a half months pregnant. I quit work at O'Connor, Moffatt and Co. Though I had enjoyed working there, my sights were set on becoming a mother, and I looked forward to it.

I made a habit of stopping by the bar to have a mocktail with lemon, lime, and soda water a couple of times a week. People at the tavern were friendly. Though over half of Andy's patrons came from the surrounding neighborhoods of the Castro and Mission Districts, Noe Valley, and Bernal Heights they also came from all parts of San Francisco and included clientele of every race and ethnicity. Andy became friends with Japanese, Jewish, and Italian Americans. One of his Italian American friends named Joey would always give Andy a bear hug and call him a mick, and Andy reciprocated by patting him on the back while calling him a dago. They would laugh and Andy would always give him his first drink on the house.

One time when I walked into the bar, I saw patrons singing. Andy, unbeknownst to me, had been given a music conductor's baton and was directing his lively and overwhelmingly inebriated clients to sing Irving Berlin's *Puttin' on the Ritz*, as if Fred Astaire were singing the song before him. I remember one part of the song:

"High hats and colored collars,
white spats and fifteen dollars,
spending every dime
for a wonderful time.

If you're blue, and you don't know where to go,
why don't you go where Harlem flits,
puttin' on the Ritz."

I had never seen Andy so happy. Running the bar was indeed his dream fulfilled.

We had our first child, a boy, in March 1934, and named him Daniel, after Andy's father. He was born at Mary's Help Hospital. Andy insisted that Daniel not be circumcised in order to save money.

When we left the hospital with our helpless newborn, I was so terrified that I wanted to take the nurses home with me to tell me what to do. Upon returning home, Andy popped open a bottle of champagne to celebrate Daniel's arrival. But his seemingly innocent celebration turned into a drinking binge. Within a few days, Andy was on a bender and had spent the money we had saved not getting the circumcision. Though emotional and upset, I had so many tasks at hand and plenty on my mind that I couldn't properly address Andy's behavior. The bender lasted about a week. Initially I received no help from him, but when he sobered up, he finally aided with diaper changing and taking the baby for a few hours so I could rest.

After a rough first month of sleepless nights and learning little Danny's different cries I got the hang of it and for the first time understood why every mother believed their baby was the most precious one. I was so enamored with my son, and life became better than ever.

Overall, times were good. However, there were some potential financial threats that year to Andy's business. In May that year, the historic West Coast Waterfront Strike occurred, and it was a hot topic at the bar. Longshoremen in every US West Coast port walked out, leaving scabs, people willing to cross the picket lines, to do the bulk of the work unloading and loading ships. San Francisco longshoremen called the Embarcadero 'the slave market.' Every morning, unemployed workers and transients would eagerly gather for work. The hiring boss would stand before them and pick those he pleased. Confrontations arose between the longshoremen and police who were present to protect the scabs. The strike resulted in the deaths of two longshoremen on what was known as Bloody Thursday, on July 5. One was a former World War I veteran and the other a union cook. Both were shot in the back by the police. This led to another strike involving over 150,000 dock workers in the Bay Area alone. Fortunately, those strikes eventually ended and there was not too much disruption to Andy's business.

On October 12, 1934, in the northeast corner of San Francisco, Coit Tower on Telegraph Hill opened to the public. The construction was made possible by a posthumous donation from another eccentric San Franciscan, Lillie Coit. When Coit was fifteen years old, she witnessed a firetruck from the Knickerbocker Engine Company No.5 respond to a call. The outfit was shorthanded, and she helped pull the engine up Telegraph Hill by rope, beating other engines trying to race to the inferno. She was nicknamed 'Firebelle Lil' and was made an honorary member of the fire department. Thereafter she often accompanied the men on fire calls.

Coit later married a man who worked on San Francisco's Stock Exchange in 1868, but got divorced by 1880. Divorce was rare in those days, with only one in 2,500 people experiencing it. She liked to hunt, smoke cigars, and wear trousers before it became socially acceptable for a woman to do so. She was also an ardent gambler and dressed like a man to get into men-only gambling dens in North Beach, where she was known to be an excellent poker player.

After Lillie Coit died, she left a third of her fortune for 'adding to the beauty of the city.' Using the bequeathed funds, a two hundred and ten-foot cylindrical art deco tower was constructed. Although we were led to believe this was not intentional, after its completion, San Franciscans could not help but notice that the building resembled a firehose nozzle. Using capital from President Roosevelt's New Deal Pilot Art Program, twenty-five artists were commissioned to paint murals within its interior. Before its intended grand opening on July 7, 1934, the most influential person on the committee, responsible for allocating the art funds, noticed that some of the artwork appeared to have leftist themes and alerted Washington D.C. That member ordered that the tower remain closed to the public, and doors were padlocked. The windows were painted over to obstruct any peering eyes. One of the frescos was painted with the communist symbol of a hammer and sickle with the caption: 'Workers of the World Unite.' Another mural depicted workers underneath a banner of the communist publication called *Western Worker*.

A journalist with *The San Francisco Chronicle* caught wind of the controversy, and on July 3, penned the headline *"Is This Red Propaganda? Murals On Coit Shaft Hint Plot for Red Cause."* Before too long, US officials ordered that the controversial murals be painted over. The artist who painted the hammer and sickle refused. He was supported by the Artists' and Writers' Union, which picketed in front of the tower for two weeks, wanting no government interference. However, sixteen of the twenty-five artists signed a statement agreeing that they were opposed to the hammer and sickle and stated that it has no place in the subject matter assigned. In the end, the two most controversial murals were painted over.

Though Andy and I were not political zealots, we, along with most San Franciscans at the time, were happy with the decision. More than anything, we just wanted to visit the tower. We celebrated in mid-October by driving to Russian Hill and traveled down Lombard Street to see the ever-changing vista now highlighting the new structure. We walked up the winding stairs within the tower and gazed at the murals. Though most of the frescos depicted everyday life, there was an emphasis on laborers, which was not an uncommon theme during the Depression.

By October 1934, Andy started drinking with patrons at the Old Keg Inn and started to come home inebriated. I tried to confront him a few times when he got home, but there was just no reasoning with a drunk person.

A few days before Halloween, I made a little Popeye the Sailor costume for our seven-month-old son Danny. I attached a pipe to his bib and stuffed rags in the arm sleeves of his long johns to give the appearance of rippling muscles, and completed the outfit with a white cap. He looked so adorable. After Andy slept off the booze from the previous evening, I brought our little boy, dressed up in the cute outfit I had made, to the breakfast table where Andy was sitting. He didn't even notice Danny's costume.

"Andy, you are out of your mind if you think you can continue to drink." I hovered over him, holding our baby. "You are going to lose the bar if you continue to do this. How are we going to feed Danny should that happen?!"

"That's not going to happen, Ann," Andy said, in an unconvincing tone.

"Please stop drinking for Danny's sake, at least." I looked into my husband's eyes as he averted his gaze.

"I'm sorry, Ann. I can cut down the drinking to a couple a day."

"No, buster." While holding Danny with my left arm, I made a fist with my right hand and briefly clenched my teeth. "You need to completely stop. You have no control over your boozing behavior. Where the hell are your priorities?"

"OK, OK, I'll stop!" Andy looked me directly in the eyes while I gave him a long, unflinching stare.

Andy did stop, but he only lasted a few weeks. When he went back on the wagon, it would usually only be weeks, not months nor years.

He gave more friends and some of his favorite patrons free drinks at the Old Keg Inn. He also got sloppy with the books. Some of his bartenders were not generating cash flow. He suspected embezzlement but couldn't prove it. The business was losing money, and we had an extra mouth to feed.

In 1935, we lost the bar. The financial commitment, sweat, and tears that went into making the Old Keg Inn happen were all for naught. He was unemployed for several weeks and it scared him dreadfully. He stopped drinking again for a while. He smoked cigarettes more often and looked older than his age of thirty-four. His hair thinned and his face began to look gaunt and weathered. Fortunately, Andy pressed his suit and got himself together. He hit the job interview trail and found a job working for Floorcraft, a carpet company in San Francisco. He became a good salesman. My unpredictable, sometimes chaotic life, appeared to stabilize again.

Bette, who often visited, gave me reports on what was going on at the White household on Nevada Street. She had caught our brother Billy exiting her bedroom before he ran downstairs and exited the house. Bette had kept some cash in one of her drawers. When she went to check, the cash was gone. When he later returned, she confronted him and demanded her money back. He cocked his fist and smashed her face with full force, knocking her to the ground. She tried to get Mama to intervene, but the theft could not be proved. So, other than scolding him for belting her, Mama told Bette to "Let it go."

Billy got in trouble with the law and had been facing jail time, but was offered a diversion plan. In exchange for not carrying out detention, he agreed to work for the CCC, also known as the Civilian Conservation Corps, which was one of President Roosevelt's New Deal Programs. It took troubled young men out of their environment to work on public land planting trees, laying telephone lines, digging flood control ditches, and building walking trails, roads, and parks. He had to live away from home, which gave my mother and sisters a reprieve both mentally and financially.

In March 1937, Andy and I welcomed our second child, a little girl named Joanne. I used to stroll Joanne in a baby carriage, while walking with Danny, to visit my Aunt Mary Ann. She was still living in a flat above her grocery store on Randall Street. She let Danny pick out some hard candy from one of the bins in her store below. I would sometimes see and chat with my cousin Elsie and her little boy Frankie Junior. It had been about seven years since Elsie had lost her husband, Frankie, back in 1930 during that awful fight.

Two months after Joanne was born, the Golden Gate Bridge was completed. At the time, it became the longest suspension bridge in the world. It was initially supposed to be painted in black and yellow colors, like a bumblebee, so it could be seen in the fog by ships entering the Bay. However, after painting some of the steel with an orange-red primer undercoat, it looked so appealing that the consulting architect chose it as the official, permanent color.

In 1938, we adopted a black cocker spaniel who had a habit of rolling in the dirt. I named him Hobo after the poor, dirty hobos my siblings and I had seen in the past while scavenging the city for firewood. Our kids adored him, and little Joanne especially enjoyed patting him, grabbing some dog food out of his dish and feeding it to him from her tiny hand.

That same year, during the summer, Andy fulfilled one of the promises he had made to me. We took our first week-long vacation. He had wanted to go to the beach town of Santa Cruz and talked about a wooden rollercoaster called the Giant Dipper, which had opened back in 1924. One of his friends said that when riding the Giant Dipper, it felt like you were going to crack your head on the wooden beams above you when the coaster dipped, then swooped upward, in one section. I had to convince Andy that it would be pointless to visit the rollercoaster when our children were so young.

"Joanne obviously can't go on the rollercoaster, and Danny isn't going to meet the height requirement. So that leaves you riding the coaster by yourself when I have to babysit the kids. Is that fair? Do you still think you're eleven years old?"

"Maybe, but how long will that take? Besides that, I can watch the kids and let you ride."

"I'm not going to go by myself on a death-defying contraption! You know I'm scared of heights. Aside from that, if Danny sees one of us go, and he isn't allowed to ride, he's going to have a temper tantrum."

"I just want to go before they tear down that ride. All these wooden rollercoasters are going to be replaced by steel ones soon. Aside from that, there is a horse carousel there that the kids can ride, and there is a lovely beach they can play on."

"Why can't we just go to the Russian River? The kids can still play with sand toys and play in the water. It'll be fun. I have longed to go back." I was going to muster up tears to drive home my wishes, but the tears flowed before I could force it to happen. "I feel like I was cheated when my family went."

Andy conceded, and we went to the Russian River that summer of '38 with Hobo in tow. Unlike the fateful trip back in 1925, with the White family I had grown up in, only good memories were formed with my new Scannell family of four. We no longer needed a diesel-powered ferry boat to cross the Bay. We ventured over the 1.7-mile-long Golden Gate Bridge, looking up at the massive towers and cables above us. We spotted ships in the Bay and wildflowers and cypress trees on the strips of land connecting each end of the bridge. Our trip was a lot quicker than the trip I took in 1925. By that time, speed limits on the highways had increased to thirty-five miles per hour. Between that and not having to take a ferry, our trip time had been cut in half, to less than three hours. On our Scannell family trip, I noticed a revival of wineries, and many of the hillsides were picturesque, with grapevines stretching for hundreds of yards. During the 1930s, Sonoma County had gained 4,000 acres of vine fruit. We stayed in the village of Rio Nido and not in an isolated cabin away from town. That year, we mostly played on Rio Nido Beach.

Every summer from then on, we took our kids to the Russian River. We all enjoyed the resort campfires with entertainment, swimming, paddling in canoes, fishing, watching big bands play at a dance hall, eating ice cream, horseback riding, and going to the movies. We developed fabulous, long-lasting memories. I didn't care for the slogan of Rio Nido, however: *'memories that linger.'* My memories from 1925, when my father passed out and didn't participate in our first campfire, and when we had to head back home due to his pneumonia, were ones that I wished I could forget.

In 1939, our five-year-old son Danny was invited by his Uncle Tim Scannell and Aunt Eileen to attend a World's Fair, the

Golden Gate International Exposition, held at Treasure Island. Treasure Island was a new island, artificially built in the middle of San Francisco Bay. To get there and back, they took a ferry. Danny came back in the evening, animated. There was an amusement section for children called Gayway. He watched monkeys driving miniature cars around a racetrack. However, the thing that excited him most was a television exhibit. Danny said, "I got to go on TV!" Television was a relatively new invention, and no one we knew owned one yet. In 1927, a San Franciscan by the name of Philo Farnsworth invented the first fully functional, all-electric television system on Green Street. The one my son saw was just some closed-circuit broadcast for fairgoers, but it made a deep impression on Danny. The other thing that impressed Danny and my in-laws was the spectacular neon lights that were turned on at the fair just as they were about to go back via ferry to the city.

My brother-in-law Tim told Andy that the NCAA was hosting their first-ever basketball tournament and that the Western Regional Final was going to take place at the California Coliseum, adjacent to the fairgrounds, on Treasure Island. He brought back a colorful map sponsored by Shell Oil showing its location. It seemed like both Andy and his brother were drooling just looking at it. I can't remember if Andy went to those finals, but he attended multiple sporting events, including basketball, baseball, football, and occasionally horse racing with his brothers. The fair would continue into 1940.

In 1940, we moved into a larger home on 28th Street in San Francisco, owned by Andy's mother Mary. It was a pleasant two-story home with detailed molding around window frames and on the interior ceilings. It had four bedrooms and two bathrooms. My children would get to have their own rooms. We paid Mary rent at a discounted rate and fixed up the home. Andy was under the impression that we would get the house in the future if he maintained it as well as the cottage in the back.

As time went on, my youngest sister Theresa, who had developed into a jaw-droppingly gorgeous young woman, did some modeling work. She also briefly became a singer, and I got to hear her on the radio. She was good, but she was no Mildred Bailey. It never amounted to a career in singing for her. Nevertheless, it was an exciting event to turn on the radio and hear my own sister singing!

Like all good Catholic families, we attended church regularly, as well as for baptisms and confirmations. However, Andy was never as committed to Catholicism as I was. He attended all the Catholic functions because that was what he felt he was supposed to do. He criticized priests, saying that most of them did not practice what they preached, then he would grab a cigarette and walk outside for a smoke. At first, I thought he felt that way because he had not experienced the same immersion in Catholicism as I had growing up. However, his parents had been incredibly committed to the church, and Andy had similar schooling through his parish, so it did not make sense to me. However, as a teenager, Andy switched high schools from a Catholic one, Sacred Heart High School, to Mission High School, a public one.

I had noticed that Andy never left our kids alone with any of the priests. He insisted that he be present when they had to go to confession. It wasn't until one evening that his behavior started to make sense. He had been out with friends drinking on New Year's Eve and came home quite drunk at about two o'clock in the morning. He came to the front door wearing a thick coat, and I could see his breath in the cold winter air. His breath was acidic and smelled like alcohol. He was making too much noise and stumbled into the house.

"Hush, you're going to wake up the kids," I chided him. "Go to the bathroom and clean up."

Andy started to walk past me. "You never can be too careful going to the bathroom at a Catholic school. One of the brothers is liable to stick it up your bunghole," he slurred.

"Wha ... what are you talking about Andy?" I spluttered. He continued walking and wobbled into the bathroom. I prodded but couldn't get any more information.

The following day, I waited until he was sober to find out what he meant. He said he did not remember saying that to me and really didn't want to talk about it. I never found out if he had been traumatized.

I couldn't fathom that a Catholic teacher, or any other member of the Catholic community, would have harmed him, especially in that fashion but I had heard stories from other people about abuses of some Catholic authorities, and it did make me suspicious. However, if you were traumatized during that time, you didn't go to the police, and surely you would not tell

Ann Scannell, née White, early 1940s

a priest. You would be excommunicated from the church just for making an allegation. A significant portion of the police officers in our community were Irish Catholic, and some attended our church, so bringing something of that nature to their attention would just bring trouble.

CHAPTER SEVENTEEN

My mother-in-law, Mary, developed poor health and moved into the cottage she owned, behind our home, the cottage where Andy and I had previously lived. Being originally from County Kerry in the town of Glenflesk, Ireland, she had a different accent than my mother's, and at times she was a bit hard to understand. Mary had been a teacher in the old country. She had become overweight, developed a respiratory ailment and used a cane to get around. She often wore a veil over her thinning, grayish-brown hair. She was inordinately regimented with her routines, such as when she ate and did chores. While she still could, she walked down the hill to church for services at St. Paul's church every morning to attend eight o'clock Mass. In the afternoon, she sat on a wicker chair on her porch and bossed us around. Especially me, since I was home more often than Andy.

Andy was afraid of her. Although she had always been a good provider, she had been a strict disciplinarian both as a teacher and a mother.

By late 1941, the United States entered World War II after the attack on Pearl Harbor. I, along with most other people I knew, had a sense of unease, worry, and trepidation.

San Francisco became a staging area and major point of embarkation for naval and army servicemen leaving for the Pacific Theater to fight against Japan. Army personnel and sailors filled the city. During the war, about 1.65 million servicemen came through its port. The whole Bay Area began to buzz with activity. Men and women went to work building ships, with over thirty shipyards and machine shops dotting the region. One of them, Kaiser's Richmond Shipyard Number Three, built an average of 1,400 vessels a day. The Benicia munitions factory produced bombs, artillery shells, and small arms ammunition. The US Army, Coast Guard and Navy also built a vast network of airfields, training grounds, storage facilities, observation posts, and underwater minefields. They installed anti-aircraft guns, radars, and searchlights used to protect the entrance to the harbor.

President Franklin D. Roosevelt banned the production of civilian automobiles during the war. The Ford Motor Company in Richmond, CA, converted its assembly plant to building jeeps for military use and aided in the final assembly of tanks, half-track armored personnel carriers, and other military vehicles.

Shortly after the beginning of the war, my mother-in-law made her way through our backyard. She came to the foot of our back porch and banged her cane to get my attention. I came running to the back of the house to find out what all the ruckus was about. I flung open the back door.

There stood Mary, out of breath, appearing perturbed. "Ann!" she panted.

"Yes, Mary?"

"Yeh 'ave ta pull doze rosh booshes oat." She scanned the whole backyard, looking at the wide, long, beautiful flower bed I had cultivated. It included several red, white, and pink rose bushes. She began wheezing. "Yeh 'ave to pull everting oat." She balanced herself with her cane in her left hand, and the other hand drifted from her thick midriff to her right hip.

"Why?"

"Yeh nee-id ta plant a Victory Gahrden for da war effort." She looked at me in consternation.

I was no stranger to a Victory Garden as my own mother had planted one during World War I behind our home on Nevada Street. I didn't mind chipping in as it was a patriotic thing to do at the time. However, the flower bed was quite large and not all of it needed to go. However, Mary insisted the whole thing come out. I remember asking Andy to intercede, but he refused to get involved. Mary told Andy's siblings that I had completely refused to put in a Victory Garden, which wasn't the truth. I eventually caved in before the rumor could gain traction. The flowers went, and carrots and potatoes took their place.

To make matters worse, one day Mary somehow sneaked past me into our house when I was talking to a neighbor outside in front of our home. I don't know why I didn't hear her as she would always wheeze. She went straight for the kitchen and rearranged my entire cabinet, in the order she thought was necessary, for me to be able to carry out my domestic duties. I don't know how she did it. She must have been on her tiptoes at some point, balancing herself with her cane. She managed to coax the dishes, drag the toaster, advance the bottles of oil, shift bags of sugar and other baking supplies, budge the flour sifters and move containers around to her desired locations. This was somehow so important to her she developed super strength to complete the task. This only annoyed me more and I rearranged everything back to its original location. Her actions were unnecessary and antagonistic.

To calm my nerves, I sang to myself as I had done in the past. To make me laugh I sang *I'll Never Smile Again* by Tommy Dorsey. It did the trick for a while at least.

One day, Mary saw Danny playing in the backyard and told him to come into her cottage where she would bake some muffins for him. She thought he lacked discipline and made him sit in a chair in the kitchen while the muffins were baking. When he started to move, she swatted him with her cane. She asked, "What's da ma'er widh ya? Do ya have Saint Vitus' dance?"

She smacked Danny with her cane on more than one occasion, to the point he didn't want to go outside in case she would spot him. I was upset about her abusive behavior and asked Andy to intervene. He took his mother's side again, reminding me she had been a respected teacher in the old country and that "she would never hit him unless he deserved it."

I took matters into my own hands. I had fended for myself well enough in my life to make it that far. I wasn't about to completely chew off the hand that partially fed me but one evening I got the courage to march right over to her cottage and confront her.

Mary answered the door wearing nightclothes. "It's moighty leht to be disturbin' me loike dis," she griped, with a sour expression. It was only a few minutes past 9:00 p.m. She was as crabby as ever.

I clenched my fists. "In regard to your cane-lashing of Danny, if I weren't getting cheap rent and did not appreciate all the things you've done for Andy and me, I might have punched you in the face already." This caught her off guard and she didn't respond. She looked quite dumbfounded.

"So, please don't use your cane on Danny. Thank you for your attention to this matter." I slowly turned around and left.

Though things did quiet down a little, unfortunately Andy began drinking heavily again. He started to develop red blotches and bumps on his face. Patches of small blood vessels erupted and facial flushing became common. Andy also developed thick wrinkles. Coupled with his now balding head, he looked weathered. His mother was bitterly disappointed in him. She heartily disliked his drinking despite the fact she herself liked to belt down a glass of port before dinner and when her appetite lagged. Andy often made the mistake of coming home and falling to the floor drunk, and he insisted on going to visit Mary over my vehement objections.

Most of the time Andy didn't drink when he was home, at least not at that time. He was good to the kids and even carved out time to coach Danny's Little League baseball team one year. He didn't drink on the days he held practices. Things did seem to turn around a little. He also attended dance performances that our daughter Joanne was involved in. Joanne had learned Irish dances at our parish and performed in a group, on a float, dancing the Irish jig during a St. Patrick's day parade held in San Francisco. Andy was an avid reader like me and often read stories to the kids.

He had a knack for fixing things. Unlike the home I had grown up in, Andy repaired our home when it needed it. He tinkered with our furnace when it broke and coaxed it back to life. He had no problem fixing cracked pipes. When our house needed painting, he erected scaffolding and painted the whole house by himself. He also helped my mother with repairs at her house, in addition to helping fix things at his mother's cottage behind. Partly for these reasons and trauma he may have suffered when he was younger, I tried to look past the drinking.

With World War II in full swing there were many other things to focus on. We sat around our Emerson radio with its glossy, grand wooden frame and listened to fireside chats given by President

Franklin Roosevelt. We heard rants of Hitler speaking in German, and he sounded like he was shouting at the world with a rapid, feverish, wrathful, crescendoing voice. It was terrifying.

There were many efforts both inside and outside the church to help with the war effort. Our whole family volunteered with many fundraisers. Metal and rubber became in short supply. Paper dolls began replacing rubber ones. Our church had us gather cans, rubber, paper, and even chicken fat to be given to the military. Chicken fat was used to make explosives.

In addition to wartime production facilities around the San Francisco Bay Area, across the United States, many industries converted into war production. Even toy companies like the Lionel train company produced items for warships, including compasses, in New Jersey.

At Westinghouse Electric in Michigan, a labor shortage occurred. The need for women to enter the workforce grew. In addition to training women for technical positions, like electrical engineering, the need for riveters, welders, and assembly line workers increased. They began depicting an image of a fictional character called Rosie the Riveter after a song by the same name. She became a patriotic American icon of a strong woman willing to do hard labor to contribute to the wartime effort.

In the Spring 1942, the US Government established rationing programs that set limits on the amount of gas, clothing, and food that we could purchase. We were issued ration stamps that were used to buy our allotment of everything from sugar, fat, meat, butter, vegetables, and fruit to gas, tires, clothing, and fuel oil. Rationing and shortages became regular topics of conversation in our community. Due to the rationing of fabric, fashion styles began to change. Men's suits became cuff-less, and vests disappeared. Women's slacks and skirts became shorter and slimmer.

Acting on an executive order signed by President Roosevelt in February 1942, Japanese Americans, as well as citizens of Japan who were awaiting American citizenship, who were living on the West Coast and parts of Arizona, were forced to move to detention centers. A significant number from San Francisco were taken to the Tanforan Assembly Center in San Bruno, CA, and herded into horse stalls, at an old racetrack, before they were sent to other camps further away from the coastline. The fear was that there could be spies among them or that acts of sabotage could be carried out by some. There was quite a bit of fear and hatred of the Japanese in general at that time. Those fears only worsened when a Japanese submarine shelled the California coast on February 23, 1942. Almost no one questioned the internment of Japanese citizens who were new arrivals to the US, even if they had good intentions. However, about two-thirds of those rounded up were Japanese Americans who had been in the United States for decades. My husband and I opposed the internment, which was an unpopular view at the time. Andy had become friends with a Japanese American named Tom, whom he had known since the days of The Old Keg Inn. His friend was interned initially at Tanforan. Our family drove out to help him with paperwork involving his property. When we arrived, we were greeted by menacing fences covered with barbed wire and guard towers.

After parking the car, Andy told us to wait. While still sitting in the driver's seat, he rolled down the window and lit up a cigarette. He smoked for a few minutes, blowing smoke out the driver's side window, before grabbing the paperwork and getting out of the car. "What's right is right," he announced. He looked at the barbed wire, and sarcastically added, "Who's wrong is nobody," before walking off.

We waited in the parking lot for over an hour. The appearance of the compound looked especially frightening to Danny. Armed guards stood inside towers. It gave him a peculiar, unsettled feeling. He wanted to get the hell out of there and was relieved when his father was done and had accomplished his mission.

In April 1942, the US Military took over Treasure Island in the San Francisco Bay. No longer were there pretty neon lights during the years of the fair. An airfield and naval base were established there. Navy personnel were trained in firefighting and chemical warfare and a training school for electronics and radio communications was developed. From certain vantage points in San Francisco, we could see airplanes, blimps, and dirigibles as well as hangars.

We would see more military airplanes flying over San Francisco. Andy taught our kids how to identify the planes. We saw the navy's F6F Hellcats, P-38 Lightning fighters, and the P-51 Mustangs. On rare occasions, we would see and hear the loud bombers like the B-24 Liberator and B-17s. Though the war made us worry, seeing those planes gave us some sense of security.

Sometime later in 1942, Andy's mother noticed that Danny was avoiding her. Andy encouraged him to go over to grandma's cottage with his little sister Joanne. Mary didn't smack them with her cane, but when they got back home, Danny let me know of a conversation he had with his grandmother. She asked him if his school was teaching them that "Jews killed Jesus." She told him: "Dat's why dey 'ave no hoomland ta dis day. Dat's why dey arr cawled wanderin' Jews."

It was hard to believe that Andy and his mother were related. They did not seem to be cut from the same cloth. I didn't know Andy's father well before he died but thought that Andy must have obtained his morals and traits from him. Being from an Irish Catholic culture, which had been repressed itself, I was surprised to hear that those words had come from Mary's mouth. My first thought was that she had been essentially isolated among parish communities in the US and that Andy and I, being first generation Americans, had greater exposure to different cultures. But I certainly could not excuse Mary's behavior. She'd plenty of time to assimilate and surely had had enough interactions that she ought to have known better.

My mother, who was similar in age, was quite the opposite. Though Mama kept her Irish traditions she made it a priority to learn about other cultures, races, and religions. She went out of her way to greet and converse with people of different backgrounds regardless if they were Black, Latino, Indian, Asian, Protestant or Jewish Americans. She gave everyone respect. Both women may have been well-meaning but had polarized views of the world.

As time went on, I became increasingly involved in following the news of the war. I had found out my brother Billy was drafted into the army and sent to the Pacific theater. I studied the troop movements and all the island-hopping that our military was involved in. All the time, good news was reported in the newspapers, but I knew all too well that everything was not always rosy. There were plenty of death announcements of servicemen who were killed during the war, and I knew some families who had lost a child in the war.

During those years, air wardens led practice drills in San Francisco in case of an aerial attack, and we had to shut off the lights when it became dark. The exception to this rule was blackout bulbs. We installed blackout bulbs inserted into lamp sockets to get some traces of light. Enough light at least to prevent us from tripping while going to the bathroom. Occasionally, bright searchlights were flashed in the sky and sirens would go off as part of the drills.

Andy continued working for the Floorcraft carpet company during the war. He had worked there for eight years since 1935, when in March 1943 I received a call from his floor manager, Lyle. I was in the kitchen, chopping onions, getting dinner ready. The day was cloudy. Danny and Joanne, then aged nine and six, were talking to me about their favorite movies and had just started to sing *Follow The Yellow Brick Road* as they had seen Judy Garland perform in *The Wizard of Oz*, when the phone rang.

"Danny, can you answer the phone?"

"Why can't you do it?" Danny whined, as the phone rang a second time.

"Can't you see I'm covered in onion juice!" I grit my teeth, and it rang again.

"OK, hold on." He picked up the phone. "Hello? Mom, it's for you."

"Who is it?"

"It's Lyle, from Dad's work." I couldn't hear Danny too well as Joanne continued singing *Follow The Yellow Brick Road* as she skipped through the kitchen.

"Did you say Daddy's work?" Danny nodded. "Joanne, stop singing for a minute." *Oh my God*, I thought. *Why would Andy's work be calling?* I hurried over to the sink to start washing my hands. "Danny, bring the phone to me." As I wiped my hands on a towel, he pulled the phone cord toward me holding the phone with an outstretched hand. I gripped the phone between my left ear and shoulder. "Hello, this is Ann, who is this?"

"It's Lyle from Floor Craft," the voice said, in a matter-of-fact manner. "Ann, I have some bad news." I shut off the water to the sink and started to dry my now trembling hands. Unsure if Andy had had an accident, I became concerned. I pursed my lips, grabbing the phone with my right hand, pushing it tightly to my right ear so I could hear.

"What happened?" I closed my eyes to receive the information.

"Your husband Andy has been drinking."

"Oh, dear Lord!" I clapped my free hand to my forehead. "I am so sorry."

"No, I am sorry, Ann, the boss fired him. He is currently sleeping on our showroom floor, curled up in a carpet roll, and we need you to come get him right now."

Worry suddenly morphed into fury. "Son of a bitch!" My whole body began to shake. Joanne started to sing again. "Knock it off, Joanne!" I barked.

I felt like hurling the cutting board full of onions across the kitchen, but I reeled that thought in. I could feel the bulging of a vein in my forehead. I put the phone down for a few seconds, clenched both of my fists, then released them and started to take slow, deep breaths. Joanne began to cry, and I grabbed the phone again. "Hold on a second, Lyle." I put the phone down and gave my six-year-old daughter a hug. "I am so sorry, Joanne, I didn't mean to frighten you." I looked up and saw Danny, who was silent and looked petrified. He also hadn't seen me so visibly shaken before. "Lyle, I can't drive. I don't know how to. Also, I don't know what to do with my kids."

"Well, someone needs to get down here and get him. The sooner the better. We can't have him here like this. We have had clientele walk out already, and he is going to ruin Floorcraft's reputation!"

"You are worried about Floorcraft's reputation? Seriously?!" Seething with anger, I started to pant. Then I briefly regained my composure. "I will figure something out. I just need to get my kids situated." I hung up the phone.

I pondered over what to do with Danny and Joanne. Most of my relatives living in San Francisco did not drive, aside from a few. There was not usually a need to, not with the extensive public transportation system in place. I called the home of Andy's brother Tim. His wife Eileen answered and said Tim had just left and taken their only car to pick up a friend and was headed to a basketball game. I tried to reach another relative, but no one answered. It was getting dark, and started to rain. I was left with very few alternatives.

I gathered my kids. "Danny and Joanne, I need you two to stay with Grandma Mary. I need to go pick up your Daddy from work."

Danny protested Immediately. "Please don't leave me with Grandma!"

"I will go," Joanne said. She had not experienced the wrath of her grandmother's cane before.

"Dad's in trouble, isn't he?" Danny asked pointedly.

"Yes, your father has been drinking again." I reluctantly called Mary, whose physical health had deteriorated even more, but could still pick up the phone and call for help in case of an emergency. I wasn't too worried about her being able to care for my daughter. She agreed to take Joanne for a few hours.

I bundled both kids into raincoats and dropped Joanne off. Danny and I walked with umbrellas to a streetcar pick-up area. We boarded the streetcar and headed for Floorcraft, changing lines once.

When we arrived, I saw Andy's car parked on the street. We folded our umbrellas and entered the store. I was fully expecting to see Andy with a cup of coffee in hand getting sobered up. Instead, the floor manager greeted me by handing Andy's coat and car keys to me and told me he was still sleeping inside the roll of carpet.

"Haven't you the decency to at least get him out of there before I arrived?!" I was about to lose it.

"We tried, Ann, but he was being belligerent, and we didn't want to cause a scene," Lyle replied awkwardly.

"A scene?" I seethed. Scanning the showroom floor, I spotted the largest tube of rolled carpet. It was a tube with a bold pattern of multicolored red, yellow, and brown leaves. Sure enough, Andy had made this tube his temporary home. I crawled into the cylinder and could smell the pungent odor of alcohol on his breath. "Let's go, Andy," I commanded. There wasn't a stir. I grabbed his shoulder. "Wake up, Andy!" He barely flinched. Pinching his nose, I repeated: "Wake up Andy!" This got his attention, and after a few seconds he woke up. We gradually made our way out of the carpet roll on all fours, only to see that a crowd of people had gathered, including customers and several other employees. He staggered to his feet. I was so livid and embarrassed, I wanted to belt him on the spot.

Lyle said, "We'll mail him his last check." I ignored him and walked out of the store with Andy, and Danny, who appeared traumatized by what he had just witnessed. We managed to get Andy to a streetcar, but he wobbled and staggered and couldn't get up into the car.

Bluntly, without allowing a second attempt, the streetcar driver said, "I can't take him, ma'am."

We started to walk back to the store, and Andy fell to the ground. He didn't appear to hurt himself, but I didn't want to have him re-enter the store in that condition.

"Danny, just stay with him for a minute," I begged.

Danny nodded, bravely. "OK, Mom, hurry!"

"Good boy. I will!" I reluctantly ran back to the store, slipping on the wet sidewalk, almost falling. There was no payphone around. Mustering what little dignity I had left, I faced the staff again. They were still huddled together, gossiping about the event that had occurred inside the store. "I need to borrow your phone and call for a taxi."

"Sure, Ann," Lyle replied, uneasily. "Just go into my office and use my phone."

I was able to get a taxi, and Danny helped me load his father into the front passenger seat of the car. Danny and I piled into the back of the taxi. We were all sopping wet from the rain. The car reeked of alcohol in no time, and it annoyed the driver, who began to make some derogatory comments. When we reached our home, I couldn't get Andy out of the car onto the sidewalk, let alone into the house. I offered the taxi driver a generous tip to help me get my husband out of the car and up the stairs to our front door. I ended up giving him $10 to get him to agree. The taxi ride itself cost under a dollar. After getting Andy settled I went to the cottage out back and collected Joanne. The nightmare of that evening finally ended.

After the job loss, I started worrying dreadfully about our finances again. This brought me back to the time during Prohibition when Papa had died, and our income was cut off. I didn't want to have to penny-pinch but was forced to start doing some of the things my mother had done, like stretching out meals.

Fortunately, Andy was able to get a job as a postal worker. He never complained about his new line of work and was characteristically good-natured, despite having lost the bar and his job at the carpet company. As far as I knew, he didn't drink at work, doing that job, but he did continue to drink by often going to a bar for an hour or so after work. However, he got home at an earlier time than he used to. He usually would sober up in time to participate in some family activities.

In 1944, Andy got free tickets to see Oakland Oaks Baseball games. After the fight in 1930 between Max Baer and Frankie Campbell, Andy kept in touch with Dolph Camilli, Frankie's brother. Dolph played Major League Baseball with four teams but was most remembered for his 1941 MVP season with the Brooklyn Dodgers. He became a player manager with the Oakland Oaks, a minor league team in 1944. Andy had no qualms about calling him up to talk about baseball. This inevitably led to Dolph offering free tickets. It made Andy feel important, as if he were contributing to something invaluable to the Scannell family.

Our whole family enjoyed going to those games. It gave us a reprieve from thinking about the war. Some of the games were played in San Francisco, and some were played across the Bay in Emeryville, near Oakland. When we traveled to the East Bay, it was an all-day affair. We went via what was called the Key System. We took a streetcar down to the Transbay Terminal near Mission and Beale Streets. Then we took a train that ran on the lower deck of the Bay Bridge to the East Bay. From there we took a series of streetcars to get to the ballpark known as Oaks Park. The ballpark was always packed. The smell of hot dogs and popcorn permeated the air. Vendors walked through the crowd, calling "Get your hot links here!" They sold other items, including ice cream, malts, and red hots. We watched players like Cotton Pippen, Johnny Lotz, Les Scarsella, and Manny Salvo lead their team to a winning record. After the games, kids were allowed onto the field. Joanne and Danny enjoyed sprinting around the bases and running through the outfield. They would later say the games were among their greatest memories of the World War II era.

During that period, my youngest sister Theresa married a serviceman named Joe, who was then shipped off to fight in the Pacific theater.

On June 6, 1944, the United States and its allies gained a foothold in Europe, with the invasion of the French coast of Normandy, in what was known as the D-Day landings.

To my delight, I soon learned that my brother Billy, William D. White, was awarded a Silver Star for bravery in combat on the Island of Saipan in the same month. He had rescued his squad leader, who had been wounded in a gun battle, and crossed an open field carrying him over his shoulder to safety while being fired upon by an enemy machine-gun nest. He had finally done something good and noble with his life.

That same year, my mother-in-law's health deteriorated rapidly. Andy's brother Tim came by often and helped Andy's mother in the cottage behind our home. He had to give her enemas before she passed away that year. I never admitted it, but I was frankly relieved she had passed on. I had enough things to worry about aside from an irritable, old woman trying to manipulate me.

Andy's siblings said, though domineering, Mary had been a good provider growing up and was especially caring when her children were ill. Andy's sister Josephine said, "She was a wonder, and I thank God for her every day of my life." Unfortunately, I never saw Mary in that light. Even if I had put on rose-colored glasses, I wouldn't have seen a cheerful, jovial, satisfied woman.

After she died, her cranky spirit arose. Unsurprisingly, when Andy and his siblings reviewed her will, she had not divided up property among her heirs equally. Why would she? That would have been notably uncharacteristic. Andy's youngest sibling, Dan, would get only one dollar because he didn't attend church. Andy, her eldest child, would receive a little over $700 in cash and stocks, which would amount to about 5 percent of the estate. His sister Josephine would get about 35 percent and Tim was left with 60 percent. Andy and I were not greedy people, and we acknowledged that Mary helped Andy purchase his bar back in 1933, and our rent at the 28th Street property had been low. However, Andy couldn't help feeling slighted and hurt, and he began to drink more. He was under the impression his mother would bequeath him the property where we were living. He was upset that his mother made Tim the executor of her will, and that she created the imbalances during the time Tim was taking care of her in her cottage. He thought something was fishy, but having known my mother-in-law didn't surprise me. Tim, in my mind, had nothing to do with it and would definitely not have suggested that only one dollar go to his youngest brother Dan. This was something only Mary would have done. Andy argued with Tim. Josephine just wanted the estate settled quickly, and thought I was behind Andy's protests. I began to be called Grand Duchess once again.

We worried about where we would go and how we would manage on a postal salary. The whole estate affair created tension between Andy and his other siblings. Fortunately, for the time being, we were allowed to stay in the house.

CHAPTER EIGHTEEN

Shortly after his mother passed away, Andy began drinking at home, hiding bottles of liquor all around the house. I discovered that he put liquor in olive oil bottles and containers of Listerine. He only did this if there was a second bottle of the actual ingredient still in use, and would hide the liquor in the spare bottles farther back from view. He also got drunk more often. Danny and Joanne became aware that I was on a mission to rid the house of any containers of alcohol. After I went through the house and found what I thought was all my husband's stash, my seven-year-old curly-haired, freckle-faced daughter knocked on my bedroom door. Andy was at work at the time. Joanne was carrying her favorite doll with a long dress and bow in her hair.

"Daddy is still drinking," she said with a worried expression.

"How do you know that?"

"I saw him drinking before work this morning. He was holding a bottle in one hand and a screwdriver in the other."

"A screwdriver?" She nodded as indignation welled up inside of me. "The son of Joseph and Mary!"

That is when I began to think like a bootlegger. Where would a bootlegger hide booze? Where would my long-dead father William

White have hidden whiskey? That's when I carried out a definitive search of the house and discovered Andy hid booze bottles in toilet tanks and behind vents that had been screwed down tightly. I poured the liquor down the drain, but this only drove him to go back to the bars to drink and once again come home drunk. He was not an angry drunk, but he swore more often when he drank. In front of our kids, he would say certain people "didn't know their asses from second base" or "they did not know shit from Shinola." Shinola was a shoe wax brand at the time. This caused a lot of friction, and I pleaded with him to stop.

I had made a terrible mistake years ago by telling Andy where I hid some cash in case we needed to pay for hospital or doctor's bills. He pilfered that emergency coffer. In addition to booze and beer, he spent the money on horse betting. He drove down to a newsstand on Mission Street some evenings to pick up the next morning's racing form. He then spent an hour or so handicapping the next day's races so he could place bets with a bookie downtown. I didn't know the extent of it until one evening in September 1944, when Bette was over visiting, and Andy came in stumbling drunk into our living room. He came in with the stench of stale beer, and he had dollar bills, mostly twenties, stuck in his hat band, shirt collar, suit pockets, and just about everywhere else. He smiled from ear to ear while wobbling and briefly took off his hat and bowed, then put it back on.

"Ann." He hadn't noticed Bette sitting on the couch at first but spotted her out of the corner of his eye. "Oh, well, hellooo, Bette." He began to slur his speech. "I juss won a crap load of money betting on horssses today!" He was sure I would be excited. When I gave him a disapproving look, he said, "May God strike me dead if I've had a dr… drinka." For whatever good reason, God did not strike him down.

"Bette, I have an idea. You stand on one side of him, I'll stand on the other, and let's grab his waist. Andy, let's get you to bed." Like picking up an injured linebacker, we grabbed his waist with one arm, hoisted his arms around our shoulders, and guided him towards the bedroom. Andy's gait was unsteady, and he staggered, causing us to nearly tip over a couple of times. Slowly, we were able to get him to the master bedroom and lay him down on the bed.

In less than a couple of minutes, he fell sound asleep, on his back, snoring loudly and steadily. Bette and I, being petite, were like the tiny Lilliputian people in *Gulliver's Travels,* having a window of opportunity to examine the giant whilst he slumbered. We pilfered Andy's clothes to get the cash he had won. The low-lying fruit were bills stuck in his hat band, shirt, and suit pockets. That was the easy part. We still had a task at hand. There were still more bills in the back of his shirt collar, waistband, and back pocket.

Unfortunately, I had not had a chance to put sheets on the bed, and there was nothing we could grab onto, to roll him over. He was not a heavy-set man, except for a bit of a beer belly he had acquired in the preceding few years. However, he was nearly twice my weight.

"Bette, why don't you get on one side and push, and I'll get over on the other side and pull?" With grit and determination, using our tiny frames, we tried to roll him over, but it was no use. We pushed and pulled for a good couple of minutes.

"What are you feeding him, Ann?" Bette demanded. She climbed onto the bed on her knees for a brief rest. A few loose hairs started to dangle in front of Bette's face, obstructing her vision. She forcefully blew her hair to the side, only to have some of it flop back. She blew again, and the second time it worked. She looked as exhausted as I was and bit dumbfounded.

"The question is, what is he feeding himself? He probably drank five or six pints of beer today … come on, we're smarter than this. We're daughters of a crafty bootlegger, aren't we?"

"I have an idea," Bette exclaimed. "Let's get some towels and roll them up and try to get them under him to give us some leverage."

"OK, hold on." I ran to our bathroom and grabbed a couple of towels out of a dirty clothes hamper. "Here you go."

Bette sniffed the towels "Ann, these stink," she groaned.

I took a whiff, and they did smell particularly musty. "They probably have an unpleasant odor because they have been sitting in the clothes hamper for a couple of days. What does it matter anyway if they smell bad? We're just using them to roll him over."

"Yeah, but I can't do it if they offend my nostrils."

I placed my right hand over my forehead and gave her a glare. "Jeez, Bette, I don't want to have to clean an extra set of towels."

"Well, do you want my help or don't you?" She fixed me with one of her serious, narrow-eyed stares.

"Oh my God!" My eyes could not help but roll upwards. What a waste of time this was. I couldn't argue with her, and as ridiculous as her stipulation sounded, I needed her help. I went and got clean towels and tossed them to her. "Is that better?"

Bette took a good whiff of the new towels. "Oh, yes. That's the *'Hustle-Bubble suds smell of Oxydol!'*" She smiled as she quoted a phrase from a detergent ad.

Exhausted and in no mood for humor, I stared straight at Bette and gave an exaggerated sigh. "Good grief," I retorted. Then I gathered myself and turned my head toward Andy. "All right, let's do it," I said, speaking to Bette from the side of my mouth.

We tried again, but Bette was only able to get part of the towel under him. Then she let out a triumphant cry. "I spotted a couple more twenties!"

"Where?!" I said with excitement as a sudden rush of adrenaline came over me.

"In his waistband."

"I have an idea, Bette. Pinch his nose and see if he'll stir. If he moves, you can jam the towel rolls under him?"

"He's your husband. You pinch his nose! It sounds like you want me to do all the work." Bette caught on to me fast, but I tried. That tactic had worked in the past on her and my younger siblings, but not anymore.

Though the mission appeared difficult, with fiery determination and the will to recover as much money as I could, I pinched Andy's nose a few times, and the trick worked. Before long, he wiggled to one side, and Bette jammed the rolled towels underneath him, allowing us to roll him over to his side. We plucked the rest of the bills out, not to mention some pocket change. I gave her a celebratory hug.

It felt like we had won the Belmont Stakes. All in all, we siphoned off over $180, and change. I offered Bette some money for her help, but she refused.

"What are sisters for?" she said, grinning. "If you think about it, we were crafty bootleggers ourselves."

Bette and I had managed to recoup enough money to cover most of what Andy had stolen from our Scannell family emergency fund.

He had been outsmarted, and I sewed the bills into one of my coat pockets. When he sobered up, I got him to 'fess-up about the stolen money and the extent of his gambling. He apologized and agreed not to do anything like that again. Somehow, he expected me to give him his winnings back, but I wouldn't allow it.

As the months went on, things started to settle down in our household again. We learned from newspapers and radio broadcasts that the Allies gained more ground in Europe and the US troops crossed into Germany in March 1945. It became clear that we would become victorious.

Franklin D. Roosevelt, who had served as our president since March 4, 1933, had envisioned a post-war organization to help maintain world order called the United Nations. He would never get to see that institution in operation. He died on April 12, 1945, at the age of sixty-three, following a stroke while on a break at Warm Springs, Georgia, where he had started a polio treatment center in the late 1920s.

Before the war ended, delegates from nations around the world were invited to San Francisco to establish the United Nations. Its main purpose was to prevent future wars, maintain peace and security, and promote cooperation on social, economic, and humanitarian issues. The conference started on April 25 at the Memorial Opera House on Van Ness Avenue. It initially included representatives from forty-six nations and expanded to fifty. The conference lasted about two months.

On a Monday, May 7, 1945, Germany surrendered to the Allies. Celebrations rang out in Times Square, in New York City, starting on May 7, and were followed by celebrations across the country, including in San Francisco on May 8. It would later become known that Hitler committed suicide a week earlier.

Fighting continued in the Pacific theater, however. Though the Allies made progress, getting closer to mainland Japan, the fight was far from over. The stark truth was that 80 to 90 percent of troops coming from the West Coast had been sent to fight in the Pacific as opposed to Europe. Anywhere from 200,000 to 1 million Allied casualties were expected once mainland Japan was breached. The general mood was not as euphoric on the West Coast as it had been in the East.

The war in the Pacific ended just three months later, in August 1945, shortly after atomic bombs were dropped over Hiroshima and Nagasaki. Some Americans were ambivalent about the atomic bombs, others were joyous, but I, along with many others, was just relieved that the war was over. The US would be victorious once again. Celebrations once again reverberated across the city. There were parades, such as one that went down the old Market Street. The liquor flowed and the celebrations continued for days. Some people climbed up lampposts and waved flags. Others set bonfires.

Further good news on a family level arrived for us: Andy's brother Tim, the executor of their mother's will, came up with a unique solution that would keep Andy's extended family intact. He decided to give us the home on 28th Street which was worth about $3,000 at that time, except that Andy would have to take a loan out for $1,500 against the house and give that amount to Dan, his brother who had only been bequeathed one dollar by his mother. It gave us only half a mortgage. Though Andy was not entirely thrilled about the arrangement, I was certainly happy. I felt like an entire chapter of my life had closed.

I celebrated the end of the war by digging up part of the Victory Garden, and planting flowers. In addition to red and pink roses, I planted a native perennial yellow flower, very aptly called *Achillea moonshine*.

CHAPTER NINETEEN

On October 24, 1945, the United Nations was officially ratified in San Francisco at the Herbst Theater Auditorium of the Veterans' War Memorial Building. Our free tickets to Oakland Oaks games ceased as Casey Stengel became the new manager of the team in 1946, but we still listened to games on the radio. We became familiar with new players like Cookie Lavagetto, Catfish Metkovich and Billy Martin. The team ended the season of 1948 as the Pacific Coast League Champions.

My sister Bette and I remained extraordinarily close. Her history was colorful, both figuratively and literally. She had grown up with the name of Bette White and married a naval World War II veteran named Allen Brown in 1946, so she became Bette Brown. She had one child by the name of Jeanette.

Not long after the war, I reconnected again with my widowed cousin Elsie. I met up with her at Aunt Mary Ann's home one afternoon. I took Danny and Joanne there, along with my mother. Also present was Frankie Camilli Jr., a high school student at St. Ignatius High School, a Catholic school in San Francisco. Frankie Jr. was about four years older than Danny. He was handsome, and years later when James Dean appeared onscreen, I could not help but notice how the actor had resembled my cousin's son. I recollect Danny complaining about having missed his favorite radio shows that afternoon, and I told him that he was being rude. Frankie Jr. stepped right in and asked Danny about them. Then, after gathering the information, proceeded to perform the scripts for all his favorite shows. He improvised by doing all the voices of the characters. I remember Danny being in awe of Frankie Jr.

Shortly after my niece Jeanette was born in 1947, Frankie Jr., still a high school teenager at the time, wrapped a baby gift for her and walked several blocks to Bette's home to deliver it. He didn't seem a bit self-conscious about having walked through the city, holding the package wrapped in pink wrapping paper with a frilly bow on top. He asked to hold baby Jeanette. We all felt Frankie was a thoughtful, caring young man.

Frankie Jr. was an outstanding football player at St. Ignatius. When his team played in the city championship game at Kezar Stadium in San Francisco, Danny sneaked into the stadium with his best friend Billy Petty. They managed to get right up to the sidelines next to Frankie Jr. After they had chatted with Frankie Jr, for a few minutes, Frankie noticed his coaches were coming toward them and he managed to get one of the trainers to escort them off the field, before they were spotted. Though I didn't condone my son sneaking into the stadium, I knew that Frankie Jr. made my son feel important.

Frankie Jr. went on to attend West Point and played football there. During his senior year, he died tragically in a plane crash on Armer Mountain, Arizona, northeast of Phoenix, along with eighteen other West Point cadets on a leg of a flight from San Rafael to New York after Christmas break. My heart ached deeply for Elsie. She had experienced two terribly painful devastating losses in her life. Both her husband Frankie "Campbell" Camilli and her son Frankie Camilli Jr. had died unexpectedly and tragically young.

In 1948, Bette moved into the cottage behind our home on 28th Street with her new family. It was the same cottage we once lived in, and where Andy's mother Mary had lived before her death. That same year, Earle Swensen, the boy who took an interest in me when we were young, opened an ice cream parlor on Russian Hill in San Francisco. He had learned how to make ice cream during World War II when he was in the Coast Guard and worked as a cook on a naval transport ship that had a freezer. With $750 in savings and a $5,000 loan, he started his business on Hyde Street, in an ideal location near a cable car line. He later opened other stores and parlayed Swensen's Ice Cream into a worldwide ice cream empire. I often wondered what my life would have been like had I been more open to dating him! Perhaps we would have been married, and I wouldn't have had to worry about finances as I got older. Then again, if that were the case, I wouldn't have had the same beautiful, intelligent children I have.

In autumn 1948 our kids dressed up for Halloween. Danny dressed as a sailor with fake tattoos. It was a far cry from the cute Popeye outfit he once wore. Joanne went as a witch dressed in a black outfit. They went trick-or-treating with a few friends, and I stayed home passing out candy. I had assembled a bag including Tootsie Rolls and Peppermint Patties. At first, several cowboys, clowns, skeletons, and Lone Rangers came to the door, interspersed with an alien, a monster, Cleopatra, and a creative kid wearing a birdcage over his face. Then the doorbell rang, and there stood a little boy, by himself, dressed as a man, wearing a baggy suit. His hat was tilted forward, obscuring his face. His shoes were too big for his feet. He immediately grabbed the whole bag of candy and began to run down the sidewalk. Startled and outraged, I chased after him.

My adrenal glands must have pumped out a quart of fluid trying to keep up with the S.O.B. "Get back here, you crook!" I roared. The little devil made it about a block and a half before I was able to catch up and tackle him into some bushes.

"Trick or treat!" I heard the voice of my sister Bette. Had she seen the scoundrel and chased him as well? Then uproarious laughter ensued. Climbing out of the bushes chuckling and chortling, there was Bette, all scraped up, wearing the man's suit.

"I would have gotten away with it had I not had to run in these damned oversized shoes!" *Good grief,* I thought. Of course, it was Bette. Who else would blindside me for pure entertainment and laughter?

Following our brother Billy's return from World War II, he moved back into the house with our mother on Nevada Street and lived with her for a few years. Though he was not as much of a troublemaker as he had been, he still gave our mother a lot of grief. In 1949, Mama turned sixty-five and was able to get onto Social Security, which made her less dependent on everyone for support.

In the early 1950s my youngest sister Theresa ran into some difficulty with her new husband. She had two young children, Jimmy and Terry, and they had no place to go. Bette, Mickey and I convinced Mama to let them move in with her and have Billy find a place of his own. He protested, but Mama finally stood up to him and kicked him out of the house. He decided he didn't want to have any contact with us any longer. We tried to reach out to him but he didn't want to talk. I felt a little guilty, but I came to terms with his decision. He had made that choice. My sisters and I would not see Billy again for close to twenty-five years.

Andy and I were able to pay for Danny and Joanne to attend a Catholic school in San Francisco, St. Paul's elementary school. I went to work in the Department of Immigration, which had been a dream of mine since my trip to Chinatown as a child, and Andy continued to work as a postman. Fortunately, our children were able to get merit scholarships which helped pay for some of their schooling. In high school Joanne graduated as senior class president, and this gave us great pride.

Mama died in 1953. Prior to her death, she had noticed that the predominantly Irish Catholic neighborhood we had been raised in was beginning to change. Asian immigrants, as well as Black Americans who had worked in the shipyards during World War II, had begun to move to the area. Irish and Italian Immigrants in Bernal Heights were ageing, and their children were starting to settle in the nearby suburbs within the Bay Area.

The five-cent price of a bottle of Coca-Cola, which I saw advertised in 1915 on Market Street, stayed at five cents until the late 1950s. It remained at five cents for well over seventy years, from 1886 to 1959, which was extremely unusual for a popular product of any kind.

The old O'Connor, Moffatt & Co's department store, where Andy, Bette and I had worked in Union Square, became Macy's in 1947. Joanne worked there in the 1950s as an elevator girl dressed in uniform while she attended Holy Name's college. Elevator girls were like flight attendants back in those days. It was a well sought-after job by young women. You had to smile, be courteous, dress nicely, and wear plenty of make-up. Joanne was often told she looked like Doris Day, and she had a similar curly short hairdo. She wore a half-length skirt and heels. The first week she worked there, Andy and I went for a ride on the elevator that she operated. As we entered the elevator she smiled and greeted us with new etiquette, not previously shown at home. We headed to one of the upper floors. With manual controls, she promptly stopped the elevator about three feet short of the floor where we intended to get off. The whole elevator

shook, and we almost fell. Andy managed to boost me up to the
landing, and we stifled our laughter as Joanne was determined to
impress us. We thought she had been given too much training in
etiquette and not enough in the actual operation! She would eventually get the hang of it, and after college she became an elementary
school teacher in San Francisco, one who thankfully did not smack
students on their hands for disobedient behavior.

Theresa also worked at Macy's, and when my niece Jeanette was
older, she was employed there as well, completing a line of six family members to work in the same building since O'Connor, Moffatt
& Co had moved to Union Square back in 1929.

Throughout the 1950s, I continued to try to persuade Andy to
stop drinking. He attended some meetings for alcoholics, but his
addiction always reared its ugly head again, and he stopped going. I
refused to do his laundry for a month if I caught him drinking. He
didn't seem to mind, so that was a bust. I got him into a treatment
program where he was prescribed Disulfiram, a medicine that had
recently been approved for treatment of alcohol dependence. He
was supposed to take the medicine every day. He did initially, but
found out instantly that he developed nausea and vomiting as well
as flushing afterwards if he drank. So, he just stopped taking the
medication. I even tried a system of rewards. I bought an extra calendar that I kept in a drawer in the kitchen, and every time he got
drunk, I wrote the word "*drunk*" under the date. If he had fourteen
days free of drinking, I let him choose some place to go on a date
night with me. Those special nights were few and far between but
did include things like eating a broiled hamburger at Zim's, dining
at the House of Prime Rib, famed for its twenty-one-day-old aged
prime rib, or going to one of the oldest businesses in San Francisco,
Boudin's, where we would pick up some of San Francisco's notorious

sourdough bread where the 'mother dough' has been fermenting since 1849.

One day, my eight-year-old niece Jeanette, Bette's daughter, came over to our home. Andy was in the back building a swing set for Jeanette. She was standing in the kitchen.

"Aunt Ann?" She was hovering over the counter.

"Yes, sweetie?"

She turned toward me with a look of disbelief. "What's this?" She lifted the calendar and pointed to the words "*drunk, drunk, drunk, drunk, drunk, drunk*," splattered all over the month.

I had accidentally left the calendar on the counter. *Oh my God,* I thought, *this is extremely embarrassing and awkward.* I just went over and put the calendar in the drawer. "It's nothing, sweetie." Andy's alcoholism had made me stoop to lying to a child; not just any child, but my own niece.

Eventually, around 1956, I called Andy's doctor ahead of a scheduled visit, and he reviewed Andy's drinking history. I'm not sure what the doctor said at his appointment, but it scared the bejesus out of him, and he stopped drinking, except for rare relapses, during the last ten years of his life. He would continue to smoke like a chimney, however.

Looking for social events that did not involve alcohol, we made a few trips out to San Francisco's North Beach in the late 1950s, to go to coffee shops and sip on a cup of cappuccino and listen to poetry, which was still a passion of Andy's. Andy loved American poets, in addition to being a fan of Edgar Allan Poe, he enjoyed reading E. E. Cummings' literature. Only the poetry coming out of North Beach was quite a bit different, having anti-establishment undertones. The Beat movement, a social and literary movement, had already found its way into that community. A collection of bohemian artists read poetry, often accompanied by the beat of bongo drums. One of its founding members, Allen Ginsberg, lived in San Francisco, and Jack Kerouac, another influential writer, visited the area often. The Beat culture rejected materialism and the status quo of American culture.

We were by no means part of the movement but certainly did enjoy some of the poetry. The ironic thing about the movement was that many started to conform by dressing similarly. Men and women often wore berets, dark turtleneck shirts, plain dark shirts, blouses, or dark sunglasses. Men often grew goatees. They frequently used terms like "cool," "cool cats," "daddio," "you dig," "man," and "don't be square." The movement had its fair share of criticism, and Herb Cain, an influential San Francisco columnist, coined the term *beatnik* to describe them. He took the term *Beat* and combined it with the Russian satellite *Sputnik*, which was in the news at the time.

Daniel went on to get a scholarship to attend St. Mary's College. He got married in 1957. Danny, who liked to be called Dan by that time, and his new wife Maureen, got a check for $500 from Elsie, which was an exorbitant amount of money in those days. Elsie had remarried shortly after the war to a man named Nick who owned a gas station. Dan called Elsie to thank her, but let her know the amount was too much.

"Dan, you were Frankie Jr.'s favorite cousin," Elsie told him. "He would have wanted you to have a nice wedding present." Dan went on to work for Kaiser Permanente and eventually became an executive working in Oakland. Dan and Maureen would go on to have six children.

In 1958, the New York Giants baseball team moved to San Francisco and the first two years they played at Seals Stadium in the Mission District, on 16th Street, close to the site where Recreation Park was back in 1930 when we saw the Frankie Campbell versus

Max Baer fight. Andy and I attended some of the games and got to watch the future Hall of Famer Willie Mays hit home runs. I kept my eye on Andy. More thoroughly than a security guard, I patted down his coat before games to make sure he did not bring any booze into the stadium. I made sure soda and not beer flowed into his cups at the concession stand. The San Francisco Giants then moved to Candlestick Park, where we continued to see games.

CHAPTER
TWENTY

On January 20, 1961, John F. Kennedy was sworn in as the first Irish American Catholic president. This became a joyous occasion in the few remaining mostly Catholic Irish communities still existing in the city.

Bernal Heights, where I had grown up, continued to change. Mexican Americans came in greater numbers. The musician and future guitar legend Carlos Santana moved to the northeast section of that neighborhood, living on Mullen Avenue in 1961 when he was a teenager.

One of the most significant events to hit San Francisco occurred in June 1962. On either the evening of June 11 or the early morning of June 12, three prisoners, Frank Morris, Clarence and Charles Anglin, escaped from Alcatraz. This was followed by numerous newspaper, radio, and television reports. We were given warnings to keep our doors locked and to be on the lookout for the three men.

Alcatraz is an island, known as the 'Rock' that sits in the middle of the San Francisco Bay. A military fortification/citadel was built at the top of the island in the 1850s. When it was torn down in 1909, a vast military prison was built. In the early 1930s that prison was modernized to become a federal prison for the most hardened of criminals and gained the reputation as the toughest prison in the US. Guarded by steel bars and a steel door, the cells were made of concrete, reinforced by twisted steel Ransome bars. Surrounded by cold ocean water, with fast currents, Alcatraz was meant to hold the very worst of the worst offenders. It housed bank robbers, kidnappers, counterfeiters, and murderers. It once held the notorious gangsters, 'Scarface' Al Capone and 'Machine Gun' Kelly.

Prior to the escape of the three men in 1962, there had been twelve escape attempts involving thirty-one men. All were unsuccessful; two resulted in drownings and six were shot and killed.

When the big escape occurred in June, through various news reports, we learned that four prisoners planned to escape, but one had been left behind. They planned their breakout several months in advance. The newspapers reported that one of the escapees, Frank Morris, had an IQ of one hundred and thirty-three. Initially, we were informed that the convicts used sharpened spoons to dig through their separate but adjoining cells and left dummy heads in their beds made of plaster and papier-mâché.

Gradually, as the days and weeks went on, more information came out. We learned that the hair on the dummy heads turned out to be real human hair and was acquired from the prison barber shop. The escapees had made a homemade electric drill and enlarged air vents in their cells, which aided in their escape. After they made their way through their cell walls, they placed false grilles over the cavities that they had created. In the weeks and days prior to the escape they set up a secret workshop above their cellblock to hide their equipment. They made wooden paddles, life vests, and a raft out of raincoats. After making their way out of the cells they climbed up a three-story unguarded utility corridor and broke through a ventilation shaft where they got onto the prison roof. From there they climbed down a bakery smokestack, hopped over a fence, and reached the shore where they were thought to have launched their raft.

Three months after the escape, Andy and I made a trip to Fisherman's Wharf as we had done, at least a couple of times a year, since the 1930s. We stood peering out at Alcatraz. A lot had changed at Fisherman's Wharf since we sat on a bench and talked about Emperor Norton back in 1934. It had started to attract more tourists in the 1960s, though it would become more popular in the 1970s and 1980s, when the wharf was renovated. We could tell tourists from the locals because the tourists didn't know how to dress for the cooler, windy San Francisco weather. They expected to sunbathe in the California climate. Instead, they were forced to go into local shops and purchase sweatshirts to stay warm.

Andy and I liked to debate with each other on everything from politics to science, religion, world and local events, and philosophy. That day at Fisherman's Wharf, we discussed whether the escapees from Alcatraz had been successful. We had most of the information by then, aside from a few details that came out later, such as additional tools used such as a flashlight, periscope, and an inflation device made from an accordion-like musical instrument called a concertina.

Andy and I had differing opinions on the matter. Andy lit up a cigarette and gazed out at the Rock.

"Ann, I don't see how they could have made it. You know that before I worked at the used car lot, I worked on Yerba Buena Island; you know, the one that the Bay Bridge runs through. With that utility company." He turned his body to the right and pointed. "I worked there long before the Bay Bridge was built in the 1930s, when it was called Goat Island because it was teaming with goats. I was given various odd jobs inspecting, repairing, and replacing cable. We were dropped off by a small boat, and I remember the currents were so strong that we sometimes had trouble getting to the island, let alone the landing dock. When I did cable inspections near the shoreline, I could see the turbulence in the water. I could see seaweed, dead bugs, plant matter, and garbage rapidly swirling within circles of sea foam and in multiple locations. And that water is ca-cold!" Andy folded his arms and made a shivering motion to drive home his point. "Even in the summer, it can be as low as fifty-three degrees. There would be no way I would've ever gone for a swim. Those prisoners drowned in the rapid currents, wind, and cold water. Just being in the Bay for a few minutes can cause you to lose feeling in your hands, and your limbs can go completely numb. They were probably bobbing and flailing to stay afloat as walls of turbulent waves struck, forcing them repeatedly under the surface. I can't imagine being in a situation like that."

"Well, you just did," I teased.

"They had to be gasping for air as their lungs filled with seawater!"

"You don't have to be so graphic, Andy."

"Sorry." Andy paused to take a puff on his cigarette. "It's definitely an unpleasant thought."

"No one has ever found any of their bodies. How do you explain that?"

"They were probably eaten by sharks ... I'll piss on your mess-kit if I'm not right." Andy had a way with words when he tried to drive his points across that could be irritating at times. I just gave him the evil eye and presented him with some counter-arguments that seemed reasonable.

"I've heard most of the sharks in San Francisco Bay are mostly harmless Leopard sharks."

"Well, people don't know their asses from second base." Andy was animated.

"How so?"

"Well, you know my family moved from Crockett, in the East Bay, to San Francisco when I was about three years old?"

"Of course."

"Well, my father, who had lived in Crockett for close to nine years, kept in touch with a lot of people in that community. In fact, he kept his membership in the Ancient Order of Hibernians in that town until the day he died. We used to go back to that area frequently. One day, at about the age of ten, I walked with my father along the shoreline of the Carquinez Strait, within San Francisco Bay. We saw a dog going out to fetch a stick in the water thrown by its master. Out of nowhere I witnessed a gigantic shark, possibly a great white, raise its head above the water, and the dog shot straight up and landed back in the water. Both the dog and the shark disappeared without a trace. So, whenever anyone tells me there are no threatening sharks within the Bay, they are full of malarkey. Aside from that, any group of sharks can devour a human being, even if they don't normally attack. You've seen dead seal carcasses in the Bay get devoured by sea life, correct?"

"Yes, but if there was a body floating in the Bay, wouldn't you see a mass of seagulls flying overhead? The Coast Guard sent helicopters up shortly after the escape, and they didn't find anything. And you saw that picture in the newspaper of San Franciscans scouring the water from shore with binoculars. Aside from that, wouldn't one person in just one of the hundreds of boats in the Bay have spotted just one body?" I was onto something.

"Possibly, but if they drowned the evening that they escaped, then by morning there may have been hardly any trace of them. Besides that, even if their bodies weren't devoured by sharks they could've been pulled out to sea by sunrise. The currents are unusually strong near the entrance to the Golden Gate. Good luck finding a body in the Pacific Ocean. That's like finding a needle in a haystack," Andy retorted, smugly.

"But you would think at least one of the three men could have swam to shore. You know that guy who started America's first televised fitness show, right here in the 1950s?"

"Jack LaLanne?"

"Yes, well, at the age of forty-one he swam from Alcatraz to Fisherman's Wharf wearing handcuffs!"

"Yeah, but that guy is a fitness buff. He's in great shape. These guys at Alcatraz are weaklings compared to him."

"True, but I heard that at least two of these inmates are good swimmers. The Anglins lived in Tampa Bay and are used to swimming in turbulent waters. I think if they aren't found and someone in the future escapes, and swims to shore, then you can't count that out."

"But that's a long shot. You know I've always been a betting man. I would say the odds are five hundred to one that they didn't make it."

I reached into my purse and gave Andy a dollar bill. "If it is ever found out that these guys have successfully escaped, then you owe me $500."

"OK, that's a sucker's bet." Andy shook my hand and put the bill in his wallet. He looked assured.

As we were concluding our conversation, we could hear the bell of an incoming cable car approaching the Bell and Hyde Street intersection. The fruits of the grip-man's labor produced a clánging, resonating sound from his tug rope.

"Andy, don't you love that sound? It just speaks San Francisco."

"I do love it, and I used to hear it a lot more of it when I was a little kid."

"What do you mean?" I gave Andy an inquisitive look.

"Well, before the 1906 earthquake, San Francisco was practically covered with cable car lines. My parents and I used to ride them all the time."

"Hmm?"

"Oh, ya. The fellow who invented it was a man named Andy like me."

"Really?"

"Yep."

Andy went on to say that he got the idea of having a streetcar pulled by cable, after watching horses struggle up wet cobblestones on Jackson Street. He, along with some partners, designed the first cable car line, and it went into operation on Clay Street in 1873. It was powered by steam engines.

Eventually, other cable car lines were built, and in its heyday, San Francisco had fifty-three miles of track and around twenty-three cable car lines. However, the 1906 earthquake destroyed many of the tracks and several cable cars.

"By the time you were two years old in 1912, San Francisco had eight remaining cable car lines," Andy said.

I looked at Andy with concern. "That number keeps dwindling. There are only three of those original twenty-three lines left. It's a shame."

"Yes, but at least we saved the remaining lines. Do you remember that mayor we had who wanted to get rid of them?"

"Oh, I definitely do. Mayor Lapham. He said something like "Junk them as soon as possible." All he cared about was the operational costs. I'm just glad there was that fellow who organized the Citizens' Committee to Save Cable Cars. Their campaign was so successful they got an endorsement from Eleanor Roosevelt and *Life* magazine ran a story about the Gripmen ... Andy, didn't we vote on it?"

"Yes, it passed by an overwhelming majority. San Francisco citizens basically told the mayor that he did not know shit from Shinola."

I looked at Andy with chagrin.

"Well, I didn't use God's name in vain, did I?" he protested.

"No, you didn't, buster." I lifted my eyes up and out, then smiled fondly at my husband. "You foul-mouthed goober."

Life went on. In October 1962, Bette called me one day, out of the blue. I answered the phone in our kitchen, where I was reading a book.

"Turn on the television," she commanded, in a concerned tone of voice.

We had a black and white console TV in our living room. Was this a major event? Was an asteroid about to strike Earth? Was it World War III? I tried pulling the phone's extension cord to the TV, but it couldn't quite reach. "Bette, I'll have to put the phone down."

"Don't worry about it, darling. Just see what I want you to watch and call me back. There is a new TV comedy show called *The Beverly Hillbillies.*"

Was she seriously making me drop my book to turn on the television for a new comedy TV series? "Pay attention to the credits. There is a name I think you'll recognize. Call me back after you watch it." I turned it on and changed the channel to the TV show, which was about midway through. I watched it until the end, and there it was. I was briefly reminded again of one of the old traumas I had once experienced. The one where my cousin Elsie's husband Frankie Campbell was killed in the boxing ring by the fighter Max Baer. I saw Max Baer's name in the credits. Only it was Max Baer's son Max Baer Junior, playing the role of a dumb, good-looking character named Jethro. A flood of emotion washed over me as I saw Max's likeness, and I briefly cried, but then I had to laugh. Life is too precious to hold grudges. After all, his father tried to make amends with a benefit fight after the horrific incident, even if it wasn't the timeliest affair. I called Bette back and we talked about the tragedies that we had lived through. Bette and I could always count on each other for comfort and support.

In December 1962, Andy had just brought in the morning newspaper and began making toast in the kitchen. I sat down with a bowl of oatmeal and read that another prisoner escaped Alcatraz. John Paul Scott successfully swam to shore with the aid of inflated rubber gloves he used for buoyancy. He swam over three miles and was discovered by teenagers at Fort Point, near the Golden Gate Bridge. He suffered from hypothermia and exhaustion, and was apprehended and treated at a local hospital. When Andy sat down with his toast and coffee, I plopped the newspaper in front of him and smiled. Andy would get the last laugh, however, as the three escapees we had discussed earlier in the year were never found.

On March 21, 1963, Alcatraz officially closed as a prison and in the fall of 1973 opened as a tourist attraction.

There was certainly no shortage of sensational news in the 1960s. Our first Irish Catholic president, President John F. Kennedy, was assassinated on Friday November 22, 1963, in Dallas, Texas. Though not a San Francisco incident, it still affected everyone I knew. There was not a dry eye in the city. We diligently followed news reports, including those given by the famous CBS news anchor Walter Cronkite. All three major television networks suspended regularly-scheduled TV shows from November 22 through November 26. Andy and I were on the phone with just about every friend and relative we knew. We attended special church services at St. Paul's church.

In 1963, our daughter Joanne started dating a man by the name of Joe Cerny. Andy thought he had introduced himself by the name of Joe Kelly, a good Irish name, and welcomed him to the family. It turned out he was Czech and not even Catholic, which created a stir. This only got worse when Joe took Joanne for a drive along the cliffs, overhanging the Pacific Ocean, on the scenic Pacific Coast Highway in his compact English Austin Healy convertible. Somewhere south of Monterey, near Big Sur, it became foggy, and as Joe pulled over, part of the front end of the car came off the cliff. Their car lurched forward and dangled for hours as they sat trying not to move. They could have been killed. Eventually, a tow truck driver was summoned, and he managed to pull them to safety. They got engaged, and Joe eventually smoothed everything over with us, promising to attend a Catholic Church and raise future children in the Catholic faith.

Andy and I got to see our daughter Joanne marry Joe in 1964. Our first grandchild, Sheila Scannell, the daughter of our son Dan, at the age of six, would be their flower girl. Both Dan and Joanne married their spouses at St. Paul's church near the elementary school they once attended. Andy died in January 1966 of heart disease. He retreated into his bedroom after eating a tamale before passing away. He thought he was having heartburn and went to lie down and rest. I discovered him shortly thereafter lying in bed, with a stack of books by his nightstand. Some were of poetry and a couple were Ian Fleming's James Bond novels, a favorite of his.

Andy's drinking had caused so much pain and stress in my life, emotionally and financially. Despite all that, I chose not to dwell on it. I can't say bad memories did not pop up, but I tried my best to suppress them. Instead, I chose to think about all the good things he had done in his life. He had kept the promises, or rather proclamations, he had given me; we had the happy family vacations that I had dreamt of. He had sacrificed to keep our children in Catholic school, and they, unlike us, became college-educated. He helped those in need, rarely complained about work, was good-natured, friendly, and kept faithful to me. Most importantly, he had been respectful to just about everyone I knew inside and outside the family.

The wounds I suffered from the alcoholic men in my life, as well as the traumas I experienced, began to heal. Following Andy's death in 1966, at the age of fifty-five, I learned how to drive and was able to purchase a white Ford Mustang. I drove around the city like a free bird riding on top of an Indian motorcycle as I had back in 1928. As I got older, after owning the car for about fifteen years, I eventually gave the car to Joanne who had since moved to the Bay Area suburbs, to the town of Saratoga. She, in turn, gave the Mustang to her sons, Joe and Dan Cerny. It would become their first car.

By 1966, people were increasingly growing their hair longer, and clothes started becoming more colorful. The Beatles came to San Francisco to perform a concert. By that time, my lifelong love of music had flourished, and I owned a number of Beatles albums. The Fab Four played at Candlestick Park, where I had attended San Francisco Giant baseball games, on August 29, 1966. I didn't attend because I didn't want to be around a large crowd of shrill voices. I didn't know at the time that it would be their last concert in the United States and their last paid concert in the world. Had I known that, I might have gone.

Around that time, I noticed blue jeans were becoming increasingly popular. Although I had seen people wearing blue jeans my whole life, they were going through a revival of some sort. I noticed that men, women, and especially young people were wearing them. Levi Strauss, considered one of the fathers of blue jeans, was a Jewish immigrant from Bavaria who moved to San Francisco during the Gold Rush and opened a dry goods store where he sold many items, including blue fabric. One of his customers, a tailor from Reno, Nevada, named Jacob Davis, found a way to make pants out of the material using rivets. Together, in 1873, they were granted a patent, and blue jeans were officially born.

In 1967, a bit of a revolution struck San Francisco. LSD had just been banned, and the Vietnam War was in full swing. Many young people opposed the war, rejected the values of older generations, and were suspicious of the government. In January, the year started off with a free event at Golden Gate Park called the Human Be-In that was organized by an artist. It was intended to promote ideas of an emerging counterculture movement and attracted many hippies who had long hair and often wore baggy, colorful, floral clothing, tie-dye shirts, beads, and sandals. Those ideas included opposition to the war and social norms, exploration of a higher level of consciousness through psychedelic drugs, environmental awareness, communal living, and expressions of self through music, artistry, and clothing. The event included speeches, political protests, poetry readings, chanting, and musical performances by local rock bands like Jefferson Airplane and the Grateful Dead. Timothy Leary, a psychologist who had gained a PhD from the University of California at Berkeley and later lectured at Harvard, gave a speech. He was known to promote LSD and told the audience of up to 30,000 people to 'Turn on, tune in and drop out.' He specifically told them to drop out of school. Before the event, an underground chemist by the name of Owsley Stanley, the grandson of a US Senator, produced LSD that he handed out at the Human Be-In.

The Human Be-In was a prelude to what became known as the Summer of Love. In the spring of 1967, in a neighborhood near Golden Gate Park called the Haight-Ashbury District, a group of people organized a Council of the Summer of Love and invited young people across the nation to come to San Francisco during the summer to embrace ideals expressed at the Human Be-In. They got quite a bit of attention, and news stations across the country began reporting on it. Newsweek magazine printed the headline: '*The Hippies are Coming.*'

In response to the upcoming event, John Phillips, a musician-song writer and member of the folk-rock group The Mamas and the Papas, wrote a song called *San Francisco*. He gave the song to his friend Scott McKenzie as a gift. The song was released in May, and a month later McKenzie played it for an enormous crowd at the Monterey Pop Festival. It became a rallying song for people to come and join the Summer of Love. The song starts::

> *If you're going to San Francisco*
> *be sure to wear some flowers in your hair*
> *If you're going to San Francisco*
> *you're gonna meet some gentle people there.'*

Young people from all over the country, and all over the world, began flocking to the city. The planners helped organize places to stay, sanitation, a free clinic, and a free store to give away basic provisions. However, they were soon overwhelmed. In all, about 100,000 people came. The mostly new arrivals to San Francisco were dubbed 'flower children.' Unfortunately, the Haight-Ashbury District couldn't accommodate everyone, which led to overcrowding and stretching of the city's resources. Though most of the young people left towards the end of the summer, there was an unwanted element that came into the district as the year progressed, and homelessness, drug problems and crime afflicted Haight-Ashbury.

During the Vietnam War era, anti-war activists began moving to my old neighborhood in Bernal Heights, in shared households and collectives. The neighborhood was referred to as 'Red Hill' during that period. Though many of the Catholic Churches remained within and around Bernal Heights, the typically Irish population, that had dominated the region in the early part of the 20th century, had mostly dissipated.

Before the end of the tumultuous decade, the year 1968 was marred by the assassinations of Martin Luther King Junior and Bobby Kennedy. Though not San Francisco events, massive memorials were held. After Martin Luther King's death, the San Francisco Mayor Joseph Alioto called for a two-minute period of silence in all the private and public schools in the city to pay respect.

Around the same time, Bette developed rheumatoid arthritis, and as a form of therapy, she took oil-painting classes. She was inspired by the oil-paint set she had acquired on Christmas Day 1922. She went on to become a well-known, accomplished artist within the Bay Area. She became known for painting nostalgic scenes of San Francisco, including cable cars, Fisherman's Wharf, Coit Tower, ferry boats, and famous hotels. She even painted scenes of the cityscape as if she were painting them from the perspective of traveling on the ferry boat that carried us in 1925, heading across the Bay toward our first and last White family vacation. Her work was featured at art galleries, wine festivals, and numerous other events. She had to turn purchasers down after she developed a six-month waiting list for her commissioned artwork. Though she initially got back into painting for her physical health, she told the newspapers that it helped her mental health. This embarrassed her family, but they knew that she, too, had been scarred in her life by our father William White. Bette later taught me and my daughter-in-law Maureen Scannell how to paint.

I eventually remarried on March 15, 1969, to Al Scully, a San Francisco pharmacist who had grown up in Hawaii, and as a child had taken surfing lessons from Duke Kahanamoku, the famous 'father of modern surfing.' I finally got to have the wedding of my dreams. Though Al was another Irish American man from a Catholic family, he thankfully wasn't an alcoholic. This gave me solace not having to worry about whether or not my husband would come home drunk.

During that period, I gradually rose through the ranks at the Department of Immigration and became one of their lead inspectors. I boarded massive cargo ships in San Francisco Bay, climbing up ladders, including the flexible rope Jacob's ladders. Though I didn't completely overcome my fear of heights, I gradually learned how to relax and yet stay focused to conquer the long ladders, which sometimes were less than vertical. One day, as I was climbing a steep ladder of a particularly enormous vessel, a helicopter flew overhead. I recall thinking I must have looked like a tiny ant on a mission to find a grain of sugar in a colossal container. I did this in my fifties and well into my sixties. The Department of Immigration worked with the port authorities and other agencies. Using the intuition and skills I had learned as a bootlegger, I was able to uncover hiding places and discover stowaways and illegal contraband. I carefully went through IDs and documents to be sure people were entering our port legally. I developed a reputation for being a tough, no-nonsense inspector with a good track record.

On June 20, 1969, we got to watch on television the first astronaut land on the moon in a lunar module called Eagle. It was a far cry from the time I rode with my father in a horse-drawn transportation wagon down Market Street in 1915. As the 1960s concluded, I was over at Bette's place discussing the end of the decade.

"Ann, if you can't beat them join 'em," my sister declared.

"What are you talking about? Are you going to smoke pot or are you just going to purchase a lava lamp?" I joked.

"No, my darling." Bette had just gone shopping and grabbed her shopping bag. She pulled out a brand-new pair of 646 Levi Strauss

Bell Bottom jeans. Those jeans had just been released in March 1969. Bell bottom pants had been around since the early 1800s, when US sailors wore them. I had seen some people wearing flared pants in the late 1960s, but it was the first time I had seen them in jean form, and it had suddenly became mass-produced. As I stood gazing at the jeans, I realized my fashion had been shaped by the 1960s as well. I wore a colorful blouse emblazoned with bright yellow flowers. "This is the new trend in clothing. It's a part of fashion that is expected to be big in the 1970s" Bette explained. "Why ... it'll be what makes up the fabric of our society!" I rolled my eyes up and smiled at her play on words. With my short frame, I imagined wearing those jeans. *Ugh, I'll look like a blue Christmas tree.* Despite that, I didn't want to be left out and ended up buying a pair.

By the mid-1970s, my sisters and I got word that our brother Billy was having health issues. We cast our animosities aside and reconciled with him. We made several trips out to Daly City to see him until he died of cancer on September 1,1976. Before he passed away, he grasped both of my hands and slipped into them the Silver Star he earned during World War II.

Throughout 1970s, a gay rights movement in San Francisco gathered momentum. The Castro District began to attract people from all around the world, and San Francisco's gay population grew from 30,000 at the beginning of the decade to about 100,000 by the end. In November 1977, Harvey Milk became the first openly gay politician in the city and was elected to the board of supervisors.

Dan White (no relation to our family), a former police officer and a board member with a history of depression, was incensed about Milk's support for placing a group home for troubled youths in White's district. He wasn't happy with his salary, either. White resigned on November 10, 1978, but changed his mind four days later. Mayor Moscone initially agreed to reappoint him but was opposed by city officials including Milk, so he reversed his decision. Enraged, on the morning of November 27, White breached City Hall, carrying a .38 caliber Smith & Wesson revolver, and gained access through a basement window to avoid metal detection. He entered the mayor's office, where he confronted Moscone and demanded to be reinstated. When Moscone refused, he was shot four times and killed. White reloaded his gun and ran down the hall. The president of the San Francisco board of supervisors, Dianne Feinstein, saw Dan White running, and called after him. White responded with: "I have to do something first." He ran to Harvey Milk's office, where he was speaking with a radio reporter. White fired five rounds into Milk's body, killing him. The last two shots were fired into his head while the gun's barrel touched his skull. White turned himself in, at the San Francisco Police Department's Northern Station precinct, the same day. Later that morning, Dianne Feinstein went before news cameras to report the harrowing events to the public. It ended up dramatically boosting her political career. On December 4 she was elected as the city's first female mayor.

In 1979, Dan White went on trial by jury for the two murders. His legal team claimed that White's depression and consumption of Twinkies and other junk food impaired his judgement. The infamous 'Twinkie Defense' led to a voluntary manslaughter conviction instead of first-degree murder, and he was sentenced to seven years and eight months in prison, of which he only served five years.

I nor my extended family members agreed with the verdict. Life could be unfair at times. Bette and I certainly knew that. However, we had to let life move on, or else we would not have enjoyed our remaining years.

CHAPTER
TWENTY-ONE

A l and I have loved living as everyday San Franciscans. Since we married, we have hosted Christmas dinners for our burgeoning, mostly Catholic-Irish extended family in our Victorian home in the Sunset district of San Francisco every year. All my sisters attend, as well as their children and grandchildren.

In San Francisco, we have taken our grandchildren to places like Sunset Beach, Fisherman's Wharf, Ghirardelli Square, San Francisco Zoo, the Exploratorium, when it opened near the Palace of Fine Arts, and to Golden Gate Park to watch the Bay to Breakers race. We also took some of them to the Avenue Theater in the late 1970s, which began re-playing old silent films. The films were accompanied by an organ player, and the kids got to experience Buster Keaton movies as I had in my youth.

Throughout the late 1960s, 1970s and into the 1980s, Al and I have attended many of our grandchildren's, nieces' and nephews' baptisms, graduations, plays, and musicals. It was not unusual for us to travel down to Silicon Valley, where my daughter Joanne's family lives in Saratoga. There, we attended many Catholic communions, confirmations, Little League games, and soccer meets.

Mother's Day is celebrated at my son Daniel's family home in the Oakland Hills every year. During the years when our grandchildren were young, it was not uncommon to see sixty to seventy relatives and friends attend! A long kiddie table was created out of numerous fold-out dining units, and the accompanying fold-out chairs were filled with rambunctious kids chatting, singing, laughing, and sometimes flicking food at each other. Amongst the adults, I can't say that alcohol doesn't flow. Their local Irish priest sometimes attends as their special guest.

Bette hosts Thanksgiving in Millbrae, CA, where she features my mother's dreaded ambrosia as a dessert salad. She has always been a favorite aunt among my kids and grandchildren. She has maintained her sense of humor, telling hilarious stories, using various voices in animated ways, acting out the characters. She finds humor in anything and almost everything, from shepherd's pies to how a fly can land on one's face in the most unusual way.

Al and I have been long-time San Francisco Giant fans. At Candlestick Park in 1982, I was at a Giants versus Reds game, and a foul ball hit a metal railing in one of the aisles. The ball caromed sideways and landed directly into my lap. I picked the baseball up with excitement, and immediately a young man practically tackled me trying to get it. I felt like slugging him, but instead slapped his hand pretty hard, and he sheepishly retreated to his seat, like a dog hiding its tail. I got a round of applause, and someone shouted: "You show 'em, sister!" which created a burst of laughter amongst the crowd. I felt a little embarrassed, but proud that I got my first and only major league baseball at the age of seventy-one! Currently, we have the ball displayed in my husband's sports-themed den.

We also have had season tickets to the San Francisco 49ers games since the 1970s. Al has about every football bobblehead doll one could imagine. We got to watch Joe Montana and Jerry Rice help lead the 49ers to victories in the Super Bowls of 1982 and 1985.

I currently lie in bed with terminal gastrointestinal cancer, awaiting my fate. Former colleagues, whom I had worked with at the Department of Immigration, stop by to say their final farewells. They tell me they aren't aware of any immigration officer in San Francisco's history who has uncovered more stowaways, hidden contraband, and illegal documents than me. Many of them are still working and wonder how I managed to accomplish that. To them, I say "Given I'm a bootlegger's daughter and a former bootlegger, I developed a strong intuition. But you don't have to have been a bootlegger to be a good immigration officer. You just have to be able to fall down seven times and get up eight."

I have several visitors every day and a family who loves me. All in all, my life has been an adventure. Whether it be Bette, my husband, God, or anyone else with me physically or in spirit, I will end with an old Irish proverb, *Giorraíonn beirt bóthar*, which means 'Two shorten the road.' Having someone by your side makes the journey easier.

AUTHOR'S NOTES

Ann Scully, (née Scannell, née White) died on September 20, 1985, at the age of seventy-four. She left behind eight grandchildren. Her cousin Elsie and sister Bette would be among the guests to attend her funeral.

Most events that took place in this book occurred. I wanted to keep the story as authentic as possible, which required researching things people might say or do during those time periods, and the way people dressed and behaved. Toward the beginning of the book, I described William White going down Market Street in 1915 in his horse-drawn transport wagon. I got the inspiration from watching an actual movie reel of San Francisco taken of street cars, horse carts, automobiles, and cable cars going down Market Street in 1906, and one man crossing the street is nearly hit by a car. This clip brings the past to the present and is so fascinating. I encourage you to watch it.

Andy Scannell did attend the World's Fair in 1915 and rode in a biplane over San Francisco Bay. A generation later, his son Danny attended the World's Fair at Treasure Island in 1939, and he got to be on closed-circuit television.

I don't know what most of the actual conversations may have sounded like, except for a few notes on-hand from long lost relatives recollecting things that were said. Their own words were used at times throughout the book.

One of the biggest challenges of the book was getting the Irish accents onto paper.

I watched numerous videos of Irish speakers and studied various Irish dialects to decipher what their accents may have sounded like. To complicate matters I had to pair the lingo to the time period. Furthermore, some of the characters came from different regions of Ireland. Andy's mother Mary had a thicker accent and was difficult to understand. I tried to reflect that in the story. I realize that I may not have conveyed their accents perfectly an am open to some criticism.

In the story, I wanted to keep the characters as accurate as possible using real names when I had the information, but there were some gaps I had to fill in. I created a few fictional characters such as Sister Pauline, Sister Magdalen, and Bertie Fink to illustrate what it may have been like going to a school taught by nuns in the 1910s and 1920s. I remember my grandmother Ann and my own mother Joanne saying that some of the nuns were strict and mean. Also, I created a fictional priest who attended Thanksgiving dinner in 1920. I don't know if something like that occurred, but I do recall that when my grandmother was older, she would invite her local priest to dinner on holidays, and this was a common practice in the Catholic community.

The most pivotal truths in the book are that my great-grandfather William White participated in a transportation business, transporting goods via horse cart through San Francisco in the 1910s, and he did become a bootlegger in the 1920s, producing and transporting his homemade White's Whisky during Prohibition. He absolutely enlisted two of his daughters, Ann and Bette, to deliver the liquor to illegal establishments using a child's play wagon carrying dolls. I don't know the full extent of the illegal deliveries made by Ann or her sister, but do recall Grandma Ann, being interviewed at my home in Saratoga, CA, in the mid-1970s. We (my family and my Grandma Ann) were all seated at our kitchen table, using a tape recorder for the interview. I was about ten years old. Unfortunately, the tape was lost, but I do recall some of the conversation about her life. I always thought her journey from childhood to adulthood was unusually interesting and tragic, yet resilient and inspiring. It gnawed at me for years to get her story out but it was not until recently that I went through a box of old photos my mother Joanne had given me, when I found interviews carried out by her brother Dan Scannell (Ann's son Danny in the story) that I was able to put together a more complete picture of her life. My Uncle Dan interviewed many of my relatives before they and he passed away, and he had collected some letters from the 1940s that he talked about. I also recently interviewed Bette's daughter, Jeanette, who filled in more gaps. Where information still lacked about Ann and Bette's involvement in bootlegging, I researched what they may have encountered and incorporated some historical fiction to describe the experiences.

Throughout the book, I used the term 'Mama' when Ann referred to her mother. I do not know what she called her mother. It could have been 'Mum,' a term which the Irish often used during that time period. She may simply have used the word 'Mom' or 'Mother.' I chose to use the term 'Mama' because it was a commonly used term in the US in the early twentieth century.

The sad events in the story such as the loss of Ann's sister Katherine and her mother Maggie's subsequent miscarriage did occur.

William White did run a bootlegging business from the White family's home. He expanded his business next door. His two eldest daughters were also tasked with checking the temperatures of the stills as well as monitoring for spills. He did indeed keep a mistress next door. I don't know the name of the mistress, but he did enlist Bette for communications between him and his mistress.

Although when I was a child, I recall my Grandma Ann, the main character in the story, saying something about having visited Chinatown when she was young, I have no notes on this and could not verify whether she went there with her family in the 1920s. I chose to include the scene primarily to talk about some of the history of the area and introduce the family members. The trip to Japantown is fictional, as are the messages that the characters in the story found in their fortune cookies. To the best of my knowledge, the history of Benkyodo producing fortune cookies is otherwise accurate.

Ann did indeed like to go to Buster Keaton movies as a child. I know this to be a fact because when I was an adolescent in the mid- to late-1970s there was a theater in San Francisco that ran silent movies, and she took me to a series of Buster Keaton shorts with live organ accompaniment.

Ann's father William White did indeed whack Bette on the back of her head when one of the stills had a spillover. He also really stuffed an artichoke down her throat when she refused to eat it.

To save money, he did line up his children and cut their hair using a bowl. His children did learn how to swim at San Francisco's Fleishhacker Pool, swimming in undershirts. There was a well-known rumor at the time amongst San Franciscans who swam there that there was a shark in the water.

I don't know if William ever slapped his daughter Ann. This was added to illustrate all the tension in the family.

The Christmas stories in the book were mostly fictional except for a few things, such as some of the Christmas gifts given, objects hidden in trees at the time, Irish soda bread, and the story about Bette smashing the doll's face in a fit of jealousy and the lesson she learned. The story about the Pig Latin 'oller-ray ates-skay' did occur but was said by Ann to her daughter Joanne when she was a child. William's father in Ireland did indeed send his sister to a convent for bad behavior, and this was given as a warning for his children to behave.

Ann's mother Maggie White did throw rocks at the home next door where her husband's mistress resided. Also, in the story, I wrote that Ann's mother started hearing voices. I don't know if this actually happened but recall my own mother saying that she remembered that Maggie had some mental health issues that surfaced after the death of her husband. I wanted to illustrate what it may have been like dealing with a parent who was going through a mental health issue, while at the same time trying to survive living in a large family with almost no income. The event where Ann's mother Maggie walked into her daughters' bedroom late at night carrying a kitchen knife sadly did occur.

Ann's father William used to toss coins to the kids in their neighborhood during the heyday of his bootlegging operation.

He also did have an illegal backroom bar at his tobacco shop on Courtland Avenue. I have it in the story that he owned it until he died in January 1926. However, the last listing in San Francisco's Crocker Langley phone directory of that store was in 1923. There is no listing in 1924 nor in 1926, the year he died. There is a listing of him as a laborer in 1925. So, I am not sure if he lost the store prior to his death and only continued his home-grown bootlegging business, or if he was trying to keep the tobacco shop hidden from the telephone directory while he continued the other business.

Unfortunately, the account of William swinging a hatchet during a bout of alcohol withdrawal called delirium tremens was true, and Ann and her siblings did laugh, thinking he was drunk and being clumsy until he accidentally chopped off one of his fingers. William did take his family to the Russian River, in Sonoma County, for their one and only vacation, and they would indeed have to return after only one day due to his pneumonia. He was found in a sewage ditch shortly before he died, and was initially identified by that missing finger.

The White family did become poor after William perished at the age of thirty-eight. They did use newspapers to stuff holes in the walls of their home, and they did find ways to stretch the dollar.

The story about Bette bringing cheaply made taffy to school and swapping it with a friend is true, though the real name of the girl she swapped it with was Joanne. Her name was changed to avoid confusion, since Ann's daughter also went by the same name. Of note, the name Bette is used throughout the book, but Bette's nickname originally was Lizzie, which she hated, as old cars were known as Tin Lizzies. By the time she reached high school, she changed it to Bette putting an 'e' at the end instead of a 'y' to separate herself from most of the Bettys during the period. I chose to use the name Bette throughout the book for character development.

Ann White played basketball as a five-foot-tall teenager and was considered quick and agile. I have a photo of her in uniform. The portion of the story of Ann getting on a rooftop using her agility and opening a bedroom window is fictional. However, I do recall she feared heights, and I wanted to illustrate that.

The description of Ann's sisters Bette and Mickey White going over to their aunt's house, while their aunt and cousins hid, was accurate. Also, Bette did lose her job at an ice cream parlor due to her exposing her boss's illegal card games. Ann White's interference in Bette's potential escapade at the Opera House absolutely happened, and Bette would never forget!

Earle Swenson, who eventually became the founder of Swensen's Ice Cream, did become friends with Ann and Bette in the late 1920s and he and his friends came over to their house and danced. I don't know the actual songs that they played. Ironically, I worked at a Swensen's ice cream parlor in Saratoga, California, in the early 1980s before I learned that Grandma Ann danced with Earle, in her home, as a teenager.

Ann did work at O'Connor, Moffatt & Co's Department Store. Before she was hired, her Aunt Mary Ann McGuire did help her get the interview, according to my uncle's notes. Bette and Andy did work there later. Bette and Ann did do some modeling for the department store to make extra money.

My grandmother's first fiancé did crash and die in a motorcycle accident. Both my Aunt Jeanette (Bette's daughter) and I recall being told that. I don't know the actual year this happened or where it occurred. I don't know her fiancé's name, or what he looked like, nor what kind of motorcycle he rode. I took some liberties in building his character, who I named James. Had that incident not occurred, little Danny and Joanne would not have existed, nor I, and neither would this book.

Mentioned in the story was a wound on Bette's leg. Her mother Maggie really did refuse to let a home health nurse enter her house to take care of her.

Near their work, Ann and Bette did attend tea dances at the St. Francis hotel, after meeting under an old famous grandfather clock in the lobby.

Grandma Ann's cousin Elsie McGuire, to whom I am related, (her grandparents Patrick Rudden and Ann McEnroe are my great, great-grandparents,) did marry a prize fighter, and the fight between Max Baer and Frankie Campbell described in the book did occur in 1930, resulting in the death of Frankie "Campbell" Camilli. I refer to Elsie's mother in the story as Ann's Aunt Mary Ann, but she actually went by the name Aunt Mary in real life. I didn't want to confuse readers because of a different person in the story, Andy Scannell's mother, who also went by the name Mary.

For any boxing enthusiast who wants a more detailed look at the famous fight and the boxers who fought, I recommend the book *Then the World Moved On* by Catherine Johnson.

I remember being told that my grandfather Andy Scannell attended the Frankie Campbell-Max Baer fight. Also, I found notes from 2006 from my now deceased Uncle Dan Scannell, which stated Andy confirmed that he was disturbed by watching the fight. In the story, I indicated Andy purchased tickets fairly close to the ring. I don't know where he actually sat, but the notes indicate he "splurged" on good seats. He was a dedicated boxing fan and usually went to fights with at least two of his friends, Johnny Sullivan and Tim Casey. I'm not entirely sure if Grandma Ann was present. I do have notes indicating she attended at least one fight with Andy and the same two friends of his, but there is no mention of which fight it was. So, I'm unsure if it was the same fight. Given Ann's willingness to attend a boxing match, which was highly unusual for a woman back then, there would be no reason to think she wouldn't have been present for one of the most major prize fights in San Francisco involving the husband of one of her closest cousins. One of the reasons I am unsure has to do with the date Ann and Andy met. Per my Uncle Dan's notes, it may have been in 1931, which would postdate the fight, but my mother Joanne said they had an unusually long courtship that spanned the time that Andy's father first became ill until they got married. This puts the date they first met more likely to be in 1930.

Ann and Bette did roller-skate through the streets of San Francisco before toe- stoppers were standard. They did skate up and down hills to visit Andy when his father was dying. Andy did laugh when they first made a trip to see him. The skating crash was fictional, but the playful banter they had with each other until Ann died was brilliantly real.

Both of my great-grandfathers, Daniel Scannell (the father of Andy Scannell) and William White (the father of Grandma Ann), operated illegal stills at different times in their lives. An altercation with a police officer in Ireland did occur in 1895, causing Andy's father Daniel Scannell to flee Ireland. He would not be able to return to his homeland. Daniel did miss his mother's funeral in Ireland a few years later. When Daniel died in the early 1930s, I wrote in the story that Ann sang *Danny Boy* at the funeral. Although *Danny Boy* may well have been sung on that occasion, as it was indeed a common song at Irish American funerals, I don't have any records of Ann singing the song solo. However, Ann may very well have sung songs at funerals as she was known to sing songs throughout her life, especially when she was anxious or sad.

Alcoholism was pervasive in the Irish culture, and my great-grandfather William White, and my grandfather Andy Scannell, had major issues with drinking.

I don't know if my grandfather Andy Scannell was sexually abused by a Catholic brother or anyone at school, but I do have notes from my Uncle Dan, who indicated that something like that may have occurred based on a conversation he had with his father. However, he was not certain if trauma had occurred.

In the story, I mentioned that when Andy was a child, he saw a large shark in a portion of San Francisco Bay called the Carquinez Strait. According to Uncle Dan's notes, his father did tell him that. He said Andy always used that as an anecdote to prove to people that there were predatory sharks in the area. Also, I mention that Andy killed three mountain lions near Lagunitas when he was a teenager. I have no way to verify this, but that is what he told his son! Even if the story is partially true, just the fact that ranchers posted large rewards for killing mountain lions in that area indicates they were apparently in abundance, and a nuisance in the 1910s, not far from San Francisco.

In the book, I mention Andy attended the Repeal Carnival in 1933. I really don't know if he attended, but given he was about to open a bar, it would not have been inconceivable that he went there to talk to liquor distributors. The exhibits mentioned in the story were true, including those of non-liquor products like Chlorox.

The story about Ann walking through Golden Gate Park with morning sickness while the song *Sophisticated Lady* played was fictional, but borrowed from a true story when my pregnant wife Wendy and I visited the Nixon Museum in Yorba Linda in 1994. Stricken by severe nausea, she ran through Nixon's birthplace, through the grounds, into the main museum hall, then into a bathroom to throw up as the song *Hail to The Chief* played on the museum's sound system.

Andy Scannell ran the Old Keg Inn on Church Street and did cook a few comfort food dishes his mother had cooked for him as a child. Union meetings were conducted in special private booths. Jack Shelly was a regular patron who later became the Mayor of San Francisco. Andy did lose his business primarily due to alcoholism and generosity. I don't know exactly when he lost the bar.

Danny Scannell was born at Mary's Help Hospital in 1934. To save money on the hospital bill, he was indeed not circumcised. Andy absolutely went on a bender shortly after his baby was born with the money saved!

Ann, Andy, and their children did indeed own a black cocker-spaniel named Hobo, and they did travel with him to the Russian River on their summer vacations.

In the 1940s, Andy really did get drunk and was fired for sleeping in a rolled-up carpet, on the showroom floor, in the carpet store he once worked at in San Francisco. In the story, a man by the name of Lyle is listed as his floor manager, but his actual name was Joe. The name was changed because there are other people in the story with that name, and I didn't want to confuse readers.

Andy did hide liquor in toilet tanks. The other hiding places I made up. He did bet on horse races and had his own bookie. He absolutely came home stumbling drunk one evening with dollar bills stuffed in multiple locations within his hat band and clothing while Ann and Bette were present.

Andy had a strict mother, Mary Scannell, who had been a teacher. She did swat her grandson Danny Scannell with a cane after she invited him over to bake muffins. Her daughter-in-law Ann had some unpleasant interactions with her, including having to tear up her whole flower garden to plant a Victory Garden. I really don't know how Ann responded to it. I wrote of an interaction where she went to her mother-in-law's cottage with balled up fists. This may not have happened but knowing Grandma Ann she would have responded to her with strength but also intelligence. I remember her as kind but feisty, and a straight shooter who would tell you the truth.

There was indeed a detention center for Japanese Americans in San Bruno, CA, at Tanforan. Andy did deliver documents to his friend at that facility. I don't know what his friend's name was, as the notes I have from his son Daniel didn't list his name. Young Danny was present and the visit to the detention center deeply affected him.

Ann's younger brother Billy, William White, did earn a Silver Star for bravery in World War II. I know this to be true because I currently have it, along with a description of his heroism, in my home in Auburn, CA. Grandma Ann must have given it to her daughter, my mother Joanne, before she died; and I obtained it when my mother died.

After World War II, Bette absolutely played the Halloween prank on Ann wearing men's clothes, and the famous chase scene did occur. My great aunt Bette told me about it, and I heard the story from other people in my extended family numerous times.

Frankie Camilli Jr., whom I am related to, did tragically perish on a flight in 1951 with several other West Point cadets. I chose not to put the year he died in the story so that I could discuss him in one large section spanning 1947 until his death, then go on to talk about events that occurred from 1948 forward.

In the 1950s, Ann's daughter Joanne was an elevator girl in the 1950s at Macy's, at Union Square in San Francisco, in the same building where Ann, and later on, Bette and Andy, worked when it was O'Connor, Moffatt & Co's department store. And yes, there was a learning curve to the operation when Joanne first started! Eventually, six family members in all worked in the same building since 1929.

The story about the Austin Healy teetering over the edge of a cliff on Highway 1 south of Monterey is true. Had the car fallen off the cliff, my mother Joanne would have been killed along with my father, and I would not have been born. Ann's story may or may not have been written by someone else!

Ann's sister Bette Brown, née White, did become an accomplished artist and was inspired by an oil-paint set she received as a child at Christmas. I don't know which actual year she received the kit.

The conversation about the escape from Alcatraz was fictional, but something like that may have occurred as I recollect having conversations about it with Grandma Ann and her husband Al shortly after Clint Eastwood's movie *Escape from Alcatraz* came out in 1979.

Ann was an inspector for the Department of Immigration and really did climb Jacob's ladders to board ships in San Francisco Bay in the 1960s and 1970s.

In the early 1980s Ann did have a foul ball land in her lap at a San Francisco Giants game, and there was a man who tried to take it away, resulting in the infamous slap. I don't know the exact year this occurred, or the team the Giants played that day, but I recall my family laughing about it on several occasions while her husband Al teased her about the strong reaction she had to the would-be baseball thief.

My first car in 1981 was indeed the white 1966 Ford Mustang that Grandma Ann once owned, and it would become my brother Dan's first car in January 1985, a few months before Grandma Ann died.

Ann's middle sister Mickey died in 1984, Bette died in the year 2000, and Ann's youngest sister Theresa died in 2006. Ann's son Danny died in 2010, and her daughter Joanne died in 2022.

I hope you have all enjoyed reading this snapshot in history, of what it may have been like growing up in a large Catholic Irish household, running a bootleg business, in the heart of a major American city during Prohibition, and how alcoholism was pervasive in many Irish American families during that period.

Ann White on the left with sister Bette modeling for O'Connor, Moffatt & Co

Aunt Mary Ann McGuire and her daughters Bernice on
the left and Elsie on the right

Daniel Scannell, Andy's father, in the early 1900s. He died in 1933

The Scannell family in the late 1930s, with Andy, Ann,
and children Joanne and Danny

Ann with the Scannells' dog, Hobo

Andy and Ann Scannell, née White, mid-1940s

Maggie's parents, Patrick Rudden and Ann Rudden, née McEnroe, who stayed
in Ireland when their children emigrated. They are the link between the author,
the main character Ann White, and her cousin Elsie Camilli, née McGuire

June 1964 wedding day photo of Joanne Cerny,
née Scannell, and her niece Sheila Scannell

Andy Scannell working in the mailroom shortly before his death in 1966

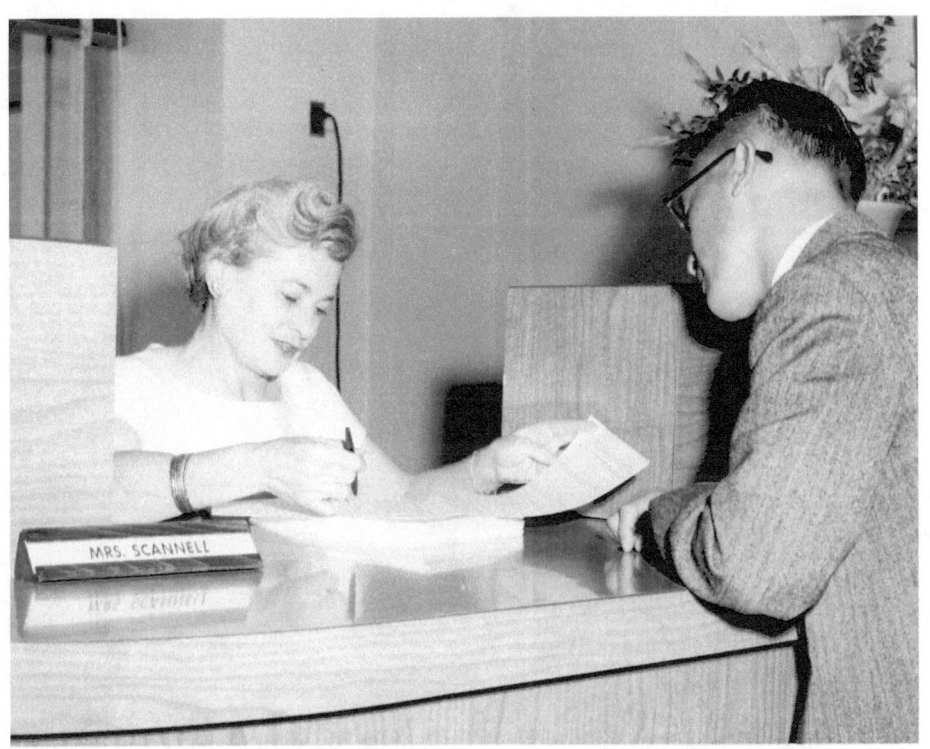

Ann Scannell, née White, working at the Dept. of Immigration
in the mid to late 1960s

SPECIAL THANKS

To my Uncle Dan Scannell, for the wealth of information he collected before his death. Without his interviews with my relatives, the story of Ann White would have been incomplete.

To my cousin Sheila Murray, née Scannell, Ann's first grandchild, whose tireless research into our family history helped shape the book. She also provided some insights and contributed to one of the stories within the book. She contributed some pictures as well.

To my Aunt Jeanette Brown Ganahl, Bette's daughter, whose interviews contributed to understanding some of the finer details, including some of the settings, in the book, as well as some stories concerning Bette.

To my wife, Wendy Cerny, née McQuary, who helped with ideas, rearranging sentences, and general editing.

To editorial assistant Pauline Panlilio for the great attention to detail in helping prepare the bibliography.

And to my chief editor, Robin Schroffel, who, after looking at my first draft, guided me through the whole process from start to finish. In addition to meticulous editing, formatting, and coordination of the book cover, she had great ideas on where I could expand or contract certain portions of the original draft. She gave so much attention to detail that I learned some new things—including the traditional order in which an Englishman, an Irishman, and a Scotsman walk into a bar!

BIBLIOGRAPHY

Aaron, Paul, and David Musto. "Temperance and Prohibition in America: A Historical Overview." In *Alcohol in America: Taking Action to Prevent Abuse*, edited by David F. Musto. National Library of Medicine. Accessed October 3, 2025. https://www.ncbi.nlm.nih.gov/books/NBK216414/

Albany Irish Dance. "What is The History of Irish Dance? Why do Irish Dancers Not Move Their Arms?" Accessed October 3, 2025. https://www.albanyirishdance.com/page/faqs/history-of-irish-dance.

"Alcatraz Escape." Federal Bureau of Investigation (FBI). Accessed October 3, 2025. https://www.fbi.gov/history/famous-cases/alcatraz-escape.

Alexander, Kathy. "World War II in San Francisco, California." *Legends of America,* January 2023. https://www.legendsofamerica.com/san-francisco-world-war-ii/.

"Ain't Misbehavin' (song)." *Wikipedia.* Accessed October 3, 2025. https://en.wikipedia.org/wiki/Ain%27t_Misbehavin%27_(song).

"Anti-Mask League of San Francisco." *Wikipedia.* Accessed October 3, 2025. https://en.wikipedia.org/wiki/Anti_Mask_League_of_San_Francisco.

"Apollo 11." *Wikipedia.* Accessed October 3, 2025. https://en.wikipedia.org/wiki/Apollo_11.

"Avenue Theater." *FoundSF.* Accessed October 3, 2025. https://www.foundsf.org/Avenue_Theatre.

"Baer in Hand Session." *San Francisco Examiner,* August 22, 1930, 22.

"Baer Knocks Out Campbell in Fifth." *San Francisco Examiner,* August 26, 1930, 21, 28.

"The Balloonatic." *Wikipedia.* Accessed October 3, 2025. https:// wikipedia.org/wiki/The_Balloonatic.

"Baseball Teens-20s." *FoundSF.* Accessed October 3, 2025. https:// www.foundsf.org/Baseball_Teens-20s.

"Bay to Breakers." *Wikipedia.* Accessed October 3, 2025. https:// en.wikipedia.org/wiki/Bay_to_Breakers.

"The Beatles Live: Candlestick Park, San Francisco: Their final concert." *The Beatles Bible.* Accessed October 3, 2025. https://www.beatlesbible.com/1966/08/29/ candlestick-park-san-francisco-final-concert/2/.

"Beatnik Glossary." *Jeff Bridges.* Accessed October 3, 2025. https:// www.jeffbridges.com/beatnik-glossary.

"Beatniks." *Wikipedia.* Accessed October 3, 2025. https://en.wiki-pedia.org/wiki/Beatniks.

"Bell-bottoms." *Wikipedia.* Accessed October 3, 2025. https:// en.wikipedia.org/wiki/Bell-bottoms.

"Bernal Heights, San Francisco." *Wikipedia.* Accessed October 3, 2025. https://en.wikipedia.org/wiki/ Bernal_Heights,_San_Francisco.

"The Beverly Hillbillies." *Wikipedia.* Accessed October 3, 2025. https://en.wikipedia.org/wiki/The_Beverly_Hillbillies.

Bierman, Harold, Jr. "The 1929 Stock Market Crash." *EH.net Encyclopedia,* March 26, 2008. https://eh.net/encyclopedia/ the-1929-stock-market-crash/.

"Black Bottom (dance)." *Wikipedia.* Accessed October 3, 2025. https://en.wikipedia.org/wiki/Black_Bottom_(dance).

"Bob Vaughn at the Mighty Wurlitzer." *San Francisco Examiner,* July 22, 1979, 91.

"BoxRec." Accessed October 3, 2025. https://boxrec.com/en/ box-pro/28183.

Burns, Ken. "Roots of Prohibition." *Prohibition.* PBS. Accessed October 3, 2025. https://www.pbs.org/kenburns/prohibition/roots-of-prohibition.

"Cable Cars On Way Out: City Orders Super Buses." *San Francisco Examiner,* January 29, 1947, 1.

"California gold rush." Wikipedia. Accessed October 3, 2025. https://en.wikipedia.org/wiki/California_gold_rush.

Campfire Marshmallows. "Campfire History." Accessed October 3, 2025. https://www.campfiremarshmallows.com/campfire-history/.

"Campbell's Last Stand and Arrest of Baer Is Ordered." *Oakland Post Enquirer,* August 26, 1930, 1.

Carlsson, Chris. "Scavengers Historical Essay." *FoundSF.* Accessed October 3, 2025. https://www.foundsf.org/Scavengers.

"Celts." *Wikipedia.* Accessed October 3, 2025. https://en.wikipedia.org/wiki/celts.

Celtic Steps. "The History of Irish Dance." Accessed October 3, 2025. https://celticsteps.ie/our-story/the-history-of-irish-song-music-dance/.

"Charles Franklin." *Wikipedia.* Accessed October 3, 2025. https://en.wikipedia.org/wiki/Charles_Franklin.

"Chinatown, San Francisco." *Wikipedia.* Accessed October 3, 2025. https://en.wikipedia.org/wiki/Chinatown,_San_Francisco.

Christmas Designers. "From Edison to LED: The Complete History of Christmas Lights." Accessed October 3, 2025. https://www.christmasdesigners.com/blog/from-edison-to-led-the-complete-history-of-christmas-lights/.

City of Torrance, CA. "1930s: A Changing Landscape." Accessed October 3, 2025. https://www.torranceca.gov/our-city/about-torrance/1930s.

"Coit Tower." *Wikipedia*. Accessed October 3, 2025. https://en.wikipedia.org/wiki/Coit_Tower.

Como, David. "August 25th, 1930: Baer vs. Campbell." *The Fight City*, August 24, 2024. https://www.thefightcity.com/august-25th-1930-baer-vs-campbell-max-baer-frankie-campbell-trage-dy-primo-carnera-joe-louis/.

Como, David. "The Death of Frankie Campbell…" Facebook post, Vintage Boxing Photos Archive, September 29, 2019. https://www.facebook.com/vintageboxingphotosarchive/posts/the-death-of-frankie-campbell-at-the-end-of-the-second-frankie-campbell-tells-hi/3113565265382600/.

"'Cons Drowned'—Prison Boss." *San Francisco Examiner*, June 15, 1962, 1, 14.

"Crash Of Douglas VC-47D on Mount Armer: 28 Killed." *Bureau of Aircraft Accidents Archives (BAAA-ACRO)*. Accessed October 3, 2025. https://www.baaa-acro.com/crash/crash-douglas-vc-47d-mt-armer-28-killed.

Creamer, Henry, and J. Turner Layton. "After You've Gone." Score. *International Music Score Library Project / Petrucci Music Library*. Accessed October 3, 2025. https://imslp.org/wiki/After_You've_Gone_(Layton%2C_Turner).

"The Day Prohibition Began." *San Francisco Chronicle*, January 17, 1920, 1, 5.

Davidiam Photography. "Traditional Irish Blessing (How to Guide)." Accessed October 3, 2025. https://www.davidiam.com/blog/traditional-irish-blessing-prayer.

"Dizzy Dishes." Betty Boop Wiki. Accessed October 3, 2025. https://bettyboop.fandom.com/wiki/Dizzy_Dishes.

"Dolph Camilli." *Wikipedia*. Accessed October 3, 2025. https://en.wikipedia.org/wiki/Dolph_Camilli.

Dornberger, Charles, and His Orchestra. "Sunshine Of Mine."
    Performance. Accessed October 3, 2025. https://www.google.
    com/search?q=sunshine+of+mine+by+Charles+Dornberger.

Dowd, Katie. "Asylums and Sanitariums of Northern California."
    SFGATE, June 16, 2016. https://www.sfgate.com/ba-
    yarea/slideshow/Asylums-and-sanitariums-of-Northern-
    California-130984.php.

Emperor Norton Trust. "The Life." Accessed October 3, 2025.
    https://emperornortontrust.org/emperor/life.

"Emperor Norton." Wikipedia. Accessed October 3, 2025.
    https://en.wikipedia.org/wiki/Emperor_Norton.

"Famous Irish Sayings in Gaelic and English." *Gaelic Matters.* 2019.
    Accessed October 3, 2025. https://www.gaelicmatters.com/fa-
    mous-irish-sayings.html.

"Fierce Beating May Be Fatal To Campbell." *San Francisco Chronicle,*
    August 26, 1930, 1, 23.

Firmrite, Ron. "Send In The Clown." *Sports Illustrated,* March 20,
    1978. https://vault.si.com/vault/1978/03/20/send-in-the-
    clown-max-baer-could-bust-them-up-with-a-right-hand-and-
    then-break-them-up-with-laughter-but-his-boxing-career-was-
    overshadowed-by-tragedy.

"First inauguration of Franklin D. Roosevelt." *Wikipedia.*
    Accessed October 3, 2025. https://en.wikipedia.org/wiki/
    First_inauguration_of_Franklin_D._Roosevelt.

"Fixed price of Coca-Cola from 1886 to 1959." *Wikipedia.*
    Accessed October 3, 2025. https://en.wikipedia.org/wiki/
    Fixed_price_of_Coca-Cola_from_1886_to_1959.

Flickr user 14024074@N05. Flatbed Sandow. [Photograph].
    Accessed October 3, 2025. https://www.flickr.com/pho-
    tos/14024074@NO5/3488984714.

"The Flu in San Francisco." *American Experience*. PBS. Accessed October 3, 2025. https://www.pbs.org/wgbh/americanexperience/features/influenza-san-francisco/

"Ford Model A (1927–1931)." *Wikipedia*. Accessed October 3, 2025. https://en.wikipedia.org/wiki/Ford_Model_A_(1927-1931).

"Frankie Campbell." BoxRec. Accessed October 3, 2025. https://boxrec.com/en/box-pro/28183.

"Frankie Campbell." *Wikipedia*. Accessed October 3, 2025. https://en.wikipedia.org/wiki/Frankie_Campbell.

"Frankie Camilli (abt. 1904–1930)." *WikiTree*. Accessed October 3, 2025. https://wikitree.com/wiki/Camilli-26.

Frishman, Dan. "Did Alcatraz convicts get outside Aid?" *San Francisco Examiner*, June 14, 1962, 1, 18, 64.

"Gee Wiz Racing Game." *BoardGameGeek*. Accessed October 3, 2025. https://boardgamegeek.com/boardgame/33400/gee-wiz-racing-game.

"General Electric Indoor Blackout Bulb." *Bulbs.2yr.net*. Accessed October 3, 2025. https://bulbs.2yr.net/ge-blackout-bulbs.php.

"George Roby Dempster." *Wikipedia*. Accessed October 3, 2025. https://en.wikipedia.org/wiki/George_Roby_Dempster.

"Gob-stick." YourDictionary. Accessed October 3, 2025. https://www.yourdictionary.com/gob-stick.

"Golden Gate Bridge." *Wikipedia*. Accessed October 3, 2025. https://en.wikipedia.org/wiki/Golden_Gate_Bridge.

"Golden Gate Ferry Company." *Wikipedia*. Accessed October 3, 2025. https://en.wikipedia.org/wiki/Golden_Gate_Ferry_Company.

"Golden Gate International Exposition." *Wikipedia*. Accessed October 3, 2025. https://en.wikipedia.org/wiki/Golden_Gate_International_Exposition.

Google AI. Search query: "what colors were offered for the 1919 flame shaped mazda light bulbs in christmas strands?" Accessed October 3, 2025.

"Great Department Store Reopens Downtown with Dazzling." The San Francisco Post, March 16, 1909, 5.

Healy, Michael C. "Key System and March of Progress." *FoundSF*, 2016. https://www.foundsf.org/index.php?title=Key_System_and_March_of_Progress.

"Hill Climber Is Widely Acclaimed." *San Francisco Chronicle*, July 22, 1923, 10.

Hill, Joseph A. "Statistics of Divorce." *Publications of the American Statistical Association* 11, no. 86 (June 1909): 486–504.

"History of San Francisco." *Wikipedia*. Accessed October 3, 2025. https://en.wikipedia.org/wiki/History_of_San_Francisco.

"History of the San Francisco Giants." *Wikipedia*. Accessed October 3, 2025. https://en.wikipedia.org/wiki/History_of_the_San_Francisco_Giants.

"Honey (Rudy Vallée song)." *Wikipedia*. Accessed October 3, 2025. https://en.wikipedia.org/wiki/Honey_(Rudy_Vall%C3%A9e_song).

"How Americans Observed V-E Day During World War II (May 8)." *U.S. Embassy in Georgia*. Accessed October 3, 2025. https://ge.usembassy.gov/how-americans-observed-v-e-day-during-world-war-ii-may-8/.

"Human Be-In." *Wikipedia*. Accessed October 3, 2025. https://en.wikipedia.org/wiki/Human_Be-In.

"Hustle-Bubble SUDS." Oxydol advertisement. *San Francisco Examiner*, March 8, 1942, 86.

"Indian Scout (motorcycle)." *Wikipedia*. Accessed October 3, 2025. https://en.wikipedia.org/wiki/Indian_Scout_(motorcycle).

Jane, Moonshine. "'Lead Burns Red and Makes You Dead.'" *MoonshineDVD.com,* April 15, 2014. http://www.moonshined-vd.com/lead-burns-red-makes-dead/.

"The Jazz Singer." *Wikipedia.* Accessed October 3, 2025. https://en.wikipedia.org/wiki/The_Jazz_Singer.

Jimerson, R. W. "Amendment Permits Hard Drinks in Eating Places/Hits Speakies/Move Calculated to Drive Out Liquor Racketeers." *San Francisco Examiner,* December 8, 1933, 1.

Johnson, Catherine. *Then The World Moved On: The Brutal Truth Behind The Max Baer-Frankie Campbell Fight.* Brown Glove Books, 2024. Chapters consulted: 1 (p. 5); 3 (p. 25); 12 (p. 95); 18 (p. 139); 27 (pp. 217, 220–24, 226–30, 232–33); 28 (pp. 234–39); 31 (p. 257); 33 (p. 282); 35 (p. 303).

"June 1962 Alcatraz escape attempt." *Wikipedia.* Accessed October 3, 2025. https://en.wikipedia.org/wiki/June_1962_Alcatraz_escape_attempt.

Kamiya, Gary. "Prohibition Meant Party Time in San Francisco." *San Francisco Chronicle,* September 15, 2018. https://sfchronicle.com/bayarea/article/Prohibition-meant-party-time-in-San-Francisco-13230852.php.

"Katherine White Death Announcement." *San Francisco Examiner,* August 14, 1917, 6.

"Keaton Turned Up Positive In 'The Cameraman'." *San Francisco Examiner,* November 19, 1978, 366.

Keegan, Timothy. "W.P.A. Construction in San Francisco (1935–1942)." *FoundSF.* Spring 2003. Accessed October 3, 2025. https://www.foundsf.org/W.P.A._Construction_in_San_Francisco_(1935-1942)

"Key System and March of Progress." *FoundSF,* 2016. https://www.foundsf.org/index.php?title=Key_System_and_March_of_Progress.

Lappin, Todd. "House Portrait: Carlos Santana's House on Mullen." *Bernalwood,* January 24, 2012. https://bernalwood.com/2012/01/24/house-portrait-carlos-santana-house-on-mullen/.

Lee, Michael. "The Surprising Origins of The Fortune Cookie." *History.com,* February 11, 2021. https://www.history.com/news/fortune-cookies-invented-chinese-japanese.

"Levi Strauss." *Wikipedia.* Accessed October 3, 2025. https://en.wikipedia.org/wiki/Levi_Strauss.

"LGBTQ culture in San Francisco." *Wikipedia.* Accessed October 3, 2025. https://en.wikipedia.org/wiki/LGBTQ_culture_in_San_Francisco.

"Lillie Hitchcock Coit." *Wikipedia.* Accessed October 3, 2025. https://en.wikipedia.org/wiki/Lillie_Hitchcock_Coit.

Little, Becky. "Meet Krampus, The Christian Devil Who Punishes Naughty Children." *History.com,* December 5, 2018. https://www.history.com/news/krampus-christmas-legend-origin.

"Livermore Lad Will Work Out At Taussig's." *San Francisco Examiner,* August 18, 1930, 18.

"Livermore Larupper: The Max Baer Story." *British Vintage Boxing.* Accessed October 3, 2025. https://www.britishvintageboxing.com/blogs/news/livermore-larupper-the-max-baer-story.

Living New Deal. "Take a Self-Guided Tour of the New Deal in San Francisco." Accessed October 3, 2025. https://livingnewdeal.org/take-a-self-guided-tour-of-the-new-deal-in-san-francisco/.

"Lombard Street (San Francisco)." *Wikipedia.* Accessed October 3, 2025. https://en.wikipedia.org/wiki/Lombard_Street_(San_Francisco).

"Macy's Union Square." *Wikipedia.* Accessed October 3, 2025. https://en.wikipedia.org/wiki/Macy%27s_Union_Square.

Martell, Maci. "What Sonoma County Looked Like In The 1930s." *The Press Democrat*, September 12, 2024. https://www.pressde-mocrat.com/article/news/sonoma-county-1930s/.

"Max Baer (boxer)." *Wikipedia*. Accessed October 3, 2025. https://en.wikipedia.org/wiki/Max_Baer_(boxer).

"Max Baer Biography." *IMDb*. Accessed October 3, 2025. https://www.imdb.com/name/nm0046368/bio/.

"Max Baer Is Charged with Manslaughter as Campbell Dies Of Fight." *Oakland Tribune,* August 26, 1930, 1, 3.

"Max Baer." *BoxRec*. Accessed October 3, 2025. https://boxrec.com/en/box-pro/12077.

McCracken, Donal P. "MacBride, John." *Dictionary of Irish Biography*. Accessed October 3, 2025. https://www.dib.ie/biography/macbride-john-a5108#.

"Meeting John Phillips." *Scott McKenzie Info*. Accessed October 3, 2025. https://scottmckenzie.info/meeting-john-phillips.

Mob Museum. "Prohibition Agents Lacked Training, Numbers to Battle Bootleggers." Accessed October 3, 2025. https://prohibition.themobmuseum.org/the-history/enforcing-the-prohibition-laws/law-enforcement-during-prohibition/.

"Moscone–Milk assassinations." *Wikipedia*. Accessed October 3, 2025. https://en.wikipedia.org/wiki/Moscone-Milk_assassinations.

"Murphy bed." *Wikipedia*. Accessed October 3, 2025. https://en.wikipedia.org/wiki/Murphy-bed.

My Irish Jeweler. "7 Ways to Say 'I Love You' in Irish: Tell Your Loved One You Care as Gaeilge." Accessed October 3, 2025. https://www.myirishjeweler.com/blog/7-ways-to-say-i-love-you-in-irish-tell-your-loved-one-you-care-as-gaeilge/.

"1906 San Francisco earthquake." *Wikipedia*. Accessed
October 3, 2025. https://en.wikipedia.org/
wiki/1906_San_Francisco_earthquake.

"1925 Indianapolis 500." *Wikipedia*. Accessed October 3, 2025.
https://en.wikipedia.org/wiki/1925_Indianapolis_500.

"1930s Men's Hats." *Vintage Dancer*. Accessed October 3, 2025.
https://vintagedancer.com/1930's/1930s-mens-hats/.

"1934 West Coast waterfront strike." *Wikipedia*. Accessed
October 3, 2025. https://en.wikipedia.org/
wiki/1934_West_Coast_waterfront_strike.

"1948 Oakland Oaks Roster." *Stats Crew*. Accessed October
3, 2025. https://www.statscrew.com/minorbaseball/
roster/t-oo13437/y-1948.

National Park Service. "Places of World War II in the San Francisco
Bay Area." Accessed October 3, 2025. https://www.nps.gov/
articles/000/places-of-world-war-ii-in-the-san-francisco-bay-
area.htm.

Navarro, J. Alex, and Howard Markel. "San Francisco." *The
American Influenza Epidemic of 1918–1919*. Accessed October 3,
2025. https://www.influenzaarchive.org/cities/city-sanfrancis-
co.html.

Nightingale, Suzy. "All That Jazz: 1920s Fragrances Still Available."
The Perfume Society. Accessed October 3, 2025. https://perfume-
society.org/all-that-jazz-1920s-fragrances-still-available-and-so-
wearable-today/.

Nolte, Carl. "Old Clam House—150 Years in Same S.F. Location."
SFGATE, February 19, 2012. https://www.sfgate.com/bayar-
ea/nativeson/article/old-clam-house-150-years-in-same-s-f-lo-
cation-3342257.php.

Nolte, Carl. "S.F. Toasts The Repeal Of Prohibition Again."
SFGATE, December 5, 2008. https://www.sfgate.com/news/

article/S-F-toasts-the-repeal-of-Prohibition-again-3182345.php.

"Oakland Oaks (PCL)." Wikipedia. Accessed October 3, 2025. https://en.wikipedia.org/wiki/Oakland_Oaks_(PCL).

"Oaks Ball Park." *Oakland Oaks Tripod Site.* Accessed October 3, 2025. https://oaklandoaks.tripod.com/oakspark.html.

Office of the Historian. *US Entry into World War I. Milestones: 1914–1920.* U.S. Department of State. Accessed October 3, 2025. https://history.state.gov/milestones/1914-1920/wwi

"Old Clam House—150 Years in Same S.F. Location." *SFGATE,* February 19, 2012. https://www.sfgate.com/bayarea/nativeson/article/old-clam-house-150-years-in-same-s-f-location-3342257.php.

"The Original Chinatown: San Francisco." *Real San Francisco Tours,* February 23, 2024. https://www.realsanfranciscotours.com/the-original-chinatown-san-francisco/

"Oscar-nominated film missed true story." *Nevada Appeal,* February 8, 2006. https://www.nevadaappeal.com/news/2006/feb/08/oscar-nominated-film-missed-true-story/.

"Panama-Pacific International Exposition." *Wikipedia.* Accessed October 3, 2025. https://en.wikipedia.org/wiki/Panama-Pacific_International_Exposition.

Panel, Tracey. "Peace, Love & Bell Bottoms: Celebrating 50 Years of an Iconic Style." *Levi Strauss & Co. History,* August 8, 2019. https://www.levistrauss.com/2019/08/08/peace-love-bell-bottoms-celebrating-50-years-of-an-iconic-style-.

Penney, David L., and Peter Stastny. "Cycles of Reform In The History Of Psychosis Treatment in The US." *The National Library of Medicine* (via PMC), 2008. https://pmc.ncbi.nlm.nih.gov/articles/PMC10302760/.

"Pig Latin." *Wikipedia*. Accessed October 3, 2025. https://en.wikipedia.org/wiki/Pig_Latin.

"Police Rum Graft Confession Hits Department Higher Ups." *San Francisco Chronicle*, April 25, 1922, 1, 6.

Price Chopper. "History of Irish Soda Bread." Accessed October 3, 2025. https://www.pricechopper.com/blog/history-of-irish-soda-bread-on-st-patricks-day/.

"Prohibition Agents Lacked Training, Numbers to Battle Bootleggers." *Mob Museum*. Accessed October 3, 2025. https://prohibition.themobmuseum.org/the-history/enforcing-the-prohibition-laws/law-enforcement-during-prohibition/.

"Puttin' on the Ritz (1930 Version) Lyrics." *Genius*. Accessed October 3, 2025. https://genius.com/Fred-astaire-puttin-on-the-ritz-1930-version-lyrics.

"Real Carnival Will Be Staged." *San Francisco Examiner*, December 6, 1933, 8.

"Ring My Nose Game." *The Henry Ford*. Accessed October 3, 2025. https://www.thehenryford.org/collections-and-research/digital-collections/artifact/202395.

"Rock Escapees Used a Drill." *San Francisco Examiner*, July 17, 1962, 1, 9.

"Roller Skating in the 1920s." *Prezi*. Accessed October 3, 2025. https://prezi.com/eziziw6m4xfn/roller-skating-in-the-1920s/.

"Roller-Skating." *Britannica*. Accessed October 3, 2025. https://www.britannica.com/sports/roller-skating.

"Roller Skates." *Wikipedia*. Accessed October 3, 2025. https://en.wikipedia.org/wiki/Roller_skates.

Roosevelt House Public Policy Institute at Hunter College. "The Death of President Roosevelt, April 12, 1945." Accessed October 3,

2025. https://www.roosevelthouse.hunter.cuny.edu/exhibits/death-president-roosevelt-april-12-1945/.

"Roots of Prohibition." *PBS.* Accessed October 3, 2025. https://www.pbs.org/kenburns/prohibition/roots-of-prohibition.

"Rudolph Valentino." *Wikipedia.* Accessed October 3, 2025. https://en.wikipedia.org/wiki/Rudolph_Valentino.

"Russian River Memories—Rio Nido." *Russian River.com.* Accessed October 3, 2025. https://russianriver.com/russian-river-memories-rio-nido/.

San Francisco Chronicle, August 28, 1930, 25.

"San Francisco Chinatown History." *Inside Guide to San Francisco Tourism,* June 28, 2023. https://www.inside-guide-to-san-francisco-tourism.com/chinatown-history.html.

"San Francisco (Be Sure to Wear Flowers in Your Hair)." *Wikipedia.* Accessed October 3, 2025. https://en.wikipedia.org/wiki/San_Francisco_(Be_Sure_to_Wear_Flowers_in_Your_Hair).

San Francisco Examiner, December 4, 1933, 4.

SFO Museum. "Flying on Display: Aviation at the Panama-Pacific International Exposition." Accessed October 3, 2025. https://www.sfomuseum.org/exhibitions/flying-display-aviation-panama-pacific-international-exposition.

"Slang of The 1920's." PDF. University of Oregon. Accessed October 3, 2025. https://center.uoregon.edu/NCTE/uploads/2014NCTEANNUAL/HANDOUTS/KEY_1991992/Slangofthe1920s.pdf.

Sonoma Valley Hospital Association. "The Evolution of Sonoma Valley Hospital." Accessed October 3, 2025. https://www.sonomavalleyhospital.org/the-evolution-of-sonomavalley-hospital/.

"The Spanish Flu." *San Francisco Chronicle,* October 11, 1918, 5.

"Spanish Influenza." *San Francisco Chronicle,* October 18, 1918, 8.

"Summer of Love." *Wikipedia*. Accessed October 3, 2025. https://en.wikipedia.org/wiki/Summer_of_Love.

"Super Bowl History: Winners." *ESPN*. Accessed October 3, 2025. https://www.espn.com/nfl/superbowl/history/winners.

"Swensen's." *Wikipedia*. Accessed October 3, 2025. https://en.wikipedia.org/wiki/Swensen%27s.

"Tanforan Assembly Center." *Wikipedia*. Accessed October 3, 2025. https://en.wikipedia.org/wiki/Tanforan_Assembly_Center.

"Three Escape Alcatraz." *San Francisco Examiner*, June 13, 1962, 1, 12–13, 60.

"Timothy Leary." *Wikipedia*. Accessed October 3, 2025. https://en.wikipedia.org/wiki/Timothy_Leary.

"Tiptoe Through the Tulips." *Wikipedia*. Accessed October 3, 2025. https://en.wikipedia.org/wiki/Tiptoe_Through_the_Tulips.

"Top 10 Candies From The 1920's." *Candy District*. Accessed October 3, 2025. https://www.candydistrict.com/blogs/sweet-talk-blog/top-10-candies-from-the-1920s.

"Topographic Map of Bernal Heights, San Francisco." *Topographic-Map.com*. Accessed October 3, 2025. https://en-gb.topographic-map.com/map-s4mdn/San-Francisco/.

"Tourette's Syndrome and The Law." *The Journal of Neuropsychiatry and Clinical Neurosciences*. Accessed October 3, 2025. https://psychiatryonline.org/doi/full/10.1176/jnp.18.1.86.

Treasure Island Museum. "WWII Treasure Island." Accessed October 3, 2025. https://www.treasureislandmuseum.org/youarehere/wwii-treasure-island.

"Ulysses (novel)." *Wikipedia*. Accessed October 3, 2025. https://en.wikipedia.org/wiki/Ulysses_(novel).

Upton, Ruth Eshow. "Avenue Theater." *FoundSF*. Accessed October 3, 2025. https://www.foundsf.org/Avenue_Theatre.

Upton, Ruth Eshow. "Baseball Teens-20s." *FoundSF*. Accessed October 3, 2025. https://www.foundsf.org/Baseball_Teens-20s.

"The US Home Front During World War II." *History.com*. Accessed October 3, 2025. https:www.history.com/articles/us-home-front-during-world-war-ii.

"V-J Day 1945: Celebrating the End of World War II." *FoundSF*. Accessed October 3, 2025. https://www.foundsf.org/V-J_Day_1945:_Celebrating_the_End_of_World_War_II.

"Vermont Street (San Francisco)." *Wikipedia*. Accessed October 3, 2025. https://en.wikipedia.org/wiki/Vermont_Street_(San_Francisco).

Vergun, David. "During WWII, Industries Transitioned From Peacetime to Wartime Production." *Defense.gov*, March 27, 2020. https://www.defense.gov/News/Feature-Stories/story/Article/2128446/during-wwii-industries-transitioned-from-peacetime-to-wartime-production/.

"What Are the Lyrics to 'Danny Boy'?" *Classic FM*. Accessed October 3, 2025. https://www.classicfm.com/discover-music/danny-boy-lyrics-history-traditional-irish-song/.

"What Sonoma County Looked Like In The 1930s." *The Press Democrat*, September 12, 2024. https://www.pressdemocrat.com/article/news/sonoma-county-1930s/.

Winslow, Cal. "The Strike That Shook San Francisco and Rocked the Pacific Coast." *CounterPunch*, July 2, 2014. https://www.counterpunch.org/2014/07/02/the-strike-that-shook-san-francisco-and-rocked-the-pacific-coast/.

Woods, Arnold. "1918 Flu in SF A Closer Look." *FoundSF*, March 2020. https://www.foundsf.org/index. phptitle=1918_Flu_in_SF_A_Closer_Look.

"Wren Day." *Wikipedia*. Accessed October 3, 2025. https:// en.wikipedia.org/wiki/Wren_Day.

"Yerba Buena Island." *Wikipedia*. Accessed October 3, 2025. https://en.wikipedia.org/wiki/Yerba_Buena_Island.

Zamora, Jim Herron. "San Francisco/ Death in the ring/ 75 years ago, renowned boxer Max Baer landed fatal punch." *SFGATE*, August 25, 2005. https://www.sfgate.com/sports/article/san-francisco-death-in-the-ring-75-years-ago-2645588.php.

ABOUT THE AUTHOR

Joseph Andrew Cerny has always been a history buff. In 1988, after graduating from the University of California, San Diego, with three degrees, including a minor in American History, he enrolled at Eastern Virginia Medical School, where he met his wife, Wendy McQuary; the two graduated from there and married in 1992.

After a career as a family physician spanning nearly thirty years, Cerny is now a volunteer for Placer County Museums in Northern California. He dresses up in period clothing and gives tours of old-town Auburn, a former Gold Rush town, in the foothills of the Sierra Mountains. He also gives tours of Bernhard House, an old hotel converted into a home, with wine-making complexes on the property. Every October, he volunteers on cemetery tours at the Old Auburn Cemetery, where actors re-enact the characters of famous locals buried there.

Cerny enjoys talking and writing about American history, of which the story of his grandmother, Ann White, is an important example. *The Bootlegger's Daughter: A San Francisco Tale* is his first novel.